Tina

I hope

entertaining & thought

provoking

Parallel

S.M. Zaccaro

Lawrence M. Zaccaro

3-13-02

Pittsburgh, PA

ISBN 1-56315-254-1

Paperback Fiction
© Copyright 2000 Lawrence M. Zaccaro
All rights reserved
First Printing—2000
Library of Congress #99-65307

Request for information should be addressed to:

SterlingHouse Publisher Inc.
The Sterling Building
440 Friday Road
Pittsburgh, PA 15209
www.sterlinghousepublisher.com

Cover design: Michelle S. Vennare – SterlingHouse Publisher
Typesetting: Kathleen M. Gall

Song lyrics by Justin Hayward. Used by permission.

Printed in Canada

Dedication

This book is dedicated to

my late father

Luke N. Zaccaro,

who died before

I ever had the chance to discuss

God, life and love

with him.

Acknowledgments

Though this book is a work of passion out of my own emotions and thoughts, there are many people who have supported and inspired me throughout my life.

I'd like to thank my mother, Marilyn, for giving me life and for giving me love;

My friend, Marilyn, who a long time ago showed me how to appreciate life;

My brothers and sister, Rick, Ed, Dan, Mike and Nancy who have tolerated and loved me, and made me laugh all these years;

The countless teachers, scientists, colleagues and friends who have taught, supported and inspired me throughout my life;

Musicians who have inspired me with their music and lyrics: John Lennon and the Beatles, Dan Fogelberg, The Alan Parsons Project, and especially Justin Hayward and The Moody Blues;

The friends who read early versions of this book and gave me invaluable feedback and suggestions: Adi, John, Kelly, Kelly, Lorraine, Pat, Sandra, Sara, Stephanie, Steve and Yvette.

And especially to my wife Cathy and children Lauren, Kristin, Mike and Eric, for being so patient and tolerant, understanding and loving.

Thank you very much.

Chapter One

s the laden donkey walked slowly through the brittle, winter air, its hooves crunched on frozen grass and clumps of dirt. With Mary riding and Joseph leading the animal by the frayed rope tied loosely around its neck, they headed around to the back of the inn. Too benign to argue with the innkeeper over the price of a room—as usual, much more than they were able to pay—they accepted a bed of hay for a minimal price. All other inns and boarding houses were full. But now, they and their donkey could sleep and get water, as long as the trough was not frozen. That would depend on what livestock inhabited the stable and whether or not they had kept ice from forming on the surface of the water. Several days past the shortest day of the year, this night had no steady wind, unlike the past few. The air was clear and cold, the stars hanging low overhead, bright and numerous. Mary and Joseph had hoped, tonight, they would sleep well in an affordable room. Now, a restful night's sleep would depend on the animals with which they would share the night, the condition of the stable, and the dryness of the hay it contained.

The fabric and continuity of their marriage was fraying. To Joseph it seemed as though Mary was in a state of confusion, unwilling to even attempt to conceive a child. And he was growing impatient, wanting a son to assist in his small carpentry trade or a daughter to help Mary tend the garden. He could not afford to hire an apprentice, and yet he was unable to sell enough wares to purchase even minimal sustenance from the greedy suppliers in the village. It had become impossible to stay in Nazareth, not having enough land to grow what they needed and no silver to purchase livestock. So it had finally become time to move on, though they did not know where to go or even if moving would be to their advantage.

Yet, he still loved Mary deeply—her beauty, her kindness—but it was becoming too much to bear in too short of a time. She had lost her enthusiasm and interest in building a shared life, and he felt she was slipping away from him emotionally and mentally. To him she always seemed preoccupied with her beliefs. He did not understand why she was unwilling to have a child, and his concern had deepened recently. Now she was saying that a god, her Lord, would "deliver" a son to them. Though they had never tried to conceive one, a son would be delivered to them.

This he did not understand at all.

Their hearts sank when they saw the stable was full—several cows and sheep, an old mare, ten fowl toward the far end. Even in the bitter cold, it reeked of manure. The ground was covered in it, and piles were heaped against the near wall, crusted with frozen hay. The saddening prospect of another sleepless night became a reality.

"Look into the manger," Mary suggested soberly in their ancient language. "Perhaps the hay through there is clean."

The animals were huddled together in the middle of the stable, attempting to stave off the cold. They were barely aware of Joseph as he walked gently between them and leaned through the opening to the manger. As Mary had suggested, the feed hay there was clean and fairly dry. There is hope that we can sleep well tonight, he thought, at least after we have become accustomed to the smell.

He led the donkey into the stable and tied it off. Again, the other animals showed no concern at this intruder's presence, not even shifting their positions, perhaps welcoming the warmth of another body. Mary and Joseph crawled through the hole in the wall that led into the small manger. They rearranged the hay slightly and lined the far corner with one of their tattered blankets. Wrapping the other blanket around themselves, they clung together for warmth and comfort.

After a while, he said quietly into her ear, "I love you."

"And I love you," she said, "with all my soul. I know you are concerned for the days ahead. But we will be fine. Things will get better. The Lord will provide for us."

To this, he remained silent.

They embraced in the darkness of the dilapidated, wood structure, animals on the other side of the wall stirring occasionally. Outside, the night remained clear and cold. Half of the waning moon rose to the east as the midnight hour approached.

Pulled abruptly from sleep, Joseph awoke with bright light on his face. His first thought was they had slept late into the morning. But the glare shining through the tattered boards cast sharp shadows across the hay, outlined in a light different than if cast from the sun. He soon became aware of the restless stirring of the animals a few feet away—cackling and fluttering, snorting and bleating, the shuffling and stomping of hooves in the manure and dirt.

Then he understood. The shadows were moving across the inside of the manger, and the source of the light came from overhead, not from a lantern or torch.

Mary was wide-eyed beside him, also well aware that their sleep had been interrupted by something neither one understood. Scrambling quickly to his feet, Joseph crawled through the wall and hurried out the door of the stable.

A harsh, glaring, blue-white light bathed the few visible trees, the entire stable, and the frozen ground as far as he could see. It radiated from a single moving source overhead, approaching slowly and smoothly from the east. He stood in amazement and watched what he thought looked like a large, moving star. The light intensified as it came closer and seemed to be heading directly for them. Moos and cries from inside the stable grew louder.

Soon Mary came out, her head and shoulders wrapped in the blanket. She stood behind her husband, watching the moving light. As fear rose within her, she whispered slowly in a cracking voice, "What is it? It looks like a star from the heavens, but why does it move? Why is it so large?"

"It looks like no star I have seen." Joseph's gaze had not wavered from the light as it moved closer to the ground, though still well above the height of the tallest trees. Fear and urgency was now apparent in his voice as he cried, "Get back inside the stable! I do not know if it is a star, but it is upsetting the animals. It may be dangerous!"

Mary moved back to the door of the stable but remained outside, mesmerized by the moving light. Its brightness was difficult to look at, yet they were compelled to watch.

Now its movement slowed, and it floated above the ground, just beyond the crest of a small hill a stone's throw from them. The light was slowly beginning to fade and a humming sound like an enormous, hornets' nest became audible. At this, the animals in the stable became even more agitated. Several loud kicks pounded against wooden boards, and fowl clucked noisily.

The light had mostly faded as it began to descend toward the ground, just behind the crest of the hill. Momentarily, the humming grew in pitch and volume.

Finally, the light had dimmed enough so Joseph and Mary could see it was shining from an object. It was longer than it was high, and they thought it might be a small fishing vessel. It landed softly just over the hill, out of their view. Then the sound diminished, and all glowing light was gone. Left in darkness, hearing only animal noises, they remained still and silent for several seconds, still completely unsure of what they had seen. Now fear consumed them both, and they did not know what to do.

A high-pitched hissing sound, like the sound of a hundred cobras threatening to strike, came from just over the hill. Mary and Joseph jumped at the sound and clutched each other in fear. The hissing reached a peak, lasted several moments, then faded quickly. They stood in confused, fearful silence again, not speaking for a long time. By now the animals were quieting down, but voices calling from the inn could be heard. Long, faint shadows were cast as a lantern was lit near the front of the inn.

And then, over the distant voices from the inn, came another sound— a broken, familiar noise coming from just over the hill where the star had landed.

It was a sound like a baby beginning to cry.

Joseph's heart thundered in his chest as he tilted his head to listen. Still fearful, at first not sure what he heard, he backed away. He then motioned silently for Mary to remain and walked slowly, carefully toward the sound. As he climbed and reached the crest of the hill, his steps became smaller and slower until he could just peer over the top.

In the dim light of the stars and moon, his eyes widened at the sight before him. A beautiful, shining cradle, the size of a small boat and lined with pillows, lay flat on the ground. Inside lay a naked baby on its back, a boy. The child cried softly, arms and legs flailing as he tried to roll over. A faint, blue aura surrounded him, giving a glow to the inside of the cradle. He had a thick mat of light brown hair and light skin, much lighter than Joseph's. Hesitating only a moment, he stepped to within a few feet of the baby. He noticed the pillows lining the cradle shimmered like silk but were of a cloth unlike any he had seen.

"Mary, it is all right," Joseph called back to her. "There is no danger. It is a baby. And he is probably very cold! Bring one of the blankets!" She hurried up to her husband, removing the blanket from around her shoulders. "It is all right," Joseph said quietly to the baby. He asked gently, though not expecting any answers, "Who are you? Where are you from? What is this bed the star has brought here?"

4

At the sound of his voice the baby stopped crying and began looking around. His eyes were bright blue, seeming to radiate the same blue light that shone around him. Able to roll over to his hands and knees and struggle to his feet, he gripped the raised side of the cradle for support. Joseph and Mary stared in wonder as the boy moved and surveyed his surroundings with an awareness that far exceeded any infants they had seen before. Soon he gained his balance and stood freely, holding his hands outward to his sides, the dim, blue light still coming directly from his skin and hair. The baby finally fixed his gaze on the two of them. After several seconds, his face was illuminated by a wide smile, exposing a mouth full of teeth.

Mary covered her mouth with both hands, staring in disbelief for a moment, but then gained a full understanding of the situation. Hearing voices moving in their direction from the inn, she handed the blanket to Joseph and said, "We must bring him into the stable. It is warmer there, and he can lay upon soft hay."

Though he did not understand anything she said, the baby continued to smile at her and calmly allowed them to wrap him in the blanket and carry him toward the stable.

Mary spoke to Joseph as they walked, cradling the baby tightly to her bosom. "He has been sent to us by the Lord, within that star, and placed within this heavenly bed. He is the son I have been praying for."

From the other side of the stable, a voice cut her off in mid sentence. "No fires! The only thing I demanded was no fires near the stable!" Then the innkeeper and his wife came from around the corner of the stable.

"We have lit no fire," Joseph said calmly as they stopped to face them.

"What was that bright light that caused the animals to stir and awoke us from sleep?"

"It was a heavenly star," Mary said quickly. "It has brought our son to us."

The innkeeper noticed the baby for the first time. It was shivering slightly and still emitting a faint, blue light, the eyes observant and very alert. The innkeeper looked back to Mary, "What do you mean by this, 'a star brought your son to you?'"

At that moment, three other men came hurrying out of the darkness. They were dressed in rich clothing, though of a style not commonly worn by people from that area. High turbans were wrapped tightly on their heads and each carried heavy sacks flung over their shoulders. "Did you see it?" one of them called. "The traveling star? It is a star that moves, and appears so much brighter than others. Did it pass over this area? We have lost sight of it."

"It came here and brought our son to us," said Mary. "He is called Jesus." Joseph looked uneasily at Mary, then back to the other men as Mary continued. "It is the name foretold to me, the name given to me by the Lord."

"The star, what has happened to it?" one of the men asked.

"It has brought Jesus to us. It has fulfilled its purpose, and the heavenly light has gone from it."

One of the men asked, "How does a star bring a son to a mother? What has happened? What manner of baby emits his own light?"

Not wanting to answer questions, Mary insisted on carrying Jesus out of the cold and into the stable. The innkeeper and his wife walked slowly back towards the inn, confused and talking quietly to themselves. Joseph remained outside talking to the three men. Soon the four of them walked back up the hill and examined the bed.

Mary helped Jesus drink water from the trough and climb into the manger. She held him within the blanket until his shivering stopped. Jesus watched her closely, calmed by her peacefulness, the gentle nature of her touch and manner. Whenever their eyes met, she would smile kindly to him, and he would return the favor. Then Jesus tried to speak, with ability far beyond his apparent age. Startled by his voice at first, she watched in amazement as he formed syllables and sounds, but they made no sense to her. In her own language, she said, partly to Jesus and partly in prayer, "Our heavenly Father has brought you to us. We will love you as our son, more than if you were born unto me. You are a sacred gift, and we will cherish you."

Several minutes later, Joseph returned to the manger. "Two shepherds who were tending their flocks on the next hill also saw the star. Like us they did not understand how such a thing could happen. The three men have been following the star for a distance, from the east. They left us these gifts, treasures from their own land, to whom they called our 'holy son.' Incense, pieces of gold, and myrrh." As he tossed the small bundles aside to the hay, he said, "Perhaps we can use the gold to purchase food, though tonight a thicker blanket would be a more welcome gift. What can be done with myrrh, I do not know." He studied Jesus. "How is he now?"

"He has stopped shivering and rests well. What of the bed he was lying on? Do you know what it is?" Mary asked.

"It is strange, indeed—like nothing I have ever seen. The outside is a metal the color of the finest silver chalices used during Passover. The top is a soft bed, like a mattress belonging to the richest of governors. One end has some symbols on it, unlike any I have seen."

"Truly it is a creation of the Lord. We have been blessed."

"I am beginning to accept your beliefs, Mary. How could a cradle be delivered by a star? I just do not understand."

Her expression changed suddenly. "Joseph, we must leave. There will be many inquiries. Soldiers will come in the name of Herod wanting to know how Jesus came to us. There was talk that Herod has foreseen this— that a savior, sent to Earth by God, would be an omen of the end of Herod's reign and lead to his death."

"This is truth. I know of this talk." He looked away from Mary and down to Jesus. "When we left our home we knew not where to go to acquire land. But, now, I believe I know of the best place. It is a long journey from here."

"To where?" she asked.

Not listening, still looking at Jesus, he said, "But another mouth to feed. We have no food as it is."

Sincerely, she said, "Now we have pieces of gold to purchase food, as you suggested, and the incense and myrrh perhaps to trade in a market. Do you think the Lord would provide us with a blessed son and then allow him to starve?"

Joseph studied her face closely. The honesty and love in her eyes was uncompromising. He smiled. "You are wise, my wife." His expression became somber, and he looked past her through the walls of the manger. "The land of the Nile. There is much fertile land where we can grow what we need, and there is abundant wood for my crafts."

"But the tribes there—their dislike for our people. Jesus' skin is lighter than ours. And eyes of his color are so uncommon. Surely we will be outcasts."

"We must try. There is nowhere in Jerusalem that is safe now. Soldiers will be searching for this child."

They heard voices outside, toward the inn. Voices in emotional, heated discussion.

Mary listened for a moment then turned to him. "Now, Joseph. We must go now," she said firmly.

He looked from Mary to Jesus. "Are you ready to travel, my son?" but expected no answer. Instead, he picked up Jesus and tightened the blanket around him. Joseph hesitated, holding the baby still for a moment, then said, "The blue light is gone, but he has a warmth, a radiance about him. Do you feel this?"

"I do. He is blessed."

They crawled out of the manger and led the donkey out of the stable. After securing Jesus upon its back, they walked alongside.

Quietly, yet quickly, they left the small village and the stable behind them, heading out into the cold darkness, traveling west.

CHAPTER TWO

Chris centered the transparency on the projector and continued. "The clitoris is truly a miracle of evolution." With a telescoping pointer he indicated the appropriate location on the screen. Out of the corner of his eye he noted the numerous smiles and glances of his students. "Its only known function is for pleasure. Some consider it an analog of the male penis, but this is not really very accurate. The penis is multifunctional: for urination, the site of sexual stimulation and arousal, ejaculation and distribution of sperm to ensure species survival. But the clitoris, while indeed having some minimal erectile capabilities, has none of those other functions. It is only for sexual stimulation, to give pleasure—" He hesitated briefly then said, "Something that doesn't happen nearly enough."

There were several laughs scattered throughout the thirty students in his class.

He held his bearded chin in his hand, waiting as they quieted down, then continued with descriptions of female genitalia, reproductive, and urinary systems. Five minutes before the scheduled end of class he took off the last transparency, saying, "That's enough for this afternoon. Don't forget, test number five on Thursday covering chapters fifteen, sixteen and twenty. I'll get them corrected and back to you on Tuesday. Then I'll wrap up the lecture, and the final exam will be the following Tuesday, covering everything since the midterm." He scanned their faces for reaction. "Anything else?"

"Will there be any essays on the final?" a boy called out near the back of the classroom.

Chris smiled. "It'll be a lot like the midterm. Same cross section of kinds of questions, including a couple short essays. And there will be an essay bonus question, but I'll talk more about that next Tuesday. Anything else?"

No one had any other questions. The students evacuated quickly in a flurry of sliding chairs and shuffling feet, and they were gone within thirty seconds.

Except for one.

"Professor Magnuson?" said a girl with long, brown hair streaked with blond highlights. She stopped in front of the table where he gathered up papers and transparencies.

"Margaret. I've been teaching you since the end of June. On the first day of class I said to call me Chris. I'm not a doctor. I'm not a professor. I'm just some guy named Chris."

"Right." She watched him with narrowed eyes for a moment. "The first day of class when you took attendance and called out, 'Margaret Lisa MacIntyre,' I asked you to call me Mac. You've called me Margaret every single class since the end of June."

He smiled, saying, "Okay, Mac. Yeah, I suppose Margaret Lisa MacIntyre doesn't exactly roll off the tongue." He noticed, again, there was something familiar about her. She was pretty—he had noticed that the first day of class—but there was something about her face that seemed—He could never quite put his finger on it. Then he remembered something he'd been meaning to ask her. "I've seen you around for a couple semesters, haven't I? Don't you work for that physics professor, the one upstairs? What's his name? Leonard?"

She hesitated and looked away for second. A distant, vacant look came to her eyes but quickly passed. "Dr. Leonard, yes. I did. Still do, I guess."

"He's the one with the Leonardo da Vinci obsession, isn't he? Or at least that's what I've heard people say."

She tilted her head, as if she had heard that a hundred times, then nodded.

"I keep hearing all these crazy rumors about him: like he quit school and moved to Europe; he got killed some mysterious way; he just vanished and no one knows how or why; he's away doing secret field work. You're still here. Do you know where he's been? Where he is?"

Again, she hesitated. "All I know is he left to do field work, at least for the summer."

Chris sensed a tone of cold rehearsal in her voice, as if she was reciting words that weren't the whole truth. "Field work? In physics? Where?"

"I really can't say," Margaret blushed. "I mean, I don't know. He's researching the new equipment he's been working on." She rolled her eyes, changing the direction of the conversation. "And he left me with enough calculations to last a year. The grant money lasts until I graduate after fall semester. So I'll keep doing his work and taking the classes I need, like this one, as long as I keep getting paid."

It was clear to Chris she didn't want to talk about it. "That's okay, I was just curious. Anyway, what's up? Can I help you with something?"

Remembering why she had stopped to talk to him, she hesitated, but finally said, "It's really kind of amazing how you can make such an interesting and enjoyable subject—like female anatomy and sexuality—sound so cold and scientific."

Chris was mentally knocked off balance for a second. Recovering quickly, he swallowed the air that had risen in his throat. "Well I, uh, it's by design. After all, I am a professional." He said the last comment with some sarcasm. While looking directly into her eyes, he wondered if she was coming on to him.

She stepped closer, but didn't say anything, until their faces were less than a foot apart.

Now he was sure she was coming on to him. He felt blood rushing to his crotch, and didn't back away, now standing so close he could feel her soft breath and smell her delicate fragrance. Swallowing, he said, "I, uh, was there something in today's lecture you didn't understand?"

She took a small step closer, her gaze not wavering, then said softly, "No, I understand it all really well." Then she added, "I like your eyes. I noticed them the first day of class. They're so—I don't know—complicated, I guess. They're bright blue, which I like, but it's how they look like there's a lot going on behind them."

"Thanks, I think." They stood close for several seconds, neither one taking their eyes off the other. Then Chris said, "You're getting a solid *A* in this class, aren't you. So you don't need help?"

She backed away a step. "I'm sorry," she said, looking down and away. "I guess I find you interesting." Then, again fixing her gaze on his eyes, she said with a hint of admiration, "I like the way you think, some of the things you said this semester. I was thinking it would be nice to get to know you better." And then, with an edge of seduction, "And you don't look too bad, either."

Chris exhaled. "Oh. Well, I appreciate that. But I—If you're asking me to—You're making a pass at me, aren't you?"

She gave a slight indication of agreement by bobbing her head at an angle in a partial nod.

"Well, I guess you know I have to say, 'thanks, but no thanks.'"

She smiled broadly. "I guess I knew you would say that. In another way, you are kind of a dweeby science guy, aren't you?"

"Kind of."

"Cute, though." She walked slowly backward, with her smile now slight but warm, then turned and headed to the door.

"See you Thursday. Hey, Margar—I mean, Mac." She stopped and turned back around. "Thanks. In a twisted way, you made my day."

She playfully bit her lower lip and narrowed her eyes slightly. "See you Thursday."

He watched her leave, all the while thinking there was something so familiar about her.

■ ■ ■

Carrying a nylon pack that contained his books and papers, Chris walked out of Lennon Hall into the stifling August afternoon air. The sun was shrouded in haze in the southwestern sky, but the temperature was still well into the nineties. As he walked across campus, he was surrounded by patchy, brown grass. Stained, pockmarked, red bricks and peeling, white paint of the colonial buildings looked dull in the heat. Withering leaves of the oak and maple trees attempted to give shade. It's hot, too hot, he thought, and it isn't getting any cooler, even though the end of summer is a few weeks away. He exhaled deeply and pushed back the straight, light brown hair that sweat plastered to his forehead. His short, full beard itched slightly from the heat, and he scratched his chin as he walked.

Algonquin State is decaying slowly, he thought. Enrollment is down, budgets are being cut, no new instructors are being hired, no new researchers are being taken on to bring in grant money, what little there is to be obtained. I wonder what I'll be doing in ten years when Mary and John are approaching college age. What kind of security will I be giving to them?

His ten-year-old Toyota waited for him, in remarkably good shape considering the 135,000 miles. With gas in abundant supply, and only $1.50 a gallon, its forty miles per gallon economy made it difficult to trade in on a new car. He climbed in, wondering what it would finally take to allow solar and battery cars to be economically feasible. The technology has been practical since 2004, he thought, but lobbyists, or unions, or someone else's personal agenda will keep gasoline powered cars entrenched as the market mainstay until every drop of oil has been found and used.

As usual, his car started immediately. He rolled down the window and pulled onto the winding street, leaving campus and heading toward Littleboro. Though 300-year-old stone walls lined the road, canopied with spreading oak and maple trees, houses and occasional businesses were packed densely on either side. For a narrow, winding road in rural Massachusetts, the traffic was very heavy, moving slowly in both directions.

The casino, what a wonderful thing to have in my town, he thought sarcastically. Well, not really in my town. In the sovereign nation that is contained entirely within the boundaries of Littleboro. The Passemannican Nation.

A former reservation that was recognized by the Bureau of Indian Affairs as an independent nation in 1999, they chose to build a casino as their means of economic empowerment. And, like so many others across the U.S., it was doing very well financially.

Chris thought, the daily income from video slots and poker alone is more than the entire annual research budget of Algonquin State. Who are all these people who pump millions of dollars a day down the throats of those machines? They come from Boston, Concord, Worcester, Providence, Springfield, Hartford. Even New York and Portland. I just don't get it. Don't they have anything else to spend their entertainment budget on? Why don't they rent a movie?

His attention was pulled back to the road in front of him as traffic abruptly braked for a red light. Cars were backed up ten to fifteen deep in all four directions. Only about six cars from the right and left made it through the light before it changed to green in his direction. Just before he reached the light, the car in front of him signaled for a left turn and slowed. Without enough room to pass on the right, he waited patiently until the car was able to turn. Chris proceeded forward, but had to slam on his brakes as a car coming in the other direction turned left across the intersection in front of him.

"Damn it!" he spat through clenched teeth. He started to move forward again, but another car closely followed the first, cutting him off again. Then another. And another. Five cars turned left in front of him, onto the road that headed toward the Passemannican Nation, before the sixth continued straight, and he was able to proceed through the intersection.

"Charming," he said aloud, "truly heartwarming. Welcome to our town."

He continued slowly toward home.

■　■　■

"Daddy!" John yelled as Chris turned right off Mourning Dove Lane and up the slight incline of their driveway. John had been bouncing a chartreuse tennis ball for their dog Dudley to catch but quickly dropped it and ran to the car as Chris pulled up in front of the garage. A short-haired mixed breed, Dudley barked loudly from the corner of the house where he was chained to a tree, his tail wagging frantically.

"Hey, Johnny," Chris called as he stepped out of the car. John leapt off the ground and into his arms, and Chris had to drop the nylon pack to complete the catch. Though he was only four, John's large frame and solid, fifty pounds made that a difficult task. Chris hugged him momentarily, then brushed some sand from John's sweaty, blonde hair and off the shoulders of his white T-shirt. "Hey, Squirt. How's it going?"

"Good. I made a castle. Want to come see?"

"Sure."

John led him to the sandbox and proudly pointed. "See?"

"Whoa! Cool!" Chris knelt to inspect it closer for a few seconds. "I really like all the sticks around the edge for a decoration."

"Those aren't sticks! They're knights!"

"Of course. Knights. Now I can tell. Hey, are Mom and Mary in the house?"

"Uh-huh. Mommy's making supper. Mary's playing on the computer, like always." He rolled his eyes.

Dudley barked loudly, impatiently waiting to be greeted, his chain just reaching the corner of the sandbox. "All right, all right, you fricking mutt." Chris walked the few steps and scratched him behind both ears. Dudley jumped up on his hind legs, extending his front legs and solid upper body up to Chris' chest. Though part of his pedigree was Husky, with his wide, brown eyes and fur with white undertones covered by henna, tipped with black highlights, he was a generic dog. "Yeah, yeah, I'm overjoyed to see you, too. And what did you accomplish today?"

Chris scratched him for another moment then let the dog's front paws fall to the sand. He called to John, "I'll come out and play ball with you in a minute," and he walked to the front door of their small, white-sided raised ranch.

As he started to climb the half-story of steps covered with beige carpeting, Sara called from upstairs in the kitchen. "Hey, Hon."

"Hey."

She met him at the top of the stairs, and he tightly embraced her tall, statuesque frame. They kissed deeply for a full five seconds. "Mmmmm, you'd better knock it off," she said, a slight, Brooklyn accent edging her voice, "you might get a boner." Her great grandparents had come to New York from Italy and Ireland and settled there. Sara had spent the first eighteen years of her life just off of Flatbush Avenue. Pulling back her straight, honey-blonde hair and tucking it behind her right ear, she revealed her soft brown eyes smiling a bright greeting for him.

Mischievously referring to her comment about a boner, he asked, "Is that bad?"

"Right now it is. We can't do anything about it."

"Who says we can't?"

"Oh, just Mary sitting about fifteen feet away in the next room," she

14

replied with feigned exasperation. "How was school?"

"I was riveting as usual. I taught them all about female anatomy."

"Did you teach them anything they didn't already know?"

"Probably not. But you'll never guess what happened. A student came up after class and made a pass at me."

She pulled her head back to examine him. "And what did you do about that?"

"Nothing. He wasn't that cute."

She laughed and smacked him on the rear end.

Mary came out from the extra bedroom where the computer was set up. "Hi, Daddy."

"Hi, Mare. Playing the maze game again?" Chris knelt to embrace her, pulling her blonde hair back behind her shoulders so he could snuggle his face against hers.

"Your beard tickles!" Then she answered his question with, "Uh-huh. I'm up to level fourteen."

"Great. That's more than I accomplished today."

Mary put her hands on her hips and said, "Dad!" then disappeared back through the door.

Sara was walking back to the kitchen counter as she asked, "Did you happen to see the paper this morning?"

"No. What's up?"

"Read it," she said, pointing with a nod of her head. "It's right there."

Chris dropped his pack in the hall and sat at the kitchen table where the *Globe* lay open to the "State" section. The headline on the first page read:

"PASSEMANNICAN ANNEXATION OF 325 ACRES GIVEN PRELIMINARY APPROVAL BY BIA"

"Jesus," he muttered and sat down slowly, unfolding the section and reading the details.

Sara eyed him carefully for reaction as he read, periodically glancing at the vegetables she was slicing. After a while she said, "It says there's a special town meeting a week from Wednesday to talk about it in more detail."

He read silently for another minute, then said out loud to himself, "Great. Just great. That's just what this town needs. To lose even more land that supplies the money for our already-feeble tax base." He pushed the paper aside and turned to face Sara. "I think I've stayed out of this for too long. Do we have anything going on next Wednesday?"

Sara smirked to herself without turning from her work. She had predicted that would be his reaction. "No. Mary doesn't start school, and I don't start work until the week after. Don't you have class?"

"It's the first day of finals week. My Monday/Wednesday General Bio just has a final the following Monday."

"I'll stay home with the kids if you want to go."

"Yeah. Yeah, I think I'll go and check it out. I know we're—"

He stopped in mid sentence when he heard Dudley barking wildly outside, louder and more frantic than normal.

And then John screamed.

Chris was down the stairs and out the door before he knew he was moving. The first thing he saw was a thick-bodied dog with ragged, gray fur standing over John, who lay face down in the sandbox covering his head with his arms. Dudley leapt at it, but the stray turned to brace for his lunge. They met in mid air, snarling, jaws thrashing at necks, teeth clapping loudly, both heads jerking violently.

"John! No!" Chris screamed as he ran over, arms waving wildly. "Get out of here! Yah! Yah!"

As the dogs moved a few feet away, still tangled and snarling and kicking up sand, John quickly scrambled to his feet. Picking up the closest rock, he threw it in their direction, but missed several feet to the right. The dogs separated, and both landed with their feet clawing the sand for balance. Dudley shook his head then lowered it, crouching, the hair along his spine and neck bristling, fangs bared. The stray held its ground, snarling, its yellow teeth filling its mouth.

John screamed, "Leave Dudley alone!" but the stray's eyes were transfixed on Dudley.

Chris ran closer and stopped a few feet away. Then the stray flinched and moved back a step, but it quickly turned to face Dudley again. They leapt, claws and fangs ripping at fur, and Chris could hear Dudley yelp in pain. They separated again, now several feet closer to the far end of the sandbox, regained their balance, and braced for another charge.

"Oh my God!" Sara screamed from the front steps of the house.

"Call 911!" Chris yelled. "No! Wait! Get me a bat out of the closet!"

After she had recovered from momentary shock, Sara ran back through the door.

Chris quickly shuffled the few steps to John.

"Help, Daddy! Dudley's getting hurt!"

When the dogs engaged again Chris picked up his son and ran back toward the house. John screamed, "Don't! Dudley!" and tried to get down.

"No, John! You have to get back! I'll help Dudley!" He ran up the front steps just as Sara came out with an aluminum softball bat. "Take him inside! That dog's going to rip Dudley to shreds!" And he grabbed the bat from her, running back down the steps.

"Oh my God, Baby, are you okay?" she cried, tightly holding John, rocking him from side to side.

"Dudley's getting hurt!" And he struggled against her hold, leaning back toward where the dogs were fighting.

"Daddy'll save him. We have to go in!" She hurried back through the door, John still protesting and struggling to get down.

When Chris returned to the sandbox, the dogs were grappling again. This time Dudley was knocked down, and the other dog clamped its powerful jaws onto his shoulder, just below his neck, ripping at his fur. Not thinking or planning, now only reacting, Chris charged. He cocked the bat high over his left shoulder, planted his feet and swung. Aluminum collided against hip with a loud thud, and the bat vibrated in Chris' hands. The dog yelped and released its hold on Dudley, who shook himself free, whining and moving back a few steps.

Chris had barely recovered from the swing, and was slightly off balance as he adjusted his footing, when the dog leapt for his throat.

He managed to parry the charge with both hands holding either end of the bat, keeping the stray at arm's length. But the weight and force of the dog were more than he expected, knocking him backward. Before he could recover, the dog was on top of him. Though Dudley clamped onto its rear right leg, it clawed its way on top of Chris. The bat was knocked from his grip and rolled out of Chris' reach. He frantically struggled to grab the dog's fur.

Now the stray's yellow teeth were inches from Chris' throat, glistening with dripping saliva, the rotten stench of its breath burning his nostrils and mouth. Chris clamped desperately onto the fur on the side of its neck, but the force of its lunging was too strong. He felt his arms giving way as the teeth snapped closer to his neck.

A shadow appeared over Chris, momentarily blocking the sun. The dog was suddenly lifted up and away from Chris, then higher, writhing and snarling, trying to reach back and bite whatever was lifting it. And then it was hurtling through the air, flying thirty feet away, landing with a crash, rolling through leaves and fallen branches. The dog staggered back to its feet, swayed left and right, shook its head. It stumbled, but soon regained its balance. Instead of attacking, it turned and bolted into the trees and down the ridge into the woods. Dudley yapped wildly, ran to the edge of the trees and stood barking, threatening, as the other dog fled out of sight.

Only then did Chris clearly see the huge figure of his neighbor towering over him. "Oh God, Crow," Chris gasped, rising to one knee. "Thank you so much." Crow extended his enormous right hand and helped Chris to his feet.

"I was pulling up a tree in my yard when I heard the commotion." His deep voice resonated, his Native American ancestors evident in the tone of his skin, his dark hair, his chiseled nose and chin. "Where did that dog come from?" He turned his six foot-nine inch frame to look down the ridge. Though his given name was Henry Johnson, everyone called him Crow. Chris had never bothered to ask him why.

"I don't know," said Chris, brushing sand and leaves off his jeans and shirt. "I just heard the barking and screaming and came running out."

"You okay?"

"Yeah, I think so. He's not, though." He knelt closer to inspect Dudley's wounds. He wagged his tail and whined slightly as Chris gently inspected the tear on his shoulder. A large chunk of fur and skin was ripped away, hanging loose and bleeding. "You poor guy. Shit." As he gently stroked the top of his head, he realized they were far beyond the range of Dudley's leash. Only then did Chris understand that Dudley had pulled the anchoring hook of his chain completely out of the tree. Otherwise, he would not have been able to knock the other dog off John. "You crazy mongrel," he whispered. "Thanks. Thanks a lot." Then Chris felt a chilling rush shoot through his body at the realization that it could have been worse, a lot worse.

"Hey, Crow," he extended his hand, "thanks again. I think you saved my neck. Literally."

"No problem. Anything you need me to do?"

"No. Thanks. Let me see if John's okay, and then I'll take Dudley to the vet."

Chris ran back into the house. "Dudley's okay!" he called as he burst through the door. "That other dog ran away." He ran up to where they stood in the living room, trying to watch what was happening through the picture window. Sara stood behind John with a firm grip on both of his shoulders, with Mary standing next to him. "Dudley got a cut, but I think he's okay. How are you?"

"He's worried about Dudley. I had to hold him to keep him from running outside. But John's not hurt or anything. Are you all right?"

Chris felt a wave of relief. "Sure. Fine. Crow threw it down the hill, and it ran away."

"I want to go out and see if he's okay," said John.

"Not yet," Chris answered quickly, knowing the huge gash in Dudley's shoulder would upset him. "That was pretty brave, what you did. Throwing a rock at that dog. I'm sure that helped to scare it away. Did you see where it came from?"

"No. All of a sudden it knocked me down. But Dudley helped me."

"Yeah. What a good dog." He looked at Sara with a wink. "I'm going to get him right to the vet. He'll need stitches."

"All right," she said. "I'll keep dinner warm."

"Thanks." He slowly walked back outside, letting the door close gently behind him. Dudley was lying on his belly, licking the wound on his shoulder. He stopped when he saw Chris come out and wagged his tail. Chris knelt next to him and scratched his head.

When Chris looked up, he saw Johnson next door and remembered he had said he was, 'pulling up a tree.' As Chris watched in awe, Johnson's muscles bulged as he pulled on a dead tree, twenty feet high, in the woods between their houses. It came up roots and all, loose dirt falling to the dead leaves on the ground. He hoisted the entire tree over his right shoulder and carried it around the back of his house. Chris suddenly realized he was very fortunate Johnson was his friend, especially today.

Chris stood, taking the loose end of Dudley's chain. "Come on, we'd better get you to the doctor."

■   ■   ■

"He's asleep," said Sara, walking into their bedroom. Chris was skimming over lecture notes, sitting up in bed against his pillow. "I think he's okay. You know? It didn't seem like the whole thing scared him much at all. As he was getting sleepy, he was more worried about how Dudley is."

Chris closed up the folder and laid it on the nightstand. "I don't know why I'm bothering. It's not like I can concentrate." He pulled back the sheet for her to join him in bed. An electric fan on the corner of the dresser across the room pulsed back and forth, rustling curtains hanging on either side of the bed. "With the stitches and antibiotics, he's going to be fine. Having his rabies booster last month saved him from getting another shot. And the vet said he could come home in a couple days."

"John knows he'll be home soon. He'll miss him a little, but I think he's more upset that he had to fight and got hurt."

"He's such a sweetheart. I swear. And such a little-tough-guy. You should have seen him jump up and throw that rock." Chris chuckled. "It missed by a mile, but it was a pretty brave thing to do."

Sara examined him with a smile. "A tough but sensitive guy, kind of like his dad."

Chris looked up and saw the love in her eyes.

He remembered the first time she had looked at him that way. They were both still in undergraduate school at Holy Cross. On a Saturday in late September, they loaded their bicycles into the back of his Honda hatchback and drove to Cape Cod. Parking and unloading at Herring Cove Beach, they rode on the bicycle trails, winding around and over the sand dunes of the Province Lands. The day was gray and cool, but the smell of autumn was in the air. When they reached Race Point and walked down close to the water, Sara unpacked the lunch she had offered to bring. Chris hadn't thought much about it, expecting something like sandwiches, potato chips, and soda. The first thing she pulled out of her backpack was a white linen tablecloth that she spread on the sand. That was followed by matching linen napkins. She then opened several containers and arranged chunks of smoked Gouda, baby Swiss and a wedge of Brie on a platter. Multigrain, whole wheat and rye crackers were next, followed by red grapes. Chris watched in astonishment as she placed a small box of Godiva chocolates to the side. Finally, two plastic wineglasses and a bottle of Merlot were pulled out, which she promptly opened and poured, announcing that it would need to breathe for a while. The wine had particularly impressed Chris since she was only twenty at the time. He remembered thinking how heavy it must have been to carry all that on her back as they rode, but she never gave him the slightest hint about what she carried.

They sat and savored the food, chewing and talking quietly, watching the waves breaking as clouds moved over them, carried by an onshore breeze. At one point, something large swam by, a hundred feet from shore. Only when it surfaced completely further along the shore did they realize it was a small, humpback whale. As they sipped the wine, he remembered how the look in her eyes had been different. Maybe it was how her warm gaze contrasted to the cool ocean behind her, or how the formality of the meal didn't conform to the natural surroundings. Throughout that day, and especially during that meal, their relationship had changed. Their first kiss, long and deep, had tasted like Merlot. And that was when he first realized he was falling in love with her. The look in her eyes told him she felt the same way.

They walked through the dunes behind the beach searching for dried wood, and built a small fire in the sand at dusk. Cuddling with Chris' blanket wrapped around them, they stayed there well past dark. And they made love for the first time in front of the fire. At one point they laughed and awkwardly fumbled to cover themselves as another couple walked by. Riding back to the car in darkness, using only one flashlight to see the trail, was an adventure. But they rode slowly and made it back, and then drove to the cottage they had reserved. There, they made love for the second, third, fourth and fifth time.

"I don't suppose the dog warden is going to have any luck."

Pulled back by Sara's comment, Chris said, "I doubt it. I've seen dogs in and out of the woods before. Seems like there's more running loose every year. They usually run away when they hear Dudley. But nothing like today. Nothing."

"It's scary. It gives me the creeps."

Chris stroked his beard thoughtfully, staring ahead. "It could have been a lot worse."

Sara studied him. "You're telling me."

"What?" he asked, focusing back on her.

"I just, well, I've never seen you like that before."

"Like what?"

"So violent. So angry. When you took that bat from me, the look in your eyes was so intense. Like an animal, I guess."

"Shit." He recounted it in his mind for a second. "Seeing John like that, and then seeing Dudley getting hurt, it was automatic. I don't think I've ever reacted to anything so easily in my life. Anyway, Crow saved my butt."

"I mean, I've seen you mad, when you've yelled at the kids a couple times. You know, when they've done things they absolutely can never do again. Like when Mary was trying to talk John into crawling under the car. Even though I hate it when you yell, I understood why you did."

Chris felt a chill. He pulled Sara against his chest and they snuggled under the sheet. After a few seconds he said, "The thought of John or Mary or you getting seriously hurt, it's the thing I'm most afraid of. It's the only thing I don't think I could get over."

She looked up at him, her expression serious. "I've never stopped loving you in the last twelve years, because you're the kindest, most understanding person I've ever known. I just didn't know it was in you to act so vicious. But I'm glad you did."

Chris was quiet for a moment, then said in a stone-cold tone, "If anything or anyone hurts anybody I love—" He closed his eyes, exhaled long and hard. "I just hope I never find out how vicious I can really be."

CHAPTER THREE

Hector Torrez woke suddenly as something hit him in the face. He became aware it was morning, and his head was heavy and clogged. Lint clung to his thick, black mustache, partially covering a mouth feeling as if full of cotton. Thick curls of black hair were in alternating patterns of being matted and disheveled. The morning sun streaming through the blinds glared brightly on his face, keeping him from fully opening his eyes. Another bottle cap flew from several feet away, hitting him in the forehead. One eye blinked slowly open.

"Hey, Buddy. Need you to get up. I have to get paid and go check on my kid." The woman sat on a stool in front of the counter in the kitchen area of the trailer. Her long, tanned legs were crossed, her tight, black dress wrinkled, one thin strap hanging off her right shoulder. She sucked long and hard on her cigarette, threw back her curled, blonde hair and exhaled a stream of smoke toward the ceiling. "Two hundred and ten."

With that, Torrez was suddenly wide awake. "What?! What the fuck are you talking about?"

She calmly inhaled again, held it for a few seconds and exhaled. "Thirty for the blow job, sixty for two fucks, a hundred for staying the night."

"A hundred for staying the night," he laughed. "What do you think this is, a fucking hotel? I was asleep, you were asleep. You think I should pay you for that?"

"House rules, not mine. And my kid had to stay there all night. I have to tip the other girls for that."

"That's not my problem, you fucking bitch." He sat up, rubbing the brown skin of his face, running his fingers through the loose curls of his hair. Then his tone changed. "I'll give you a hundred and twenty." He looked up at her, and his eyes glowed as he remembered. "You were good. Real good."

"Gee. Thanks. How charming," she smirked, and snuffed the cigarette in an empty coffee cup. She just wanted to be out of there, remembering how hard he had pulled her around in the bed, thinking he might hurt her if she pressed the issue. "A hundred and forty."

Glancing at the clock on the small table next to his bed, Hector noticed it was 8:35. "Shit. I have to go. Sure, sure. A hundred and forty." He pulled his wallet out of the worn jeans flung over the chair near the foot of the bed. From a thick wad of bills, he unfolded seven twenties and handed them to her.

"Thanks," and she forced an insincere smile while opening a small, black purse, stuffing in the bills and snapping it shut.

"Do it again? Next week?"

"You got the number. Call two days ahead. If you want me, ask for me by name."

"Yeah, yeah." He watched her butt as she let herself out, the aluminum screen door slamming behind her.

"Shit." He remembered the time and dressed quickly. The empty coffeepot, cemented to the coffee maker by a burnt crust, was buried behind dirty dishes on the kitchen counter. He badly needed a cup but didn't have time to brew any. With less than twenty minutes until his meeting with his supervisor, the vice president in charge of maintenance, he grabbed a pack of cinnamon gum and ran out the front door of his trailer. Climbing into his worn, black pickup, he drove out from the trailer village and headed toward the Passemannican Gold.

Driving quickly along the winding road that entered reservation land, he passed driveway after driveway leading up the ridge to enormous homes owned by Gold employees. Most of them were upper management, and their houses were richly landscaped and appointed, often with swimming pools, gazebos, and large decks or sunrooms. Behind them, on the highest, level land on top of Passemannican Hill, the casino stood tall and majestic, the many levels of its gold roof glistening brightly in the morning sun.

He thought, those lazy assholes sit all day in fancy offices and shuffle papers, making a million bucks a year. Guys like me do all the work and make next to nothing. They live in mansions, and I live in a fucking trailer. And everything I make goes to that bitch ex-wife of mine.

He turned left into the entrance of the Gold and headed up the hill to the parking lot.

■　■　■

Torrez was ten minutes late but was told by Brown's secretary, Pamela Nixon, to have a seat and that Brown would be with him in a minute. He examined her suspiciously but understood, sitting in the chair farthest away from the door to Brown's office. As he waited, he watched Nixon as she acknowledged people that passed through the reception area. Occasionally she spoke briefly on the phone or checked herself in a small mirror, verifying her hair and makeup were still as she desired. When she looked toward Hector, he avoided eye contact. Often his gaze found its way to water colors hanging on the walls—crude paintings in pastel colors, depicting scenes of eastern Native Americans fishing or harvesting corn. As his eyes wandered, he soon spotted a coffee maker in the far corner. He stood again and walked the few steps to Nixon's desk.

"Can I have some of that coffee?"

She eyed him with mild annoyance and said, coolly yet politely, "Certainly. There are cups in the cupboard just above the percolator. Help yourself."

Hector nodded once without a word and served himself, taking a cup of hot, black coffee back to the same chair. Between sips, with the cup held in his right hand and resting on his right thigh, he sat in silence as his mind idly thought of what he wanted to discuss with Brown. Without realizing it, his left fingers found their way to the pattern of scars on the underside of his right forearm. As they often did, his thoughts went back inexorably to how he got them.

He could still remember the first scar clearly, having received it when he was nine. Riding his bicycle through the apartment parking lot on the way home from school, Hector had tried to maneuver between parked cars, but the end of his handle bars had nicked his father's Camaro on the driver's side. Since the old bike had no rubber handle grips, it left a thin scratch eight inches long just above the door handle.

"Give me your fucking arm!" his father had yelled later. "Hold it out! Now!"

More angry than scared, Hector put out his right arm. Grabbing firmly and extending it fully, his father held it with one hand while puffing several times on his cigarette until the ash was glowing red and hot. Hector clenched his teeth and winced in anticipation, trying to struggle free, but his father held firm. The pain was worse than he had expected as his skin sizzled briefly, a small wisp of smoke curling upward. And the smell. He would never forget the smell of his own flesh burning, especially that first time. He had cried out only for that second until his father loosened his grip, and Hector was able to pull free. And all the while his mother and Rosie, his little sister, sat quietly in the next room, fearful, knowing full well what was happening and knowing they couldn't do a thing about it.

"There. That's one," his father had said. "Every time you do another fucking stupid thing, you get another mark. When you've got enough marks, then you'll be a real, big, total 'asshole.'"

As he stared across the room at nothing, Hector's fingers passed back and forth over the scars, mostly unnoticeable under the hairs on the bottom of his arm. Eight small circles completed the A and seven more made the first

S. The composition of the second S had gotten only as far as the first four marks. That was when Hector was thirteen and had been big enough to fight back.

Pulling his arm free and running to the kitchen, he pulled the largest carving knife from the drawer. "Don't you ever do that to me again!" he yelled, brandishing the knife at arm's length.

His father's first reaction had been to laugh. But that quickly transgressed to fury. He yelled, "You little shit!" and moved toward Hector to punish him for such audacity. Stabbing wildly, first at his father's arms and then at his chest, Hector had sent him to the hospital in serious condition. Once social workers were involved and evaluated the entire situation, Hector and Rosie were immediately placed in foster care. Over the next several years they moved from home to home. And Hector was constantly in and out of trouble. First at school, then with the law.

Rosie, thought Hector. These scars are bad enough, but what that shit father of ours did to her. Hector could still hear her screams. "No! Don't Daddy! That hurts! Ow! Ow! Ow! Ow!"

And still their mother did nothing, pretending not to know what was going on.

"Mr. Brown will see you now," said Nixon, forcing a smile.

Hector stood, remembering why he was there. "Oh. Okay" And he opened the office door.

"Hector, come on in," Richard Brown said as he stood and walked from behind his large, mahogany desk. He extended his right hand, glittering gold rings on all four fingers, each studded with large gems. His navy blue, silk suit fit perfectly, accented with a pink handkerchief, and was open enough to reveal the pink shirt underneath. Open buttons exposed a thick, gold necklace and a thick mat of chest hair. "How are you?" Brown asked.

"Okay. A little tired. I was here until one last night, rewiring the track lighting above the Pacific Slots. I think we got it all ready to go."

"Great. Great. Well, sit down. Right. There is good." Brown returned to his thickly padded, leather chair. "So, what was it you wanted to talk about?"

Torrez briefly fidgeted in his chair, his hands clamped over the vinyl arm rests. "I think you know I been here since we opened, for six years. And I been electrical floor supervisor on second shift for almost two years."

"Sure."

"What I wanted to ask is, uh, we're doing real good. I see on the TV how much we make every month. But I haven't got a raise since last year."

"Ah. I see. This is about more money." Brown thought a second, his

25

fingers intertwined in front of his face. Then he calmly and sincerely said, "Well, I know you have been doing good work. But it's just not that easy. If it was up to me, I'd be happy to give you a raise today."

"I know you can do something about it if you want to." Torrez became angry, his hands clamping tighter around the arm rests. He had been expecting a denial like this.

"But you must know we have organizational policy. These things are done across the board, so to speak, when the executive committee approves it."

Hector look confused for a second, then shook his head. "And when's the next time that's going to happen?"

Brown thought a moment. "You know, with the preliminary approval of annexation, that will open up so many opportunities. For you, for all of us."

Hector's brow crinkled. "I don't get what you mean."

"You know the annexation plans, right?"

Torrez nodded, but then said, "Well, some of them. What I saw on TV."

"When we annex all 325 acres into the reservation, we'll build the new hotel and the huge, new theater. And we'll triple slot, poker, and blackjack space."

"That's going to take years. What difference will that make? I need more money now."

Brown noticed the white of the man's knuckles, the change in his expression, the tone of his voice sharpened with anger. He knew Hector and his reputation at work and thought maybe he should just move him along, humor him, tell him what he wanted to hear. Reports from other floor supervisors and electricians occasionally came in about him, describing him as mean and ill-tempered. He would harass others, making their working conditions unbearable. And whenever things were accomplished, he would take the credit with no acknowledgment of his coworkers.

"I can tell you a few things for sure," Brown said. "The plans are pretty much finished. Once construction begins, you can imagine how much wiring will need to be done. Most of it will be done by contractors, but they'll need in-house people to help, to make sure the work meets our criteria."

"Our what?"

"Up to our standards. As good as we need it. I think you and others will fit right into that."

"Will that pay more?"

"What it will be is overtime. Once construction begins, we'll need it to get finished as soon as possible. You're on second shift now, right? I think many extra hours during the day at time-and-a-half would help, don't you?"

Torrez had calmed down some. "But that's more work, and it still won't be for a long time. They won't get to the wiring for at least a year."

"And I think some preliminary consulting, you know, talking to the architects about what we have now, would be in order."

"I don't know anything about how to do that."

Brown, now, was saying anything to appease him just for the moment. "That's okay. They'll work with you. And once expansion is complete, your job as supervisor will expand. More people under you, more pay."

Torrez grinned slightly, but then said, "But what about now? I make nine fifty a week, and that bitch wife of mine, and that brat kid, they take four hundred of it. For doing nothing."

Brown waited a few seconds, then said sympathetically, "I'll tell you what I'll do. I'll talk to Mr. Aiello. Of course, he's busy running this whole place, so I can't promise you when. But I will talk to him. I'll see what I can do."

"Okay." Torrez smiled, nodding his head. "It's just so fucking hard to get by on five hundred a week. And this place wouldn't get too far without electricity."

Brown laughed. "No, it sure wouldn't. We all appreciate the work you and your men do." Then he remembered something. "When are your days off?"

"Tuesday and Wednesday. Why?"

"There's a town meeting next Wednesday, at Littleboro High School. The town council and some of the tribe executives will be trying to encourage community support for the annexation." He laughed again. "Not that it matters. Once annexation is approved, construction will begin. It's more like a neighborly gesture. You know, try and get everyone calmed down so things can go as smooth as possible."

"What does that have to do with me?"

"I thought maybe you'd like to go to it to learn more about the expansion that will happen when annexation gets final approval. They'll be talking about when things will happen, what will be built, how many people will be hired, how much they think Gold income will increase, how it will help the town. Things like that. It'll be a good way for you to learn more about it."

Hector shifted uneasily. "I don't know if I should go. I don't like crowds like that."

"You won't be saying anything. You can just sit and listen."

Torrez thought for a while. "I guess. Maybe you're right. It would be good for me to know what's going on. The high school, you said?"

"Right. And I'll talk to Mr. Aiello." Brown stood, indicating the meeting was finished. "I'll let you know what we come up with."

Torrez stood and they shook hands. "Thanks, Mr. Brown. That meeting is a week from tonight, you said?"

"Right. I won't be there, but a few people from these offices will."

"Okay." Torrez turned and left the office.

Brown sat down and watched him go. What a loser, he thought. With all the money we're making, we should be able to hire anyone we want, to get the best there is. But he is a tribal member. Too bad he can't live up to the standards we're setting.

■   ■   ■

Torrez walked down the wide staircase and into the large, gaming room, thinking he should score big again, as he had the week before. That win was helping to tide him over until he got paid on Friday. The room was a bustle of activity though it was a weekday morning. Video slot and poker machines whizzed and beeped. He heard a cascade of coins fall simultaneously with a yell of excitement. The voices of dealers calling the progress of their games blended into a low murmur to add to the din. Smoke clung to the ceiling before being removed by heavy exhaust fans that hummed overhead, and cocktail waitresses moved to-and-fro between tables and machines.

Careful not to let security see him (employees were not allowed to gamble in-house), and knowing where to sit so surveillance cameras couldn't get a good shot of his face, Torrez chose an empty video slot machine next to an elderly woman. Sitting alone, she had a gold, plastic bucket in her lap, half filled with silver dollars. Just as Hector sat down, she hit a large jackpot. Lights flashed around the outward edge of the machine and silver dollars began pouring down. Her expression didn't change as she watched, waiting patiently for the coins to fall. When they stopped, she picked one out of the bucket, deposited it in the machine, hit the "pull" button, and watched the losing result. She took another coin, hit the button, waited. Another. And another. Her expression never changed.

Seeing the big win next to him, Torrez grew more excited in anticipation. He pulled two twenty dollar bills from his wallet and fed them into the slot of the bill acceptor, causing *40 credits* to appear on the small, green monitor. He began playing, always choosing a two dollar bet per pull in anticipation of double the payoff.

The first seven tries were losers. He muttered a quiet "fuck it" after each loss, watching the indicated credits counting down on the monitor. The eighth spin hit two bars and a cherry, causing a light to flash and the credits to rebound to thirty-six. He smiled, bobbing his head slightly and saying, "Come on, come on. That's it."

But the next thirteen were all losers. Following each loss, he slapped the side of the machine, swearing louder and louder, hitting it successively harder. But he played a hunch with the last ten credits, the maximum bet allowed by the machine, and bet it all on the next spin. He watched with genuine expectation as the three columns stopped in succession. When it came up bar—apple—star, a loser, he stared for a moment in disbelief. He finally realized he had lost it all and yelled, "You fucking piece of dogshit," while punching the front of the machine full force. It gave no ground, and nothing broke, but he felt stinging pain shoot up his right arm. "God damn it!" he cried, shaking his hand vigorously until the stinging subsided. He remembered how much security didn't like that kind of behavior, so he refrained from punching it again. He stood, fighting an urge to play more. There were only four more twenties in his wallet, and they had to last until Friday.

Walking away quickly while muttering, "I should've given it to that whore instead," he left the building and drove back to his trailer.

Chapter Four

undreds of torch flames shimmered off the peaks of the pyramids, giving an orange glow to the clear night air. The reflections danced and sparkled on the water of the Nile delta. Birds called from all directions, their cries echoing across the flood plain.

Jesus sat in front of their small shelter, gazing in awe out at the majestic man-made structures. Though a child, having seen them for a few short months, he had a sense there was something familiar about them. Mary and Joseph had stood, night after night, gazing across the water in wonder. How could men build such a structure, standing higher than the hills that lined the far bank? Magnificent, they had said aloud. Truly man's greatest accomplishment. Yet Jesus had a feeling of uneasiness about them. Though he said he agreed with his parents that they were spectacular, he sensed something about them that brought restlessness, almost fear, to him. He did not understand how or why he felt this, but he did.

Jesus walked back inside to find Joseph sitting in the corner of their one room, sharpening his knives and saws on a thin slab of slate. He inspected each one carefully, delicately. Mary sat at the table, separating individual strands of flax and wrapping them neatly around a large, wooden spool. The two lanterns they owned lighted each of their work areas as a small fire crackled in the stone hearth.

"Beautiful evening, Son," Joseph smiled, looking up.

"It is." He walked over and sat across from Mary. "May I help you?" Though he had been with Mary and Joseph only a year and half, Jesus had easily learned their language and was fully conversational. His physical stature and mental abilities were those of a six or seven-year-old boy, growing and maturing at a rate well beyond any other children Mary or Joseph knew.

"Certainly. Here, take the spool. When I separate a strand, you wrap it around tightly. See how I have done the others?"

"I see. I can do it."

Mary smiled. "I am sure you can."

There was little conversation as they all worked peacefully in the dim light.

Recently, Joseph and Mary had heard that Herod, King of Judea, had searched for a male child soon after Jesus had arrived with them. This child, it was said, was not of Earthly creation and was a sign that foretold the end of the reign of Herod. When this child could not be found in spite of extensive searching, Herod ordered every male child under the age of two, in and about Bethlehem, to be put to death. His soldiers faithfully, savagely, carried out this order.

Joseph and Mary did not speak of this with Jesus or with any of the people who lived near them. Quietly, they thanked their Lord for delivering their son, and sparing him this horrible death.

Jesus clung to Mary's tunic as they worked their way through the streets of the large village. People belonging to many of the local tribes of Egypt swarmed the marketplace where vendors sold fruit, grain, fish, and fowl from their carts. Most had been pulled to the village by donkeys or camels still harnessed to the carts, patiently waiting in the midday heat as business was conducted. People and animals scurried in all directions like ants gathering crystals of dried honey from a fallen branch. The smells of animal dung and fish were oppressive. Noise and dust permeated the air.

Mary had stopped at a cart, saying to the vendor, "One piece of silver for those two herring."

The vendor eyed her spitefully and looked insulted. "I would ask no less than five," he said impatiently.

"One is all I have."

He dug to the bottom corner of the wooden box and pulled up a large, thick-scaled fish. "One will buy you this carp." As soon as it was pulled clear of the other fish, Jesus could smell its fetid odor above all the others.

Mary's expression and posture sank in disappointment. Again, she thought, it is always the same. But it would supply them with the meat they needed. She could grind it and bake it in cakes as in so many other meals.

"Two carp for one piece of silver, especially for your wares you will cast out tonight anyway."

The vendor shouted, "How dare you insult my catch, vag! One carp or none at all!"

"The one then." She took it, wrapped it in a torn piece of flaxen cloth and placed it gingerly into her tattered, jute sack.

The vendor took the coin and inspected it carefully, flinging it loudly into his moneybox. "Off with you," and he motioned her and Jesus to continue down the street.

Jesus was very much aware of the nature of the interaction that had just transpired, similar to so many others that had occurred in the past year. He noticed everything and understood it all. He also was beginning to understand the best way to react, no matter the situation. "Carp will be fine, Mother. You make it taste like herring when you bake it in your breads." He smiled up at her.

She instantly forgot her frustration and looked down. Remembering who he was, she smiled and felt the same warmth she always felt toward him. "You are wise beyond your years, my son."

They continued along the street, purchasing dates, wheat and a section of horsehide. They loaded their donkey and walked alongside, back across the flood plain of the Nile and up the gradual slope of the eastern bank to their land.

That evening, after helping Joseph clean up around his work area, collecting the small scraps of wood to burn in cooking fires, Jesus sat alone on a rock outcropping above their small garden. The sun had set across the river, leaving gold on the horizon fading to a deepening, cobalt blue. Occasional flocks of birds darted by, just visible in the remaining light. A chorus of crickets began their serenade from the tall grass above. Jesus noticed a small rabbit scurry in front of him and stop short in full view. He smiled widely and watched closely, speaking gently to it, beckoning softly with his voice. The rabbit's ears surveyed the air constantly, turning in his direction when he spoke. Its tiny nose moved up and down, then it took a couple steps closer to Jesus. He stood, moved closer himself, and squatted patiently, speaking to it, holding out his hand in a greeting.

The rabbit suddenly tensed in fright and quickly scurried up the slope into the bushes that lined the crest of the hill. Joseph soon appeared from below and walked up to sit next to Jesus.

"It will be dark soon. You should come in out of the night air."

"Why, Father? I have heard you and Mother say that before. What is in the darkness that we should avoid?"

"It is understood well that many of the morbidities that afflict people are caused by breathing the night air. It is a time of bad spirits."

Jesus considered this, but within his mind his father's words only caused him confusion. "What are 'bad spirits?' I do not understand this."

Joseph looked out across the river, thinking. "Forces, I believe. Forces that have the mind and likeness of people, but without the flesh of our bodies."

"I do not understand how that could be."

"They are not Earthly, not meant to be understood, nor even possible to be understood. They are beyond what is real to us."

Jesus looked at Joseph, then said, "If they exist, are they not real?"

Joseph was silent, not knowing how to respond to this.

Jesus was thoughtful for a few moments. Finally he said, "Father, I know things, I understand things. There are thoughts in my mind, and I know I have not learned these from you or Mother or any of our neighbors. It is as though I remember another place, another life. My memories are as if I was in a different land, among different people."

Joseph hesitated, then said, "We have told you how you came to us."

"Yes. But I do not remember that happening. It is like I remember— what was before I came to you."

"How you came to us is truly the work of spirits, of things beyond the abilities of people."

"But I do not understand how there could be things such as spirits. There are many things people do not understand, but they are still real. Many things that can be seen, heard, tasted, touched, but still not understood." Jesus thought a moment. "It is as if I remember I was once among other people. People who knew many things and did many things we do not do. I think it is some of these things that I am remembering."

Joseph genuinely considered what his son was saying. "To this I do not have an answer for you. Both your mother and I have always believed you were given to us for a reason. And there have been some who have said you have been sent here for a reason, to help people, teach people. Perhaps it is these things you remember or these things you understand. Things that you are meant to teach."

"But these things seem so unclear to me now, almost like remembering a dream after I am awake."

Joseph cradled Jesus' shoulders in his strong, right arm, his callused hand touching him lightly. "If you are meant to teach people, you will know what to teach them when the time comes."

Jesus snuggled into his tunic, the smell of sawdust and sweat strong in the cotton. "I know this to be true as well."

"How do you feel you know these things? People must be taught almost everything they know from the time they are born. And yet, it has not been necessary to teach you very much. As you say, it is as if you already know many things."

"Do you remember in the fall you told me of the geese that live here in the winter? In the summer they fly to lands far north and then return to the very same spot the next summer. Or how a bird knows how to build a nest, though its father and mother have never taught it? Or how bees know to gather nectar and make honey, again, though they were never taught?"

"I remember."

"That is what it feels like to me, I think. I know things, but I have always known them, without having to be taught."

Joseph thought a moment. "We started to talk of morbidities. If you do not think sicknesses are caused by spirits of the night air, then by what?"

Jesus thought. Memories were there, though it took a moment for him to visualize those thoughts. "It seems like there is some truth to this. But the words are vague to me. Perhaps I just do not know our language well enough yet." And then a different idea came to him. "Or maybe there are words to describe these things in a different language. What I am thinking now is that living things have a spirit, that spirit is the difference between what is living and what is not."

"Does not every thing have a spirit? Every tree, every bird, every rock?"

"Trees, birds, donkeys, people—yes. Rocks, no. Rocks are just rocks. It is what lives and dies that has a spirit, not what has never been and never will be alive, such as a rock."

Joseph considered this, thinking these were truly complex thoughts for any person, let alone a young boy. "The more time you are with us, Jesus, the more I believe you are not of Earthly creation."

Jesus smiled. "This spring when I cut my hand helping you lathe cedar, did I not bleed? I also remember feeling very cold this past winter."

"Perhaps. But you are unlike any person I have known."

CHAPTER FIVE

The sprinkler shot diverging streams of water skyward as it slowly rocked back and forth. John and Mary in bathing suits squealed with glee as they ran through the shower, laughing and yelling, daring each other to go through again. Water collected in small pools in the uneven texture of the lawn, and their feet splashed through the puddles as they ran. Chris was at the corner of the house near the garage, crouching as he nailed flange to the siding that held the drainage spout in place. Sweat beaded heavily on his forehead in the humid, hot air. His T-shirt was soaked in the armpits and along the front from neck to belly. Dudley lay content in the sandbox, happy for so much activity around him, his eyes moving to follow what was most interesting at any given time.

Chris finished his chore with three more hits of his hammer, each landing squarely with a loud, metallic thud. He stood as he wiped his forehead with the top of his forearm, dropping the hammer into the toolbox nearby. It landed with a loud clunk among the other tools. "Hey, guys," he called to John and Mary, "maybe we should turn that off soon. There's a water saving alert, you know."

"But Dad," Mary protested, "it's so hot! And there's only one more Saturday before school starts!"

"I know. But you've cooled off enough."

"Nooo!" she cried. Realizing she may have taken her protest too far, she quickly put her hands over her mouth.

Chris watched her reaction, then called out in mock annoyance, "Excuse me, young lady. I know I couldn't have heard what I thought I just heard."

Mary just stood silent, grinning wryly.

Chris quickly strode across the driveway toward where they were playing. Halfway there, he bent at the waist and extended his arms, saying, "What did you say? What did you say?"

John and Mary both screeched in playful fright and took two steps away from him. But he ran straight through the sprinkler and grabbed them both, hoisting one under each arm. Carrying them back until they were directly under the falling water, he stood there, holding them as they laughed and struggled to get down.

"Now, what are we going to do with this sprinkler?" Within seconds his hair and shirt were completely soaked with the cold water.

"We'll turn it off!" cried Mary, laughing.

"That's the answer I wanted to hear." He gently placed them back on the wet grass.

As soon as her feet hit the ground, Mary ran over and turned off the spigot on the front of the house.

"Why don't you dry off with the towels on the railing there, then go inside and see what Mom's up to."

"All right." They hurried to the front steps, dried themselves quickly and inadequately, and went inside with water still falling from their hair, bathing suits, and backs.

Chris rolled his eyes with a smile. Lifting his face to the sky with his eyes closed, he slicked back his hair with his hands, savoring the refreshing feel of the cool water on his skin. Just as he began walking across the driveway to pick up his toolbox, he saw Crow limping up the small incline from his house.

"Hey, Crow. How goes it?"

"Good." He noticed Chris was wet and then saw the puddles on the grass and driveway. "Aren't you a little old to be playing in the sprinkler?"

Chris just laughed and clamped the lock on the toolbox cover.

Dudley was standing now, wagging his tail in greeting. "How's he doing?" asked Crow, pointing to him with a thumb. "Seemed like he got hurt pretty bad the other day."

"He's okay. The stitches are holding, once we got him to stop biting at them. And he's been taking antibiotics twice a day. I don't know what they put in those things, but he likes their taste better than he likes his food." Chris noticed Crow was carrying a brown paper bag. "What do you have there?"

"Oh." He lifted it as if surprised Chris had seen it. "Six from my latest batch."

"Great! What did you make this time? More stout, I hope. That was the best beer I've ever had."

"No, this time I tried a new one, an experiment. Blueberry-honey-wheat."

"That sounds ambitious. And good."

"The only one I opened was okay, but a couple more weeks of aging wouldn't hurt. I picked the blueberries myself, back in July. Got the honey at the orchard, too."

"Thanks a lot. I'll stick these in the fridge and pull one out in a couple weeks, maybe to celebrate annexation." He shook his head and looked down.

"Sure looks like it'll happen, doesn't it?" said Crow. "If it does—whatever. If it doesn't, oh, well. I'll be security at the Gold either way. A glorified bouncer for life."

Chris studied him. "You don't care whether your tribe gets more land, to expand and all that?"

"Like I said, I'll be security until I die. Or until I get too old to throw jerks out on their butts."

Chris glanced up and down at his massive size. "You could be an offensive lineman for the Patriots."

"Maybe ten years ago, if I wasn't so slow. Why'd you mention annexation?"

"There's that town meeting on Wednesday. It's been on my mind a lot lately." Chris looked down at Johnson's feet. "You were limping. Ankle again?"

"Yeah. Would you mind?"

"No, sure. Here," he said, kneeling, "kick off your sandal." Johnson did so and balanced his weight by putting a hand on Chris' shoulder, who took the massive foot in his hands. "Like I told you before, I might as well put those three years of pre-med to some good use if I can." He carefully felt, found the misplaced tendon, applied pressure to the heel, and gently manipulated until the tendon slipped back beyond the bone to its proper position.

Johnson grunted and then immediately sighed in relief. "It's amazing how you do that. That chiropractor I went to last year charged a hundred and twenty bucks, and didn't do it as good or as fast." He slipped his sandal back on and tested the full weight of his three hundred and twenty pounds on the newly adjusted ankle. "Mmmm, great. Good as new. And all it cost was a six-pack."

"Great. Glad to help. I don't remember much from pre-med, but I do remember where all the bones, muscles, and tendons go. Cutting those cats and pigs to pieces was so much fun." Chris thought a second and laughed. "No wonder I couldn't hack those courses, trying to remember all those Latin names. Every one had at least fifteen letters. All I know now is parts is parts, no matter what they're called."

Not really understanding, Crow said, "Whatever. Glad you live next to me now."

"Just keep those home brews coming." Chris held up the bag and licked his lips.

"Hey, I have to go. Need to be at work by four."

"Yep. Thanks for the beer."

"Thanks for the ankle. See you, Dudley." Crow lumbered down the hill.

■ ■ ■

Hector tipped the shot glass, swallowing the tequila in one gulp. "Hit me one more time, Mel," he called to the bartender. Mel refilled the glass and waited while Torrez finished it quickly. His cigarette sat in the glass ashtray to his right, the thin column of smoke rising to the ceiling.

The floor of the small, dark bar was uneven, worn hardwood, warped and stained from decades of spilled beer and muddy feet. Pictures of New England sports heroes sparsely decorated the walls in select locations. Not autographed glossies, but shopping mall posters, framed in black plastic and covered with thin glass. A half dozen neon signs hung behind the bar, advertising various brands of beer. Only one other man and woman, both in their fifties, sat at the bar, far to the left of Torrez. They both wore red T-shirts with white lettering, advertising *Will's Truck Plaza*. Matching red and white caps coordinated their uniforms. They sipped quietly on beers.

"That'll be eighteen-fifty, Hec," Mel said.

Flipping a twenty onto the bar, he crushed his cigarette in the ashtray and stood, pushing the stool back with his legs. Wavering slightly, he waited until he gained his balance. "See you tomorrow." He walked slowly to the door, out into the afternoon heat.

Within five minutes he was parking his truck in the maintenance employees' lot behind the west entrance of the Gold. He unwrapped two sticks of mint gum and began chewing, then walked through the service entrance toward the locker rooms. Soon he was stringing wire to a bank of soon-to-be-flashing, gold lights being installed over the newest row of blackjack tables.

■ ■ ■

"Hey! Lockwood! What the fuck are you doing?" Torrez yelled a half hour later. He quickly walked straight at the young man who was on a stepladder and twisting a wire nut around two exposed ends.

Lockwood turned with a start, saw who it was, and thought, now what? He shook his head slightly and said, "Connecting these wires," then turned back to his work.

"Hey! I'm talking to you! What the hell are you doing? Aren't those part of the new wiring?"

"Yeah," Lockwood said. Now he turned to face Torrez. "What's the problem now, oh, Mighty Supervisor?" He took the two steps down the ladder to the floor and stood face to face with Torrez.

"Lose that tone with me, shithead," he growled. "I told you last week to use the red nuts on the new wiring. How else are we going to keep track of what we done with the high grade copper?"

"Some of us don't come to work stinking of tequila, asshole. We can tell by looking at it what's high grade and what was put in five years ago."

Torrez grabbed a fistful of Lockwood's shirt and pulled him to his face. "Don't you ever talk to me like that again," he hissed. "I'll break your fucking neck."

Lockwood threw up his hands, over-dramatizing the fact that he wasn't fighting back. Two other electricians who had been working nearby hurried out the employee entrance and into the gaming room. "Hey, I'm so scared," Lockwood laughed. "Why don't you take a swing at me, Supervisor. Do us all a favor and get yourself fired. That would be worth taking one of your pussy punches."

Torrez shoved him hard, back against the ladder. Lockwood fell into it, knocking it over, sending tools falling in a shower, clanging noisily against the wall and floor. As he fell, his momentum carried him over one leg of the ladder and brought him thudding against the wall. Torrez was on top of him quickly, picking him up by his shirt, then throwing him back in the other direction against wooden crates that were stacked nearby. Lockwood yelled in pain as wood splintered under his weight.

"Now, you gonna use the red nuts?" Torrez threatened, standing over him.

"What's going on?" a deep voice came from behind him.

Torrez turned to see Crow standing there, his hands on his hips, wearing his blue shirt with gold trim and dark blue necktie—the uniform of security. His brow was wedged into an angry V.

"This is none of your business, Crow," Torrez said, then turned back to Lockwood. "I was just making sure Jimmy and me understand each other. Right, Jimmy?"

Lockwood groaned and tried to get up.

"You okay?" Crow asked, looking past Torrez to Lockwood.

Torrez sneered, "Sure he is, he's just getting back to work."

Crow tried to walk past him to help Lockwood up, but Torrez quickly stepped in the way. "He's fine, I said."

"Back off, Hector," Crow said firmly, and tried to walk past.

Torrez grabbed his arm by the shirtsleeve. "Leave him alone." But when

Torrez saw Crow's eyes look at his hand holding the shirt, then move back up to his own eyes, with growing anger and diminishing patience in his expression, he tried to make light of the situation. "Look, aren't there any card counters you can haul off in cuffs," he laughed nervously.

"Let go of me."

Torrez released his shirt, but persisted, stepping completely between Crow and Lockwood.

Crow looked down in disbelief. "Either you move, or I'll move you."

"This is between Jimmy and his boss. It's not a security issue."

With his left hand, Crow took a fistful of shirt and lifted Torrez easily off the floor, swung him around against a finished section of wall and held him there, three feet off the floor. Torrez struggled to get loose but couldn't move. Crow said, in a low tone, "You made it a security issue when you hit him," and then moved his face closer. "It's bad enough we have people in here who get mad when they lose all their money. Or they think they got cheated. That I can understand. When workers are fighting between themselves, well that's just embarrassing." Then Crow growled at Torrez, nose to nose, "Now back off. Get it? And it'll save me a lot of paperwork and you a lot of blood loss."

It was then that Torrez stopped struggling. When Crow felt him relax, he put him down then moved over to Lockwood, helping him to his feet. "You okay?"

Lockwood shook his head, twisted and stretched his back left and then right. "Uhh, I guess so. Damn it! I can't even do my god damn job without my own boss screwing me up."

"I really don't feel like writing this up," Crow said. "Why don't you two just kiss and make up and do your jobs."

"Fine with me," Lockwood said. "That's what I was doing."

"Yeah, yeah," said Torrez.

Crow slowly turned and walked out to the gaming room.

"Fucking gorilla," said Torrez under his breath, while straightening his shirt. "Mind your own fucking business." Then he turned to Lockwood. "Use the fucking red nuts."

■   ■   ■

"'Bitsy Bunny ran over the grassy hill and into her burrow, as fast as she could,'" Chris read from the book.

"A bureau?" John asked, laying next to him on the small bed. A lamp emblazoned with Boston Red Sox logos on the small night stand gave the room a dim, yellow glow. "She lived in a bureau? Like what my clothes are in?"

"No, a burrow. It's a hole in the ground that small animals live in, like a rabbit or a mouse."

"Oh. Okay. Keep going." He looked expectantly at the pages.

"'After brushing her front teeth, she snuggled into bed and said her prayers before—'"

"What are prayers?" John interrupted.

Chris thought a second, then said, "It's when somebody thinks about things they want to happen, but they think about them as if they are asking some big magic person to make them come true."

John looked at him and then his face crinkled up. "Huh?"

Chris laughed a little. "I guess I made that sound kind of silly, didn't I?"

"What big magic person?"

"Have you ever heard people talking about God?"

John thought about this, then said, "Sometimes, but I don't—" Then his face lit up. "Oh yeah! The god dam! I heard about that on movies."

Chris laughed again. To himself, he said, "I guess we should cancel cable." Then he turned to John. "No, see, a lot of people think that a great big—person, I guess, or something in the shape of a person, made the whole earth, all the people and animals, all the stars, everything. Sort of by magic."

John asked, "How? Where is this person? Like in a factory? Is it a boy or a girl?"

"I guess everyone who believes in God has a pretty good idea about what He—He looks like. Most people think God is like a man. There's a way of thinking called religion."

"I know what reledging is. My friend at school, Jason, he goes to church. He told me about that."

"Right. Church. People go to a church or a temple to worship God."

"War ship God? Why?"

"I—Let's see. I guess when you think something or someone is so special, you try to do things you think they will really like."

"Like when you brought Mommy flowers on her birthday?"

"Well, I did that because I love her." He hesitated, but John was watching him, waiting. "Can I tell you a secret I usually only tell my students?"

John looked excited. "Okay!" he whispered, and leaned closer.

"There are millions of people all over the world who believe in a god, but it seems like they all have a different idea of what God is like, even though there probably is only one thing or person called God. Some people think God

41

is like a great big magic person who lives somewhere called Heaven who makes everything, and makes things happen. God made the stars, the Earth, everything." Chris watched John's reaction. "Does that sound real to you?"

"It sounds like a TV show. Like a cartoon."

Chris laughed. "Yeah, I guess it does. But you know what? Here's the secret. Sometimes I think I know exactly what God is."

"Really? What does He look like?"

"It's not a he or a she. God is everything that's alive. God is just life. Not stars, or wind, or lightning, or anything like that. Just what is alive."

"Plants are alive. Mrs. Reid told me that in school. A long time ago, before my birthday."

"She's right. Plants are alive, so are bugs and animals and people. Everything that is alive is made to look like the part of God they have in them."

"Huh?"

"That might be getting too hard for you to understand."

"How did you get to know that?" John asked.

"Well, I'm not really sure of all the reasons. I know I started thinking about it a lot when my daddy died, just before I started going to college. I was so sad when he died, but it helped me understand how lucky it is to be alive. In college I learned a lot about living things, like how they work, all the different kinds of plants and animals, all the things inside them that keep them living and growing. It always amazed me how complicated living things are, but they all still work so well. First I understood that the thing people think is God can only be what makes things alive. And, after I met Mommy, and Mary and you were born, then I really understood what love is."

John had been thinking about what Chris had been saying, then said, "Dad?"

"Yeah?"

"Why don't we go to church?"

"Well, church is something called a ritual. Something people do to worship God."

"Then why don't we go?"

"Because I think that God doesn't need to be worshipped, God needs to be loved. You only can do that by being a good person. By trying to make everyone you know a little happier, if you can. You don't do that at church. You have to live your whole life that way, all the time, everything you do, everything you say."

"Sometimes you don't make me very happy. When you get mad and yell really loud."

"Sometimes you have to be mean, or mad. If bad things happen, or people do bad things, you can't always think it's okay"

John suddenly looked sad, and was thinking about something.

"What wrong?" asked Chris.

"There were some boys at my school last year. They were mean."

"Mean how? What did they do?"

"They pushed people down a lot. Or took toys I was playing with, or Tim, or Janet was playing with."

"What did your teachers do?" asked Chris. "Didn't they stop them?"

"Those boys always waited until the teachers weren't looking."

"Pretty sneaky. What did they do to you?"

"They took my toys a lot of times and pushed me down to get ahead of me in line for the slide."

"What did you do? You were one of the biggest kids in your class. Did you stop them?"

"I wanted to hit them, but I didn't. I don't like to be mean to people. It just makes me mad."

Chris thought a second. "Well, you're right. You should always try to be nice whenever you can. But it's okay to stand up for your rights."

"What does that mean?"

"If someone is being very mean to you, you don't have to let them. Never start being mean to anyone, and never start a fight. But it's okay to try and stop fights. If someone is being mean to you, or someone else, for no reason, it's okay to try and stop them, even if you have to be a little mean yourself."

John thought about this, then yawned deeply and rubbed his eyes.

Chris said, "Hey, let's finish reading. Where were we? Oh, yeah. 'She snuggled into bed and said her prayers before turning off the light and lying down on her pillow. It had been a long, busy day, and Bitsy just wanted to sleep. And she did!'" He closed the book.

"I want to sleep, too."

"Great idea." Chris pulled back the sheet and John crawled under.

"Thanks for reading the book to me, Daddy."

"You're welcome. Good night, Johnny. Tomorrow we can practice throwing the ball some more."

"Okay. Good night."

Chris turned off the lamp and left the room.

Sara was sitting on Mary's bed with her, talking about school.

"Hey you two," Chris said quietly as he entered the room, sitting on the foot of the bed.

"Mary's worried that second grade will be too hard," Sara said with a smile only Chris could see. "She's heard they're going to learn cursive, and that's scary."

"It is!" Mary emphasized.

"Well, you probably don't remember," Chris said, "but you said the same thing about learning to read last year. Was that hard?"

"That was easy! Only babies like John can't read."

"Right, because he hasn't learned how yet, like you did last year. And if I remember right, you were in the highest reading group in your class most of the year."

"But cursive is weird. There's all these new letters that look funny."

"They're the same letters, you just make them a new way," Sara said.

"Right. I think that'll be a lot easier than learning to read," added Chris.

"She's also a little concerned that I'll be working, too," said Sara.

"Mom's just going to be at the hospital from nine until one, taking care of the kids of patients while they're in the hospital. You'll be in school the whole time she's working, and John will be in preschool."

"But what if I get sick and have to stay home? Who will give me medicine or take my temperature?"

"I worked it out with the boss there," said Sara. "I can stay home sometimes if I have to."

"And most of my classes are in the afternoon, so I could go to the college later sometimes."

Mary finally accepted. "Al-l-l-l-l right."

"Let's get some sleep," said Chris.

When both kids were asleep, Chris and Sara sat quietly in the living room. As Sara read her favorites from *The Complete Robert Frost*, Chris reviewed lecture notes. Dudley lay content and asleep at their feet.

Chris suddenly said, "So. You want to strip naked and boink?"

Sara looked at him out of the corner of her eye. "You romantic fool."

Chris waited patiently, for a moment, then said, "Well?"

"Umm. Okay." But she continued to read.

After a few seconds, Chris said, "Are you horny?"

"Umm. Kinda."

"Cool."

Suddenly, notes and books were tossed aside and the sofa was cleared of everything except their bodies.

Ten minutes later, when Sara cried out for the first time, Dudley looked up to see what was going on.

By the time they both cried out simultaneously, twenty minutes later, Dudley had already gone down into the family room in the basement and was sleeping in peace and quiet.

Chapter Six

he caravan of six wooden carts and several donkeys plodded along slowly, returning from Jerusalem to Nazareth in Galilee. A high cloud of dust rose behind the procession as hooves and wheels pounded the dirt road. Since Herod had died several years earlier, Joseph and Mary thought it safe to return to their homeland and had been living near Nazareth for the past three years. Now, after participating in the celebration of Passover at the temple in Jerusalem, they returned, with friends and neighbors, back to their home. Though it was a late afternoon in early spring, the air was warm and dry, the sky clear blue.

Joseph was concentrating on maneuvering the donkey-drawn cart around the many holes and ruts in the road. He didn't hear Mary's question the first time she asked, so she repeated it.

"You left Jesus with Peter and Martha?"

"Yes," confirmed Joseph. "He was back in their cart, talking to their children."

"Perhaps after the next watering rest he should ride with us, and sup with us, eating our own bread. You know Peter lost several of his flock over the winter. We should not allow Jesus to eat their food when we have much bread and salted fish. Perhaps we should give some of our fish to Martha since our catch this year has been good." Mary turned and looked back over the procession, trying to spot the cart of Peter and Martha, the last one in line.

"That is a good idea. And, I would feel more comfortable with Jesus at our side, within our sight. Though Herod is dead, Archelaus has some of the beliefs and superstitions of his father. I do not trust him."

Mary eyed Joseph silently, thoughtfully. Then she said, "Your caution and concern are for the best, Joseph. Jesus has been with us for just these few years. And though he approaches manhood in size and strength, he is still vulnerable."

"And trusting of everyone."

"As you and I have taught him to be."

He took his eyes off the road and turned to her. "I think it was his nature before he came to us, but we have reinforced it. That is good, but it can be dangerous. Not everyone is to be trusted."

"Jesus would tell you differently." She smiled.

Joseph smiled as well, knowing she was right. "Still, he should ride with us. And I would like to be in his company for the trip home."

"He is not with us," said Peter. He pulled the rope and led the donkey to the edge of the small, sandy pool where water seeped from beneath the ground. Without hesitation, the donkey bent and began drinking.

Joseph's expression quickly changed from inquiry to concern. "He did not ride from Jerusalem with you?"

"Just before we left he was talking with Daniel and Thaddeus. As we started the ride back, he got out of the cart. I thought he went up to be with you."

"No." Joseph quickly scanned the other carts and small groups of people in their traveling party. If Jesus had been among them, Joseph would have seen him.

"Thaddeus!" Peter called to his ten-year-old son, standing nearby at the water's edge.

"Yes, Father?" Thaddeus said, hurrying over to them.

"Was Jesus with you before we left?" Peter asked him.

"He was—" Thaddeus hesitated and looked uncomfortable. "Daniel and I were very confused by what he said." He looked at the sand, kicking restlessly with his sandals.

"Tell me, Thad!" Peter scolded firmly.

"Daniel said to him, 'I understand nothing of what you say.' That made Jesus sad. He got out of the cart and said he needed to talk to people who could understand of the things he spoke."

Peter looked at him for a moment, then asked, "Did he say where he was going?"

Thaddeus continued to look at the ground. "No, Father."

Peter looked to Joseph, then said, "Do you know what this means?"

"Not exactly. But I think he must still be in Jerusalem." Joseph gripped the edge of the cart, his knuckles white. Frustrated, he made a fist and pounded the edge of the wood. "By all that is evil!"

"What would you like us to do, Joseph?" Peter asked.

Joseph thought for a second. "Mary and I must go back. Tell everyone what has happened. You should all continue toward home."

"Would you not like us to return and help you search for him?"

Though Joseph realized this was a good idea, he felt strongly that he should not cause inconvenience to his friends. "No. But, thank you. We will find him and return as quickly as our Lord will allow."

"As you wish. When we arrive in Nazareth, I will see that your house is secure and tend your garden." Peter moved off along the edge of the spring to tell everyone what had happened.

"Thank you, my friend," called Joseph over his shoulder, running back to his own cart, panic welling up inside him.

As fast as their donkey would pull the cart, they hurried back to Jerusalem, arriving in half the time it had taken them to travel the other direction. For more than two days they searched. In the market area, the temple, the docks and boats, wealthy neighborhoods, poor areas, the gardens and woods of which they knew Jesus was fond. As each hour passed, their fear rose, believing that something bad had happened to their son.

During the third day, at wit's end and considering confronting Archelaus himself, they returned to the Temple of Herod where they had spent the two days of Passover.

"The sun is but a star," said Jesus, his arms spread wide. "But much closer to Earth than any other."

He was surrounded by five men, each more than thirty years his elder. Teachers and philosophers who either taught in the temple of Herod or spent many hours a day there, they listened to this unusual boy who was no more than fourteen, sitting in their midst.

They talked among themselves for a moment before Michael, a teacher of philosophy in the temple, questioned him. "But child, surely you understand that Earth is the center of all that has been created? God has created all men in His image and Earth in the image of Heaven. These are basic truths known for centuries. The sun is another of God's creations, to provide warmth and light for Earth, for our use and comfort."

"Some of what you speak is truth, wise Michael." Jesus paused, searching his mind for the ideas, for the words. "But I speak of new knowledge, of a new understanding. We are indeed made in the image of

God, and He has given us life, and is the—essence of our life." Jesus felt frustrated. The ideas were in his mind, but there were no words to describe them. "God has made life in such a form so as to use the sun, to harvest its warmth, its energy."

"God has made all things," said Gabriel, another teacher. "This is known to be true."

"I do not understand this to be true," said Jesus. "God is alive. God is life. God did not create the sun and the stars. But all that we are, all that we do, all that we think, are an expression of the—" He couldn't find a word to describe his thought. "—the spirit, the essence, of God. The image of God."

"Yes, we are made in God's image," agreed Michael.

"We are an expression of the essence of God. He is a real, physical part of us, not a magical, spiritual thing." Jesus tried to think of a way to describe the thoughts in his mind. "Just as a son is created in the image of his father, when the essence of the father is offered to his wife to create a son or daughter, so are we the expression of that essence of God within us. But there is another—spirit—" Jesus stopped, his face contorted in confusion. He felt intensely frustrated.

"Continue, child," said Samuel, a wise man from northern Jerusalem. He thoughtfully stroked his long white beard. "Of what you speak is intriguing."

"Our language is beautiful," said Jesus. "But there are no words that describe the nature of what we are."

"Are not words such as *spirit* and *god* accurate enough?" questioned Joshua, sitting to Jesus' right, an accusatory edge in his voice.

"No," said Jesus quickly. "These suggest magic, things that are not real. God is very real. We, and all living things, are the expression of the part of God that is within us."

"That is an accurate description," said Michael, as Gabriel nodded in agreement.

"But it is not complete." Jesus spread his arms, waving his hands to accent his words. "God is within us, making us have the appearance and abilities that make each of us different. God's knowledge is brought outward by another spirit, another force, from the source where it is stored. And this force then translates this knowledge to make the living, breathing, working parts of our body. Just as you would translate a scroll from Rome into our own language to understand it, so does this—trinity of forces, these spirits within us, make us who we are so we can live in the realm of the Earth, find comfort in its heat and its cold, its day and night. Yet, still, completely the expression of God's image."

Gabriel held up his hand and looked down, trying to grasp and understand what Jesus had just said. He then spoke slowly, deliberately. "So, just as a son is created in his father's image, so are we created in God's image, with this third spirit doing the holy work of translating the will of God into the flesh of our bodies?"

Jesus nodded slowly. "Yes, wise Gabriel, you have repeated it well. Yet, I understand this in different ideas, ideas for which there are no words. It is not a magical thing. For God is a living force, a force within us all, within all that is alive."

"Within all things in Heaven and all things on Earth," said Samuel.

"Not all things, Samuel," said Jesus. "The force of God is what separates the living from that which does not live. The Sea of Galilee does not live, but the fish within it contain the force, the spirit of God."

"But men move upon the Earth with the grace of God within them," offered Michael. "It is what separates man from beast."

"What separates man from beast," added Jesus quickly, "is the ability to love. But by the gift of love from God do men have the choice, the will to make Earth a paradise, where goodness shall govern all that men do."

"Jesus! My son!" called Joseph, his voice loud with anger and relief. He ran across the large hall to where Jesus and the men sat.

"Father! Here!" Jesus called back, standing slowly.

With Mary several steps behind, Joseph ran to him. Slowing to a walk as he approached the circle of men, he said, "Jesus! Where have you been? Your mother and I have been frantic with worry. Every imaginable horror has entered our minds! Why do you make us sick with grief? Have you no compassion for your dear mother or for your father?" The other men in the discussion circle examined Joseph with mild concern, in fear that he would punish his son. Mary came up behind him and stood silently.

"I have been in this very temple for these three days, my father," Jesus said calmly. "I am quite unharmed and at peace among these many wise men." With a sweeping movement of his arms, he motioned to acknowledge them.

"Why did you not tell someone?"

"I apologize for this." Jesus hung his head.

At this, Joseph calmed, catching his breath and taking Mary's hand in his own. She smiled slightly in relief, but could not easily dispense the fear she had experienced the past three days.

50

Jesus looked up again, into his father's eyes. "You have been aware of my growing frustration over my desire to share the knowledge with which I have been blessed, have you not?"

Joseph nodded. "I have."

"I have not felt such comfort as I have among such men as these who not only listen to this knowledge, but try to understand it, and help me to understand it as well. The knowledge of God is such to be shared, not kept within me." He then said, firmly, "I have not felt such completeness, such fullness within myself as I have in these days. As you have suggested, to share this knowledge is why I am on Earth."

Joseph nodded. "And you will teach. But, now, we must travel back to Nazareth. Our friends and neighbors tend our garden and flock for us. We must relieve them of this burden."

"Yes, Father." Jesus made eye contact with each of the men seated before him. "I thank you all for sharing this time and for talking with me. May the love and peace of God be with you, and may you share it with all you meet." He walked through the circle. Embracing Mary, he said, "I am truly sorry to have caused you this torment, Mother."

She held him silently, nodding, as a tear of relief welled in her eye and rolled down the side of her nose. The three of them turned and walked slowly across the hall.

Watching them go, and turning to the other men, Michael said, "Surely no child has ever been blessed with the knowledge Jesus possesses."

"Or perhaps any man," added Gabriel "His eyes are illuminated with such a light, such an awareness."

"He is blessed," said Michael. "As if not of Earthly creation."

The others vocalized varying levels of agreement.

CHAPTER SEVEN

The phone ringing at 12:30 Monday afternoon tore Hector Torrez from sleep. It took him a few seconds and two phone rings to get his bearings, squint open his eyes, and reach for the phone on the table. "What," he mumbled.

"It's me," Angela, his ex-wife, said.

"What do you want?" He closed his eyes, lying back down with a sigh.

"What do you think I want?" she snapped. "You're three months behind."

"Oh, fuck," he grumbled, reaching for the pack of cigarettes next to the phone. He sat up, lit one with a red butane lighter, inhaled deeply. "Why don't you tell me where you are, and I'll bring it right over."

There was a brief silence, then, "What do you think, I'm still a complete idiot? I've gotten a lot smarter since I married you! Maybe when I met you I was a total loser, fucked up on crack and your live-in whore, thinking you were cool because you had a steady job and a truck. But, since I had Priscilla, I get things way better. Way better! Look how smart leaving you was!"

Hector firmly rubbed his forehead, the phone wedged between his shoulder and ear, cigarette smoldering in his right hand resting on the bed. "I'm not going to give you any more money, you lazy bitch. I already told—"

"Yes, you are! You have to! Look, I shouldn't even be calling you, but I can't wait for the courts. They take forever."

"Well, you can just wait forever," he said, then inhaled and exhaled as he spoke, smoke spitting out around the phone receiver. "I didn't want no kid, and you don't do a damn thing to deserve any of my money. I work all night at my pain-in-the-ass job with a bunch of assholes, and I barely make enough to get by myself." He inhaled again.

"Barely get by," she said evenly. "But you can afford to have prostitutes over every week."

His jaw dropped slightly, and he was silent for a moment. The phone started to slip out from his shoulder. As he reached up quickly to catch it, the cigarette brushed against the edge of his pillow, knocking off the entire hot ash. It landed on the sheet just under the edge of the pillow, but he didn't see it. "What are you talking about? No, I haven—"

"Don't even bother lying. I know all about it. If you try and argue in court that things are hard for you, I'll slap that in the judge's face."

"What, you been spying on me?" He lifted the cigarette to inhale, but sucked in cold air. Swearing, he quickly relit.

"Mail three month's worth to the box number the court gave you."

"No fucking way. You take all my money and then spy on me? I'll be damned if—"

"I'm not going to argue!" she interrupted "Send it now, or the courts call next." And she hung up.

He heard the loud click on the other end but still yelled into the receiver, "Don't you hang up on me! I'll find out where you are, you bitch." And when he finally accepted she didn't hear him, he slammed the phone down. "Fuck it!"

He stood and paced back and forth, smoking rapidly, swearing under his breath as he thought. "Fuck her," he said finally, reaching a decision. "I'll fix her."

After pulling on his pants and boots, he hurried out of the trailer and into his truck.

■　　■　　■

"That's all I wanted to cover in the book this semester." Chris turned off the overhead projector with a loud click. "You all know the final is a week from today at 3:30. Any specific questions or comments on anything that'll be covered?"

There was silence for a few seconds. Chris looked around at the faces of the forty-five students in his General Biology class. "Okay, then. Now I'd like to talk about something a little different. I kept pretty close to the book all semester. But just for a few minutes I want to talk about some things that aren't in the book."

Someone asked, "Is this stuff going to be on the final?"

Chris tightened his jaw in a knowing smirk. "It will be directly related to the bonus essay question on the final." He began by lifting the projection screen, exposing the entire chalkboard. Taking a couple steps to pick up a large piece of white chalk from the dusty tray, he turned to face the class. "What I would like to do now is present my point of view. I think some of you may agree with it, or strongly disagree with it. What I would like you to do is, at least, consider what I say. Take it with you and think about it. See how it fits into your perception of the world around you."

Chris paused for a second and then continued. "I think there is a great deal of denial by people around the world. As a matter of fact, it seems to be so prevalent that it's almost automatic. The first thing I want you to consider is that, by definition, there is no such thing as 'supernatural.' There can't be. If something exists, it is real and therefore natural." He paused again. "There are plenty of things that people don't understand, things that seem to be unexplainable by known, 'natural' processes, but that doesn't make them supernatural. There is no magic, no omnipotent beings, nothing that defies physical or time parameters and constraints of the universe. They may seem supernatural to some of us, but we just don't know everything there is to know. As a matter of fact, we really don't know very much about the Earth, about life, let alone the rest of the universe." He spread his arms apart. "In spite of the way I so confidently explained the material this semester and how your text makes it all sound like bottom line fact."

"If there's no supernatural," a boy asked, sitting in the front row, "how did everything form in the first place? All matter, all life. There has to be some higher power that created everything."

Chris noticed one of this student's front teeth seemed misshapen, something he hadn't noticed earlier in the semester. "Well, Mike, let me ask you this in response: Do you think by assuming there has to be some higher power, that can explain everything away? I'm asking you to try considering that all matter, all energy, has always been, instead of assuming there is some intelligent force that created everything. Matter and energy just are, the way they have always been, long before people existed, and regardless of what people think or believe or know."

Mike had his hand raised again, but then spoke without being acknowledged. "When I was in high school, I sort of figured out that the structure of atoms and our solar system was so similar it's too weird to be a coincidence."

"What do you mean?" asked Chris.

"Well, like, in atoms, all the weight's in the nucleus, and the electrons orbit around it. And our solar system is the same. The sun has most of the weight, and the planets have very little, in a relative way. And not only that, but the number of electrons in the different shells of atoms match the pattern of the relative weights of the planets. Like, the first four shells have two, eight, eight, and two electrons. That's just like relative sizes of Mercury, Venus, Earth and Mars."

Chris nodded. "That is pretty interesting."

Mike said, "When I realized it, that was the first time I ever considered that a god could have created everything, since the design was so much the same. There had to be some sort of plan to everything."

"That definitely is one way to look at it," said Chris. "But what I'm asking you to consider is that those similarities between atoms and the solar system are because that's just the way matter and energy are, it is the way they behave. It is their nature. Scientists don't know all there is to know, believe me. Maybe there are gravitational, or other, forces that apply to all matter, regardless of size. That's just a guess. But just because there is a pattern, seeming like there is a design, doesn't necessarily mean they were created by a god."

Mike was silently considering this when another student in the middle of the room asked, with accusation in his voice, "In fact, we are created in God's image. And the rest of the universe has been created for our use."

Chris looked up then said, "So, Derek, a god who looks like us, or certainly has some human-like qualities, created the entire universe? Every galaxy, an absolute infinite number of stars?"

"He did."

Chris smiled, realizing that Derek had led into the next part of his discussion, as if on cue. "And God exists everywhere, in everything?" he asked.

Derek nodded. "Of course."

"And you believe this because it is written in a book, and that's what you've been taught?"

"The Book, yes. It is the direct translation of God's word."

"Remember, if you would for a second, that it is a book that has been written and translated by men. Over many generations, across several languages. There's a lot of room for error and interpretation in that whole process. Another thing I wanted to point out is that people exaggerate. We tend to see things in our own way, from our own point of view, influenced by where we live, what we've been taught. We tend to think that because we have an idea in our mind, or believe something to be true, it must be true. Seeing another person's point of view is a very difficult thing, especially if the influences that have shaped our lives are very different from that person. Sometimes we can't even look right in front of us and tell the difference between what is real or what isn't." Chris noticed his own voice was starting to rise in pitch, edged with emotion. Realizing that if he continued he wouldn't accomplish what he wanted, he paused and tried to talk more relaxed, more deliberately.

"God is the only thing that is real," Derek said.

"As I was asking you to consider," Chris said slowly, "there is no such thing as supernatural. I'll talk more about God in a second. But I want you to consider another important aspect about our nature. That is, many people seem not to be able to accept that they will die. Maybe a lot of us are in denial about it. It is a very, very hard thing to come to grips with. But all living things, even people, die."

"Life is eternal," Derek protested.

"I agree, to a point. Life is essentially eternal. But you are not. Neither am I. And nothing else is, either. When we die, we are gone. Just like we didn't exist before we were conceived and born, we will not exist after we die. Our molecules will be used in other life forms. But that won't be us, just our molecules."

"And how do you know this?" asked Derek. "No one really knows what it's like after you die. God tells us it can be wonderful and peaceful, depending on how we have lived our life on Earth."

"You're right, I don't really know. But I'm offering it as a pretty reasonable extrapolation of being alive. Since we are organic, biological organisms, and all organisms die, we do, too. And, in death, the individual person that is each of us ceases to exist."

"What a cheerful discussion this is turning out to be," said Mike.

Chris chortled. "Sorry. What I'm trying to give you is a sort of reality check about living."

"But doesn't the human spirit live on after the body dies?" asked Mike. "Don't you think our spirit is more, I don't know, more divine than other animals?"

"Stop and think about that for a second. What does *spirit* mean?" Chris asked. "We use words like *soul* and *spirit* as if we know exactly what they are, that they're clearly defined, like *chair* or *blue*."

"The human spirit is our essence, our soul. And, yes, it lives on after we die," Derek said.

"Where? In what form?" Chris asked him.

"In Heaven."

Chris smiled. "Like I said, a lot of you will disagree with me. But try considering, for the sake of this discussion, that that point of view could be denial on a cultural level. Consider that you will die and be gone. Things you have made will remain, people you have influenced and loved will remember you, but you will be gone." He paused a second. "What we are really talking about is self-awareness, isn't it? That, even after we die, we still want to be self-aware, wherever or in whatever form we take. Hopefully, we'll still be self-aware, know that we are ourselves, remember our life on Earth. Right?"

Only Mike shrugged a reluctant agreement.

"Again, consider that could possibly be nothing more than denial. An idea to give hope and a different purpose to our lives. To make living mean more than a mere biological existence. Consider that ideas like heaven and hell, reincarnation, multiple lives for the same spirit, all have risen from that denial, and persist because of denial, from our failure to accept our own mortality.

"Remember," Chris continued, "that the universe really is billions of years old, as far as we can tell. And that life has existed on this planet for at least a billion years. That is long before people evolved with the ability to think about their own existence, about their own meaning or purpose."

"That's kind of a depressing view of life," Mike suggested. "It makes us sound like we're just another species of animal running around the planet, just living to eat and reproduce. Trying to avoid getting killed by forces of nature."

■   ■   ■

Hector checked that his .38 caliber pistol was secure in the black leather holster. He picked it up off the seat and put it in the glove box of his truck, periodically glancing at the road while driving toward home. The small box of cartridges he had just purchased was in the back, left pocket of his jeans. Rushing air blew in the open window, tossing his hair wildly about while music from the radio played loudly. His knuckles were white, tightly gripping the steering wheel. All the while he was trying to think of a way he could find out where Angela lived (he knew it was around Boston somewhere) and teach her a lesson, permanently. He had remembered that one of her friends still lived nearby. What was her name again? Maybe if he called her she might accidentally give something away.

The first thing he noticed was several cars parked along the entrance to the trailer park. A few people were standing near their cars and a few hurried along the entrance road. As he turned in and drove back toward his trailer, thick billows of black smoke became visible over the few trees scattered in the park. He wondered, just for a few seconds, who was burning garbage. But then he saw one square, red, rescue truck and one small, pump truck that had apparently just arrived. Firemen hurried about, connecting a hose to a hydrant nearby.

When he rounded the final corner, his heart sank as he saw his trailer completely engulfed in fire.

In the scorching afternoon heat, with no wind, the smoke was thick and rose straight up. Firemen ran back and forth, yelling commands, telling neighbors and spectators to stay back. The hoses were connected to the truck, and two men controlled each length of output hose, yanking them toward Hector's trailer. When they were close enough to the flames so their black protective suits reflected dancing, orange light, each pair of men planted their feet, braced into position, and turned the chrome nozzles until a hard stream of water shot out. As Torrez slammed on the brakes and jumped out, he saw them starting to douse neighboring trailers, not his own.

"What the fuck are you doing?" he yelled, running frantically towards them. "Put it out! Put it out! Get my trailer!"

One of the other firemen ran up from the side and grabbed his arm. "Get back! Now!"

Torrez yanked his arm away and growled, "My trailer's on fire! Put it out! Why the fuck are you wetting those?"

"No kidding your trailer's on fire, Einstein," the fireman yelled back, over the noise of the water and flames. "Your trailer is gone. Gone! We can't stop it! It's too late! The siding on the others is melting, and the grass and trees are close to igniting. We've got to cool them down! Now get back!" He reached for Hector's arm again.

But Torrez pulled free, grabbing the fireman by the coat. "Put out my trailer! Now!"

"Tom! Butch! Get this nut case out of here!" he yelled to two men monitoring the pressure on the truck. He turned and yelled at Torrez, a foot from his face, "Get the hell out of the way!"

Quickly, Tom and Butch intervened, both tall and broad-shouldered. "Let's go, pal," one of them said. "Get back. Let us do our work."

"God damn it! Fuck!" yelled Torrez. He stepped away, but walked back and forth along the length of his trailer, thirty feet back, pacing like a caged animal between the two teams spraying the other trailers. Soon, the heat became too intense, and he backed away farther, all the while pacing and swearing.

Two other trucks arrived, then a police car. The police kept the crowd back and kept traffic moving on the road outside the trailer park. A third crew of firemen connected to another hydrant, first wetting more surrounding area and, then, beginning to spray Hector's trailer. The flames sputtered quickly as water drenched the blackened remains.

As it came under control, the gathered crowd began thinning. Cars drove away, and neighbors returned to their trailers. Some stood in small groups, speculating on how it started, how it could have been much worse if it spread.

"Who started it?" Torrez asked Butch, who had stood between him and the trailers while monitoring pump pressure.

"I got no idea. That's not what I do. But when we took a quick run around when we first got here, I didn't see anything obvious. It probably started inside."

"Inside?" Torrez repeated, disbelieving. "It didn't start inside, someone must have set it."

"Look, I don't know. The inspector will talk to you later. When it's cooled down enough, she'll take a look. She's not even here yet."

Torrez walked closer and inspected the smoldering skeleton of his trailer. Slowly, the reality of what this meant to him was sinking in. "Oh, no," he said quietly. "Fuck me. Now what the fuck do I do?" He walked back to his truck, sat in the driver's seat with the door open, lit a cigarette from the pack sitting on the dashboard. Finishing one, he lit another and continued to smoke while watching the crews working. They inspected and felt trailers and trees nearby, talked to witnesses, emptied and rolled hoses.

"Hector?"

He turned to see a neighbor, an elderly woman cradling a white, longhaired cat, standing at his truck door. "Hi, Mrs. Gilbert," he said.

"Are you okay?"

He laughed a single syllable, looking through the windshield at the trailer. "No, I'm pretty god damn far from okay. I'm royally screwed. I have no idea where I'm going to live now."

"But you're not hurt?" she asked.

He looked back at her and shook his head.

"Well, insurance will cover it all," Mrs. Gilbert said with enthusiasm. "It may take a while, but you should be able to get a new trailer."

"Damn it," he said through clenched teeth. "Damn it." He looked back at her and said tensely, "I don't have insurance. I can barely afford the payments, let alone insurance. Fuck."

"Oh," she said, then when she really understood, "Oh my!" She put a hand over her mouth. "That's simply awful!"

"Yeah. It sure is."

"Of course, I'd offer to let you stay with me. But with my five cats, I just don't have the room."

"Yeah, whatever," he said. After a while he said, but not to her, "It's not like it matters."

■　■　■

Chris smiled at what Mike had just suggested. "Okay, then, consider this:

Being alive is being self-aware. Every living thing is aware of itself, if even only at a cellular level. Not in a way we can really understand, and certainly nothing like our state of consciousness. But cells know exactly what they are doing. The mechanisms necessary to maintain life are the result of a very pointed, controlled process." He paused for a moment, letting the students think about that. "And, now, consider what an amazing gift that is. We are so gifted to be alive in the first place. Think about how lucky you are just in terms of your own conception, of the 200 million sperm in your father's ejaculation. Any other one, fertilizing any other egg, would not have been you, or me, or any of us. Everyone who is alive has won the luckiest lottery of all. If your parents had had sex on a different day, or twice on that day instead of once, your brother or sister would be alive instead of you. Or no one would have been conceived at all, at that particular time."

"But that's just a biological point of view," Derek said. "You don't even believe in God and all He's done for each of us."

"Who said anything about not believing in God?" Chris said. Then he reconsidered and said, "I was going to bring this up in a second, but now is a good time." He thought a moment. "You're right, I don't believe in God. That's an interesting word, believe. Using it in reference to something is like confirming you don't think something is real or that something will happen, but you want to *believe* it is real, or that it will happen."

Mike's brow wrinkled in confusion. "I don't get that."

Again, Chris noticed his tooth as he spoke. "Do you believe in Santa Claus? Do you believe in ghosts? Do you believe in aliens? Do you believe in God? Do you want to believe that global warming isn't really happening? Implied in each of those questions is the answer. All those things are either out of the normal parameters of our existence or, at least, at a level we don't understand. Hoping they are true gives us some sort of comfort or hope, regardless of the apparent level of truth involved."

"So you think there is no god?" someone else asked.

"Well, as a matter of fact, I know there is a god. I know that God did not create everything, and is not omnipotent. And, even though I can't see it directly, or prove it scientifically, I know it because all evidence supports it. I don't believe the Earth revolves around the sun, I know it. Just like I know I will die. Just like I know the process of photosynthesis is real and has been going on long before people understood it, or even knew about it. I feel confident saying *know* because all those things are quite within the realm of the natural world. There's nothing magical or supernatural about them, and there is evidence supporting them. The best evidence supporting the existence of God is essentially every culture on Earth has come up with the idea independently. To me, it doesn't seem like an intuitive concept, that there is some force that made us, or controls everything. The fact that this idea has been a part of just about every culture is the best evidence there is truth to the concept."

"So, you talk as if you know what God is," said Mike. "If He doesn't look like us or, as you say, isn't omnipotent, don't keep us in suspense. What is He like?"

Chris thought for a moment then spoke as he wrote on the chalkboard. "Let me explain it this way, as a bridge across the current gap between science and religion, the parallel between the two. I think this is primarily a Christian point of view, but have you ever heard of God stated in these terms?" And he wrote on the board in large block letters:

FATHER   HOLY SPIRIT   SON

Derek said, "Sure, that's the Holy Trinity."

"Ever stopped to think what it means? I mean, what it really means, if it means anything at all? If these things are real, and not supernatural, what could they be? Plenty of people would say they mean nothing at all, depending on what their religion is. But since so many people, for so long, believe there is a god or gods, let's assume they are real. So then it just depends on what each person wants to call them, depending on their point of view, their culture, their education." Then he wrote on the board:

FATHER   HOLY SPIRIT   SON
DNA   RNA   PROTEIN

"This is the parallel. That's my interpretation based on all supporting evidence. In general, science and religion have been mutually exclusive disciplines. But, regardless of our point of view, there really is only one underlying reality, one actual truth. Remember, the processes that make our cells work, that give us the ability to live, that give us form and function, have been going on for a billion years or more. That's long before we figured out what we are made of and put names to it all. It all goes on without our conscious input, by a power that is at a level of awareness and has a design well beyond our consciousness or intelligence. Hell, we only figured out what most of our components actually are, from a chemical standpoint, in the last few decades. But, they are what is real, and we are an expression of that reality. What we call *proteins* are, in fact, what make us look like we do, behave and function as we do, live as we do. No matter what we call them, proteins are what do the work in our bodies, in our cells, that make each one of us an individual. Enzymes, membrane receptors, whatever function we think they have based on our experimental evidence, they are doing what they do to keep us alive every second of every day, without our conscious input. And it's not just a few chemicals in our body. We're talking about thousands of functional proteins in every cell, hundreds of different kinds of cells, trillions of cells in our bodies, all working simultaneously—pretty much without mistakes." He emitted a one-syllable chuckle. "What an amazingly complex, intricate system we are. That is what is god-like: The design, knowledge and control to keep us running and alive for our eighty or ninety years. Maintaining the balance and control to keep us healthy and functioning."

Chris paused a second, looking at the faces of his students. For the most part, he had their undivided attention. "And remember, the source of the information—deoxyribonucleic acid, DNA, or whatever you choose to call it—transcribes its message to ribonucleic acid, RNA. Then, through translation, RNA strings together an exact sequence of amino acids reflecting the exact sequence of the nucleotides of DNA—in the image of the DNA. It is a commonly held belief that we are created in God's image. You, and every other living thing, is exactly that, the expression of the information in your DNA, in your genes, translated into very specific proteins that give your body a specific form and function. If that information is changed, then the form of the expression changes. And whatever the life form is that is being expressed will then look or function differently. And, not so surprising then, the concept of a god has been so prevalent in human history. That same system is also the source of the design and process of our thoughts, exactly where the idea of a god has been conceived, in so many different minds, in so many different cultures."

"So you think DNA is God?" Mike asked.

"Not exactly. All components that allow life to exist all need to be in place for the system to function. DNA, itself, is the source, the storage location of the information. That sequence is transcribed to RNA that holds and carries the 'message' to the right location in each cell. Then it translates it to string together amino acids to make proteins. And proteins do the work to give each plant or animal their unique form and function. So, the whole idea of fragmenting the system into components is pretty inaccurate. You can't have one without the other and be alive. Of course, to study them scientifically you need to separate them, at least, with our current crude methods. But the whole natural system only works when all the parts are together to make a complete, functioning cell."

Derek was incredulous. "So, let me get this straight. You think DNA created the universe?"

Chris stifled a sigh. "Try and consider that energy and matter have always been in existence, and that has nothing to do with any god, whether you believe God is in a human-like form, or any other form. One critical point is that only life is self-aware. That is the difference. That is one characteristic that separates the living from the non-living. Only things that are alive are aware of themselves."

"Single-celled animals are self-aware?" asked Mike.

"I know they are. Not like you and me, with what we call a consciousness, but at a cellular level, maybe a chemical level. One I can't explain and don't pretend to understand. But I can tell you that I've been studying living things for twenty years, and one thing I'm sure of, no matter what we call anything or what function we think the parts have, is that cells know exactly what they are doing. They are a lot smarter than people. Incredibly complex processes go on in cells—pretty much, without flaw—never stopping, for as long as the cell is alive. Compared to what people know, cells have had at least a billion years head start accumulating 'knowledge.' This is the knowledge that is stored in genes and expressed, through RNA and then as proteins, to make all the life forms on Earth. All the different plants, animals, and bacteria that live in the environment."

Derek asked, "Did cells conceive of and build the internet, satellite systems, all the amazing buildings and bridges and utility systems that keep everything running? Everything throughout history, all the technology and art that people have made? Can cells do all those things?"

"Cells did do those things. What do you think we are but that amazing conglomeration of trillions of cells, all originating from the same fertilized egg at conception. Everything we are, everything we do, everything we think, is, in fact, cellular. Whether you call it, 'Father—Son—Holy Spirit' or 'DNA—protein—RNA' or 'Tom—Dick—Harry,' the system is really there, giving us form and function, allowing us to live. It is the source and nature of life. And it is self-contained. Consider that there doesn't need to be an outside force to make it live. The source of design and control and purpose is within the life system itself. It is who we are, what we are, what we do, what we think."

"So where does spirit, or soul, fit into cellular processes?" asked Mike.

"They are cellular processes. One way to look at it would be that soul or spirit is the cumulative awareness or activity of our cells while we're alive. But to fragment the whole concept of life into components, except to study specific parts of it in a lab, is an inaccurate assessment of how the system works. You may think a soul is one thing, spirit another thing, body another thing, mind another thing, but they are all part of the same system. To separate them with different words, according to some vague concept or perception, is kind of pointless. The living system is created at conception, exists as a complete, homeostatic entity throughout life, and is disassembled after death, becoming non-living molecules to be used by other life forms. Just like bricks from a demolished house being used to build a new one. Try not to think that we're here in some kind of rehearsal for the hereafter, or whatever. Life is really all we have. It's the time you are alive that is important. Making the most of it, making it as good and productive as possible, and making it better for as many other people or animals or plants as possible is the best you can accomplish while you are alive."

He glanced around the class. "Anyone want to add anything else?"

The class was silent for many seconds, either thinking about what Chris had said or poised and ready to leave.

Then someone asked, "So will all that be on the final?"

Chris sighed, and a sinking feeling quickly came into the pit of his stomach. "Like I said, the DNA—RNA—protein part, transcription and translation, will be part of the test. I'll ask a bonus essay question about the rest of it, maybe along the lines of how what I said fits into some other aspects of the semester we've already talked about. It will be something like, 'give me your opinions, supported by telling me how much you've learned this semester.'"

There were no other questions so he said, "Okay. Thanks for listening. See you next Monday."

As the class filed out, he stopped Mike before he could leave. "Excuse me, Mike. Hey, thanks for your input. It really helped the discussion flow well."

"Oh, sure," he said. "It was interesting. It sure gives you some different things to think about."

Chris nodded. "Yeah. That's the point." Then he said, "I couldn't help but noticing your tooth. Are you okay? Did you break it or something?"

Mike smiled, exposing it fully. "No. It's E.S. I got it done a couple days ago."

Chris gave him a blank look. "Excuse me?"

"Enamel scrimshaw. See, it's an eagle, on a perch. Look close." He opened his mouth wider.

Chris leaned forward and could see the design. "You had your tooth carved, into a sculpture?"

"That's what E.S. is. It's the latest thing. Pretty cool, huh?"

Chris resisted any judgmental comments and said, "I'll be damned. Well, why not? When I was your age, the rage was body piercing. I guess this is just another step toward the extreme."

"Yeah. I suppose." Mike moved toward the door. "See you Monday."

"Sure." Chris watched him go. "Enamel scrimshaw. I'll be damned. What will they think of next."

As he collected his papers and books, he wondered if anything he had said made sense to his students. And he wondered how many he had pissed off.

■   ■   ■

Hector tossed and turned, while lying in the front seat of his truck. Unsuccessfully, he was trying to get comfortable.

The inspector had said the fire started on his bed, probably by a cigarette ash or butt, igniting the sheets and feathers in the pillow. It had quickly spread to the curtains hanging on the small window above the bed. He hadn't believed her and argued briefly, until she said it didn't much matter what he thought. Upon talking to the owner of the trailer park, Hector discovered he would be responsible for the cost of cleaning up the area around the burned trailer and having the remains removed. Or, at least, his insurance company would. Hector assured him he would get right on it, that he would call his insurance company right away. He then threw a few tools, and other odds and ends of value, in the back of his truck. As he drove away, he realized all he owned was his truck, the clothes on his back, and a few hundred dollars in the bank.

No cars came into the small park where he spent the night. He had pulled back away from the parking lot, hidden among the trees. It was warm and humid, with very little wind. He left the windows open halfway, to get whatever breeze he could, but mosquitoes were constantly flying into the truck. He could see them banging incessantly against the glass of the windshield or hear them buzzing past his ear. His sleep was broken and restless as he thought about where to go and what to do.

CHAPTER EIGHT

"**H**e's not in," said Pamela Nixon. "He's not in a meeting or didn't say he doesn't want to see you. He's simply not here."

"Where is he then?" insisted Torrez, both hands gripping the front of her desk. "Just don't jerk me around."

"He's at a meeting in Atlantic City, and he won't be back until tomorrow evening. Would you like to set up an appointment? Perhaps early next week?"

"Next week?!" he laughed, then muttered, "Shit."

"Was that a no?"

Torrez looked at her through narrowed eyes, noticing how every piece of her clothing, every hair on her head, all her makeup was perfectly in place. He wondered if she had ever spent a night in a car, except to get laid. "Yeah. Monday. Before I come to work. Three o'clock."

She moved the computer mouse to scroll through the appointment program. "How about 2:20?"

"2:20. For how long?"

"He can talk to you for about twenty minutes. Will that be sufficient?"

"Wha … uh, yeah. That should be long enough."

In the locker room, Hector flipped through the uniforms hanging on the rack just inside the door and pulled out the three that had his name printed on a small, blue patch above the breast pocket. Currently, it was in the middle of first shift, so the room was empty. After showering, he dressed in one of his clean uniforms. Though the clothes he had been wearing didn't have his name on them, he threw them into the dirty laundry barrel. He put the other two uniforms in his locker and left.

As he started his truck, he remembered that the annexation town meeting was that evening. Then he remembered how Richard Brown had said it would mean overtime, maybe a promotion. And, what the hell, he thought, maybe they would be serving free food.

For a minute he couldn't think of where it was, then remembered Littleboro High School. It didn't much matter what time. He'd go have a couple drinks and then wait in the parking lot until people started to show up.

■ ■ ■

Chris arrived at the high school a few minutes before seven, but the parking lot was already overfull. Cars were parked in any extra room at the end of the rows of painted spaces, on the small dirt islands separating sections of the lot, on grass at the edge of the football field, two hundred yards along the street on the shoulder. He squeezed his Toyota into half a space at the end of the lot just inside the entrance and walked the hundred yards to the main lobby, passing a television remote truck parked directly in front of the door.

The lobby was full of people, most standing in small groups of three or four, in serious discussion. This resulted in a low murmur of voices that coursed throughout the enclosed area and echoed off the tile floor and cream-colored cinder block walls. Chris said hello to several people he knew, mostly parents of Mary and John's friends. The auditorium was close to capacity when he walked in. There were several people filing down the two center aisles, each located a third of the way in from the side walls. Both were equipped with a microphone on a stand near the front. The total seating accommodated 600, though he thought there had to be more than that there already, including those he had passed in the lobby. It already felt stifling hot inside and probably would get worse as the meeting progressed. As he searched for a seat he heard someone call, "Chris!" just behind him to the right, and turned to find the mother and father of one of Mary's friends.

"Hi, Diana, Vin," he said to them, walking back.

"There's a seat on the aisle here," said Diana, her tinted, brown hair turned upward and makeup well placed. "My purse is here, but it's not saved for anyone. Where's Sara?"

"Keeping an eye on the offspring. Is Leighton home with a sitter?"

"Yeah, our neighbor," said Vin, who was tall and well-groomed, still wearing a suit and tie from the day at his private practice as a urologist. He smiled knowingly, having performed the vasectomy on Chris a year earlier, but refrained from mentioning it in front of Diana. "Go ahead, sit down."

"Thanks," Chris said, waiting until Diana picked up her purse.

"Leighton still talks about how much fun she had in tee-ball," Diana said. "She thought you were a good coach, and she really learned a lot."

"Well, thanks. She's a good kid. It was fun having her. I don't know much, but I do know the mechanics of how to swing a bat and how to throw."

"Are you as mad about this annexation as we are?" asked Vin, leaning across Diana's lap.

"Mad? Well, let's just say I don't think it's the best thing for our town in the long run. I have to admit that I'm glad we live across town from the reservation. We don't have to deal with it all directly, except traffic once in a while." He looked around at the faces in the crowd. There were no smiles, no laughs. Only looks of concern, restlessness, even anger.

Chris talked quietly with Diana and Vin for a few more minutes. Soon three men, all wearing ties and dark suits, walked across the hardwood floor of the stage in front of the drawn curtain. They took seats behind the table there, microphones on short stands placed in front of each chair.

The man in the middle spoke first, his voice emanating from two large speakers hung on the wall on either side of the stage. "If everyone could find a seat. We should get started since I'm sure there will be plenty of questions. Thank you, if you could, please."

Several people who were standing quickly returned to their seats, and the murmur of the crowd quieted some. The television cameraman, carrying the unit on his shoulder, was standing on the floor of the auditorium in front to the left. The reporter talking quietly with him was a tall, thin woman wearing a dark green pants suit. Keeping their hands cupped over their microphones, the three men on stage talked among themselves. Finally the man in the middle spoke again, once the crowd noise had reached a lower level.

"Thank you all for coming. As you may know, I am David Fontaine, Chairman of the Town Council of Littleboro. To my right is Rodney Diaz, manager of the Gold Growth and Expansion Task Force." He acknowledged with a brief wave to the crowd. "And to my left," Fontaine continued, "is Thomas Aragones, a member of the Passemannican Executive Committee."

There was a slight increase in the noise level of crowd.

"The purpose of tonight's general town meeting," Fontaine said, "is to outline the details of how annexation, if it is approved, will take place, and how it will impact the residents who live on the affected land, particularly how they will be compensated if it becomes necessary for them to move. Also—"

He was interrupted by the voice of an older man yelling from the audience, to the far left, "We've lived in our house for thirty-five years! We're not going to move!"

"Excuse me!" Fontaine called. "Apparently at this time it is necessary to discuss protocol for this meeting. Under no circumstances are there to be comments made from the audience that have not been recognized by me and, then, only by using one of the microphones set up in the aisles. First, Mr. Diaz, Mr. Aragones, and myself will briefly outline details of the proposal, and then comments and questions will be welcomed from the audience. But only from the microphones in the aisles. And if we could have no more than three people waiting in line to use each microphone, and limit your comments and questions to three minutes each. That way, we can maintain order, and everyone who wants to will get a chance to speak."

He paused briefly, scanning the audience. The same elderly man who had yelled out the comment stood and walked around the front of the auditorium to the microphone standing in the left aisle. He calmly took his place in front of it, folding his arms behind his back, standing patiently and looking at the stage expectantly.

"Excuse me, sir," Fontaine said, "but it will be quite a while before we solicit questions from the audience."

"I'll wait," was all he said, and stood quietly again.

Fontaine scrutinized him briefly and decided to continue. "Also, tonight we will briefly discuss compensation the town will receive from the state to offset the lost revenue from the depleted, real estate tax base. Then we will address any concerns or questions you have."

Diaz started off by explaining how, if annexation reaches final approval by the Federal Government, the 325 acres will be added to the Passemannican Nation over the span of three years. Plots of 137, 82 and 106 acres will be annexed, on the first day of each fiscal year of the town, July 1st, in 2009, 2010, and 2011. The largest, and first, section to be annexed, which adjoined the existing reservation, had already been surveyed. Development plans included a 650-room hotel, another 1.2 million square feet of gaming space, and an 8,000-seat, multimedia theater. This brought a multitude of comments and discussions from within the crowd. People shifted uneasily in their seats. The elderly man at the microphone in the aisle stood quietly, now with his arms folded across his chest.

Chris shifted in his seat. Though the plans had been discussed in local newspapers and on websites for years, hearing them outlined in person made him understand that it was real. It was going to happen.

"Please, could we have quiet," said Fontaine sternly. The talk within the crowd only partially subsided.

"May I point out," added Diaz, "that this will produce as many as twelve thousand new jobs for the area."

Chris noted the tone in his voice spoke not with a sense of pride or accomplishment, or even defense. He spoke with absolute arrogance, as if he was doing the biggest favor in the world to everyone in the room and knew he was doing it. Chris immediately did not like the man. He couldn't help notice his expensive suit, and glittering, gold jewelry on his wrists and fingers but was surprised by how cheap and out of place his hair weave appeared. Chris smiled to himself.

Fontaine spoke again. "Now, this will require some zoning changes to the roads and land approaching the Gold, additions and upgrades to existing utilities. The town council has already discussed in some detail, with the state and the tribe, how this will be accomplished financially. In a nutshell, the state has agreed to cover ninety percent of these costs up front, some sixty three million dollars, in exchange for certain compensations."

"What compensations?" someone yelled from the audience.

"Again, may I remind you," Fontaine yelled angrily into the microphone, "no unsolicited comments from the audience!" He glared in the general direction of the last comment. "As I was about to explain, in exchange for the initial investment for upgrading roads and utilities, for adjustments to local zoning laws, and by release of real estate tax liability to homes and land purchased prior to incorporation into tribal reservation land—" The crowd stirred again. "Excuse me!" And he waited a few seconds. "The state will received a portion of the slot and other gaming profits from the Passemannican Nation. The percentages will increase in a sliding scale over the course of the next ten years, from an initial take of eight percent of the profit in 2009 to a maximum level plateauing at nineteen and a half percent in 2016."

"That's a bribe!" came a yell from the audience, behind Chris. "The state and town took a bribe!"

"That is enough!" Even from where he sat, Chris could see Fontaine turning bright red. "There will be enough time for orderly comments at the end!"

Diaz interjected calmly, "It will greatly increase the income of the state and the town, and other local towns, as a matter of fact. Similar arrangements have proven quite profitable for other states and communities." Chris felt his blood pressure rising but still tried to remain calm and rational and listen thoughtfully. It was clear to him that tension was high for most people in the auditorium, including himself.

"Thank you for pointing that out, Rodney," Fontaine said, calmer now. "That's correct. Approximately fifty to sixty percent of those funds will be redistributed to towns in north central and northeastern Massachusetts. To use as the towns deem appropriate."

A few more details were outlined about how the funding would be collected and invested, how local contractors and companies would benefit, and the cross section of new jobs that would be created.

Hector Torrez, sitting in the back, smiled at this last news. Brown had been right, he thought. Annexation will mean more money. And, since Angela's monthly payment is fixed, that means more for me. After all the crap that's gone wrong for me, at last, something good.

"Now," Fontaine said, taking a deep breath, "orderly and quietly, we would like to alleviate some of your concerns and try to continue to show you that this will benefit the Passemannican people, the local communities, and the state. When you address Mr. Diaz, Mr. Aragones, or myself, if you would identify yourself and politely and succinctly state your issue or question. Remember, only three people at each microphone at a time, and we will alternate, first to my right to the gentleman already waiting and then to my left."

"George Tomlins," the man at the microphone said immediately.

About fifteen people stood and worked their way to the microphones. A few stopped and sat back down when they saw how many people were getting in line. Others reached the line, realized they were fifth or sixth, slowly backed away and returned to their seats, or stood further up the aisle. Though Chris was anxious about the proceedings, he didn't feel he had anything specific to say. It seemed to be mostly an economic and political issue, and his home was not directly affected. Besides, it was going to happen. Anything he had to say probably wouldn't change a thing.

In the meantime, Tomlins had continued, "And my children grew up in this house. It's the only home they ever had. We have no intention of giving it up."

Diaz interjected, "Your home, and any house on land to be annexed, will be purchased at a fair market value."

"I don't want a fair market value!" Tomlins yelled into the microphone, his high-pitched voice cracking. "I've been hacking away at the mortgage for thirty years. Fixing everything that's been breaking on our house, scrimping to make every monthly payment. And now, a couple years after we've finally paid it off, it's going to be taken away! How are we supposed to start over in a new place? Answer me that!"

A few people started clapping, and there was a single call of agreement from the audience.

"Well, frankly, Mr. Thompson, was it?" Diaz said. "Fair market value, based on assessment values in the neighborhood, is what you will be paid. Period."

Chris folded and unfolded his arms. He felt his cheeks flush as his pulse rate increased. He felt sorry for Tomlins, thinking how he would be forced to move from the home he had maintained for his family, regardless of what he would be paid. And there was nothing he could do. This situation sucks, Chris thought, the whole thing is such a travesty of how things could be, what is really needed.

"Well, damn it!" Tomlins yelled, "I won't move. I won't! You can threaten me at gun point, and I still won't leave. Shoot me and carry my dead body out! It's the only way I'll leave my home!" He abruptly walked back around the front of the seats, glaring at the stage, and returned to his seat. A few people applauded again. On stage, Diaz and Aragones made eye contact with each other and smiled slightly.

From the right microphone a middle-aged woman said, "I think most of you know me. Lynn Harris, principal of this school. One of your reported advantages is the creation of thousands of new jobs. But what kind of jobs are we talking about? Card dealers? Cocktail waitresses?" She waited for a response from the stage, but only Aragones shrugged. "Great. All through our children's education we're training them for college, especially when they get to my school, to be prepared for the formal schooling it takes to become a professional, an engineer, a doctor, a scientist, a computer technician. Not only should we be questioning what message we're sending to our kids, that these are the kinds of jobs to look forward to, but we should look long and hard at the kinds of jobs that are actually being created. Most of these things require almost no education at all. A week or two of training, and they've got it. And what? Someone just out of high school is going to be dealing cards for the next forty years?"

"Mrs. Harris," Aragones said. "First, there are plenty of other kinds of jobs besides waitresses. There are security people, facility maintenance people, many administrative and management positions. And the pay they will receive is competitive with many other professions."

"Competitive with other professions? What does that mean? The same as a waitress at Pizza Shack? And where are all these people going to come from? I mean, what are they doing right now, before they get hired? You say you will create all these new jobs, but there are not that many unemployed people between here and Boston. Most likely you will have a huge influx of people doing service jobs into an area where water and space is already in short supply. The roads in this area just can't handle that many more people. And these are not jobs that will pay enough for people to afford to own a home. I just don't think there are twelve thousand rental units in this area, or the space to build many more."

Someone else asked about money for schools. They pointed out that the education budget was already critically low and that the student to teacher ratio in the Littleboro system was about the worst in the state. If this huge part of the real estate tax base was lost, how would that affect the budget?

The answer, given by Fontaine, suggested that at least part of it would be defrayed by the slot and blackjack revenues gained by the state.

"What about the increase in crime?" the next person asked.

"Your name please?" Fontaine insisted.

"Jackson Hanley. There has already been a significant increase in murder and robbery in the last seven years—"

"Not significantly more than the national average, per population." said Diaz.

"The national average?" Hanley exclaimed. "Is that something we want our town to have? The fact is, there were twelve murders in the last seven years, and in the fifty years before that there was only nine. That's not even talking about the robberies, assaults, vandalism. Cripes, every week mailboxes on our street get knocked down by vandals."

"And you think having the Gold in this town is responsible for having mailboxes knocked down?" asked Diaz.

Chris was fuming and could barely sit still. God, how he felt contempt for that man. So completely arrogant, he thought.

The crowd was growing more restless. More comments were being yelled out from the audience, and Fontaine wasn't even bothering to remind people anymore. And there were six or seven people in line at each microphone.

Someone else asked about crime, giving more details about personal assaults. She also pointed out that, on several occasions, parents who were gambling in the Gold had left children, sometimes infants, unattended in their cars for hours. When caught, these people had been arrested and the children taken away and put in foster care. She also asked about the increase in suicides and committed gambling addicts in the area in the last several years. This discussion also brought much murmuring from the crowd.

The next person to speak was someone Chris knew. She was the mother of a friend of John's from his preschool class.

"Erica Houston," she said. "I'd like to question you about something a little more, uhm, philosophical."

Chris noticed she sounded very nervous. The little he knew of her made him think that it was probably very difficult for her to speak in front of so many people. She seemed so shy to him. Even saying *hi* to him while he was dropping off John made her blush.

"That's okay," said Fontaine. "It's your three minutes."

"Well, I, I was wondering. Why does the tribe get all these advantages? I mean, not paying taxes, even on the land you own." She was blushing, and her voice seemed stuck in her throat. "You use our roads, our sewers and water, the Passemannican children even go to Littleboro schools. Why do you get advantages when we're … we have to pay taxes to support road repairs, police, everything else in the town?"

"Simply," said Fontaine, "it is a matter of federal law. They are a sovereign nation."

Diaz answered more bluntly. Sensing her insecurity, he attacked like a dog smelling fear. "How dare you! You complain about advantages that we have! After all you people have done to us, these are small compensations—"

"Who are 'you people!'" Chris heard himself yell, anger propelling his voice so everyone could hear clearly. He was on his feet in the aisle and repeated, loudly, "'You people!' You said 'you people.' Who do you mean?" He glared at Diaz as he took three steps down the aisle. Seeing Erica being verbally attacked while making a valid point had pushed him beyond control.

"Wait your turn, sir!" Fontaine cried angrily.

"No! I want Mr. Diaz to explain himself." Chris walked close to the microphone.

Houston saw who it was, and her face lit up. "Hi, Chris," she said, away from the microphone. "I didn't know it was you."

"Sorry to interrupt your time," said Chris quietly to her. "I couldn't help myself."

"I'm glad you did. I felt like I was ready to cry." Then her expression changed. "I've got two minutes left on my time. Do you want them?"

Chris eyed the stage anxiously. "You don't mind?"

"I'd be more than happy to let you use them." She turned to the microphone. "I've decided to forfeit the rest of my three minutes and let Mr. Magnuson speak in my place."

Fontaine whispered to Diaz and Aragones briefly, then said, "That's within guidelines, as long as you realize you are forfeiting your own time."

Erica stepped aside and let Chris move in behind the microphone. "Thanks, Erica." He then turned to face the stage. "Magnuson. Chris Magnuson. So, Mr. Diaz, who are 'you people?' Am I one of them?"

Diaz hesitated, but quickly regained his confident manner. "Yes, as a matter of fact you are. Everyone of your race. All the white men who took land and kept my people repressed."

"Your people? My race? White men?" He pointed both thumbs at his chest. "I didn't do it! No one else in this room, or this country did it!" Chris said, his voice raised in pitch. Then he caught himself, taking a deep breath. He unfolded his arms and held his chin for a second. "I know this is beyond the scope of these proceedings, but I've got two minutes. And this is what I want to say.

"You said race. Race," Chris began, "is a totally fabricated concept. The whole idea is only one of human perception. Nature doesn't care about race. It's simply how we decide to categorize people based on the amount of pigment in their skin, or other characteristics. Originally, continent of national origin was a factor, but that just isn't true anymore. Mr. Diaz, you said 'white men.' What does that mean, really? You're skin is barely different from mine. Actually the same when I've been working on my tan." There were a few laughs from the crowd.

"It is a matter of ethnic background, sir," Diaz said. "You're of European descent, I am not. Where have you been living, in a cave?"

"Don't you dare criticize me, you pompous ass," Chris said calmly.

"Order!" Fontaine yelled. "We'll have none of that kind of talk in these proceedings!"

"I've been living with my eyes open, Mr. Diaz. What I see is that everyone on Earth, every single person, has brown skin. Everyone. Some are very dark, some are very light. But everyone is brown. Imagine how far it would go to eliminating racial tension if we did something as simple as call ourselves brown and beige, instead of black and white. Besides being more accurate, it would break down the divisions between us."

Diaz smiled smugly on stage, his arms folded in front of himself, saying nothing.

"You have less than a minute left," Fontaine said.

"Any time that people fragment the world by thought, or by action, it decreases the quality of life for everyone concerned. Maybe not right away but, definitely, in the long run. So, what do you hope to accomplish, Mr. Diaz, by this annexation? Do you really pretend that this is some sort of 'get even' action to right all the cultural injustices done in the past? What a bunch of crap! Not only is this giving an advantage to a select ethnic group, but it's racism across time. Yeah, what was done four hundred years ago in this area to Native Americans was wrong. But it was four hundred years ago. To pretend you, or anyone else, should get some kind of an advantage to compensate for that it is a bunch of crap. To even consider, for a second, that this project is anything but a way to abuse federal law for quick and extreme profit is a joke. And it will do nothing but increase the ethnic tension around the country and in this area."

"Your time is up," interrupted Fontaine. He looked to the other microphone. "Next question?"

The man there looked at the stage and said, "He can have some of my time," and he looked back at Chris. "My comment will only take a minute."

Chris waved across the audience at him. "Thanks."

"Each person is only entitled to three minutes time," said Fontaine.

"I'm giving my time to him," said the man at the other microphone.

"And it will only increase problems in this area," Chris continued quickly. "The more we fragment things, here or anywhere else, the worse problems will get. For God's sake, look around this area, the world. Water is in short supply, arable cropland is decreasing. Global warming is a confirmed reality, and there are already droughts in central Asia and serious erosion along both the Atlantic and Pacific coasts. Carbon dioxide levels are double what they were a hundred years ago. This summer, the hurricanes have caused the worst damage ever, and it's only late August. Bridges, roads, schools in this area are in horrible shape. And what is being accomplished? A bigger casino is being built. Does that strike anyone but me as being totally absurd?" He turned to the audience.

There was a fair amount of applause.

"So, what are we going to do about that? Just sell off our homes and move?" He paused a second. "When are we going to get it? When? Why don't we take a stand? For once. This is the only place we'll ever live, this planet, and it's falling apart. Here, and everywhere else. The last thing we need is more entertainment. Yes, it will create jobs. But wouldn't those twelve thousand people be better off working in areas that would improve the world, instead of ways to entertain us. What a great epitaph for the human species: They were playing blackjack while the polar ice caps melted. I know that sounds absurd, but that's exactly what we're talking about. That's really what is happening." Chris looked directly at Diaz. "How do you respond to that, sir?"

"The Federal Government of the United States is in agreement with me on this. What you think doesn't make one bit of difference."

"That doesn't make it right," Chris said calmly. "Here, right now, let's stop it. Let the town council know, let the state representatives know, let the national government know. Don't put up with it. Wrongs of the past cannot be corrected by giving advantages to certain groups of people today. Everyone in this room was born here, in this country, on this land. The more we fragment ourselves by law, by action, by thought, the worse things will get." He stopped, realizing he had probably said more than enough, and walked slowly back to his seat.

There was a spontaneous eruption of applause.

"Order! Order!" called Fontaine.

Many people called out in agreement. Some were standing, waving hands and fists at the stage.

"Order, I said! ORDER!"

But the noise continued. Chris sat quietly, looking around, amazed at what he had incited.

"I call this meeting adjourned!" yelled Fontaine. "No further questions!" He, Diaz and Aragones stood and hurried off stage. The level of crowd noise raised in volume and intensity.

Chris noticed Diana and Vin staring at him with their mouths hanging open. He just felt flushed and shrugged his shoulders. Several people walked past him, one nodded, one gave him a thumbs up. He stood and was starting to leave but saw the television cameraman and reporter working their way toward him through the thickening mass of people in the aisle.

Hector Torrez sat in the back, his hands gripping the back of the seat in front of him. What the hell had just happened, he thought. Everyone is mad. Does this mean they don't want annexation?

He thought about what that would mean to him, or what it wouldn't mean to him.

His anger rose. It was that last faggot who talked, he thought. That pretty boy with the beard, just like some fudge-packing fruitcake from Provincetown. I didn't understand anything he said, but it sure made everyone pissed off about annexation.

As Torrez watched, he saw Chris and the reporter follow the cameraman through the crowd and leave the back of the auditorium.

He thought, what did he say his name was? Mathewson? Masterson?

■   ■   ■

Chris and Sara lay in bed, propped up on their pillows, Sara snuggled against the hair on his chest, her arm across his stomach, his arm down along her side. They watched the 11:00 news airing on the independent Boston station that had covered the town meeting. The small television sitting on the table off the foot of their bed gave the room its only light.

After a brief lead-in by the anchorman, the reporter came on, saying, "That's right, Dennis, I was at Littleboro High School for the town meeting this evening where residents voiced their opinions on how they felt about annexation. And opinions were not mixed. Several residents spoke out against it, pointing out several negative aspects, and some asked accusing questions. We'll have the complete story tomorrow at 6:00, but we did have a chance to talk briefly with Chris Magnuson, a science professor at Algonquin State, who was one of the most vocal opponents of annexation."

The scene shifted to Chris in full camera view, standing in front of a brick wall. The glaring light that shown on him caused him to squint. His skin and hair looked much lighter than they actually were.

"I look horrible!" he whispered.

Sara lightly slapped his chest and said, "Shhh!"

From off camera, the reporter asked, "Why were you so against annexation tonight?" and then a microphone was thrust in front of his face.

Chris looked at her and said, "Well, besides all the reasons everyone else was giving, which are all valid, it's a lousy idea to give an advantage to one particular ethnic group for no reason other than they are of a particular ethnic group. All it will do is serve to strengthen the barriers and tensions that are already between people. And that's exactly what is happening." He turned and looked directly into the camera. "Mistakes or abuses of the past won't go away by further separating groups of people by action or by law. Trying to make up for those mistakes will just make things worse."

The scene abruptly changed to the reporter standing alone in front of the same brick wall. "As if this summer wasn't hot enough, Dennis, the annexation debate in Littleboro is heating up as well."

"Hey, they cut me off!" Chris said in bed, faking annoyance for the benefit of Sara.

The reporter finished, "We'll have more interviews and a detail of the annexation proposal tomorrow at six. Dennis?" And the scene switched back to the anchorman in the studio.

"That was good," Sara said, "you sounded good. What else did you say?"

"I guess you'll just have to wait until tomorrow at six," he teased.

She was studying him, then sighed.

"What? What was that for?"

"I was just remembering, that's all," she said, laying her head back down.

"Remembering what?"

"When I was a kid in Brooklyn. I can remember how divided all the communities were. There was an Irish section, a Chinese section, a Puerto Rican section, a German section. Lots of others. We stayed in the Irish part of town and really didn't mix with other ethnic groups very much."

Chris waited for her to continue. "Yeah?"

"After we had been dating for a few months, you talked about some of your views, like you did tonight. I remember you struggling with it all, thinking about things in new ways. Well, at least, they were new to me. I had never heard anyone talk with attitudes like that." She laughed. "Even my own father called blacks *jigaboos* and Asians *chinks*. I don't think I ever heard him call them anything else."

"Isn't that sweet."

She lifted her head again and looked him in the eye. "Back then, you were so—restless, I guess. Trying to find a better way."

"What better way? All I did was give a point of view."

"But no one thinks about it that way. It always seems to be, 'I belong to this race, this religion, this club, this country, this political party.' People seem to go out of their way to find new ways to separate themselves from each other. Why do they do that?"

"I don't know," he answered. "For a sense of identity, maybe. A sense of comfort and belonging."

"Maybe. Tonight, you seem like you are so—confident. So sure of yourself. Ten years ago you weren't."

"I've been watching people for the last ten years, I guess. Thinking about the way people are, the way they act, some of the things they say." He sighed. "The whole black and white thing for skin color—that's such a joke to me. I've never understood that. Nobody is actually black, and nobody is actually white. Well, except for maybe albinos."

She laughed a little.

"But," he continued, "saying black and white is so automatic to so many people, no one even considers what color skin really is. I've always been amazed by that, and never really understood it."

She was quiet for a moment, then said. "You remember I told you about the time when I was a kid, walking home from school. I walked with a friend and dropped her off at her house and then had to cut through a couple of blocks of, uh, the 'black' neighborhood. Some boys threw rocks at me and chased me down the street, I guess just because my skin wasn't the same color as theirs."

"I remember."

"I've never understood that."

"It's not really much of a different attitude than saying *jigaboos*. It's just expressed differently."

"I guess." They were silent in thought for a second until Sara said, "So, anyway. Your attitude, even back then, really caught my attention. I think it's one of the reasons why I wanted to raise a family with you."

He held her tighter. "You've never told me that."

"No. I guess I never thought I needed to."

"Thanks, I guess. Then, again, it's just the way I am."

"Why are you that way? I mean, how come you've been able to step back and look at sort of the whole big picture?"

"I guess, at least partly, it's because I really don't belong to any groups."

"What do you mean?"

"I'm not in a political party. I'm not part of an organized religion. My Mom took me to Catholic church when I was a boy, but I stopped that in my early teens. I'm a mongrel when it comes to ethnic groups. You know, part Italian, part English, part Polish, part Greek, part Native American—"

"You're part Native American? I never knew that."

"Yeah. You know Aunt Helen traced our family tree all the way back."

"I know you had direct descendants on the Mayflower, but not Native American relatives."

"Hey, not just on the Mayflower. In charge of the Mayflower. William Brewster. He wrote the Mayflower Compact and was a governor, or captain, or something. And John Cotton, too."

"Never heard of him."

"Some Pilgrim priest, or something. I don't know, he's in the encyclopedia. And, yeah, there was a branch of the family tree that was part Native American, about a hundred and fifty years ago."

"Huh. Hey, maybe you have a claim to land rights somewhere!"

"Yeah, whatever. No, thanks. Not interested. Anyway, like I was saying, I'm an ethnic mongrel. I'm a man, but it could be argued that I have some female qualities, like being sensitive and emotional."

"Okay. I'll give you that one."

Chris laughed. "Hell, I'm not even left-handed or right-handed. I do half things one way and half the other."

"You mean ambidextrous."

"No. That's doing things with either hand. I do some things right-handed, but can't do them at all left-handed. And it's split right down the middle as far as how many of each."

"Huh. That's weird."

"I've always thought it was pretty efficient. Anyway. That could indicate some kind of balance in my brain, or something. You know, using both sides equally."

She looked at him, tilting her head and narrowing her eyes. "Now you sound like you're full of shit."

"Well, I don't know! You asked me why I'm the way I am. That's the best I can come up with!"

She smiled and laid back down. "Mmmmm. I've never slept with a TV star before. Left-handed, right-handed, underhanded. Anything." She tightened her grip around his belly and began gently kissing his chest.

He closed his eyes and laid back as she slowly worked her way down his stomach. But he stopped her, gently pulling her face up to him, kissing her hard and deep on the mouth.

Their bodies became more intertwined, and there was no more conversation.

Chapter Nine

esus lifted the full weight of the heavy, rough-cut boards from the cart, hoisting them to his left shoulder. He carried the load around to the back of the small shed where he and Joseph built and repaired chairs, tables, ladders, carts, and other items. Most orders came from their neighbors who lived in the hills above the southwestern shore of the Sea of Galilee. The sun was hot in the afternoon this day in late spring, the sky bright blue, save for the few clouds casting shadows across the trees and hills. As Jesus approached the pile against the rear wall where the boards were stored, Joseph stood from his work of lashing together sections of a small stool. Wiping the sweat from his brow, he smiled as he watched, ever thankful that his son had grown to manhood so quickly. Joseph had always hoped for a son, but he could not have imagined one who would grow so rapidly and become so strong. Now the size and strength of a man of twenty-five years, he had been with them only half that time. With each passing year Joseph became less capable of the heavy labor required in his carpentry trade. With his broad shoulders and solid arms, Jesus easily could do all that was required. And Joseph had never seen a man swing a hammer so easily, with such power and aim!

The boards clattered loudly as Jesus dropped them on the pile. Without hesitation he turned to retrieve another load. As he approached the cart, he noticed a young woman walking up their road. He smiled broadly as he recognized her immediately.

"Mary! How good to see you!" he called when she was still a fair distance away.

She waved silently, smiling as well, but then hurried her approach. A small bundle wrapped in cloth hanging under her right arm swung back and forth as she quickly walked to him.

"Jesus!" and she ran into his arms, against his bare chest covered with dark hair. They embraced tightly for several seconds. "I was afraid you might not be here," she said with relief.

"I have just returned from the village, purchasing boards from the mill. I am afraid I may smell much like a donkey, working in the sun as I have." He pulled back and smiled at her, admiring the sparkle in her large, brown eyes. Her long, dark hair was tied loosely and hung down her back.

"Even when you sweat, you still smell sweeter than most men I know," she said. "Never have I met anyone who bathes as often. And whose mouth smells as yours."

"That is the mint plants from our garden. I chew on a leaf several times a day for my own comfort. Do you like the smell of it?"

"It is far better than the smell of decay in so many of the people I know in Magdala."

He continued to admire her beauty, his solid arms holding her close. "But surely you have not come to talk of the cleanliness of my body. How is your home in Magdala? Have you not found a husband yet, or do you still tend to your house and garden alone?"

At this she released him, stepping back and looking down. "I still live alone, yes. Though I have visitors often." After remaining silent for a moment, she looked back up into his eyes and said, "And, as for a husband, I believe I know a man who would be as good a husband as any. But I do not believe he knows this."

Knowing exactly what she meant, Jesus studied her silently. He was aware of Joseph standing nearby, so, instead of discussing this further with her, he motioned at the package under her arm. "What do you carry with you?" Joking with her, he asked, "Surely it must be some dear gift you have brought for me."

"It is such a beautiful day. I have brought bread, dried fruits and dried meat, and a sack of wine. I was hoping you would walk with me to the top of the hill that overlooks the village to the north and the sea to the south. I have also brought a blanket upon which to sit."

"I would enjoy that very much. Let me first carry this last load of boards to the pile and then put on a toga."

Joseph had walked closer and now spoke. "Hello, Mary. What a nice surprise." Though his words were pleasant, his tone was cold.

"Hello, Joseph. May I borrow the company of your son for the remainder of the afternoon?"

"He will be leaving to attend synagogue with us, in Nazareth, when the sun is close to setting."

"Father, you know how I feel about synagogue," said Jesus. "I do not understand why so much importance is placed on this ritual."

"We have had this discussion before. For the worship of God. You know this well." Impatience edged his voice.

"I cannot help but think this ritual is a substitute for a life of goodness, as God has intended for all men. God needs love returned by all men. God does not need to be worshipped."

"We express our love for God in synagogue, through worship." Joseph looked from Jesus to Mary of Magdala, who stood silently, knowing it best not to get involved in this discussion.

"We express our love for God in every thought we have, in every action of every day, in what we do to, and for, others."

Joseph studied his son for a moment. "You are a man, and you now make your own choices. Your mother and I will be going, and we would like you in our company."

"Mary has been kind enough to walk the distance from her home to spend time with me. I will return that kindness to her by sharing the meal she has brought for me."

"As you wish, my son," said Joseph. "I thank you for traveling to the village and purchasing the wood and unloading the cart."

Jesus noticed how tired his father looked. "For this you do not need to thank me. I love you and respect you, Father, but my love of God can be expressed in the company of a good friend this afternoon."

Jesus finished chewing a small piece of dried lamb, then took the leather wine pouch from Mary and drank deeply. As he swallowed, he looked off over the Sea of Galilee below them. The setting sun behind them cast sparkles that danced over the surface of the water. The blue of the sky deepened.

"Mmmm," he exclaimed, taking another short drink. "It is so pleasant up here. The village looks peaceful, the Sea looks calm, the sky is beautiful." He turned to face her directly. "And so is the friend with whom I share the evening."

Mary smiled widely and looked away. "Thank you."

"Thank *you*," Jesus said quietly, with a smile. The slight breeze had tossed some of his long, brown hair over his shoulder. He pulled it up and flung it back behind his neck. "And how is the fever you had the last time we spoke? I sense it must be gone."

Mary looked back to him. "I had forgotten completely about it. The small, green plant you said would relieve the fever worked very well."

"You dried it, ground it, dissolved it in wine, and then drank the mixture with warm water?"

"As you suggested. I was strong within two days."

"I am glad it restored your health. I remember how dusty your skin looked."

"That plant resembles what grows on my bread when it has gone bad."

"It is similar. And the same will help to heal leprosy. It is truly an amazing plant, though it is so small."

She studied him closely. "Word of your abilities to heal are spreading throughout Galilee. People speak of the power of God within you that allows you to heal."

"The knowledge I have surely is from God, but it is not my power."

"Other men do not know of these things, even men who have studied medicine for the whole of their lives. Most people say it is the magic of God that allows you to heal."

He smiled, "It is not magic, but knowledge. God has allowed me to know what plants will help reduce fever or cure leprosy, how to set a crippled man's leg to allow him to walk, how to cleanse a child's ears that she may hear. I know I do possess this knowledge by the will of God." He looked away, across the sea. "And, yet, it is always as if I remember these things from another place, another life. A place where many people have this knowledge."

"A place where there are others like you? Could this be the kingdom of God of which you speak?"

"I do not know. But I think it is important that I do not question these things. It is much more important that I share them, to help everyone I can. To make their lives better."

Mary watched him closely, then reached out and took his hand. "People say you are the chosen one, the Son of God who has come to lead all people down a path of righteousness."

"All people, all living things are the children of God, are made in the image of the spirit of God within them. I think the only difference between me and all others is that I know this, and other people do not."

"You are different," said Mary, still holding his hand, staring at his face. "You are so much a better man."

He turned to meet her gaze. "If I am different, or better, it is by the will of God. I only hope I can use my abilities to make life better for as many people as possible."

Her throat felt tight, but she said, "Never have I met a man so strong and yet so gentle, so wise and yet so humble, so beautiful of both spirit and of face, with so much knowledge and the desire to only give it away." She looked at him hard. "And, yet, still with such a deep sadness."

"Perhaps you know me better than anyone, Mary. Though I know these good things of which we have just spoken, I still have such a sadness. The reason for which I do not understand. I am certainly not able to put words to whatever it is."

"You told me once that it is a sadness for the difference between the way things are and the way things could be."

"That is part of it. But there is a sense, a remembrance of loss, that I feel."

"I do not understand."

"Nor do I. As I said, I cannot put words to it. It is like trying to remember a dream upon awakening."

She squeezed his hand tighter. "You have said you find me beautiful."

"You are the most beautiful woman I know," he said without hesitation.

"And you know of the many men I have known. Men who have wanted only to share of my body and not of my life. And yet you remain my friend."

He looked deeply into her eyes. "I can understand why many men would want to share of your body, but they are at a great loss not to share of your life. You have a goodness about you, within you. Your beauty is truly not only upon the surface of your skin."

"I think, perhaps, I feel a sense of sharing, of giving myself to these men, because I know it gives them such pleasure to look upon me, to touch me."

"You have so much more to share with everyone. It is sad that they only look upon you and not within you."

"Do you think I do wrong for pleasuring these men?"

"Complete love between a man and a woman is of mind and of body, Mary. I do not think the way you live your life is how all people should live. But you are my friend, and I will ask you not to change to suit my judgment."

"I feel about you like no other man, Jesus. The things you say, the things you do, radiate such beauty."

"Thank you," he said, taking her other hand in his.

"You find me beautiful to look upon, and yet you have never asked to share of this, to touch me."

"No, I have not."

"Is it because of the other men I have known?"

"No." He looked away.

"Why then? Do you not think you would enjoy my touch?"

"I know I would very much. I think it is because of this sadness I feel.

Touching you has not felt like the right thing to do. I think perhaps you know I have not touched any woman in this way. It has not felt right with any woman. Though I have sensed there are many others I have met who would have liked to have me touch them."

"Does it feel right at this moment? Here with me now?" She leaned closer.

He swallowed hard. "More than ever before. But I would want to share of myself so that you would have pleasure from my touch as well. This is more important to me than the pleasure you would make me feel."

"I would like that," she said gently. "No man has ever bothered to ask what I like." She kissed him lightly on the cheek, once, twice, then moved closer and kissed him on the lips.

"Mmmm, your lips are truly soft, and you taste sweet."

"And you, Jesus, taste of mint." And she laughed.

He smiled slightly and pulled his head back, looking into her eyes. "What would give you pleasure, Mary," he whispered.

"Kiss me, Jesus. Please, kiss me, and then touch me with all the love you have in your soul."

The sun had set and twilight darkened the sky, the first stars becoming visible over the eastern shore of the sea. Birds darted in the still air, snatching their fill of insects close to the surface of the water. Jesus and Mary lay together wrapped in the blanket, needing the added warmth in the rapidly cooling air. Still naked, they clung to each other's warmth.

"I have never reached completion in such ways as those," said Mary quietly. "So many times, so easily." She kissed him lightly on the neck.

"It filled me with great joy to see you in such pleasure," he whispered. "I enjoyed that very much."

"How do you know to do such things? You have said you have never been with a woman before. And yet, you know to do things I have never heard tell of being done."

Jesus searched his mind. "I feel as though I know it of memory, just like the other things I know of and talk about."

"Ohhh," Mary sighed, embracing him tighter. "I have reached completion only once or twice previously, but seven times in such a short amount of time, I would have never believed it could have been like that."

He lifted his head slightly and smiled at her. "You asked to be touched with all the love I have in my soul. For this evening, you, and only you have received exactly that. I was more than happy to give it to you."

"Oh, Jesus," she sighed again, "will you be my husband? Would you find me worthy to spend the rest of your life sharing your love with only me?"

Jesus closed his eyes and swallowed hard, feeling suddenly saddened. "No," was all he said.

Her heart sank, but she waited a few moments. "That is all? Just *no*?"

"Oh, Mary, in some ways I wish I were simpler and easily able to partake of the riches of all life has to offer, like other men and women do. But I am not like other men. Even you have said that people talk more and more of me, of the things I teach, of the things I know. This is why I am here, to teach of these things. And I am just beginning to do this. The time of living with my parents grows short. I will not be able to help them much longer. Soon my teaching will be my life. People will travel from afar to hear me, and I will travel as well. I will not be able to keep a garden, a flock, a home. And I will ask no woman to follow me on this life."

"I want to, Jesus," She lifted her head and looked him in the eye. "For I love you, as I have loved no other man."

"And I love you," he confessed.

"Why do you have such sadness when you say that?"

"It is sadness not for the love of you. The answer is, 'No, I cannot give my love only to you.' I am here to share all of my love with every living thing. I know in my heart that a wife and a family cannot be part of that. It would be unfair to them."

She laid her head softly on the hair on his chest, considering this. "That does not change the way I feel about you, my love for you. Hear me and understand this when I say that from this time forward I will be with no man other than you. I devote the rest of my time to you, your life, your teachings."

"You must not, Mary. Though I would enjoy spending much time with you, I will not be able to."

"Even if I cannot be with you, I will be with you in thought, in spirit. No other man has cared for me as much. And though you care for all things, I accept this. Some of you is better than all of other men."

"Do not say such things. There is goodness in all men."

"You are willing to share all you have, all you know, only for the reason of making other people's lives better. Few people can that be said about. If

88

you will allow me to follow you whenever it is possible, I will be honored to be at your side, at any place, for any reason. If I cannot be your wife, I will still devote my life to you."

Jesus was silent. He felt the softness, the warmth of her skin, heard the sincerity and commitment in her voice. In her company he felt at peace.

"Thank you, Mary. All should be as loving and devoted as you."

The full moon began to rise and appeared huge and luminous just over the tops of the hills above the eastern bank of the Sea of Galilee. They watched in silence until Jesus said suddenly, "And yet, there is more than a great sadness within me. There is a great fear as well."

She propped herself up on her elbow and looked at him. "Fear? Of what do you have fear?"

"Fear that I will fail. Fear that people will misunderstand what I say. Fear some will not believe that my motives and my compassion are sincere. They may despise and fear me, because I will threaten the way they live now." He held her tighter against his chest. "I know that people have the ability and love to make Earth a paradise. I fear, most of all, that this will never happen, that I will not be understood. That is how I may fail."

She was silent for a moment and then said, "A person cannot fail if they are motivated by love."

Jesus thought about this, and then said, "What if others do not share of that love?

CHAPTER TEN

Crow opened two bottles of blueberry-honey-wheat home brew, the pressure releasing with a hiss and the caps falling to the wooden deck with a tinkle.

"I'll pour it," said Chris. Smoke from the black, spherical grill swirled about them in the slight breeze. Dripping grease from the skirt steaks spit on the coals as Chris flipped and positioned the meat over the heat. He took the bottle from Crow. "I'm glad you have a couple days off so we can partake of the riches of the Earth together." He raised and tipped the bottle toward him. "You start first shift later in the week?"

"Monday," said Crow. "Hey, be careful with these. There's a little more sediment than normal. And settled pretty loose. I think it's pectin from the blueberries." He looked at the fire. "You're the only person I know who doesn't use gas, let alone cooks on wood. Wood! Who the hell barbecues over a wood fire? It's 2007, for Christ's sake."

"That's some way for a Native American to talk. What a novel idea, using wood to cook. Would you prefer I use buffalo chips? Anyway, being the efficient geek that I am, I can clean up the yard and get energy for cooking at the same time. All this wood is dead branches I picked up." He turned and called to the kitchen, "Sure you don't want some of this beer!"

Sara and Kathy, Crow's wife, were inside boiling corn on the cob and making tossed salad. "No thanks," called Sara, "we'll stick with the red wine!"

Chris slowly poured down the side of the glass, but quick enough to allow a layer of foam to fizz to the top. "Ahhhh. Nothing like good head."

Crow guffawed. "And this from the pillar of the community? Is this the same man who so firmly set an example for us all to follow? The image of my hero has been shattered."

"Hero? You mean you aren't sticking to the beliefs of your tribe, your people, oh, mighty Crow? There is talk afoot that I have wronged them, that I speak with forked tongue."

Crow spit a laugh out his thick lips. "To hell with that. My job won't change and neither will my pay. Actually, I don't have a warm, fuzzy feeling for plenty of people who work there. In one way, I'd like to see the business not do real well so some of the people would get laid off. One or two in particular."

"That's kind of harsh, isn't it?"

"It's my income, but I don't have a lot of friends there. And besides, a few years back, when I had a chance for a big promotion, they passed me over and went outside to hire somebody new. Now I'm on a career plateau, destined to be a security guard forever. I've never quite got over that."

"I remember that. You were kind of crabby." Chris drank, savoring the flavor of the beer, waiting for the full effect of the aftertaste. Finally he said, "I don't think I've ever had a beer taste so tart. And there's a different mix of flavors I don't recognize."

"That's probably the honey. When all those weird carbohydrates ferment, there's no telling what kinds of end products and flavors you're going to get."

"Hmmm." He took another sip. "Very unusual, and very good."

"Thanks."

"So anyway, back to your job. Why don't you leave if you don't like it?"

"Oh, I like the work just fine. And I'm good at it. My natural ability to look intimidating and all. There's just some people there I don't like very much. And personally, I think you're right with what you said about unfair advantages to ethnic groups, just because they're part of an ethnic group." Crow took a drink, then grinned. "But, then again, if I got paid by commission based on how much The Gold made, I'd kick the living shit out of you. You know, for disrupting future growth and expansion and all that."

"Ha. I'd like to see you try. You barely out-weigh me by, what, a hundred and thirty pounds. And you're not that tall. Hell, you can't be more than a foot taller than me. And anyway, I can run way faster than you, so you couldn't catch me."

Crow laughed and took another sip, watching the meat cook.

"Hey, Crow," said Chris after a moment. "I've got to ask you something."

"You sound so serious. Sure, anything."

"Your name, how did you get it? Is it some Native American importance?"

As Chris was speaking, they heard crunching leaves and breaking twigs in the woods. They both stopped and looked into the trees. Neither saw them at first, but at the next movement, a moose cow and her calf could clearly be seen moving among the leaves. Fifty feet from the edge of their back lawn, they were leisurely browsing on tender plants growing in the moist soil in the shadows.

"You see that?" Chris whispered.

"Sure," Crow whispered back.

"Hang on, let me get the kids." Chris quietly opened the sliding screen door and hurried into the house. "There's a moose in the woods," he said to Sara and Kathy. "Right in the back yard. Where are the kids?"

Sara said, "A what? Really? Uh, they're on the computer."

As Chris continued through the kitchen, Sara and Kathy hurried out to the deck.

Chris found John at the keyboard and Mary sitting next to him.

"No! Not that way!" Mary was instructing him.

"I can go any way I want!" John argued.

"Fine," she said, crossing her arms, "you'll die. The Lava Serpent is in there."

"Guys! Guys!" Chris whispered. "Come out back! Quick!"

"I'm in the middle of a game," said John, annoyed.

"There's something really cool in the woods!"

"What?" asked Mary, getting up.

"Come on. I'll show you. But, be quiet."

They slunk through the kitchen and out on the deck. Sara waved them over, frantically but silently.

"Look straight in through there," she said quietly, pointing. "Under that one branch and a little to the right of that patch of sunlight."

"What? What is it?" said John, too loudly.

"Not so loud," whispered Chris urgently, "you'll scare them away! It's a moose and her baby."

But at the sound of John's voice, the cow and calf both froze and looked up, startled. The mother took several quick steps forward, crashing through saplings and branches. The calf tried to follow but couldn't get good footing, its tiny hooves treading wildly on the loose soil and leaves. As the mother leapt over a fallen tree, she sideswiped a limbless, dead tree still standing. Her weight caused it to wobble momentarily. With a crunch, insect-riddled wood splintered and the tree fell over, landing first on a small sapling, then rolling off. It fell onto the calf as it still tried to run, landing across both its rear legs with a thud. The calf collapsed to the ground with a bleat of pain and began crying loudly, scraping at the leaves with its front hooves. The cow immediately turned and came back, but stopped several feet away and called to the calf in a series of low, hollow bellows, beckoning it to follow her.

"Damn!" said Chris. "That baby is hurt."

"Daddy! Save it!" cried Mary, hopping up and down while holding onto the railing of the deck.

"Yeah, yeah," he said, but not really to her. "Hey, Crow, let's go." He motioned to him and they hurried down the steps to the grass below. The cow caught sight of them and hurried farther away, up a short incline. As Chris and Crow reached the edge of the trees, she had stopped and again called to the calf, higher in pitch and more insistent. The baby's struggles increased. It cried louder, but couldn't move, the weight of the dead tree pinning it down.

"We'll have to lift it off," said Crow. Pointing to the smaller end, he said, "You get that end, I'll get this one."

"Right." As Chris moved past the trapped calf, it eyed him with panic. He began speaking to it in soothing tones. "It's okay. We're just going to help. That's it, just relax." As he came around in front of the calf, continuing to speak, it still eyed him suspiciously, but its struggles slowed. By the time he took the few steps to the far end of the fallen tree, it had stopped struggling and seemed to be waiting patiently. Up the slope, the cow's calls continued, though they became less urgent when the calf stopped crying.

"Whenever you're ready," said Crow, positioning his legs on either side of the tree and taking hold with both hands.

Chris reached down and found a firm grip. "Okay."

"On three," said Crow. "Lift it off and away behind it. Got it?" And he indicated which direction with a jerk of his head.

"Yep. Ready."

"One, two, three!" And they both easily lifted the tree off and swung it away.

Before they could put it down, the calf was up on all four hooves, trying to walk. It staggered at first, dragging its rear legs. But it regained its balance and hurried forward with only a minor hitch in its gait. By the time Chris and Crow had put the tree down and brushed the dirt and rotten wood off their hands, the calf had rejoined its mother. They hurried up over the rise and disappeared into the trees, the sound of crunching leaves fading quickly. Chris and Crow gave each other a congratulatory nod and slowly walked back to the deck.

"Whoa! That was cool!" exclaimed Mary as they reached the top of the steps. "It didn't get hurt?"

"I guess not too bad," said Chris. "It seemed like it was okay."

Mary turned to John. "You scared them!"

"I didn't know there were mooses in the woods!"

They both headed back into the house, arguing.

"Moose in Littleboro," said Chris. "Who would have thunk it?"

"I know their range has been expanding again, maybe for the past thirty years," said Crow. "But it's still something to see them right in the middle of our neighborhood."

"They didn't seem to be scared, until John yelled," observed Kathy. At four feet eleven inches and under ninety pounds, her and Crow made a physically mismatched pair. She pulled a strand of her long, black hair away from her face. "My hero!" she cooed sarcastically, tilting her head and batting her eyelashes while looking at Crow.

He jammed both thumbs into his pants above his hips, elbows out, and threw out his massive chest. "It was nothing, nothing at all. Just another good deed down on the ranch." He laughed and picked up his glass of beer.

"So, when are the steaks done?" asked Sara, lifting the cover off the grill, waiting for the smoke to clear a little, smelling the rich aroma.

"Soon. Very soon," said Chris.

"Well, hurry. It's almost six o'clock."

"Hey, this is man's work out here," Chris said. "We'll take care of the charred, animal, striated muscle, you take care of the vegetative matter."

"You make that sound so delicious," said Kathy. "And, anyway, skirt steaks are diaphragm. Seems like a science teacher should know that." She gave Crow a parting glance and wink before following Sara back into the kitchen.

The two men watched them go, each taking a sip of beer.

Chris soon said, "How did a couple of losers like you and me ever wind up with great women like those two?"

"My charm, my rugged good looks, but mostly it's because I'm great in bed."

"Right. And I'm sure Sara only likes me for my money." He picked up the empty plate off the railing and pulled steaks from the grill with a pair of tongs. After a moment he said, "So? What's the answer?"

"To what?"

"Crow. How did you get that name? Did a black bird appear to your mother in a vision just before you were born?"

Crow laughed. "Uh, no. Not nearly that colorful. When I was a baby, I cried a lot, or so my mom tells me. Probably because I could never get enough to eat. Anyway, I cried so much, and so persistent, that my voice reminded her of a crow cawing. They've been calling me Crow since I was a baby. And it's stuck all these years. Anyway, I like it a lot better than Henry."

"What? Because your baby cry sounded like a crow? That's it?"

"That's it."

"That's pathetic," Chris laughed.

Crow laughed along, and they both took another sip of beer.

■ ■ ■

John and Mary were sitting on the floor of the dining room, plastic trays in front of them. Small cubes of steak and half-eaten ears of corn were on plates next to covered cups of Pepsi, straws protruding from the top. The four adults sat around the dining room table facing the television turned away from its normal position so they could see.

The lead story on the six o'clock news concerned the severe drought in sub-Sahara Africa, the worst in forty years. Though grain supplied by Canada and the United States would provide temporary relief, political unrest was preventing overland transport to areas in greatest need. The next story described military activity escalating around the construction of the Kazakhstan oil pipeline. It was being laid along the north shore of the Caspian Sea, through the southern region of Russia, north of the Caucasus Mountains, to the Black Sea port city of Tuapse. Fear of terrorist activity in retaliation for perceived, inequitable economic benefit from the oil was prompting mobilization of forty thousand Kazakhstani troops. Two United States aircraft carriers were speeding to the Mediterranean Sea to provide air support. Completion of this pipeline would ensure a consistent supply of crude oil for the next twenty to thirty years, since the huge reserves there had barely been tapped.

"Yes," said Chris, to no one in particular, "a bigger casino is clearly what this world needs."

Tropical storm Jeremy had quickly become a hurricane, with sustained winds over ninety miles an hour, and was expected to continue to strengthen. It was currently 450 miles east of San Juan, Puerto Rico, and was heading west by northwest at nine miles an hour.

"When's Daddy going to be on?" asked Mary, restless.

"Be patient," said Sara, "just a minute."

After a commercial break, Passemannican annexation was the first local story. The same reporter talked briefly about the details of the proposed expansion. Videotape of Lynn Harris, the high school principal, was shown as she briefly talked about the jobs that would be created. The reporter made a couple comments and then said, "And Littleboro resident Chris Magnuson made these remarks."

The scene changed to Chris standing in front of the same brick wall, his name in white letters at the bottom of the screen. The original scene was shown, and he continued with, "What we need to be doing is constantly improving the quality of life for future generations, both short-term and long-term, looking beyond the benefits for just us, or whatever our particular group is. Love on a cultural level is the mutual sharing of resources that improves the quality of life for everyone involved. Compared to other animals, people have so much power to make life on Earth so much better, or so much worse. It's our choice, and we each need to make it, individually. We need to take a hard look around and start putting together a world that can be functional, sustainable. A huge casino doesn't fit into that scheme of things."

The reporter summarized by discussing some of the action that was happening as a result of the town meeting. A citizens group was forming, with the support of a local law firm, to explore every possible way to legally fight annexation. There was also movement to organize boycotting patronization of the Gold.

"That's already started," said Crow. "When I was out today, I saw yellow signs with bright red letters saying *Annihilation for Annexation*. Someone must have got them printed and hung them all over town."

"See what you started!" said Sara, her tone teasing.

"Did I say 'annihilate?'" said Chris, laughing. "I thought I said things like *love* and *sustainable*."

But, with his joking tone, he didn't let them know he was scared, truly concerned, that all he had done was widen the differences between the people involved. Exactly the opposite of what he had intended.

■ ■ ■

Dealers, waiters, waitresses and various other employees sat in the lounge area, taking their fifteen minute breaks. There were a few cloth, reclining chairs along the wall, but the furnishings of the room were dominated by round, wooden tables and brown and white, wooden chairs. Several vending machines were along the near wall, offering snacks, soda, coffee, and cigarettes.

Hector hurried in, made a purchase of cigarettes and coffee, and sat alone at one of the tables, facing the big-screen television in the far corner. He wasn't paying close attention to it until commercials ended and the news came back on and he recognized the front of the auditorium and Lynn Harris. When Chris came on, he stood and turned up the volume, crouching on the floor near the set, watching and listening.

He said to himself, "What the fuck is this faggot talking about?" His anger rose as Chris spoke, and he noticed Chris' name across the bottom of the screen. Hector remembered the signs he had seen on trees while driving to work from Mel's, *Annihilation for Annexation*.

He turned to two waitresses sitting at a table nearby and asked, "What's annie-hillation mean?"

They stared at him for a second, one trying to keep from laughing while the other said, "Excuse me?"

Impatient, Hector snapped quickly, "Annie-hillation! I saw it on signs. They said, 'annie-hillation for annexation.' What does it mean?"

Then the one waitress understood. "Oh! The signs! Annihilation! It means to kill, like, wipe out completely."

"Thanks," he grumbled, giving a dirty look to the other waitress. He turned back to the television and heard the reporter saying organized action was being taken in town to legally fight annexation. "Damn it! What the hell." He stared in anger at the television for a few seconds.

Pulling a pen from his breast pocket and picking up a dirty napkin from the table, he wrote *Chris Magnuson* and stuffed the napkin in his pocket.

■   ■   ■

Crow put down his coffee cup with a clink. "No, I don't think you're weird, except when you ask me if I think you're weird."

Sara and Kathy looked at each other knowingly. John and Mary had long since gone to bed, and the four of them sat around the table talking quietly. A cooling breeze coming through the screen door freshened the room.

Chris fiddled with his empty cup, gripping the handle and swinging it back and forth. "I guess I only get in this self-examination mood when I've had a few drinks. Good thing I don't do it very often."

Crow said, "Hey, I'll grant you that you don't think about things like anyone else I know. But it's okay. That's you. The things you say make sense, even though I never think about stuff like peace and harmony and shit like that. Then again, you can be as crude and obnoxious as the next guy."

Chris looked up and said with sarcasm, "Gee thanks, Bud."

"And I only married you for your cute butt," said Sara, smiling, "I don't care what you think or say."

Crow laughed a single syllable. "No accounting for tastes. Some people like big, rugged men, some people like scrawny wimps."

"Again, thanks," said Chris, raising his cup as if in a toast. Then he shook his head and said, "Aaaahh, it's just that sometimes I can't figure out, for the life of me, why things are the way they are. Even stupid little things."

"Like what?" asked Kathy.

"Well, like the calendar."

"The calendar?" she asked. "What's wrong with the calendar?"

"It's all out of whack with the Earth's cycles."

"Isn't it based on Roman days, or something?"

"Yeah, whatever," said Chris. "But just a simple thing, like when the first day of the year is. Or how many months there are."

Crow said, "Aren't they kind of the way they are for a reason?"

"Nothing but some arbitrary dates assigned a long time ago." Chris put down his cup. "Look, if you divide 365 days a year by twenty-eight, you get thirteen months, with one day left over. Twenty-eight days in every month would follow the phases of the moon better, women's menstruation cycles better." He faked excitement, as if experiencing a revelation. "Imagine that! Women would know the exact day when they were ovulating, when they could expect P.M.S. Full moons would basically be on the same day each month. The elegance and simplicity of it boggles the mind!"

Kathy looked at him curiously. "Maybe you are weird. So, what do we do with the extra day?"

"New Year's Day. Maybe make it on the shortest day of the year, or whatever, so it wouldn't change too much from when it is now. And make it a huge holiday. With feasts, and reflection of the past year and looking ahead to the coming year, and a time to be with family and friends. Like a Thanksgiving, Christmas and New Year's rolled into one."

"And on leap years?" asked Sara.

"A two-day party! No problem there. And every month would still have the same number of days."

"Thirteen months. Sounds unlucky," said Kathy.

Chris looked at her sideways and said, "Whatever!" Then reconsidered. "No, you're right. And that would be the reason we will never change to a universal, celestial calendar—because of some arbitrary superstition. That's exactly the kind of thing I'm talking about." He smiled. "People, got to love 'em."

"And what would the thirteenth month be called?" smiled Crow. "Chrisember?"

"Sure. Works for me," he smiled.

"I think maybe you think too much," said Sara, sipping coffee.

"I can't argue with that. Unfortunately," he laughed, "I can't just turn it off. It sort of just happens, and I go along for the ride." They were quiet for a few seconds, until Chris said, "But it's the big things that really drive me crazy. The fragmentation of the world by the way people think, or just how they choose to perceive it. The whole concept of race, like I said at the meeting. What a crock of dog shit. Political parties. A hundred different religions. A thousand different ethnic groups. What's up with all that?"

"They aren't exactly planned divisions," said Sara. "Everything sort of evolved socially around the world in different locations, by different people, for different reasons."

"I know, but isn't it time to reassess everything? We really are becoming one, big interconnected planet. Don't you think the more we're all on the same page, the less conflict there would be?"

■　■　■

The phone ringing at 12:45 in the middle of the night rudely tore Chris from sleep. He lifted his head slightly and felt his heart thundering in his chest. As he gained awareness, he quickly grabbed the receiver on the night table as the second ring began.

"Hello?" he said in a gravelly voice.

There was a brief silence and then—click! The caller hung up.

Chris swore and awkwardly put the receiver back on the phone, drifting back off to sleep within a few seconds.

CHAPTER ELEVEN

"**N**o, it's not canceled," Hector said angrily to Pamela Nixon. "Yes, it is," she said calmly, though the look in his eyes caused her fear. "He's not seeing anyone and has had to reschedule all appointments."

"Not mine, he hasn't," he growled at her. "Tell him I'm here."

She looked at him briefly then picked up the phone, dialed and waited. "Mr. Torrez is here for his two-twenty," she said into the receiver. "… I know … I told him … yes, sir. Okay." She hung up and said to Hector, "He can't see anyone."

Hector spun angrily and opened the door to Brown's office.

Nixon immediately picked up the phone and dialed for security.

Brown was on the phone when Hector burst into the office. He stood and started to complain until he saw the look in Hector's eyes, then calmly said into the receiver, "I'll have to call you back in a few minutes. No, it's okay. Just go through those names I told you about. Yeah, a couple minutes. Thanks."

Brown hung up, but, before he could speak, Hector said, "I had an appointment. I need to talk to you right now."

"Hector. Look," Brown said evenly, "it's not you. I've had to cancel all my appointments. We've had to, well, we've had to change some plans and address some new issues."

"What issues? What's so fucking important?"

"There's a lot of public dissatisfaction with annexation. And we have to address it the best we can. Immediately."

"What. You said before annexation is going to happen no matter what."

"It is," said Brown, "but there are a couple of things going on now that could interfere with patronage at the Gold."

"What?"

"Uh, with the number of customers coming here. And public perception could be hurt. We've had to form an emergency task force to nip this in the bud."

"I saw the signs around town. Is it something to do with that?"

"Yes, it is. That's one of the things we need to take care of immediately. We'll have people out first thing in the morning taking them down, at least the ones on telephone poles and along state highways. The signs on private property may be more complicated. As a matter of fact, that's what the phone call was about when you came in. Don't you think you should let me get back to that?"

"I need to ask you something first. It's important."

Brown hesitated and was ready to refuse but, again, changed his mind. Even though he had burst into his office unannounced, he thought it might be best to keep Torrez calm. "Sure, but make it quick."

"I need somewhere to stay. Somewhere to live for a while."

"Uhh ... okay," Brown said slowly, indicating he needed to hear more.

Hector hesitated. "My trailer—" Then he remembered it was up to him to get the trailer off the property. "I can't stay at my trailer for a while. I need somewhere to live."

"Surely you don't expect to stay at my house." Brown's impatience grew quickly, not believing the gall of Torrez.

"No. I don't know. I was thinking, maybe, I could stay in one of the hotel rooms for a while."

"That's out of the question, unless you were to pay regular guest rates."

"Shit. I can't afford that! One night cost almost as much as a month for space at the trailer park."

"One of the reasons we need annexation and expansion is because our hundred and fifty rooms are almost booked solid until after the first of the year. I can't just give you one."

"Well, what then?" said Torrez, his anger rising. "Damn it, aren't there any empty construction trailers or something I could just sleep in for a while?"

"Nothing yet. Construction won't begin—"

There was a knock on the door, and it quickly opened. Crow entered, asking Brown, "Everything all right in—" And then he saw it was Torrez.

"It's okay, Henry," said Brown. "We're almost through."

Hector turned full around and glared at him. "What do you want?"

Crow looked past him to Brown. "You sure everything is all right?"

"Just get the fuck out," said Torrez. "Why don't you quit butting in where it's none of your business."

Brown looked at Torrez, then to Crow, then back to Torrez. "What do you mean, 'quit butting in?'"

Torrez felt his stomach tighten as a rush shot through his body. "I, uh ... nothing. Nothing. Just get out, Crow. We were—"

"I'll tell him when to get out!" barked Brown, suddenly furious. "What's going on?"

Both were silent, but Torrez flashed Crow a threatening look.

"Johnson, tell me exactly what's going on," said Brown, stepping out from around his desk. "Now!"

Crow hesitated, but then wondered why in the world he was protecting Torrez. "Well, Mr. Brown, last week there was a disagreement."

Very impatiently, Brown asked, "What kind of disagreement?"

"It was nothing," said Torrez. "Just a little problem—"

"I'm talking to Henry, Hector!" Brown interrupted, "Shut up!" He looked back to Crow. "What disagreement? Between who?"

"Hector and one of his workers, Jim Lockwood, had a disagreement. Last week, I think it was."

"What was the nature of this disagreement?" Brown asked. When Crow hesitated he said, "Let's go! Let's go! For God's sake, don't I have enough on my mind without this bullshit!"

"Best I could tell," said Crow, "Hector and Jim had an argument about what type of equipment to use. When Jim disagreed, Hector got physical."

"What do you mean, 'physical'? He punched him?" Brown was fuming mad, his face a flaming scarlet.

Torrez began to panic. "Hold on a second! I just—"

"Shut up!" yelled Brown. "Johnson, what do you mean?"

"No, not really. What I saw was Hector pick up Jim and throw him into some crates."

Brown's teeth were clenched. "Did Lockwood get hurt?"

"Nothing serious. He's okay."

"Why wasn't this reported?" asked Brown.

Crow hesitated, then said, "Well, like you said, you have enough to worry about. We solved it there. They got back to work, I didn't want to write a report, and I knew you wouldn't want to deal with it."

"I appreciate your concern for my time, but I still need to know what's going on in my own department. I know something like this with Hector happened about a year ago. Have there been any other times besides that one, and last week?"

"Well, I ... yes, Mr. Brown," said Crow, feeling pressure to talk about it. Even though he didn't like Torrez, he still didn't want this all to come from him. "There was a minor argument about a month ago. And one other time, I'm aware of, maybe six months ago. That one got pretty ugly. A couple punches were thrown."

"Damn it," said Brown, rubbing the back of his neck, looking down.

"Okay, thanks Henry." He turned to Torrez. "For Christ's sake, Hector, all the chances you've had. I've had it. I really have. I've got important things to deal with, real problems. These invented crises you create. I can't stand it. I just can't stand it! " He threw up his hands in frustration. "That's it, this meeting is over. I've got important calls to make. Listen, Torrez. Once more. Just one more time I hear about any of this bullshit, and you're gone. You're history. You got that?"

Seething mad, his teeth clenched behind tight lips, his hands curled into fists, it was all Hector could do to say, "Yes, Mr. Brown. I understand."

"And, no, I don't have a place for you to stay. Figure something out for yourself. I've got real issues to work through. Both of you get out. Now."

Crow opened the door and went out as Hector followed him. As soon as the door of the office closed, Hector growled at Crow, "You fucking pig. How dare you fuck me up like that." They stopped near Nixon's desk, who looked up uneasily.

"Back off," Crow said calmly. "I didn't say anything that wasn't true. You keep fucking yourself up."

"I swear, one more time," said Hector, sticking a fist in Crow's face, "you screw me one more time, and I'll fucking kill you."

The office door opened, and Brown was walking out saying, "Pam, could you call—" until he saw they were still there, and Hector's raised fist. He came out in time to hear, *and I'll fucking kill you.*

Hector dropped his hand and turned to face Brown.

"What the—" said Brown, and then exploded. "That's it! Torrez, you're fired! Get the hell out of here! Now! God damn it! God *damn* it!"

Crow turned slowly and walked around the corner, but Hector stared at Brown dumbly.

"Was there some part of that you didn't understand?" cried Brown. "Get out of here! You're fired!" Then he looked at Pamela and said, "Get West on the phone again." And he turned and walked back into his office, mumbling to himself, "Annexation is stalling and I've got to deal with maggots eating us from the inside out." And his office door slammed closed.

Hector turned slowly and left.

■　　■　　■

"Okay," said Chris to the four remaining students, "school guidelines say you have two hours for your final. If you haven't got it by now, you probably won't."

Mike was the first one to flip closed the pages of his test, stuff his pen into his backpack, zipper it closed, and walk to the front. Handing his test to Chris, he said, "I was just trying to add a little more to the essay. I know it's a bonus, but it really got me thinking about some of the things you said this semester, especially last class."

"That was the idea," said Chris. "Science doesn't all have to be hypothesis testing. Well, it does by the definition of the scientific method. But religion, philosophy, and science all really cover the same stuff in the real world, just different ways to study them, or discuss them."

"Right," said Mike, "like what you said on the news the other night?"

Chris flushed slightly. "Oh. You saw that?"

"I did, too," said another student, handing her paper to him.

"So, Amy," Chris asked her, "did it make sense?"

"Sure it made sense," answered Mike, "but it's not something you hear talked about much, especially on the news. Last week you said we're basically an expression of our cells, our cellular processes."

"Right."

"On the news you mentioned love, improving the quality of life, or whatever. What has love got to do with cells, the fact that were made of cells?"

He took the tests from the other two students. "Thanks." All four lingered to listen. "Regardless of what you call the cellular processes, they are the source of all our thoughts, emotions, choices, everything. They're the source of love, too. Love is expressed by those same cellular processes."

"Do you have any idea how cold and inhuman that sounds?" asked Amy.

"However it sounds, whatever you call it, the things we call cells are the source of everything we are. Even love."

"So, if love is cellular, why are people the only animals that can feel it?" Mike asked. "Cells have been around for a billion years, like you said, and all animals are made of them."

"Part of the confusion," Chris said, "comes from the use of the word *love* so much. It means so many things to so many people in so many situations and relationships. You heard my definition of love on the news. But like I said, a lot of other people would define it in a completely different way." He paused for a second, and then said, "In its most universal definition, love is the mutual sharing of resources that improves the quality of life for everyone involved."

The students were silent for a moment until Amy said, "Boy, does that sound romantic."

Chris and the other students laughed, and then Chris said, "Obviously,

I'm not talking about that kind of love. But that's a real good example of how overused the word love is. What a man and woman feel when they are thinking about each other all the time, and are committed to each other, is pretty different, at least in some ways, from what a mother feels for her baby. But *love* is the word used to describe both. But, then again, the definition I just gave describes both. In each one there is an exchange of resources to make everyone's life better."

"What resources? I don't get that," one of the other students said.

"Anything. Time, knowledge, feelings, money, food, equipment, anything."

"So when countries trade stuff, like food for minerals, that's an act of love?"

"Yeah, it is. Both countries benefit. Obviously it's not romantic love, but it does fall into the definition I said."

The other girl said, "I have to go. It's been pretty interesting, for a science course and all."

"Thanks, Brittany," said Chris, shaking her hand, "it was great having you."

Mike watched her go and asked, "So, plants or animals that live in symbiosis, where both benefit, that's an act of love?"

"That's a fair statement, sure. And I think that is the meaning of life—the constant quest to improve the quality of life. Whether it's more efficient photosynthesis that allows better use of the sun's energy or countries trading food for cotton. Constantly improving the quality of life for each successive generation is the meaning of life."

"Oh, yeah," said Mike, "you said something about that on the news. So, you talked about God last week when you were talking about cells. If love is 'a gift from God,' like every religion sort of says, does that make it more than just a cellular process?"

"Let me ask you this. How has just about every other organism in the history of the Earth lived? I mean, under what kind of control?"

Mike thought a second. "You mean instinct?"

"Exactly. Instinct. Direct cellular control. Knowledge at the cellular level, at the genetic level, that can be passed on from generation to generation, without each new plant or animal having to learn it. That's pretty efficient, but pretty limiting, in a way." He paused. "So, how are we different, in a way that's mostly different from other organisms?"

"We don't behave much on an instinctive level. Most of what we have to know to get by in the world we have to learn."

"Right. So we can have the flexibility to do more things, all the things that people do, instinctive control has been forfeited. I mean, things like deductive reasoning, intuition, creativity to make art, music, literature, invent technology, build complex buildings and cities. Those are all things we couldn't do if we lived under strict instinctive control. I don't want to put human judgment or value on cellular processes. But, by having that flexibility, by cells giving up direct, instinctive control over our actions, that has allowed a tremendous increase in the quality of life for both the cells, themselves, and us, too. Even though, of course, we are one and the same. In that way, it's the ultimate, the original act of love. And if you accept the way I defined God, it is God's love. God, that is life processes at the cellular level, has given up total control for the potential to greatly improve our quality of life. That sacrifice, that act of love has made life better for us and better for those processes that are expressed as us. In other words, better for God."

The three students were silent until Amy said, "You sort of make it sound like cells decided all this on purpose. Doesn't that go against the theory of evolution, that it's because of random mutation, and the best plants and animals survive better?"

"Like I said, it's kind of hard to imagine what the processes are really like, because we can only think about them from a human point of view. But they've been going on long before people were around, long before anything could 'think' at the level we do. Personally, I don't see how a process as complicated as photosynthesis could have evolved by random mutation, even given a billion years. But, however the evolutionary changes occurred, we have that ultimate gift of love. And we have the ability to love."

Mike asked, "So why is everything so screwed up? If God has given us love, the flexibility to do so many different things, why is there so much hate, murder, pollution, greed? Are things really better for us, or for God?"

"We absolutely have to return the love we've received from God. It must be the priority of our life, to try and improve the quality of life in any way we can, for others and ourselves. We are abusing the love God has given us. God has sacrificed control of our behavior to give us a chance to make things better on Earth, better than they have been for any other life form. We have so much power and flexibility to either make life on Earth better, or totally screw things up. That choice is something we all need to make, individually. And it's not done in a church or temple or prayer or confession, or whatever. It *has* to be a way of life for everyone. It has to be an automatic process, a timeless commitment, without keeping score, without reflection. It has to be the core of our lives."

A student appeared in the door. "Is this the calculus final?"

"Whoops," said Chris, "I guess we'd better get out of here." He smiled at the three of them. Shaking each of their hands he said, "It was great having you. I think this was about the most enthusiastic class I've ever had."

"It was interesting," said Mike. "For just a biology course, you made it really about *life*, not just things that are alive. Not only memorizing genus and species, and crap like that."

"I'm glad you got something out of it. I hope you can find a way to use some of the stuff I talked about in *your* life."

CHAPTER TWELVE

The radio alarm woke Chris at 6:45 with a loud commercial expounding just how good were the car dealer's prices and cars. Swearing, he groaned and hit the button. As he lay for a moment, waiting for his head to clear, he noticed he had sweat in the night and his legs were sticking to the sheets. Slowly sitting, he remained in that position for a moment before standing. Dudley, on the floor next to their bed, only raised his head slightly to give a sleepy look, then laid back down. Chris was wearing only a T-shirt so he put on his bathrobe and walked across the hall to Mary's room.

To his surprise, Mary was not in her bed, and it was neatly made as if it hadn't been slept in. A mild feeling of alarm crept over him, and he quickly walked down the hall towards the living room. When he saw she wasn't watching television or at the computer, his pace quickened. He hurried around the corner and then saw her, sitting calmly at the dining room table. She had her new assignment book open in front of her, the calendar from the kitchen wall down on the table to her left, and she was meticulously filling in the correct dates for the coming months on each corresponding page. She was completely dressed in her new first-day-of-school, white dress, white ankle socks, and new, white sneakers.

"Oh! Hi!" exclaimed Chris. "What are you doing up already?"

"Hi, Daddy. I woke up at five-thirty, and I couldn't go back to sleep. I'm getting ready for school. I sorted my new pencils and erasers and wrote my initials on them, and now I'm getting my homework book ready. We're going to start getting homework in second grade, you know."

"Wow. Great. Well, I'm going to take a shower, and I think Mom will be up in a minute. What time does your bus come?"

"8:05."

"Oh. So we have plenty of time, right?"

"But I don't want to be late."

"Okay. I'll make sure Mom's up before I get in the shower."

Chris returned to his room where Sara was still curled up under the sheet. The fan swung to and fro, moving air in the room, but it still felt hot and muggy. Chris crawled on top of her, pulling back her hair from her face and kissing her gently, just in front of the ear. "Hey, aggregated bee vomit. I mean, honeybunch. You taking a shower?"

"Mmmmm. Do I have to get up?" she said sleepily without opening her eyes.

"There's an anxious little girl, already dressed and ready to for school. I think we owe it to her to get up and be ready."

Sara smiled. "Aww. She's too cute." She rolled over and opened her eyes. "Ooo, smashing hairdo. You look like a nutty professor."

"Thank you. I am a nutty professor. And it's your first day of work, so you'd better get your cute buttocks in the shower, too. I'm going in now. Should I tell you when I'm rinsing, or would you care to join me?"

Sara was quiet for a second, then closed her eyes again and rolled her head to the side. "You'll just wait until I bend over to wash my feet and then you'll—"

He was smiling broadly. "Uh, so what's your point? Is that a yes or a no?"

"With that hair. Tell me when you're rinsing."

The morning was a flurry of activity. Four lunches were made and stuffed into lined, nylon sacks. Chris and Sara drank more coffee than they had any other day all summer. John was soon up and dressed and at the dining room table with the others. For the first time in weeks, they ate breakfast together. While Sara finished dressing for work, Chris cooked pancakes on the electric griddle, and, between the four of them they drank two quarts of orange juice. Syrup and crumbs left on plates were mixed with dog food nuggets that Dudley thankfully gobbled up.

By ten of eight Mary was extremely concerned she would miss her bus and insisted on waiting at the stop at the end of their driveway. Chris walked down with her while Sara got the video disc camera ready. The sun had already burned away the light fog that had formed overnight. Squirrels ran back and forth across the yard while numerous songbirds combined in a disjointed chorus. A mourning dove cooed from the next yard.

"When will it come?" asked Mary a few minutes before eight.

"Probably in a little while," said Chris. "It might take a little longer today because the driver is probably learning the route. And other kids might be a little late getting ready."

"Mrs. Swain already knows the bus stops," Mary said, matter-of-factly. "She won't be late."

"What if Mrs. Swain isn't the driver this year?"

Mary's eyes widened. This possibility had not occurred to her. "She has to be."

"Don't worry," reassured Chris. "Even if it isn't, I'm sure whoever it is will be nice."

Sara led Dudley on a leash to the end of the driveway, with John walking slowly behind.

"What's wrong?" Chris asked John as they approached, and he took the leash from Sara.

"I want to ride the school bus, too."

"Next year you can," said Chris. "Today Mom has to drop you off at your school."

"Why? It's not fair."

The straining of a diesel engine, rising and falling as each gear was shifted, could be heard further down the street. Dudley's ears raised slightly, and a low growl rumbled in his throat.

"Here it comes," said Sara. "Now don't forget to stop halfway up the steps and turn around so I can take a good video."

"Yes, Mom," Mary said, exasperated, "you only told me a bazillion times."

As the bus drew closer, Chris could see a column of three cars that had collected behind the bus as it intermittently stopped along their street. A fourth car, a black, pickup truck, pulled onto the street a couple hundred yards down and joined the rear of the procession.

Dudley barked wildly and strained against his leash. Chris had to hold on tightly and brace his legs to keep from being pulled over. Brakes groaned loudly as the bus stopped in front of them, the doors opened, and Mrs. Swain greeted them with a bright, "Good morning, Mary. Mr. and Mrs. Magnuson! How are you?"

Mary turned to Chris and announced, "See!" and climbed aboard, stopping and turning around as per Sara's instructions. Dudley was making various vocalizations as his tailed wagged wildly and his feet fidgeted on the asphalt.

"Thanks, honey," called Sara, waving with her free hand, holding the camera with the other, the small disc inside whirring. "Have a great day! See you when the bus brings you home!"

Once she was aboard and had selected a seat, the bus lurched forward, the engine racing and transmission grinding as Mrs. Swain found each gear. As the other cars drove past, Chris made eye contact with the driver of the pickup truck, who looked at Chris intensely for those couple seconds. It struck Chris that he had never seen him before. He wondered who he was.

"She's so cute!" chirped Sara, turning off the camera.

"I wanted to go!" whined John, almost on the verge of tears.

Dudley began barking again once the vehicles were past them.

"Hey, you two better get ready," said Chris. "You should be leaving in twenty minutes or so."

"Are you going to school?" Sara asked Chris as they walked up the driveway.

"In a little while. I just need to finish correcting all the finals and then calculate the grades. There's no hurry. I don't have to turn in the grades for a few days."

"Yep," Sara said to John, "both of you will be getting on the bus next year." Then she turned to Chris. "Imagine that, our baby will be riding a school bus to kindergarten next year."

"I guess that means we're getting to be old farts," said Chris.

"I wanted to go today," said John sadly, dragging his feet.

■   ■   ■

Hector had nowhere to be, no place to go, and was enjoying each stop the bus made, watching all the fucking children come from their fucking, pretty, little houses taking the fucking, nice, clean bus to their fucking, quaint, little school. His anger was rising with each stop, thinking about Magnuson and annexation. He had plenty of time in the last couple days to think about it. Again and again. He had assumed he wasn't allowed to go back to the Gold to shower, or to get the few things out of his locker. There was less than a hundred dollars left in his bank account, and his last paycheck wouldn't be ready until the following Friday.

The way he figured it, he had nothing to lose. He might as well have some fun.

As the bus continued out of the neighborhood along Jefferson Drive, a squirrel darted onto the right edge of the road. The bus and the other cars applied their brakes slightly and swerved to the left to give the squirrel clearance. It crouched, its tail twitching nervously, then it scampered back off the edge of the pavement to the sand on the shoulder. Hector accelerated briefly and swerved sharply to the right. As the tires of his truck crushed its body, the only sounds audible to him were *tick—tick* and the tinkling of sand hitting the inside of the fenders. "Got you, you bushy-tailed rat," he said, swerving back to the left.

The bus pulled onto the town road and headed down the hill towards Route 14 with Hector still behind it. When it pulled into the driveway of the school, Hector turned right and slowly drove along a side street that ran parallel to the schoolyard. As the kids filed out of the bus, a teacher standing nearby directed them to the playground to the side of the school where they were to play until all the buses had arrived and school started. Hector parked on the shoulder of the street near where the kids were playing, only a six-foot-high chain link fence separating them.

He sat and watched. Watched them all playing. On the swing set. Basketball. Kickball.

He just watched.

Mostly, he watched a little girl with blonde hair, in a white dress, white socks, and white sneakers.

■　■　■

Jamie Hudson, Sara's supervisor, led her around to the desks of various people. She filled out W-4 and employee I.D. forms, had her picture taken and embossed on a plastic I.D. card, was given a parking sticker and completed various other administrative chores that would allow her to begin employment. That completed, Jamie escorted her to the hospital daycare center. Sara had talked about details of her responsibilities before she accepted employment, had seen the actual room where the children stayed, and even met some of the other caregivers. But, still, she really didn't know how the days would proceed.

"You never quite know who's going to be here, or what's going to happen," said Jamie. "Of course, there are some regular kids who might have one parent working somewhere, and another coming in for regular treatments or tests. Some kids have a parent on a regular schedule of chemo, and the other parent might need to be with their spouse and give them support. Then there's plenty who come in only once while their parent is having a test done. They stay for half an hour, and we'll never see them again. What you basically need to do is give attention to whoever needs it the most at any particular time. Infants will need the most attention, of course. Play with others if you want, keep fights to a minimum, help them with their food at lunchtime. Whatever's needed. It's a free service we provide to patients to help make their medical problems just a little easier, so, however you can help these kids, whatever they need, that's your job."

"Got it," nodded Sara, scanning the large room.

She was introduced to Tiffany, the other caregiver in the room, an overweight woman in her early twenties. After a hurried hello, she returned to the cribs along the back wall where she picked up a crying baby and began rocking it. Jamie wished Sara good luck and left her to her new job.

The room was actually quieter than Sara would have ever expected. In the far right corner, a group of three small children were playing quietly with cardboard bricks, carefully building a series of small walls into a little fort. Another girl, perhaps around seven years old, sat reading at the small, wooden table in the center of the room. At the same table, another boy colored with crayons on white paper. The only other child was an older girl sitting alone against the wall to the right, not doing anything. Her long, brown hair was knotted and dirty, her clothes old and tattered, and she looked very sad.

Sara walked over and stood in front of her, forcing a tentative smile. "Hi."

The girl looked up. Her expression didn't change, but she also said, "Hi."

"Can I sit down for a minute?"

"You can if you want."

"Thanks. I'm new here. I just started today. My name is Sara."

The girl pulled back strands of hair away from her face and forced a smile, "Laurie."

"You don't have school today?"

"No. It starts tomorrow."

"So you must live in Kingsboro," Sara said.

Laurie nodded, and said, "I'm going into sixth grade."

"So that makes you eleven, right?"

She nodded again, then seemed to really notice Sara for the first time, studying her up and down briefly. "You're pretty. Are you a model?"

"Awww. No, not at all. But thanks." Sara then asked her, "So, is one of your parents getting tests done?"

Laurie shook her head and the depth of her frown increased. She seemed on the verge of tears. "My mom. She ... "

"It's okay if you don't want to tell me. You don't have to."

"My mom gets chemotherapy every Wednesday and Saturday. Every week for the past two months."

Sara watched Laurie briefly, seeing the deep sadness in her eyes. "What kind of cancer?"

"Breast."

"I'm sorry," Sara said, and then didn't know quite what to say. After a moment she asked, "And does your dad have to work?"

"They're divorced. He lives in Chicago. Since she's been sick, he hasn't even called once."

"I—that's too bad," was all Sara could think to say, her pity for this poor girl growing by the minute. "But, hopefully, your mom is getting better?"

"After the operation on her breast, they found more in her limp system, but the treatments are making it better. She's sick a lot, especially after the treatments, and her hair all fell out. But her wig covers that. She gets tired and sleeps a lot at home, you know? But the doctor said the cancer is going away."

"Well, that's good."

"We used to do a lot together. Play cards, play games, even shoot baskets in the driveway. But now all she can do is sleep. I usually have to make my own food."

"Well, do you want to play a game with me? I love games. What do you like to play most?"

"My favorite is hearts. But I was hoping my friend Tommy could play with me. He knows I'm going to be here today, and this might be my last day for a while. Maybe he just didn't feel strong enough today. He's pretty late."

"Strong enough? Is he sick?"

There was a rattling sound coming from the doorway, metal clinking against metal, and Laurie quickly looked that way. Her expression instantly lifted with expectation when a boy entered the room, maneuvering an IV stand on wheels through the door. Laurie jumped to her feet and ran to him. He was about her age, dressed in a hospital-issued, blue and white checkered bathrobe. Thin and pale and limping slightly, his head was completely devoid of hair. Dark blue veins were plainly visible under his skin, even from where Sara sat. In spite of all this, his face broke into a beaming smile when he saw Laurie running to him. They hugged warmly, their faces glowing, and they began talking incessantly. Sara watched the two of them for several seconds. It was all she could do to keep from crying.

After a minute or so she walked over and stood near them until Laurie noticed her. "Tommy, this is Sara, my new friend who works here."

"Hi, Sara," Tommy exclaimed, and he reached for and shook her hand.

To Sara, his grip was light and cool to the touch, but his smile was so bright it appeared as if his teeth had back lighting. "Nice to meet you, Tommy."

"He has to stay here for a long time while he gets his treatments," said

Laurie. "I met him my first week visiting, and we've played hearts every Wednesday and Saturday at nine-thirty ever since."

"Sorry I was late," said Tommy, "the nurse was having trouble getting the right flow in my tube."

"You ready?" Laurie asked him, pulling a pack of cards out of her pants pocket.

"Let's play!" he exclaimed. Then he turned to Sara. "Want to play?"

"I'd love to. I'm not very good, so go easy on me."

They both laughed, and Laurie led the way to an empty table along the near wall.

"You know," said Sara to Tommy as they sat down, "If Laurie can't come, and you still want to play sometimes, I'll be here every weekday from nine until one. If I'm not too busy, I'd love to play with you."

"Okay!" he gleefully blurted out.

Laurie shuffled and dealt, and they began playing.

All the while, Sara watched their faces as they absolutely reveled in each other's company, constantly talking, smiling, laughing. With all they have going wrong in their lives, they still can be so alive and happy, she thought. She had never enjoyed playing a game as much as she did that game of hearts with Laurie and Tommy.

And what she realized most of all was how good her own life was, ever thankful that her children were healthy and bright and that her family really didn't have any serious problems.

■　■　■

Chris hung up the phone and sat back down at the dinner table.

"What the heck was that all about?" asked Sara.

Chris explained his phone conversation with Melinda Hanley, the organizer of LACTELL, the Littleboro Action Committee To End Land Loss. She had described the demonstrations and had asked him to come speak, if he would, since he was so vocal against annexation at the town meeting.

"Oh, yeah," said Sara. "I got a call from them a couple days ago. I just said we weren't interested."

"I told her I'll go and check it out. Maybe say a few words."

Sara's eyes narrowed. "That's what you said about the town meeting. And look what happened when you just went to 'check it out.'"

"What can I say. I can't keep my big mouth shut." He smiled at Mary and then John and then asked, "So, where were we?"

Mary said with excitement, "I heard that hurricane is really strong now!"

"Oh, yeah. Jeremy," said Sara. "It's got winds sustained at 160 miles per hour, and gusts over 180."

"180?" asked Chris. "I don't think I've ever heard of one that strong, at least not in the Atlantic."

"The strongest one since Mitch in '98," said Sara. "It could have the fastest winds in an Atlantic storm since they've been naming storms, if it keeps strengthening."

John said seriously, "Of course they have fast winds, that's why they're called hurry canes."

Chris smiled. "Oh. I didn't know that." Then he asked Sara, "Where is it? Which way is it going?"

"It's something like 400 miles southwest of Bermuda, heading northwest."

"Isn't that kind of right for us?" asked Chris.

"It is, but it's predicted to turn north, and then northeast, and then out to sea."

Mary looked concerned. "You mean it might come here?"

"Oh, don't worry, sweetheart," said Sara. "Even if it comes anywhere near us, it has to go over land, and that would make it weaker by the time it got here."

Mary didn't look particularly convinced.

Chris finished chewing and then said, "Even hundred mile an hour winds will knock over trees and knock out power for a while. Maybe I should stockpile some wood, so we'll have something to cook with."

"Whatever. I guess it wouldn't hurt," said Sara. She then changed the subject. "So, Mary, anything exciting happen in school today?"

"No," she said, looking down at her plate, "it was boring. It was good seeing my friends and teachers. But nothing exciting ever happens at that dumb, old school."

Chapter Thirteen

"Those who hear and understand the words I speak, and follow in the example by which I lead," said Jesus loudly, "would build the foundation of a world that shall be as a paradise. Beware of false prophets who would preach of their own goodness for the sake of their own reward.

"I am not here to contradict the laws that are written, but to uphold them. All should understand the laws, question their intention, yet obey them. Change of unjust laws should begin from within the spirit of the good, through peaceful, merciful means."

The crowd continued to grow in size, now numbering close to two hundred, as people traveling to the village walked over from the road to see why so many were gathered. They were of all ages and occupations. Fishermen and shepherds sat next to each other on rocks above the shore of the sea. Weavers and carpenters, farmers and merchants stood intermingled on and around the larger stones. Some of the children had climbed a few of the trees that grew from the exposed soil. None who listened had heard such a voice, powerful yet soothing. Many had stayed and listened, even those who initially were disappointed that it was only a man speaking. They became interested by his tone, by his words, by the very presence he projected.

Seeing the thickening mass of people straining to hear and see him, Jesus paused and walked further up the hill. The largest rock was flat and protruded from the hillside, being the size of one of the carts that had pulled off along the road. Jesus nimbly climbed upon it, stood tall, and, once again, addressed the crowd. The thickening gray clouds formed an ominous backdrop as he spread his arms wide, gesturing often to emphasize his words.

"We have received the greatest gift of any living thing. It is the gift of choice, to behave as we choose, not as the Lord instructs every other living thing. It is because of the love of God that we have this ability. By giving us this choice, this timeless gift of love, God has faith in us as His children, made in His very image, to make Earth as a paradise. Hear me, now, when I tell you that to return this original gift of love is how we all must lead our lives."

Even now, after speaking of these things for years, an edge of frustration haunted his mind. Though he knew the words he spoke were inadequate to describe the concepts, he had no choice but to use words the people could understand. Other words simply did not exist to explain the thoughts in his mind.

"Let the love of your spirit, the good qualities that are in each of you, shine out like the stars in the sky. Would you light a lamp and then place it under a bowl where its light can shine upon no thing? No. As you would place a lamp in the open for the most to see, so let the love that God has given you shine out to do the most good. Do these good things so not to boast of them, but as you would have the goodness returned to you by your neighbors. In whatever way you may make the life of a friend or neighbor better, so shall you make the life of an enemy better. All would help a friend, but only when an enemy, or a stranger, is shown such goodness has the love of God been returned."

The crowd continued to thicken. Mary of Magdala had arrived and sat most of the afternoon just below where he stood. Whenever they made eye contact, Jesus would pause in his speaking and smile down to her. She would return the favor. Though they had not been together since their time on the hill above the sea, other than to talk or for her to listen, as now, her love of him had continued to strengthen. She remained true to her vow to be with no other man and to follow him as he traveled and taught the people that lived in and around Nazareth. Today she listened for as long as possible but had to return to her home in order to tend her garden.

"Should someone strike you across the face," Jesus continued, "it is better to turn away and try to understand why they have struck you, and not to simply strike back. The old law speaks of 'an eye for an eye, a tooth for a tooth.' Yet this will leave a world of people who cannot see and cannot speak or eat. If you do not strike the first blow, then none shall be struck.

"Worry not about what you wear, or of the size of your house, or whether you have five loaves in your cabinet and not ten, or how much wine you may have to share among friends. If all share of this love of which I speak, if all share of what they have, so shall all be provided for. This is as the man who must choose to build his house on rock or on sand. Though the sand may be easier to dig in, and softer to walk upon, so shall it shift when the waters rise or the winds blow. And how strong is such a house, then? Let us build our home, this Earth, upon a solid foundation of the love of God, just as a man would build a house upon rock. Though it may require more work, more effort in the building, it will be a home that will stand strong against any storm, any flood."

Jesus spoke for several hours. People came and went, some listened all afternoon, some listened for a few minutes. When his throat grew sore and his voice would not carry, he walked down from the stone and talked quietly among the people who remained.

Having finished a morning fishing sail, Simon Peter and his brother Andrew had arrived earlier. Now, they worked their way through the people and stood close to Jesus. When he had a chance to speak, Simon Peter said, "Master, would you not like to sail with us this evening, upon the sea?"

Jesus frowned. "As I have told you before, my friend, I am the *master* of no man. Only a teacher chosen to speak of the bidding of our lord."

"You are much more, Jesus," said Andrew, bowing his head. "We would be honored by your presence upon our vessel."

In a raspy voice, Jesus said, "I have been speaking for a long while and am quite tired. I am afraid I would be of no use hauling in nets."

"We would hear of no such thing!" exclaimed Simon Peter. "The Son of God hauling fish from the sea! We would only like to be in your company for this evening, since we have not been able to be with you this spring when the fish harvest has been high."

"As I have said, all people are children of God, not only myself. Of what I teach explains this. One difference between others and myself is that I have been blessed with the knowledge of why, without having been taught. Others may know as I do by listening to me."

Simon Peter and Andrew waited for a few seconds, but Jesus did not give an answer about the boat. Finally Andrew asked again, "Then you will come with us, Master?"

Jesus sighed to himself but said, "Yes, I would enjoy that. If you would be so kind as to let me sit in the stern and rest, I would find the motion of the water soothing to my legs and back."

"As you wish," Simon Peter said, then motioned with his arm. "Here, come with us. Our boat is lashed to the dock below."

After making a few parting comments to people who had come close to talk with him, Jesus followed the two brothers through the thinning crowd. James and John, friends of Simon Peter and Andrew, joined them. They all walked across the road, along the shore a short distance, to the dock where their fishing vessel rocked gently in the small waves, the thumping of the wood of the boat against the wood of the dock resonating a hollow sound. As Andrew leaned over and held the boat securely, the others climbed in. Jesus stepped to the rear and sat quietly, looking out across the water, as the four others picked up oars and slowly rowed away from the dock. Further out, the sail was hoisted and secured, and the small vessel headed toward the middle of the Sea of Galilee.

Deep in thought, Jesus relaxed and sat back on worn pillows piled in the stern. He watched the canvas sail hang loose and then fill in rhythm as gentle gusts of wind moved them quietly over the water. Though he often had trouble sleeping at night because of the thoughts that occupied his mind, now his eyelids grew heavy. Comfortable, knowing his friends were experienced sailors, he allowed himself to drift off to sleep.

Jesus was wrenched from sleep as thunder crashed overhead. The sound rumbled low and rolled across the water, echoing from the hills along the near shore. As he lifted his head over the side of the boat, he saw a crooked streak of lightning stab the highest hill, followed an instant later by another deafening roar of thunder. A wave poured over the stern, drenching him in warm water. Wind tore at the top corner of the sail, ripping it free from its lashings, and the canvas flapped loudly. The next sounds Jesus heard were the shouts of Simon Peter to the others.

"Secure the riggings on the port side! Secure the oars! James! Andrew! Fasten the nets! Then bail! Bail!"

The small vessel rocked wildly as white-capped waves rose and fell all around them, flooding over the sides and quickly filling the bottom with water.

"Master!" called Simon Peter, "Master! Our boat is close to capsizing! We fear we may have led you into danger!"

"Andrew!" yelled James, "lash the last corner of the net, there at your feet! I will begin bailing with this pot!"

Lightning flashed again, striking somewhere behind the hill on the far shore. The crack of thunder took several seconds to reach them.

"Help us, Master!" called Andrew. "Can you not lead us out of this storm?"

Slowly, Jesus stood. He maintained his balance, keeping his legs and arms spread apart as the boat rocked from side to side. As he scanned the clouds with his head lifted skyward, wind blew his long, wet hair wildly about his face. Lightning flashed again, still further away than before.

Jesus sensed something about the wind, the color of the clouds beyond the near shore. The wind changed direction suddenly, coming from straight above them. With his arms still spread, Jesus called out, "Fear not, my friends! The storm will end now! Prepare to lower your nets once again!"

An instant later, the wind abruptly fell away to nothing more than a slight breeze. Rain now fell gently, and waves on the sea, though still occasionally capped with white, lessened significantly.

Simon Peter stood near the rudder to the left of Jesus, staring at him wide-eyed, his mouth hanging open. "Truly you are all-powerful, Master!" he said, his voice trembling. "Even the wind and rain obey your command!"

"My friends," Jesus said, sitting again on the pillows in the stern, "the wind and rain are as they are. No man or thing commands them. But, as I have said, to know of the nature of these things is the closest we may come to commanding them. This allows us to use them to do the most good, and the least harm."

But Simon Peter had turned to the others and was saying, "Did you see? Bare witness that Jesus, the Son of God, has the power to command the lightning, the wind! Surely there is no man greater!" He fell to his knees trembling, overcome with emotion.

"I have the knowledge to have known when the storm would end. I did not command it to end," said Jesus quietly.

"We are blessed to know him, to be called his friends!" James was saying, bailing slowly with the clay pot, his eyes never wavering from Jesus.

In the distance, a rumble of thunder could be heard. The setting sun split the fragmenting clouds and sent rays of light fanning earthward in all directions.

As the others spoke excitedly to each other, seeming to have forgotten that Jesus was still in the boat, he sat quietly for a while, noticing how beautiful the sky had become. The beams of light widened through the clouds, reaching the surface of the sea, causing a million dancing sparkles on the water. Jesus sighed at the breathtaking sight, pulling his wet hair back from his face.

After a while he said, "You would best be served by casting your nets upon the waters now. The fish will be active and feeding after such a storm."

CHAPTER FOURTEEN

"**W**hat do you mean I can't play?" protested Mary, incredulous. "I'll tell Mrs. Linder you're not letting everyone play!"

"Girls suck at kickball," said Brendan Scott, a fifth grader.

"I don't suck," said Mary, "I play soccer. My father is the coach. I'm one of the best players on my team, girls or boys."

"Aaaa, go jump rope with the other second graders," said Brendan, punting the ball to one of his friends near home plate.

"Just pitch me one ball, let me kick it, and I'll show you," said Mary. "If I don't kick it good, I'll go jump rope."

Brendan considered this. "Okay, sure. Go ahead and get up."

Mary trotted to home plate. While grinning at her, the other boy bounced the ball back to Brendan. He corralled it, wedged it in his right wrist, and cocked it back, ready to let it roll. Mary took her place, pulled up her jeans slightly, and shook the stray hairs off her face. With her right leg slightly behind and her left knee bent, her body was poised and ready. "Okay. Pitch."

Brendan stepped forward and purposely tossed the ball hard, bouncing it towards Mary on three big hops, crossing home plate two feet off the ground. She caught the ball and threw it back to Brendan, yelling, "Come on! Pitch a good one, a real pitch!"

Brendan smiled and got ready to pitch again. This time he rolled it low, along the ground, flecks of dead, yellow grass kicking up in its wake. Mary took three steps, planted her left foot and kicked. With a loud thud, the ball lifted in a rising linedrive and sailed straight out over Brendan's head, over second base. It landed in center field, rolling several yards farther. Another boy retrieved it and threw it back into the infield.

"See! I can kick far! Now let me play!" she yelled.

"That would have been an easy out. The center fielder would have caught it," said Brendan.

"Would not! It was a liner. No one would have caught it."

"Okay. Whatever. You have to be able to catch in the field, too. Go out in center field and I'll throw you one."

"Fine." Mary confidently trotted out to center field and turned to face the infield. A few other boys standing in the outfield eyed her with amusement.

"Mary! Hi!" a man called from the other side of the fence behind her.

She turned to see a black, pickup truck parked there, an arm out the driver's side window waving at her. Looking confused and squinting in the sun for a minute, she wondered if she was supposed to recognize the truck. She didn't and turned back toward the field.

"Mary! I need to tell you something important!" Hector called. "Your mother told me to come get you!"

She turned around again. "You know my mom?" she called back.

"Sure! We've been friends for a long time! She told me to come get you!"

Mary walked within a few yards of the fence. Some of the other boys eyed Hector suspiciously. "What did she say?" asked Mary. She was now able to see that the man sitting in the truck had curly, black hair, a mustache, and a blue shirt.

"She said she got in a car crash and needs me to take you to see her in the hospital."

"What! My mom is in the hospital?" she said, alarmed, her voice high-pitched. She ran to the fence and clutched the metal links.

"She's not hurt too bad," said Hector quickly. "She just wanted me to come get you so you can visit her."

Mary unconsciously sensed a change in the tone of his voice, and that something wasn't right. She released her grip on the fence and slowly took a step back. "Do you work with her?" she asked.

"Near her, but not with her. She called me from the hospital."

"Wait a minute. She works at the hospital." Looking at her little pink and white watch, she said, "it's only twelve-thirty. My mom doesn't get off work until one."

Hector looked away, thinking as quickly as possible. "She had to leave early and go to the store. A car couldn't stop and hit the side of her car."

Mary looked at him suspiciously. "What's my mom's name?"

Hector suddenly got angry. "Hurry up! Come on! She needs you to come right now! There's a hole in the fence by that tree over there. Let's go!"

Mary took two steps backward. "No. I don't believe you."

"Come on, you little brat! I'm doing your mother a favor, and you won't even come. She's going to be mad at you."

"My mom doesn't get mad at me." She stepped back farther.

Brendan called from the infield, "You going to play or not, kid?"

Mary turned to look at Brendan. "Yeah, I'm going to play. In a minute."

"Who is that guy? Is that your father?" asked one of the other boys.

"Hurry, Mary! Your mother's waiting!" Hector called angrily.

Mary came to a realization. She looked at Hector, to Brendan, to some of the other boys, then back to Brendan. "Hurry! Tell Mrs. Linder there's a stranger here. A stranger!"

"A stranger?" one of the other boys exclaimed.

"Stranger!" someone else yelled.

"Quick," said Mary, "get Mrs. Linder. Stranger!"

Hector saw a couple of the children running away from the field and Mary trotting further from him, towards home plate. "Mary! Get over here!" he tried again. But she was too far away to hear him. Then he saw some of the children running up to two women standing closer to the school building. They had been talking with each other and not paying attention to what had been happening. When Hector saw the children pointing towards him and the women turn and look, he swore to himself. Putting the truck in gear, he accelerated rapidly, the tires spinning on dirt lining the road as the truck pulled away.

"Who was that?" Mrs. Linder asked Mary with concern in her voice as she watched the truck vanish around the corner.

"I don't know, he was a stranger."

"What? What did he say to you?"

Mary recounted what had happened, and finished with, "And he wanted me to get in his car with him. But I figured out that he was probably lying."

Mrs. Linder's jaw had dropped, and her eyes flew open wide. "Kids!" she called to all the children within earshot. "Everyone come over here quickly! Hurry now!" Some of the children looked up, some ran toward her, most slowly began moving in her direction. "Hurry! Everyone!" A few more moved faster. "That's it! Now, line up by class, in your assigned spots. Quickly!" She turned to one of the children. "Rebecca, would you run into Mr. McCullough's office and tell him to come out here as quick as possible. Mary, if you could go with her, and tell him what happened. He might want to call your parents, or the police."

"Okay," said Mary. "Let's go, Becca." They ran through the double doors.

"Everyone stay in line, in your positions, while Mrs. Casey and I make sure you're all here. That's good, right. Quickly now. All right, now start reciting your names. Let me know if anyone is missing." Each line of children began saying their names in alphabetical order.

When they had finished, everyone was present or accounted for.

■　■　■

124

"Of course I want to tell the police!" cried Sara, pacing back and forth in the living room. Chris sat on the edge of the sofa. "Oh, my God! My God! I can't believe someone tried to kidnap Mary! Why would someone do that? Who is this guy?"

"I—don't—know," said Chris, accenting each word. "I saw the truck following the school bus yesterday, and I saw the guy's face. I don't know who he is. I've never seen him before."

"You said he pulled out of a driveway right down the street. Right?"

"I saw him pull out from somewhere, but I wasn't paying that close attention. It could have been the woods between Reid's and Sullivan's or either one of their driveways. I really didn't think much about it." Chris' right hand was clenched into a fist, and he was rubbing it absent-mindedly with his left. "Why?" he asked himself. "Just some random guy, for kiddie porn, to get something we have, what?"

"Kiddie p—!" Sara gasped, covering her mouth with her hands. "No! Oh my fucking God!"

Chris realized he had been thinking out loud. "Oh. I'm so sorry. I shouldn't have—Damn it. I don't think that's it. I was just running possibilities through my mind."

She pulled her hands from her face and looked at Chris angrily. "Call the police. Now," she hissed.

"Mary is in the other room, getting totally weirded out. We need to talk to her first."

"I'll talk to her. You call the police. Now." She walked down the stairs into the family room in the basement.

Chris watched her go. He went to the phone and dialed the non-emergency number on the orange sticker on the receiver. It rang once.

"Dispatch," a woman's voice answered.

"Hi. Chris Magnuson calling, Mourning Dove Lane."

"Yes, sir. What can I do for you this afternoon?"

"I, uh," he stammered, not sure what to say. "A stranger, someone we don't know, tried to kidnap our daughter today. At least tried to get her into his car. I'd like to talk to someone about that."

"Hold on. Officer Crooks is on call. She's right here in the office." The phone went silent for a second.

"Liz Crooks."

"Hi, Liz. Chris Magnuson here. Mary's dad."

There was a pause, and then she said, "Oh, hi! Sure. Mary. She was in D.A.R.E. last spring. Right?"

"Yeah, that's right."

"Precocious, confident little girl. I loved having her." She paused. "She hasn't started taking drugs, after all the things I taught her in class, has she?" she chuckled.

Chris could not even bring himself to smile. "No. I'm, uh, I'm sorry, but I think we may have a problem."

"What's wrong?"

"Well, it looks like someone, someone we don't know, tried to talk Mary into getting into his car today. But thanks to your 'stranger' training she had in first grade, she knew enough not to get in."

"Oh, thank God," she said. "Tell me more. Hold on, let me get my notebook. Okay, so you're sure you don't know him?"

"Pretty sure. I got a quick look at his face."

"So this happened in front of your house?"

"No, actually at school. I saw him yesterday, following her school bus. Of course, I didn't think anything about it at the time."

There was a pause as Liz wrote. "What kind of car?"

"A black, pickup truck. A Dodge, I think, and kind of old. Maybe eight or ten years old, from the late '90s."

"License plate?"

"I don't know. Like I said, I really didn't think about it. No one at school got a good enough look. I do remember a few things, though. It had two yellow, fog lights on the roof of the cab, and it had back fenders that stick out just a little beyond the width of the bed."

"Mm—hmm. What did he look like? You said you got a quick look at him."

Chris described what he had seen, and then said, "And Mary said about the same thing. She noticed he was wearing a blue shirt and thought she saw an oval patch above the left breast pocket, like it would have a name on it or something."

"Right, right. Maybe a uniform. Okay. Anything else?"

Chris thought a second. "Not that I can—Well, one of the teachers said there was several cigarette butts on the ground next to the school yard where he had been parked, like he had been parked there for a while."

"Why her? Do you think he randomly picked her, maybe just because she's a pretty, little blonde girl?"

Chris said evenly, coldly, "He called her by name."

"Oh. I see."

"What should we do?" he asked. "What can you do?"

"I'll run the truck information through the computer and see what falls out. Even if there's something clear, we just can't run over and grab him, even if he lives around here. We can put out an APB, so, at least, our officers are aware."

"What about us, our house, the school?" Chris asked. "Can you have a car stay at the school, or cruise our neighborhood?"

Crooks laughed. "I wish we could, believe me. But you may have heard we're extremely understaffed. We can barely handle Gold traffic and the increase in crime in the last few years as it is."

"Damn it," Chris said softly. "Well, what should we do?"

"Keep a close eye on her. You have another kid, right?"

"Yeah. John, a son who's four."

"Right, right. Don't let them out of your sight. Don't let Mary ride the bus. Take her to school. If John goes to kindergarten, or nursery school—"

"Uh huh."

"Take him there yourself. I guess the teachers at Mary's school already know, but tell your son's school as well. Don't let them play in the yard alone. You know, common sense things like that. Lock doors and windows—"

After Chris had hung up with her, he walked down to the family room. John was playing with plastic blocks on the floor, Mary was curled up in Sara's lap on one of the old, brown recliners.

"Hey! I just talked to Officer Liz," said Chris. "From D.A.R.E. Remember?"

Mary nodded silently.

"She's so upset," said Sara. "I'm trying to make her feel better, but she keeps thinking she's done something wrong."

"Wrong?" said Chris. "Oh, sweetheart. You did exactly the right things. You were so smart not to go with this creep. Why do you think you did anything wrong?"

She shrugged and snuggled her face deeper into Sara's blouse. "I'm afraid," she said meekly.

"It's okay to be afraid," said Chris. "You can be afraid, but Mom and me are not going to let anything happen to you. And Liz is telling the other police to watch out for this guy."

"What if he comes into our house in the dark? And tries to get me?"

"Ohhhh," Sara groaned. Chris noticed tears forming in the corners of her eyes, and she clutched Mary tighter, softly stroking her hair.

"Officer Liz has a gun," piped in John. "I saw it at your D.A.R.E. graduation. She can shoot the bad guy."

127

"Right, John," said Chris, "all the police have guns."

"We should get a gun," said John.

"No, I don't think we need to do that," said Chris, "but we can lock all the doors and windows in your rooms while you're asleep."

"It'll be so hot," said Mary.

"You can have our fan," said Sara.

"And you know what else?" smiled Chris. "We have something better than a gun, because he'll let us know if anyone ever comes into our house. Right, Dudley?" Lying on the floor nearby, at the sound of his name, Dudley lifted his head and tilted it slightly, his ears cocked. His tail began wagging slightly. "That's right. You're such a good boy." His tail wagged faster, and he stood and walked to Chris, who scratched behind his ears. "He's got real good hearing. He'll bark if there's anyone around," Chris said to Mary. "Remember how he helped fight that other dog to keep it away from John?"

Mary smiled slightly, looking from Dudley back to Chris.

"Hey, why don't we order pizza for dinner," said Chris. "I turned in my grades today, so we should have a little fun. Okay?"

"Can I get a mushroom with extra cheese?" asked Mary.

"Anything you want," said Chris, winking at Sara. "I'll go call right now."

As he walked up the stairs, the anger he had been hiding behind his facade of calmness and comfort, for the sake of his family, was churning to the surface. Lines on his forehead deepened. His knuckles were white on the handrail, his brow wedged low into an angry V.

Damn it, he thought. Who is this guy? Why would he do this? I can't stand it when a huge problem is created that is totally avoidable. Everyone is upset. Mary is scared to death. So is Sara. So am I. Damn it.

God damn it.

Chapter Fifteen

"This young donkey has never been ridden," said James, tugging forcefully on the rope around its neck, desperately trying to coax it forward. Jesus stood calmly waiting as the animal bucked and fought. "Your friends immediately agreed to let you use him, as you suggested they would, but he is a colt and is not trained in the ways of riding."

"Thank you, James," said Jesus quietly, taking a step forward. "You have done exactly as I have asked. Do not worry about the age of this animal. He will suit me well."

Hooves pounded the ground, sending gravel and dust flying in all directions. Foaming saliva had collected in the corners of the donkey's mouth, and its eyes darted about in fear, wildly scanning the gathering crowd. "But I am concerned for your safety, Master," said James, between grunts. "If you try to mount him, surely you will be kicked or thrown."

Calmly, Jesus moved forward several steps as he spoke softly. "I will be able to ride this donkey if he understands I mean him no harm." Then he said directly to the donkey in a soothing tone, "Is this not so, my friend?" He stepped alongside and reached out his hand, but the donkey flinched and snorted, backing away a step. Jesus continued to speak. "There is no need to fear. I only have wish of your service for but a day to travel to Jerusalem." Within a few moments, the donkey stopped fighting against the tension on the rope and stood still. It soon allowed Jesus to move around to its front. As James passed the rope to him, Jesus reached out and gently stroked the fur on its neck, continuing to speak quietly. "You see, there is no need for such anger, such fear. I would be grateful if you would do me this one service." Knowing the words he spoke were not understood, but that it was the tone that was important, Jesus continued to soothe the animal by speaking to it.

To the astonishment of all, Jesus easily laid a blanket across the donkey's back. He then swung his left leg over and mounted, all the while continuing to speak. Loosely holding the rope in his right hand and stroking the donkey's neck with his left, he turned the animal around.

"You see, my friends," Jesus said to the people standing about, including James, "with gentleness and kind persuasion, instead of force and fear, tasks may be achieved. If your motives are sincere, and the best for all is truly desired, all others will know this and follow."

There was murmuring among the crowd.

Jesus gave the donkey a gentle nudge forward, and it began walking toward Jerusalem.

The friends and followers of Jesus who had accompanied him into Jerusalem had gone off to purchase goods in the market area, or visit friends and relatives. Others had gone to the temple to worship.

It had been years since Jesus had gone into a temple. Though he spoke constantly of God, he maintained his ideals that God should be loved and not worshipped, and spoke of this as the way each person should live their lives. He had never condemned those who worshipped, but he felt a quiet sympathy for those who sought solace and comfort in a God they did not comprehend. And, yet, he knew the answer was as simple as: each person is the expression of the essence of God, and everything they need, spiritually, can be obtained from within themselves.

On this day, he walked alone to the temple in Jerusalem, unrecognized by the people there. He was surprised to find that the center courtyard of the temple was a mass of swarming people, loud voices filling the air. Carts and tables were lined in rows from front to back, ten across. Fish, grain, and fruits were being bought and sold. Men and women haggled over the price of cattle, sheep, and donkeys. Though he didn't think temples were important in the expression of the love of God, he was alarmed to find this huge display of commerce in a house of worship.

To his immediate right were several tables where people were obtaining shekels in exchange for currency of other countries, allowing travelers to make purchases from the vendors in the courtyard. Two men standing behind the closest table were talking to a young man about the rate of exchange on this day. The latter carried a small satchel around his waist. His beard and hair were well groomed, and his toga was lined with silk on the neckline and cuffs. Jesus listened to their discussion with interest.

"Two thousand shekels for one silver talent is the rate today," said the elder man behind the table, folding his arms across his chest.

The young man laughed. "I was here but a few days ago and the rate was 3,500 to one. Do not waste my time with your insults. If you will not give me 3,500 for one, I will go to the next table." And he started to walk away.

"Wait, my wise friend!" the moneychanger called quickly. "All tables will tell you the same today. The rate is actually three thousand to one."

The young man turned and came back. "Then why did you offer me two thousand to start?" he asked, only mild annoyance edging his voice. Now he stood against the table, leaning forward.

"Good sir," the moneychanger grinned nervously, "I need to feed my family as much as the next man." He waved a hand at the young man next to him, apparently his son. "Would you not forgive me for trying to earn a living, just as you clearly have done?"

"It is being aware of men such as you that has allowed me to make a living, selling my wares, but always for a fair price." The man reached into his satchel and pulled out a small sack of silver coins. He laid it on the table. "Here are ten talents worth of silver. That is thirty thousand shekels. At least, today it is, I believe."

"Very good, Sir," the elder man said. He opened the sack, spread the coins on the table, and began counting.

Jesus felt a sadness grow within him as he watched the exchange. Though he realized the necessity of the system, given the different currencies in the region, the basic premise of exchanging money for money gave him an empty, cold feeling. He did not know why, exactly. Perhaps a vague memory, again. Perhaps, to him, the cold exchange of coin for coin seemed so lifeless, so inhuman. The fact that the moneychanger had tried to get more than the true exchange rate clearly added to his sadness.

The young man counted the shekels he received, placed them in his satchel, and walked off into the crowd. As Jesus watched, a young woman, no more than twenty-five years old, walked in through the courtyard entrance and made her way through the crowd. Clinging tightly to her tattered wrap were two very young children, a boy and girl, perhaps four and two years old. All their clothes were stained and worn. The bare feet and faces of the children were coated with dust, and their hair was tangled in knots.

The woman spotted the same money exchange table, now empty of other customers, and quickly made her way to it. She meekly looked around, then at the elderly man. She pulled out a worn piece of cloth and unfolded it on the table to show it contained several coins.

"I have one talent of silver I need to exchange for shekels. How many?"

The elderly man scanned her up and down with contempt, eyeing the children briefly. "The rate today is five hundred to one. I will give you five hundred shekels."

The woman's expression sank. "Five hundred? Oh no. I need to buy my children food for many days of travel, and new sandals to walk a great distance. Five hundred will barely feed us for a few days, even if I buy only bread."

"This is no concern of mine, and there is nothing I can do," said the moneychanger. "I do not set the rate, I only use it in my exchanges. Five hundred to one."

As he watched, Jesus felt his sadness boil to anger. He stepped closer, watching the face of the elderly man, hoping to make eye contact and cause him to feel remorse and, perhaps, give her the correct rate. But the man glared at the woman as she looked around nervously.

"I do not have all day!" the man said after a few seconds. "Either make the exchange, or be off with you!"

As the woman slid her silver forward, agreeing to make the exchange, and the moneychanger started to count, Jesus was consumed by anger. Rushing forward, he yelled to the woman and children, "Stand back! Away from these thieves!" Seeing the anger on his face as he ran at the table, the woman grabbed the two children and leapt to the side. Leaning across the table, inches from their faces, Jesus said to the men, "You lowest of the low forms of life! Is it not bad enough that you conduct business in a temple erected for the glory of God?! But you must rob the meek and helpless as well?!"

"Away with you!" the elder man yelled back, though fearful, taking two steps back. "How we conduct our business is no concern of yours!"

"It is my concern! I have made it so! And so has God!" With that he reached his hands under the table and violently lifted and threw it up and over. Coins scattered in a shower in all directions, bouncing off the moneychangers and upon the ground with a loud burst of tinkling. Most coins rolled away many feet as the table landed on its side at the feet of the two men. They leapt back just in time to avoid having it land on them.

The younger of the moneychangers spoke for the first time, threatening and stepping forward, "How dare you—"

But Jesus cut him off. "Out! Get out of this sacred building! How dare you question what I do!" The crowd near them had fallen silent and turned to watch. Jesus addressed them all, yelling at the threshold of his voice. "You have turned this house, built to glorify God's love, into a nest of thieves!

Have you no respect for yourselves, or other men? Or for God, who has given you all you have, including life itself?" And he turned to leave, sickened and angered by what he saw before him.

But he caught sight of the young woman and her children, who now regarded him with terror. He paused for a moment, remembering her coins were on the table as well. Quickly, he stooped and scanned the coins on the ground around his feet. Finding a combination that added up to three thousand shekels, he stepped to her and held them out. When she backed away, he said quietly, "Do not fear me. I am Jesus. This is what your silver is worth today."

An expression of recognition flashed across her face as her eyes widened. "Jesus? The young prophet from Nazareth?" At this, a wave of murmuring flowed through the people in the courtyard.

"I am from Nazareth, yes. Here. Do not fear me." She held out her hand, slowly, and he gently placed the coins in her grasp. Smiling kindly, he said, "I am sorry I have frightened your children."

Turning, he walked slowly away and out of the courtyard, still alone.

On the small stone wall in front of the temple, Jesus sat thinking about what he had just witnessed in the courtyard, and how he had reacted to the moneychangers. A silent tear welled in his eye. *Even I am not above anger, perhaps even hatred,* he thought. *It is in every person.*

"Master!" called Philip. He and Bartholomew had just hurried through the arch that led from the courtyard. Spotting Jesus, they ran to him. "We heard the commotion," said Philip. "When we saw you in the middle of it, we feared someone was hurting you! Are you all right?" They stopped directly in front of where Jesus sat.

"Someone hurt me deeply. Though they did not touch me, they caused me great pain." Jesus looked away, watching people hurrying by on the street, unaware of him sitting quietly. He turned back to Philip and Bartholomew and recounted what he had seen at the table.

"This does not surprise me," said Philip. "The moneychangers in Jerusalem very frequently get as much as they can in their exchanges. It is so common, I do not believe people think much about it, or do anything to change it."

Jesus moved his eyes to look at him without turning his head. "This does not give me comfort. That is even worse." He paused, thinking for a moment. "And why do people allow this to happen?"

"Though the rates are set by the local governors," suggested Bartholomew, "there is no one to enforce that they are upheld. And even when moneychangers are accused of not offering the fair rate, if they give the guards a small part of what they have made, all is forgotten."

"My God," said Jesus, to himself, "maybe Your confidence in us is too great."

"What did you say, Master?" asked Philip.

At first Jesus shook his head and remained silent, then decided to explain what he was thinking. But a child's voice called from the street, interrupting him. "He is here, Mother!" yelled a girl of age five. "The rabbi from Nazareth!" She ran over and stood a few feet away, staring at him with wide eyes, smiling. Her long, brown hair was braided and hung down her back.

Jesus smiled back, warmed by the way she looked at him with admiration, the way one might admire a mountain towering over a plain, or an eagle soaring on the wind.

A woman walked over, carrying a baby. Two other young children followed close behind. The mother acknowledged Jesus meekly with a nod, then spoke to the first daughter. "You may ask him, Martha. Go ahead."

Martha continued to smile, but, now, she was flushed with shyness, her feet kicking in the dirt. Then suddenly she ran the last few feet between her and Jesus and put her arms on his knees, preparing to speak.

But Philip quickly stepped forward and took hold of her arm, pulling her away, saying, "Do not bother Jesus now, child. Many troubles weigh upon his mind."

Timidly, she looked up at Philip. Her bottom lip quivered, and she looked ready to cry.

"Philip!" scolded Jesus, "No! Do not push away an innocent child who seeks anything from me!" He looked back to Martha, smiling. "Come here, Martha, my dear. Ask your question."

She stepped back to him, forcing a smile. Confused by everything that had just happened, she hesitated.

Jesus gently reached for her, picking her up and setting her on his knee. He touched her hair, continuing to smile at her as she looked up at him, warmed and overcome by his genuine tenderness. Jesus looked up at Philip and Bartholomew, at Martha's mother, at other people who had gathered, and spoke. "Look at this child. Study her face, her eyes. She knows nothing of deceit, of treachery, of lies. The only way this will become part of her life is if she learns it from those around her. Until all people can look at the world through the eyes of a child, the eyes of children such as this, then will the Earth become a paradise. The world can be such a wondrous place. Only when people who, now, do not understand or accept the love that God has given them are willing to view the world for what it could be, by returning this love—only then will love be the power and source by which we lead our lives."

He paused a moment, still saddened that, over and over, he had to repeat these things to his friends, and to those who heard him speak. And he knew full well that he would have to say these things again. And again.

Through the archway leading to the courtyard, the sounds of coins rattling and voices yelling could clearly be heard. Jesus shuddered, then turned back to Martha. "Please, child, go ahead and ask your question. If I can answer it, I will be glad to do so."

Martha hesitated, still feeling overwhelmed to be sitting on the knee of Jesus of Nazareth. Then she looked up at him and quietly said, "I was going to ask you about love, my Lord, and how I can make it the biggest part of my life. But you have already answered that question for me. Thank you."

CHAPTER SIXTEEN

"I'm glad you're taking me to school, Daddy," said Mary, an edge of fear in her voice.

"Me too," said Chris, turning to her briefly as he pulled the Toyota onto Route 14.

"Don't you have to go to your college today?"

"I'm going in a little late. Classes are over, and the next ones don't start for more than a week. I'm just going to do a few things. When Mom is home tomorrow, I'll go in and do a little more."

"Do you like teaching college?" asked Mary seriously.

"Yep."

She waited for more, then asked, "Why?"

"I like having a positive influence, uh, what I mean is, I like making some people's lives a little better, by teaching them things. Even if it's just a little better."

"How do you do that by teaching college? Aren't the subjects in college way harder than regular school?"

Chris laughed. "Yeah, I guess they are. But sometimes I teach my students something they really use in their lives, or something they've never thought about before, maybe things that are really interesting, or ideas that I have that nobody else has thought of before."

Mary was silent for a few seconds, watching cars passing by in the other direction. Occasionally she turned and looked behind them, and strained to look over the dashboard to see what kind of cars were in front of them. "I want to be a teacher," she said.

"That sounds like a good idea," said Chris. "Hey, are you looking for the bad guy's car? Is that why you keep looking around?"

"Mmm—hmm," she acknowledged with embarrassment.

Chris felt a wave of anger rising in him, but refrained from letting her know. "Oh, Mary. I know it's hard, but try not to worry. I'm taking you to school so he won't follow us."

"What if he comes to school again?"

"The teachers already know to look out for him. And I'm going to talk to Mr. McCullough when we get there to make sure they're taking this seriously."

"What about John? What if the stranger tries to get him at his school?" asked Mary, extremely concerned.

"Mom's taking him. She's going to talk to John's teachers so they know what's going on, and to make sure they understand how serious it is."

Chris pulled the car into the school parking lot, just behind a town police cruiser near the front door. Mary noticed the police car and said, "Are the police here to watch the school?"

"I don't know. Let's go find out."

And as they walked from the car to the front door, unconsciously they both scanned the parking lot and the side streets that were visible from the front of the school, looking for a black, pickup truck. When they walked into the principal's office, they saw Officer Crooks standing at the counter, talking to Mr. McCullough and one of the secretaries.

Chris said, "Hey. Liz. Russ." He shook Crooks' hand, feeling her strong grip. She had short, straight black hair and an attractive, non-descript, slightly masculine face.

She said pleasantly, "Hi, Chris," and then knelt down, saying, "Hi, Mary. How are you?"

"All right. A little scared."

"I bet you are. But you did the right thing by telling the teachers there was a stranger there. I guess you were paying attention when I was talking to your class last year, weren't you?"

"Mmm—hmm," she nodded, and turned to bury her face against Chris' leg.

Chris was shaking hands with Russell McCullough, saying, "What a way to start a new school year."

Russ nodded in agreement. "Even when you think you've taken precautions, have aids on the playground—That's one of the main reasons we had that fence put up a few years ago. That, and to keep balls and kids out of the street."

"So, are you all set?" asked Chris. "I mean, have all the teachers and aids been told what's going on?"

"Not yet. I'll talk to each one as they come in."

Liz stood and said, "I can't stay here all day, but I'm going to talk to as many teachers as possible, at least in the morning. Then I'll be out on patrol."

"Can any other police drive by once in a while?" asked Chris.

Crooks shook her head. "Besides routine patrols in other parts of town, the other two units need to keep an eye on those demonstrations near the Gold."

"Oh, yeah," said Chris, remembering he was supposed to go speak some time. "I've heard about those. How are they going?"

137

"More people are coming every day. They're starting to affect traffic."

"You can't break them up? Make some of the people leave?"

"They're mostly on private property, in someone's yard just outside reservation land, just below the casino. There's not much we can do. Constitutional right for people to assemble, and all that."

"Right. Anyway," said Chris, "so no one can patrol the school area?"

Crooks said with a smile and a wink, "I'm patrolling today, until five. I may just happen to swing by once in a while."

Chris grinned with an understanding nod. "Thanks. Thanks a lot. Anything you can do. I think Mary will feel better, and so will Sara and me."

"We all will," said Russell. "Believe me, we'll all be on our guard today, probably to the point of distraction. Since this is the first confirmed incident like this we've had in years, I think all the teachers and students will be all too aware."

"I guess that's good, sort of," said Chris solemnly. "Okay then, I guess I'll head out." He knelt and gave Mary a big hug. "I'll pick you up at three. Okay?"

"Do you have to go?" she complained.

Crooks quickly spoke up. "Mary, I need you to do something with me. Will you help me with an important police investigation?"

She looked up, "What do I have to do?"

"Can you walk out to the school yard with me? I want you to show me and tell me everything that happened. Do you remember very much?"

Mary looked insulted. "I remember everything." She took Crooks' hand. "Come on. I'll show you," and led her away.

When Crooks turned to look back over her shoulder, Chris gave her a thankful wave and watched them leave. Kids are so sharp, he thought. That's one thing about being a parent I never expected. How smart and alert children are. I wonder why there are so many adults that constantly screw things up.

■　■　■

Chris was rounding a corner in the hallway of Lennon Hall, thinking about Mary and John, when he almost collided with a girl carrying an armful of books. He side-stepped her effectively, but she was startled sufficiently to drop the top three books from her stack. They crashed to the floor, falling open, bending the cover of the one that landed on the bottom. Chris stooped quickly to help her pick them up, and suddenly noticed who she was.

"Margaret! Hi! Uh, sorry. I guess I wasn't looking where I was going."

"Hi, Professor Magnuson," she blushed, stooping next to him. "It was my fault. I was hurrying back upstairs to the lab." She set the other two books down and picked up the bent one. "Damn. And it's a library book, ordered from out of town."

"That's too bad." Chris picked up the other two and was setting them on top of her stack on the floor when he noticed the title of the top book, *Florentine History*. He looked at the other title in his hand and was surprised to see, *Rare Writings and Paintings of Leonardo da Vinci*. Looking up at her, he tilted his head and raised his eyebrows inquisitively. "Unusual books for a physics student to be reading, don't you think?"

Margaret looked mortified. Fumbling for something to say, in defense she quickly blurted out, "I had to order these on loan from Harvard. They just came in today."

"Has your missing professor's obsession with Leonardo rubbed off on you?" Chris teased. But, then, he saw she was genuinely upset and looked to be on the verge of tears. "Oh, I'm sorry. I was just kidding. I don't think it's a big deal that this one got bent. Books get damaged—"

"It's not that," she said, then looked away.

"God, Margaret, what's wrong? Do you want to talk?"

"I don't know what to do. I don't know who I should talk to, if I should let anyone know." Tears welled in her eyes. She sniffled and pinched the bridge of her nose. "Shit."

"Come on. Let's go into my office. I was just going to reorganize some notes for next semester and make sure the new texts are at the bookstore. I've got some time." Chris stood, holding her five books. "Let's talk. Is it because Dr. Leonard is gone? Did you hear anything?"

She laughed slightly. "How ironic you should say that. Yeah, I guess you could say I've heard something."

Chris looked at her with confusion. "I don't get it."

"Of course not. I don't even know if I 'get it.'" She stood, looking at him, studying his face, gazing at length into his eyes.

He returned her look, but was confused. "What? Are you making another pass at me?"

She looked down. "I'm sorry. No." She looked back up at him. "Though that's not a bad idea."

Still not understanding what was happening, Chris said, "Uh, does that have anything to do with why you're crying? Because I said 'no thanks?'"

"No, not at all. I was just deciding."

"Oh. Well, whatever it is you were deciding, did you reach a decision?"

"Yeah. Let's go to your office and talk."

In his small, cluttered office down the hallway, Chris put her books on his desk and pulled a chair around to face his. "Have a seat."

"Thanks," she said as she sat. She pulled a tissue from a box on the back corner of his desk and blew her nose loudly, giving a finishing wipe and tossing the tissue into the basket behind her.

There was an awkward silence until Chris said, "I guess I'll let you start, since I don't know what to ask."

"I'm just trying to decide what's the best way to tell you. I haven't talked about this with anyone, so I don't really know what to say."

"Take your time. I can't promise you any answers, but I'll listen." Chris smiled compassionately.

Feeling a little better, she said, "Thanks," and took a deep breath. "Dr. Leonard is not really missing. I know what happened to him."

Chris hesitated. "What. Did he die?"

"Probably not. All evidence suggests otherwise," Margaret said, completely serious.

"Uh—"

"I know, I know. I'm being vague. It's just hard for me to say."

"Like I said, take your time. I'm here to help."

"Dr. Leonard got a grant four years ago to work on designing some new physics equipment. He's been working on it since then, and made good progress. I started working with him two years ago under the condition that I keep everything confidential."

"No papers, no talks? Don't grants require publication to get renewal? What kind of equipment?"

"One of the reasons Dr. Leonard stayed here was to be able to work anonymously, without a lot of, oh, investigation, without much accountability for the money he received. If he'd been at a bigger, higher profile university, he wouldn't have been able to do that."

"But isn't he working on the equipment, like you said? Hasn't he made progress?"

"Oh, he made great progress. It's just that the equipment he's been working on isn't what he proposed in the grants. He wrote up a detailed proposal about developing a new energy source, the initial steps for developing a type of nuclear, radioactive energy. I guess you could call it more of a slow release mechanism for the energy contained in radioactive nucleotides. So not to create an explosive chain reaction like in a bomb, or nuclear fission like a power plant. It's a very efficient reaction, and supplies amazing amounts of power. I still don't understand it all, but I know it can revolutionize energy use." She paused. "The grant proposal was very convincing for a good reason."

"What's that?" asked Chris.

"He outlined the details of development very well in the grant because he had already developed it."

"He had already developed an alternative form of nuclear energy?" Chris asked in amazement.

"And it worked, I mean, it works. Very well. But he's only used it as a mechanism to power the other equipment he had been working on."

"It works? How does it work?"

She thought a second. "Oversimplified, because that's the only way I understand it, the huge amounts of energy in atoms of common materials, like the radioisotopes of most metals, is sort of drawn out slowly, almost like diffusion. This is channeled into whatever type of equipment you want to power—lights, heating elements, whatever."

"Do the materials change, to different isotopes or whatever? Does the radioactivity decay?"

"Not significantly in the lengths of time we worked with anything. Over time though, it probably would, yeah. Anyway, that was what he got the money for, but he had already done that. So in a way it was fraud, sort of." She looked away, as if she had just admitted something horrible.

"Why didn't he do more with that? It sounds like such a useful idea. An alternative energy source for the world, or something."

"To him that was just tinkering. He figured that out so easily, and got it working so quickly, it wasn't even a challenge. He just needed it to do other things he wanted to accomplish."

Chris was thinking about the little contact he had with Dr. Leonard. "I don't know him well, but he always struck me as a very talented guy. I've seen him running, playing basketball and touch football on the campus green. I remember at a faculty Christmas party a few years ago he sat down and played the piano beautifully. I had never heard such a beautiful rendition of 'O Holy Night' before. All this, and alternative energy as a hobby?"

"He was the most brilliant man I've ever known," said Margaret, with a far-away look in her eyes. "But I have to admit that I went to work for him for the wrong reasons. He was so handsome, even with his long hair and graying beard. And he was so persuasive. He convinced me that what he was working on would work. And he convinced me not to talk about it with anyone."

"Why do you keep referring to him in the past tense? Did he die?"

She looked at Chris silently for a few seconds. "Did you ever see his paintings? Dr. Leonard's, I mean. His drawings?"

"He's an artist, too?" Chris was amazed. "Was there anything he couldn't do?"

"Actually, no, there wasn't," said Margaret, looking away. "He was even a tremendous lover." She looked back at him. "I guess I have to admit, that's one reason I feel so attracted to you. In some ways, the two of you remind me of one another. Not physically, but you both, I don't know, seem to think a lot differently from anyone else I know. Much deeper. I guess I thought maybe you would be as sensitive and considerate in bed, even if you are married." She sighed. "I've never been touched like I was by Dr. Leonard, before or since. I miss it."

"Since. Since," Chris repeated, annoyed a little. "Where is he?"

She looked directly into his eyes. "All evidence I can find points to the fact that Dr. Leonard didn't have a Leonardo da Vinci complex, like so many people have been saying, like you said after class that day. He is Leonardo da Vinci. Or was Leonardo."

Chris stared at her blankly. "Excuse me?"

"The equipment he was working on, that he designed, built and tested, was time relocation equipment." Her gaze was piercing.

"Time reloca—What does that mean, exactly?"

"Like time travel, except it's not really travel. Just relocation. Kind of a one-time thing. You go there and you stay there."

Chris didn't know how to take what she was saying. "Time travel? You're serious?"

"Does it sound like I'm joking?" she asked, tension and truth undeniable in her tone.

Chris' mind was suddenly spinning with the implications of what she was saying. "So you're telling me Dr. Leonard made equipment, a machine that can take people anywhere in time, to the past, to the future?"

"Not the future, at least that was his hypothesis. Again, all evidence and calculations suggest that he was, or is, correct."

"Not the future? Why not?" Chris felt as if he was humoring her, not really believing what she was saying.

"It's a matter of calculation. Of setting the machine to the right time, the right place. Since the future hasn't happened yet, there's no way for the computer to calculate where to go. And since the events haven't happened yet, there really isn't anywhere *to* go."

"Right place? I don't understand. Why is that important?"

"Every event has taken place in a specific place, in time and space. The computer is programmed, by Dr. Leonard, to figure out exactly where you want to be brought to. The time and the place."

"So, like, if I wanted to see, oh, the sinking of the Titanic, you can program the machine for April, 1912 in the north Atlantic, and I can go there?" He now knew, at least, she was completely serious with what she was telling him.

"No, that's not what I mean by location. It's more of a calculation and relocation in a four-dimensional grid system, with where and when we are now being the origin of that grid. The Earth, everything for that matter, was in a totally different place in the universe yesterday than it is today. That's the location the computer is able to calculate. It takes when you want to go back to and calculates where that place is in space and time, and takes you there. Any variation in location on the surface of the Earth isn't that important, since that changes minute to minute, hour to hour, as the Earth spins on its axis. But where the Earth is in space, that's the critical thing." She paused a second. "I don't understand how it works, exactly. Like I said, Dr. Leonard was the most brilliant person I've ever known. Not only did he conceive of the idea and design the equipment, but he built it, too. I've been doing mostly support work. But when it was ready for testing, that's when my role became critical."

Chris was trying to understand what she was explaining but couldn't quite grasp the reality of it. "And he tested it on himself?"

"Eventually, yes. But he wasn't—isn't—stupid. He made several smaller prototypes that he tested first, with my help, mostly on mice and rats." She watched Chris intently. "Well, Professor Magnuson, I mean Chris, since your very expressive eyes betray your disbelief, would you like to see the relocation equipment for yourself?"

"Uh, okay, Mac. I guess. I'm sorry if I seem skeptical. It's just that my thinking is fairly rooted in reality. Time relocation isn't part of that reality, except maybe when students fall asleep in my class, wake up later, and don't know what happened to that hour of their life."

Margaret smiled as she stood, picking up her books. "Come on. It's on the seventh floor."

Chris followed her out of his office and down the hallway to the stairs. Since it was between semesters, the building was mostly empty, except for one custodian they passed as he came out of the stairwell. Their footfalls echoed off the metal and cinder blocks as they slowly climbed to the top floor of the building. Soon they stood in front of a dark green, steel door without windows. The dimly lit hallway was completely empty except for a few empty boxes and paint cans stacked in the corner at the far end. Chris held her books as she fumbled with several keys until she found the right one and jammed it into the silver knob. Turning it sharply, a click could be heard as the bolt disengaged. Margaret pulled the door open and they entered.

When the dim fluorescent lights flickered on, Chris was surprised to see the lab was mostly empty. There was some electronic equipment along the far, left wall, but it was small and unimpressive. A table stacked with papers and books was straight in against the back wall, and to the right was a desk housing a small, outdated personal computer and piled high with papers. Chris' eyes were immediately drawn to several paintings and drawings against the back and near, right walls. They were framed in simple, stained oak and covered with glass that made seeing them difficult, light from overhead reflecting with a harsh glare. As Margaret put down her books on the desk, Chris came closer to examine the paintings. One he recognized as Dr. Leonard, his long hair and full, flowing beard occupying most of the frame. Another he recognized immediately as Margaret. As he looked at it for several seconds, something about it seemed very familiar, but not because it was Margaret. He couldn't quite put his finger on it, just as he couldn't understand why Margaret had looked familiar the first time he had met her.

"Who did these?" asked Chris. "They're quite good."

"Who do you think?" Margaret said, walking over to him. "Dr. Leonard, of course."

"But that one is him, isn't it?"

"Sure. It's a self-portrait."

"Aahh. Right. And you posed for this one?"

"Sure. After I got to know him a little better, he asked me if I would do a sitting. Having seen his other work, I was actually pretty flattered. Like you said, he's quite good." She paused, and said to herself, "More evidence to support the hypothesis."

"Hmm? I'm sorry. What did you say?" Chris had been lost in thought examining the painting of Margaret.

"Would you like to see the equipment?" she asked.

144

"Definitely. It's not in here?"

"Follow me." She walked to another, dark green door in the back of the room and unlocked it with a different key. She led him into a huge, open, circular room with a very high ceiling. Before she turned on the lights he recognized where he was. "This is the old observatory, isn't it?"

"Right. The telescopes have been gone for years, though. Kind of useless at this altitude with all the particulate matter in the atmosphere." She flipped a switch, and a bank of recessed lights around the perimeter of the room came on, giving it a dim, yellow glow. A large panel of electronic equipment filled the far side of the room. The facing of the equipment was covered with small buttons and dials and dark, rectangular displays. Cables and wires ran a few feet along the floor and connected to a console on the end of a silver, bullet-shaped cylinder about the size of a coffin, or a water heater laying on its side. There was a second, empty stand next to this one, without the cylinder or wires making the connection to the main equipment.

"That's it," said Margaret. "That's the relocation machine."

"Well, fire it up!" joked Chris. "Let's take a trip back to October, 1986. The Red Sox losing the World Series when I was a little boy is one of the most traumatic moments of my life. We can get seats at Shea and yell out to Bill Buckner, 'Get that glove down! Get it down!'"

Margaret just looked at the equipment.

"No? Okay, then. How about going back to the time of dinosaurs? We could study them and then write definitive papers on what they were really like."

She looked at him with mild annoyance. "We couldn't get back to the present to do the writing. Anyway, the capacity of the machine is only the last two thousand years or so. *BC* doesn't mean anything in the calculations. Just the numerical years of the period we've all been calling *AD.*"

"Why is that?"

She sighed. "That's the extent of the capacity Dr. Leonard programmed into it. I guess that was enough range for how he intended to use it." She continued to look at him. "You're beginning to make me regret I'm showing this to you. You don't seem to be taking it very seriously, let alone believe what I'm showing you."

"I'm sorry," Chris apologized. "It just that I'm a little overwhelmed by this. I don't know quite how to react to it all. How does it work?"

"As you might have guessed, that cylinder is the transportation vehicle. Once the date is entered into the main unit, it calculates where it's going. The cylinder takes that information and, well, I guess you could say, it relocates itself and whatever is in it to the location on the four-dimensional universal grid. I have no idea how Dr. Leonard figured out how to do that. And the atomic diffusion energy powers the cylinder. Once the power reaches maximum, it begins to move, eventually reaching the speed of light, traveling though space and, therefore, time. Exactly what physically happens to the atoms of the cylinder and its contents as they travel at the speed of light, I really can't say."

Chris listened more seriously now, taking it all in. "It looks like there used to be a cylinder there. Dr. Leonard?"

"Got into it, and I sent him off."

"To when? I mean, where?"

"Like I said, all evidence supports that Dr. Leonard is—was—Leonardo da Vinci. His intelligence, his musical ability, his obvious artistic ability, his scientific, mechanical, natural knowledge. Everything. Even the self-portrait out in the other room looks like the self-portraits of Leonardo I've seen."

"But Leonardo was born and lived kind of a normal life, at least from a physical or biological standpoint. Didn't he?" asked Chris.

Margaret hesitated, then said, "Some of the first trials with mice, and then again with rats, in small prototypes of the relocation equipment indicated that there would be some cellular regression in anything alive that was sent in the cylinders."

"What does that mean?"

"Relocation would cause the contents of the cylinder to have regression, to revert back to an earlier, younger form. Rats in particular, in the three prototypes we were able to recover, had regressed to very young rats, younger than they were when the cylinder relocated them. They were about six months old when they were sent, and only a few weeks old when they were recovered. We didn't know exactly how or why that happened, but the results were pretty clear."

Chris didn't get it. "If they went back in time, to another location as you say, how did you recover them. How did you get them if they went into the past?"

"Like I keep telling you, Dr. Leonard was pretty bright. We recovered the prototypes several months before we sent them."

"What?"

"We recovered three of the cylinders, but we recovered them before we sent them. Actually, once we thought of the idea, once he thought of the idea,

146

it really wasn't very hard. We tracked their location with a radio transmitter. We had to just pick a date and, then, go looking for them. We found the three, but one of the rats was dead. We don't know what happened to the other five cylinders. Maybe they got burned up, landed in the ocean, we don't know. Then, months later when we were ready to send the prototypes with rats inside, we sent them back to the correct dates. We recovered one in southwestern Texas, and another on a mountain in the Pyrenees, on the Spain-France border. One was in northern China. It was kind of weird, like circular logic or something, since we already knew it was a successful test, but we still had to send them. And we knew we were going to send them, and nothing was going to go wrong, since we had already successfully recovered them. And we sent the other five knowing we hadn't recovered them."

"This is too weird," said Chris, his head spinning, his thoughts confused by the sudden drastic change in his reality. "Weren't you afraid of screwing up the world, of messing up history?"

"What do you mean?" asked Margaret.

"Well, not so much with the rats, but by sending Dr. Leonard back. Weren't you afraid that an intelligent man with modern knowledge and abilities in the past would change everything, change history?"

Margaret smiled. "You're too cute," she said, "and you've been watching too many movies. No, Chris. All things, all events only happen once. If somebody or something, like Dr. Leonard, or a rat, relocates in time, he was there the one and only time those events happened, whenever that may have been. The rats' prototypes landed in Texas, in Europe, in China, ten months ago. Nothing can change that."

"Why those locations? We're in Massachusetts. The Pyrenees, China, and Texas seem pretty random to me."

"Not quite random," said Margaret. "Two of those locations are about equal distance north and south from here, and Dr. Leonard thought it was just random variation, that the calculations just 'missed' by a little. The one in Europe was pretty close to our latitude."

"And he still tested it on himself? Thinking that the calculations may have missed?"

"A slight deviation in the initial direction of relocation could have a big impact on final location. So even if the calculations were off by hundredths or even thousandths of one degree of arc, it could have a huge influence over the final relocation destination."

Chris shook his head. "So, what did happen to Dr. Leonard?"

"You still really don't get it, do you? Dr. Leonard made the relocation successfully. He didn't have a Leonardo da Vinci complex. He was Leonardo da Vinci. His capsule landed near Florence, Italy in 1452, which is when we set it for. It was found by a peasant woman who claimed him to be her son conceived to her by a Florentine notary. The rest of his life and accomplishments are fairly well-documented, most of which I'm sure you're aware of."

Chris stood staring at her with his mouth open. "But, so, you mean he regressed to a baby and then grew up again in Florence, or wherever Leonardo lived?"

"Probably a baby, but I don't know for sure. That's why I'm doing a lot of this research, getting all these books. The details of his birth are not documented. The first available details of his life start when he was living with his grandparents in Vinci."

"So, as a baby, he remembered everything he knew when he was alive, now, in the present?" Chris asked, realizing how silly it sounded when he said it out loud.

"Not really," said Margaret. "Dr. Leonard was very bright. I think what Leonardo accomplished was just a small fraction of what Dr. Leonard knew. That was one of the things Dr. Leonard wanted to study. He trained some of the rats with a conditioned response. You know, getting food by slapping a switch. The one recovered in Europe retained that ability, which, of course, we had to verify before it was born later and we trained it."

"Born later, errrrr!" Chris shook his head.

"But, the most important thing I'm trying to find in my research, the thing or things that I'm really trying to document, are hints that Dr. Leonard may have given me as Leonardo, to indicate how much he retained following relocation."

"What does that mean?"

"Well, it's pretty clear all his physical and intellectual abilities were retained, at least to a point. But that's not really confirming data. Though I know some things, I'm trying to find others I might have missed."

"What things have you found so far?" asked Chris.

Margaret hesitated. "You saw some of his paintings in the other lab, right?"

"Yeah."

"The one of me, you saw that one?"

"Yeah, I noticed that one the most. I guess because it's of you. It's really good."

"Did it seem, oh, I don't know, familiar to you. As if you had seen it before, or something like that?"

"Yeah, it did. It definitely did. Why was that?"

Margaret untied her long dark hair and let it fall around her shoulders and face, hanging down straight and loose. She walked over and sat on a chair near the corner of the main unit, facing to her right slightly, folding her hands in her lap. And she smiled slightly, ever so slightly. "Except for my blond streaks, does this look familiar?"

Chris looked at her for a second, and his eyes flew open wide. "Oh my God! You're, you're not—No! This is too weird!"

"Except I think my eyes are a little bigger. And my lips are a little fuller. Do you remember what my middle name is?"

Chris stared at her.

"Lisa. Margaret Lisa. I never really thought about it until a few months ago, after he painted me, but he's the only person who ever called me by my middle name. He always called me 'his Lisa.' But, actually, when he said it, to him I was 'my Lisa.'"

"Oh my fricking God. This is too—" Chris had to sit down.

"Anyway, that was very strong confirming data for me. He retained the memory of a pretty good likeness of my face and my name." She smiled. A very delicate, yet knowing, smile.

Chris stared at her. "My Lisa," he repeated. "I'll be a son of a—Leonardo da Vinci taught physics at Algonquin State."

Margaret looked at him thoughtfully as she stood and walked closer. "I guess now you understand why I'm so upset. And why I feel like I just need to make sure somebody else knows about this besides me."

Chris looked up at her. "What do you want me to do?"

"Nothing, at least not yet. Just listening and understanding while I was telling you is a huge help. Talking about it, getting it straight in my mind, helped me a lot."

"What are you going to do with the other cylinder? Do you have plans to relocate?" Chris asked, completely serious.

"No. Not at all. I feel no connection with the past at all. I would probably end up being a poor peasant somewhere, or die during relocation. No, I like it just fine right here, right now. And I don't think I could build another cylinder by myself. The protocols are all well documented, at least in Dr. Leonard's messy handwriting, but I guess I just don't know who to tell, what to do next. I've been pretty confused since he went." She looked away and, suddenly, looked very sad.

149

"What?" asked Chris. "Is there something else?"

Margaret was looking away, tears welling in her eyes, shaking her head slightly, biting her lower lip. "I guess you already figured out from what I said before that I was kind of in love with him. I think I still am. I feel empty, kind of lost without him. I don't know what to do—about the equipment, about anything." She broke down and began crying openly, sobbing loudly, covering her face with her hands.

Chris stepped closer, reaching out to comfort her. When Margaret saw where he was standing, she opened her arms and embraced him in a hug, burying her face into his shirt just below his collar. "Oh, Margaret, I can't even image what you're feeling," he said quietly. "You've just explained it all to me, and I don't even know what to think. And I sure don't know what to tell you to do."

"Thanks," she said, muffled into his shirt. They embrace for a few seconds as her sniffles gurgled in the cotton of his shirt. Soon she relaxed her grip and pulled back until they separated slowly. She looked up into his eyes. "Thanks," she said again.

"You don't have to thank me," Chris said gently. "Thanks for telling me. I'm not sure how I'm helping you, or how I'm going to help you."

"You already have. Just by listening and believing me."

■ ■ ■

"You know what, Daddy?" John asked as Chris pulled the sheet over him then sat on the edge of his bed.

"What?"

"Did you hear that the hurry cane is even stronger and might be coming this way?"

"I did hear that. Doesn't it have winds that are gusting over two hundred miles an hour?" Chris said as he reached for and turned off the light.

"I think so. How fast is that, anyway? As fast as a cheetah can run? They're the fastest animal, you know."

"I do know that. Well, you know how fast we drive on the highway when we go down to Grandma's house in Virginia? That's about sixty-five miles an hour. Jeremy, that hurricane, is three times faster than that. Way, way faster than that."

"Wait. What's a virgin?" asked John.

"A what? Where did you hear that word?"

150

"You just said Virginia. But I heard virgin in class before."

"From your teacher? "

"Kyle said his mother was a virgin. What does that mean?"

Chris laughed, then caught himself. "Well, a virgin is someone who has never—" he grimaced, "had sex with anybody."

John took this in stride. "Oh. Okay." Then he asked, "Is your mother a virgin?"

Chris laughed again. "No, she isn't, and wasn't. But I was born in Virginia." He thought of something else and tried to gradually change the subject. "In Arlington, Virginia. Do you know what that city is most famous for?"

John shook his head.

"Dead people. The thing in Arlington that most people know about is the National Cemetery." Chris laughed. "We lived in Falls Church, but I was born in Arlington. I've always thought it was pretty funny that I was born in a place that's most famous for dead people. That's pretty ironic, don't you think?"

John just looked at him with confusion.

Chris tried to get back to the original subject. "So, about this hurricane—"

"Uh—huh. What if it comes here?" John asked, concerned.

"We're a little ways from the ocean, so it would have to cross land to get here. It would get weaker."

"Could it still blow our house down?"

"No, it couldn't. It'll get rainy and windy, but we'll just stay in the house."

"What about Dudley? Won't he get hurt?"

"He can stay in the house, too. For a few days if he has to."

"What if he has to go poop?"

"If it's too windy, I'll let him go on some newspaper on the floor."

"And then one of us would have to bring it outside in the wind."

"Or we could just flush it down the toilet, like your poop."

John thought about this. "Oh. Okay. Well, good night, Daddy."

"See you tomorrow."

Chris walked out into the hallway, realizing he was exhausted. It had been an emotionally draining couple of days. His head was spinning from what Margaret had showed him, and he wondered if he should tell Sara, or anyone else, about it. He decided he'd have to think about that some more and talk to Margaret about it before deciding what to do.

What he needed the most at the moment was sleep.

Chapter Seventeen

"e has done nothing wrong. He has hurt no man, woman, or child," said Caiaphas, the high priest of the Jewish Council. As on most days, today he was surrounded by a dozen elders of the Sanhedrin who advised him. Now, they sat in his house, discussing the man who had come to Jerusalem, the man people were calling the Son of God. The glow of several lanterns hanging in the archways and on the walls cast dancing shadows when each man moved and gestured.

"He has blasphemed God by calling himself His son. It is a crime punishable by death!" one of the elders cried, his voice cracking and reaching a high pitch.

"Is this true?" Caiaphas asked the others, his eyes moving from man to man, searching their expressions expectantly.

"This is what all people are saying," someone else said.

Caiaphas looked hard at the elder, his dark brown eyes were piercing below his shock of snow-white hair. "But what has he claimed about himself? What other people say often does not represent the truth."

Other members of the Sanhedrin were silent. Several looked down or away from Caiaphas' questioning stare.

"What do we have against this man, other than hearsay? We cannot convict a man of blasphemy on what other people have said! We must have witness against him for this blasphemy."

"Lord?" came a meek voice from the hallway leading to the entrance of his house.

Caiaphas turned to his servant and angrily thundered, "Not now, Deborah! Can you not see the importance of our discussion?"

She cowered, on the verge of tears, then said in a whisper, "But Lord, the man at the door claims to be one of the followers of the man of whom you are now speaking."

Caiaphas paused, composing himself. After a moment he asked calmly, "Do you know this man?"

"I do not, Lord, but he says his name is Judas."

"Is he bearing sword?"

"No, Lord."

Caiaphas considered, wondering why a follower of Jesus would be coming to his house. No one other than the council of elders knew they were discussing Jesus and what could be done to stop the raging waves of unrest he was causing throughout Jerusalem.

"Send him in," he said finally.

The man was led to the meeting room, coming slowly around the corner. His eyes darted nervously about, beads of sweat on his forehead glistening in the pale light. Pausing briefly, he walked into the midst of the other men. They all eyed him suspiciously. He waited for several seconds, his feet shifting uneasily, his arms and hands seeming not able to find a comfortable position.

Finally Caiaphas asked impatiently, "Who are you? What is it you want? We are discussing important matters."

"I am Judas Iscariot," he spat out nervously. "And it is what you want which I have come to discuss."

Caiaphas waited for more. When it was not offered immediately he said, "I know not of what you are speaking. We are discussing private political matters."

"Jesus of Nazareth, the man you seek. I can deliver him to you."

"You know this man?" one of the other elders quickly asked.

"I know him as well as any man. I have traveled with him and listened to him speak for much of the past several years."

Caiaphas' interest was aroused. "Tell us then, Judas, does he claim to be the Son of God?"

"Yes. That, and much more."

"You have heard him say these words himself?"

Judas' eyes shifted from side to side, yet he did not look at any man in the room. "I have heard him say this many times. He also talks of knowledge he possesses that no other man has. As he explains it, this knowledge has come from God, and his purpose on Earth is to teach all people of these things."

"How does he say God has granted him this knowledge?" asked one of the elders. "In a dream? In a vision? Has a spirit visited him?"

Judas hesitated, trying to recollect. "The best I have been able to understand it, he has said he remembers living in another place, before he was a child in Jerusalem."

"What is that? Another place?" asked Caiaphas. "I do not understand this. Knowledge from another land, before he was a child?"

"Nor do I," agreed Judas. "But he says it is as if from another world, but his memory of this is quite unclear. And the knowledge that he teaches is possessed by all people who reside in this other world." He looked around at the confused expressions of the men. "These are some of his very words, I swear to you."

"And God is present in this 'other world?'" asked one of the men. "Is this Heaven of which he speaks? Does Jesus believe he was conceived as the Son of God in Heaven?"

"Though he has not said those exact words, I know this to be what he believes."

Caiaphas studied him with narrow eyes. "How do you know this?"

"As I said," Judas answered quickly, "I know him as well as any man. Much of what he knows, as he explains it, is beyond our knowledge and needs to be translated to our common language, so we all may understand. What I have just told you is but one example of such knowledge he has translated. This, he says, is knowledge God has bestowed upon him."

"We have heard enough!" one of the council yelled. "Surely this is enough to convict Jesus of blasphemy, for insulting God with such vile and irreverent claims!"

But Caiaphas was still closely watching Judas. "Jesus will not walk into our house, as you have, and ask to be arrested. Do you know where he is?"

"I will do better than tell you where he is," said Judas, now anger edging his voice. "What will you give me if I deliver him into your hands?"

"Can you do this?"

"I am with him much of every day. I can do this."

Caiaphas thought about this. His mind calculated how many guards it would take to search for Jesus, to find him, to bring him before the Sanhedrin. How many hours, possibly days, it would take, and the wages the guards would need to be paid. Finally he said, "I will give you thirty pieces of silver."

Judas looked puzzled for a moment, then an expression of understanding flashed across his face. "Agreed. I will tell you in a day or two when and where I will deliver him."

"Very well," said Caiaphas. He motioned for one of the servants nearby to retrieve the silver from another room. After he had counted out each coin one by one and given them to Judas, he said, "I will have Deborah escort you out," and she directed Judas back toward the hallway. "Just a moment!" Caiaphas called out suddenly.

Judas stopped and turned. "Yes, Lord?"

"Why have you come to us? Why are you betraying one you have accompanied for so long?"

"As you correctly state, he has blasphemed God. I know not of all things, but I do know this to be a crime."

But Caiaphas heard the edge of insincerity in his tone. "This is not the reason. I hear it in your voice. Speak frankly with me, these are serious matters."

Judas flushed, the sweat still thick on his brow. He bowed his head slightly. "Most wise Caiaphas, you accuse me correctly. Part of the reason is personal injustices against myself, my friends."

"These injustices must be most cruel and harsh," said Caiaphas.

"It is years of his arrogance, his blasphemy, of which you have correctly accused him. To hear a man claim to have knowledge granted him by God is a troubling chorus to have repeated to my ears, day after day, season after season. The attention and catering that is given him, by all who meet him, is truly a crime. To see so many men, women, and children swooning at his feet. So many beautiful women who would gladly give him anything, and yet he pays them the slightest attention, other than to acknowledge he is pleased they have heard him speak." The anger rose in Judas' tone, his face becoming contorted and turning a glistening red.

"This I understand," said Caiaphas calmly, a faint smile curling his mouth. "You have your thirty pieces of silver, Judas. Deliver to me this Son of God."

Judas composed himself, breathed deeply. "I will honor our agreement," was all he said. He then turned and followed Deborah down the hall to the door.

The elders watched him go, and began talking among themselves, excitement and approval in their voices. One said directly to Caiaphas, "This will curb the unrest that disrupts our quiet land. Perhaps now we will be at peace."

Jesus picked up the crusted loaf and broke it in half, crumbs falling to the blanket on which he sat. He took a small bite and chewed briefly as his friends sat patiently, waiting for him to speak.

"I have eaten this bread," he said, "and just as it will become part of my body, so must what I have been saying these past years be a very part of your life. So much a part of you, you need not choose to think or to act in such a way, just as I need not think about this bread becoming part of me."

Several of his friends murmured quietly while continuing to watch him.

Jesus reached for his small clay cup, slowly lifting it to his lips and sipping the deep red wine. He let it flow over his lips and held it in his mouth for a moment, then swallowed deeply. "This wine will become part of me, and I will feel its effect in my own blood. So should you feel the flow of the gift of God's life and love in your own blood. The gentle touch of it, always there, always giving you breath, will warm you more than any wine ever can. Remember what I have told you as you go about your lives. Teach others what I have said."

Thomas looked from Jesus to the others, back to Jesus. He was preparing to take a bite of his loaf, but stopped and asked, "Master? You speak, now, as if you are leaving us. Is this so?"

"It is so, young Thomas. One of you will betray me, and I will be taken from you all."

They all looked aghast, their eyes opening wider, and there was much movement and talking. Thaddeus dropped his cup of wine, and it spilled over his crossed legs and feet.

"How can this be?" cried James. "None among us would think of hurting you!"

"And yet, James, it is already done." Though he knew this, again, he did not know how. Though he had not observed anything or heard anyone speak, he knew it as if from a memory.

"But who, Master?" James pleaded. "Which of us has done this? And what has he done?"

"Fear not, my friends. I am but one man. What is done to me will affect only me. But what I have taught you can affect all men, women, and children yet to live. It can help all who follow from this day forth, to make the lives of all people better." He paused, thinking a moment. "I know, now, I will live again. But I know not when or where this will be. I only feel it to be so. I will be conceived from within a land—" He paused, closing his eyes as if to see the thought better. He then said, "of a virgin. And I will rise and live again from within the domain, a land of the dead. In that life I will also teach as I have in this life, but few will hear or understand what I say. As well, in that life I will be hurt deeply as is soon to happen in this one. And if the teachings of that life are not heeded by men and women, the entire world will burn with the pain and scars that we will leave in place of all God has given us. Earth can be a paradise, but if we do not return God's love, all people, all beasts, and all plants, will suffer from the pain and death of burning wounds."

His followers had not been listening very closely, still in shock that he would accuse one of them of doing him harm. They continued to talk among themselves until Philip demanded, "To accuse us of such a thing is a terrible insult!"

"Yes, Philip. But to do such a thing is even worse."

"Who, then? Who has betrayed you?"

All eyes stared at Jesus as he bowed his head slowly, and a silent tear fell from his eye. He then looked up directly into the eyes of Judas, and offered him the other half of his bread. "Here, my friend, share bread with me one last time."

Judas looked at the bread but did not take it. He glanced back up to Jesus, and then nervously looked around at the other men who all stared at him.

"You have been my friend these many years," said Jesus. "I do not know why you do this, but whatever it is you must do, do it quickly. There is no need to prolong any suffering, or to hurt any of my other friends."

Judas stood with a start and backed away. He quickly ran out of the room as the others watched in shock.

Overcome with emotion, Jesus wept bitterly, tears falling into his wine.

CHAPTER EIGHTEEN

Dudley growled low and guttural as the glow of headlights moved across the wall, casting shadows of the wooden dividers in the glass through the bedroom windows. He leapt to his feet and hurried across the room near the foot of the bed. With a hop, his front paws clutched the windowsill, and he peered out through the screen. The hair along his spine stood on end when he saw the headlights. Convinced they were stopped at the end of his driveway, his barking shattered the silence of the house.

This instantly woke Chris and Sara. Chris was to his feet quickly, seeing the lights on the wall. Sara rolled over and sat up. Her heart began to race.

"Good boy, Dudley," said Chris, kneeling beside him. "What's happening?"

Dudley looked at Chris, continued growling, then turned and barked out the screen again, louder, more insistent. Chris saw the headlights, the beams shining high and fully on their house, illuminating the front yard in raw white light.

Chills ran up his back when he saw the pair of yellow fog lights on the roof.

He swore, watching intently, sure his and Dudley's silhouettes were plainly in view. The engine revved every few seconds, but the truck didn't move.

"What is it?" whispered Sara, alarmed. She asked hopefully, "Is somebody turning around?"

"I don't think so," was all Chris said.

Slowly, the truck began to move in reverse. The lights shown more fully on the grass in the front lawn, less on the house. After the headlights had moved about thirty feet back, so the truck was lengthwise across the street, it stopped again. And waited.

"It looks like he's going away," said Chris, then instantly regretted saying it.

"Who? Who's he?" Sara asked, the tone of her voice rising. "Oh, my God, it's not—Oh, my God." She froze where she sat, her eyes wide as her fear rose.

"He's leaving. He didn't do—"

The truck raced forward toward their yard, the engine roaring, all four tires screaming against the pavement. Then a loud, *Wham! Wham!* and the truck stopped a few feet into their grass.

As the volume of Dudley's bark increased, Chris stared, not moving, not realizing what had happened right away. Not until the truck backed up again did he see the flattened mailbox on the ground.

"That bastard crushed our mailbox, and drove on our lawn!"

Sara sat, her eyes wide and staring, as Dudley continued barking.

"Mommy? Daddy?" Mary called from her room. "Mommy?"

This momentarily snapped Sara out of her shock. "I'll go tell them it's okay." She leapt out of bed, threw her bathrobe over her naked body, and hurried out into the hallway.

Chris stood away from the window and pulled on his shorts that were on the chair near the bed. "Come on, Dudley! Let's go find out who this asshole is!" Dudley turned and watched Chris heading for the bedroom door then turned and looked back out the window. "Come on! Let's go!" Chris repeated. At this, Dudley turned and hurried to follow him out of the room, still growling, hair along his spine still erect. They ran down the hall and down the stairs toward the front door. Chris reached into the front closet, pulled out an aluminum softball bat, yanked open the front door, and ran out.

The truck was already straightened out on the street. Before Chris and Dudley could get halfway across the front lawn, the tires spun quickly, and the truck accelerated away. By the time Chris reached the curb, all he saw were the taillights fading toward the end of the street.

"Damn it!" he called loudly. "You son of a bitch! Who the hell are you?" He stood watching for several seconds. Dudley growled at his side, also peering intently down the street.

Chris walked over and inspected the damage. Two deep, tire ruts started in the lawn at the edge of the pavement, evenly straddled the fallen mailbox, and ended about twenty feet further in. The four-by-four, wooden post that formerly supported the mailbox had been snapped cleanly off at ground level. A deep gash exposing splintered wood indicated where the front bumper had hit. "Damn it," Chris said quietly, as he looked at Dudley sniffing around the tire ruts and mailbox, still growling. Chris let him learn the smell and then said, "Come on, Dud, let's go see how Mom and the kids are."

Inside, Sara sat with John in his bed, Mary sitting there as well. Sara cradled them both in her arms. "They're kind of scared," she said. "They mostly got upset because you ran outside in the middle of the night in your shorts, carrying a baseball bat, looking really mad." Only then did Chris see it was 2:45 in the morning.

"A car just ran over our mailbox," Chris lied, in a feeble attempt to appease his family.

"It was him, wasn't it?" exclaimed Mary. "That bad stranger!"

"Who is he?" asked Sara evenly. "Why is he doing this?"

"Did Dudley bite him?" asked John, excited. "Or did you smash his car with the bat?"

"No, John, he drove away too fast. Like I told you, he's afraid of Dudley."

"And of you. Right?" John looked at his father in admiration.

"Oh, I don't know. I don't even know who he is."

"Call the police again," said Sara. "Tell them that the school yard thing was not random. Could you, Chris? Call them now?"

"Yeah. Sure. You guys should try to get back to sleep."

"Back to sleep?" laughed Sara. "That's not likely. Not for a while."

"I'll tell you all what. Why don't the three of you sleep in Mom's and my bed, and Dudley and me will stay in the living room. I'll watch TV, and Dudley can stay with me. We'll keep an eye out the window."

"Sure," said Sara, "that's a good idea. We'll bring the fans back into our room, close the windows, and John, Mary, and I will all cuddle in our bed." She looked first at Mary, then at John. "Okay?"

"Okay, Mommy," said Mary.

"Yeah, and Daddy and Dudley will get that bad stranger if he comes near our house," said John.

"I'm going to call the police now. Why don't you guys go ahead and get in bed."

Sara led the children across the hall with her arms around their shoulders. John and Mary each had their own pillows clutched tightly in front of them.

Who is this, thought Chris, walking down the hall. The question ate at his mind as he dialed the local police.

■ ■ ■

Chris jumped on the shovel, but again it crunched on a buried rock that wouldn't budge from the force of his weight. "Another one," he said to John, who was standing patiently near by. With Chris digging for the past hour and John picking up the small rocks and putting them in a plastic bucket, they had nearly exposed the bottom of the broken support post for the mailbox. The morning was clear and seasonal, less humid than it had been in recent weeks, and the sky was mostly a clear, bright blue. Chris' shirt was soaked with sweat, and the small of his back was tightening as his work progressed. A portable radio sat on the grass, quietly playing music broadcast from a classic rock and roll station. Dudley lay content near them, tied to a tree, occasionally raising his head when he caught sight of a bird or a squirrel or when a car drove by. Like Dudley, as soon as the engine of a car became audible, Chris looked up quickly until he could see what kind of car was driving up their street.

"Can you get it out?" asked John, stepping closer and peering down the hole, his hands resting on his knees.

"It'll take a minute." He straightened his back, sticking his stomach out, stretching and groaning slightly. "Hmmm. I'm ready to be done with this job, aren't you?"

"It's okay. I don't mind helping you," John smiled up at him. Then his expression changed and he asked, "Daddy?"

"Yeah?"

"The policeman who came a little while ago?"

"Yeah?"

"Why did he get mad at you? He said you shouldn't be wasting his time. Why did he say that?"

"They have a lot of other things to do. Too many things. There's more traffic problems, robberies, fights, things that are more trouble than a broken mailbox."

"Don't they know it was the bad stranger who did this?"

"I told him, but I guess he still had a lot of other things to do. He said he had to go to the casino and make sure all the people there, at the demonstration, didn't start arguing."

"What's a demin stray shun?"

"Oh, when people are complaining about the way something is, and they all get together to kind of tell people about it."

John thought about this. "I think I get it. Like when Jason, Samantha, and me talked to our teacher about how we thought we needed more time to eat our snacks?"

Chris laughed. "Yep, that's sort of what a demonstration is."

"I bet Liz wouldn't have been mad. I bet she would have been nice and cared about our mailbox."

"Yeah, I bet she would. To us, our mailbox is important, but there are a lot of other bad things going on that the police need to take care of." Chris stood quietly for a few seconds, looking around. Bird songs could be heard in all directions. The leaves of the large oaks and maples in and near their yard swayed gently in the slight breeze. Small, puffy, cumulus clouds moved across the blue overhead, racing on high winds. Chris smelled the air, the sweetness of late summer, the faint smell of freshly cut grass reaching him on the breeze.

Two squirrels sprinted across the street and scurried up a tree, under the attentive eye of Dudley.

"Everything is so beautiful, isn't it?" Chris asked aloud, not to John.

"What?"

Chris remembered he was standing there, looked down at him, and sighed. "Oh. I was just noticing everything around us. It's really a nice day out. Too bad we have to do this crappy job."

"Let's keep going and put the new post in the hole."

A song began playing on the radio. Chris noticed it right away, a driving, rock and roll song, written before he was born. After a brief, electric guitar lead-in, the lyrics of protest and prophecy began:

> I've been thinking 'bout our fortune
> And I've decided that we're really not to blame
> For the love that's deep inside us now is still the same
> And the sound we make together, is the music to
> The Story in Your Eyes
> It's been shining down upon me now, I realize
> Listen to the tide slowly turning
> Wash all our heartaches away
> We're part of the fire that is burning
> And from the ashes we can build another Day
> But I'm frightened for Your children
> That the life that we are living is in vain
> And the sunshine we've been waiting for
> Will turn to rain

"The Story in Your Eyes," Chris thought to himself. That is what we are, the expression of that knowledge, that story inside of us, the story that is us. We are the music to the story in His eyes.

And what a lousy song we're all playing. It could be so much better. He breathed deeply, suddenly moved and very sad.

> When the final line is over
> And it's certain that the curtain's gonna fall
> I can hide inside Your sweet, sweet love
> For ever more

"What's the matter, Daddy? You look like you have to cry."

162

Chris inhaled through his nostrils, the accumulating liquid gurgling in the incoming air. "Yeah, I guess I sort of do feel like crying."

John said, "We don't have to finish this today if you don't want to. The mail lady can bring our mail on Monday instead."

Chris looked down at him, his sweet, completely serious, innocent face. "Oh, John, what did I ever do to deserve a great kid like you." He knelt and gave him a long, firm hug.

John didn't really understand what was happening, but hugged him back, tightly.

A single tear formed in the corner of Chris' eye and rolled down his cheek.

■　■　■

"Hurricane Jeremy is now believed to be the strongest Atlantic storm on record," said the announcer on The Weather Channel. "It is now moving north at seventeen miles per hour, with maximum sustained winds of over two hundred miles per hour. With the eye centered four hundred and fifty miles west of Bermuda, it is expected to maintain its strength and continue northward. Right now, best predictions have it making land over Montauk and then Watch Hill, Rhode Island, some time Sunday evening."

Chris had been thinking about the black, pickup truck. And then his mind had gone to Margaret, wondering how it could be true that Dr. Leonard's equipment had been upstairs from him all that time, and he had no idea it was there, or even that such a thing was possible. Margaret had even been in his class, and he still hadn't known. The news of the storm shifted his attention. Sara, John, and Mary all sat watching intently.

The announcer continued, "Evacuation plans and procedures are quickly taking shape as authorities rush to deal with this probable killer. At the moment it looks as though everyone from New York City to Cape Cod will be encouraged to evacuate, as far north as Worcester and Boston, with mandatory evacuations from New Haven to New Bedford. There is no reason to expect the course of this storm will change direction at this time."

"Oh, my God," said Sara, "it's going to go right over us."

"At least we're far enough inland so it won't be catastrophic," said Chris. "We'll get some serious wind and rain, but I don't think we'll be in danger."

"Should we leave?" asked Sara. "Go to your mother's in Virginia, or just inland more. To your Aunt Helen's in Springfield, or maybe upstate New York?"

"I don't know. I think all the highways around here will be a mess tomorrow. Maybe we should just close up the house and stay downstairs for the night, and Monday, or however long it lasts."

Sara looked at him for a moment, unconvinced that was the best course of action.

The announcer said, pointing to an enhanced radar image on the screen, "And already two more storms are strengthening east of the Caribbean, moving west. Lawrence is already a category two hurricane, with winds approaching one hundred miles an hour. Marilyn is now a tropical storm and is expected to continue to intensify, possibly becoming a hurricane as soon as Monday morning."

"I've never seen anything like this, all the storms this year," commented Sara.

The Weather Channel shifted to a studio shot with two meteorologists sitting behind a desk, discussing the extreme Atlantic hurricane season, the most severe on record, with the most named storms by such an early date.

"Why is that, Kevin?" one of the announcers asked the other.

"Jeremy illustrates the point well. Simply put, the water in the Atlantic is significantly warmer than it was ten or fifteen years ago. With warmer water, and more warm water further north, the storms have much more of an opportunity to form and strengthen."

"Why is the water so much warmer?"

"It's not only in the Atlantic. It's global. The average temperature worldwide has risen over one degree centigrade in the last ten years. That doesn't sound like much, but it's a huge difference. As we all know, this directly correlates with a continuous increase in atmospheric carbon dioxide, and other gases, which have contributed significantly to this warming. We're approaching global temperatures that could be warmer than anything the Earth has ever seen in the last billion years."

"What's caused the increase in carbon dioxide?"

"The burning of tropical rain forests, to be cleared for agriculture, besides causing massive species extinction, has contributed huge amounts of carbon dioxide to the atmosphere. But, primarily, it's been caused by fossil fuel burning over the last one hundred years. There is evidence, now, that suggests glacial ice fields in Scandinavia, Greenland, Baffin Island, and the Brooks Range in Alaska, that have been intact since the last ice age, have now decreased in size by as much as forty per cent."

"I want to watch something else," said Mary. "Can you switch it, Daddy?"

"Hold on a sec," he said, listening to the TV. "I wonder if there's anything about the highways and traffic on the Boston station." He pressed buttons on the remote.

"—significantly lower than it was fifty years ago," the anchor on the local news said. "Once again, the Ogallala Aquifer, the seemingly endless underground water supply for much of the breadbasket of the central and western United States, now appears to be at critically low levels. Once containing many times more water than all surface bodies of water on the entire Earth, it is now clearly dry in many areas, and only a few feet deep in others. Unregulated, center pivot irrigation use is believed to be primarily responsible for this decrease. The future impact on agriculture in this area can only be speculated at this point, but it could have devastating effects on crop yields within the next few years."

"Jesus," said Chris, "What next?"

"Dad!" said Mary. "Can we please watch something else?"

"Just a minute, please," he said.

"Locally," the announcer continued, "demonstrations at the Gold casino on the Passemannican Reservation in Littleboro turned heated today when verbal exchanges occurred between protesters and employees passing on their way to work."

Chris watched, listened. He felt his stomach tighten, seeing the angry expressions and hearing the words of the people on the screen.

"I've got to," he said aloud.

"What?" asked Sara, turning to him.

"I've got to go tomorrow," he said. "I have to try."

She studied his expression, seeing a look of intense conviction in his eyes. Now it seemed more intense than she could ever remember. "You don't have to if you don't want to. It's really not your place."

"It is. I have to try. I have something to say that I think might help." "Different than what you said at the town meeting?"

"Yes. And no. I was too emotional then. Too angry. I need to say something, and say it rationally and plainly. Maybe it will help, maybe it won't, but I have to try." He looked into her eyes, his gaze piercing. "I have to."

"Ohhh," she groaned softly. "What about us?"

"What? What about you?"

"That creep in the truck. What if he comes around again?"

"It'll be the middle of the afternoon, for an hour at the most. Just stay with the kids and keep Dudley close by. He won't do anything in the middle of the day."

"He did at the school yard," she said coldly.

"If you all stay together, it'll be okay." Then Chris thought of something.

"Want me to have Crow come over and hang around? And Kathy?"

"That would make me feel better, yeah," Sara said.

"Dad! Could you please turn to something else!"

"Oh. Sure. What do you want?"

"See if there are any cartoons on channel thirty."

■ ■ ■

"I'd like to go with you, if you don't mind," said Crow over the phone.

"You would?" asked Chris. "Why?"

"I've seen them all out there every day this week, on my way into work."

"And?"

"I've been interested in it all, but I have mixed feelings, like I told you. I've never left enough time to stop and see what it's like. Tomorrow might be a good time to do that."

"With the storm coming and all, you're still going to work?"

Crow laughed. "The Gold never closes. Unless there's a mandatory evacuation. Then I guess they'd have to do something. But, since there isn't, the doors will be open, and I'm sure the crowds will still be there. They'll still need security. Maybe a little more sparse than normal. But it's kind of amazing how much of a priority gambling is to some people. Anyway, the storm won't even get bad until later in the night."

Chris thought a second. "I guess we'd have to meet there, then. If you're going right up to work, and I'll only stay an hour or two. You start at four?"

"Yeah. Why don't we drive together, I mean, you follow me in your car?"

"Sure. But I am actually concerned about the family. We don't even know who this guy is."

"They'll probably be fine," said Crow. "It'll be the middle of the afternoon on a Sunday."

"That's what I thought. But it's more for their own peace of mind. I mean, Dudley's not really a guard dog, but, at least, he gets the 'dog thing' right. You know, barking at strange cars and stuff. But, then again, he barks at robins."

Crow laughed.

"But at least he barks loud enough to scare most people away."

"You know what? I think Kathy is pretty flexible tomorrow. Maybe she could come over for moral support."

"That'd be great," said Chris. "So, when? Want to go at two-thirty?"

"Works for me.

CHAPTER NINETEEN

"**W**e'll be all right," said Kathy. "You guys go and do your thing. Chris, set them all straight." They were standing in the Magnuson's driveway.

Chris looked at her, forcing a smile. "Thanks."

"You're sure you want to do this?" Sara asked him. "With the storm coming and all? Why don't you stay home and help us get the house squared away before Jeremy gets here."

"There's really not that much to do around the house. Just bring in stuff from outside. It's not like we need to board up the windows or anything." Then he said solemnly, "I know it's hard to understand, and it's hard for me to explain. It's just something I feel, I know, I have to do. If I don't, I'll feel like I didn't do something that I could have, something that could make a difference."

This was the part of her husband that Sara didn't always feel comfortable about. She knew it was part of him, but sometimes wished it wasn't. Though he was always good with the children—supportive and helpful, firm yet tender, authoritative yet compassionate—he seemed to have something else on his mind, preoccupied with larger, deeper thoughts and ideas. "Do you really think you can change people's minds?" she asked.

"Not many, no. Anything I have to say is almost theoretical, philosophical. You know, I tell a few students some things a couple times a year, but the more I hear about what's going on in the world, the more restless I get to tell more people. And I know that if any change does come of it, it will have to be by a cultural evolution. It's up to each person to understand it and change their life by their own choice. One person here, two people there, four people way over there." He looked at her intensely. "Does that even begin to make sense?"

"In a way. But sometimes I feel a little selfish. I want all of you, all your love for just me and the kids."

He studied her momentarily. "I really don't know why I feel like I have to do things like this. Yeah, I think about things differently than most people, maybe all people. I guess that's just me." Then he said, only half joking, "I'm the person my cells are designed to express. My genetics. It's just who I am."

Sara let the last comment pass, not knowing how to respond. "Just be careful. And hurry home. Hurricane's a comin'," she joked, imitating a ship's lookout. "And I'm glad Crow will be there with you."

"I'll keep him out of trouble," Crow said. "Besides, I want to see what everyone is saying myself."

"You be careful, too," Chris said to Sara and Kathy. "Keep Dudley near by, and don't let the kids out of your sight." He turned to look at Mary and John playing in the sandbox. "You guys behave for Mom and Kathy. Help them bring your stuff in before it starts raining. Okay?"

"We will."

Crow backed his old, green Ford Expedition out of the driveway as Chris followed in the Toyota. With Crow leading, they drove toward the Gold. Chris noticed Crow's car listed slightly to the left. Then it occurred to him that having over three hundred pounds always sitting on the same side would do that to a set of shock absorbers, even heavy duty shocks like those on the Expedition. Though traffic was light moving in their direction on the state road, cars were thick and driving much slower in the opposite direction, toward the interchange of the interstate highway heading west. Many people in the area had decided to avoid the storm, or were leaving the Gold after a short weekend of entertainment.

Gray clouds were thickening overhead, blocking the sun, and the air was cooling rapidly as increasing winds lightly rocked the trees. The roof of the casino was soon within view, its bright gold roof a gleaming contrast to the gray sky. Crow and Chris turned their cars onto Passemannican Drive and headed up the hill. Traffic was now heavier in both directions, crawling up and down the access road into the reservation. Soon it stopped completely, and they had to wait several minutes before moving again, inching forward at a pace slower than a walk.

Further ahead, Chris caught sight of some people standing near the road, and others walking past. As he drove around the curve where the road entered reservation land, a crowd of people became visible to the right, clustered in front of one of the houses. Cars were parked on the shoulder further ahead, in driveways, and scattered on other lawns. Crow pulled off to the shoulder and parked. Chris followed his lead.

"I don't think we're going to get much closer," Crow called back, stepping out of his car. "Let's just walk the rest of the way from here."

As they did, Chris realized there were as many as a hundred and fifty people jammed into the small area of the house's front yard. It was a white, one hundred-year-old Victorian with a covered front porch, the roof of which was supported by white pillars. Trimmed evergreen shrubs and mountain laurel were growing along the front. A small, wood podium was set up at the top of the steps, with a single microphone on a chrome stand curving up from the wood. Two rectangular speakers were on the roof of the porch, one on either side of the stairs, and two smaller ones were on the steps just below the podium. About fifty people were clustered around the front of the house, and another hundred were scattered back toward the street. A van emblazoned on the side with *Channel 16* in large, blue letters was parked across the street. A cameraman and reporter stood in front of it, talking to themselves, having either finished filming or not having started yet. Two police cruisers were parked directly in front of the house on the shoulder. One officer was attempting to keep traffic moving. Two others were standing in the back of the crowd, calmly watching the proceedings. Chris saw Officer Crooks standing alone near the far cruiser. She was talking on the car radio, but she didn't see him as he moved toward the crowd.

The person currently at the podium was a woman, and she became clearly audible as Chris and Crow approached, working their way toward the front of the crowd. She spoke slowly, awkwardly, with many *ums* and *ahs* disrupting her delivery. It was clear she was nervous.

"Uh, and I just think it will cause too many, uh, traffic problems, you know, like there is right now." And she pointed behind the crowd, with a nervous laugh. "And that's all I wanted to say."

Another woman moved to the microphone as the first stepped away. "Thanks for the comments, Mrs. Platts. I think we may need to close up here for the day fairly soon, since it will probably start raining in a couple hours. Andrew Warren is going to say a few things in a minute. I'm Melinda Hanley, representing LACTELL. If you would like to talk, no matter what your opinions are, please come up and see me. The only thing we're asking everyone is to limit their time to ten minutes. And now, Mr. Warren."

Chris remembered Melinda from the phone call earlier, the person who had asked him to come. Warren started to speak, opening with an angry tone, saying, "I am so sick of this traffic, of the crime, of these god damn Indians wanting to take our land."

Chris said to Crow, "I'm going up and talk to her for a second, to tell her I'm here."

"I'll follow you up. Go ahead."

"If you don't mind, I'd like you next to me when I talk. More people might listen, on both sides of the argument, if they see a Native American standing with me."

"I'm with you all the way," he said.

They moved through the crowd slowly, Crow's head and shoulders towering over the mass of people. Some were reluctant to move for Chris, but once they saw Crow standing behind him, saying, "Excuse us, please," they quickly stepped aside.

Someone from the crowd yelled at Warren, "Our land? Our land? Whose land is it?"

"Hear me out! It's my turn at the microphone!" yelled Warren angrily.

The crowd murmured among themselves. Chris hadn't noticed before, but the faces on the crowd were distorted with emotion. Some were clearly angry. Some were restless or sad. Several people shifted their weight back and forth between their feet, or crossed and uncrossed their arms, or talked among themselves.

"Sit down, you loser!" someone else yelled at Warren.

Chris reached Hanley who was standing to the right of the steps in front of a mountain laurel, and he made eye contact with her. "Hi, Melinda. Chris Magnuson."

She looked at him blankly for a second and then a look of remembrance flashed across her face. "Chris! Yes, of course! Good of you to come." She shook his hand briskly, then her gaze shifted to Crow.

"And this is a friend of mine, Henry Johnson."

"Mr. Johnson, good to meet you," she said with hesitation, her hand dwarfed by his, examining him as someone looks up at Mount Rushmore.

At the microphone, Warren yelled, "I refuse to have my tax bill go up to help line the pockets of some rich men who don't even pay any taxes to use our water or our streets!"

There was a chorus of angry responses from the crowd.

"Has there been any trouble?" Chris asked Hanley, concerned, as he looked around.

"What do you mean? Fights, or something like that?"

Chris nodded, eyeing Warren at the podium.

"Not much. Yesterday there was a lot of shouting and a couple people got into a shoving match. That's about it. Then again, there's been a lot of shouting ever since we've been out here."

"Well, when do you want me to talk?" asked Chris.

"How about next? There were a couple of people who said they wanted to speak, but I don't see them anymore. They could have left."

"Next? Uh, I guess so." Chris suddenly felt a little nervous. This was quite a different audience than students in his classroom. He looked to Crow for support, but he was scanning the crowd. Even he looked a little anxious.

Chris looked back to the podium in time to hear Warren say, "You know what? It's not worth it. It's not going to do a damn bit of good, anyway. They'll do whatever they want, and they won't care about anything we have to say. I'm moving out of this screwed up town as fast as I can sell my house!" He stepped down quickly and disappeared into the crowd.

Hanley moved back to the microphone, eyeing Warren briefly as he walked away. Then she said, "Thanks, Mr. Warren, for those thoughtful comments. Don't forget we have a stack of literature up here on the steps. Please come up and take some, and become better informed about what's legal and what's not; what can be done to keep from losing our homes, if we don't want to; what you can do, individually, to help stop annexation of more land." She paused and looked down to Chris, raising her eyebrows to question if he was ready. When he shrugged and nodded, she said, "Next to speak is Chris Magnuson, a science professor at Algonquin State. Chris?"

It had all happened so fast, Chris didn't feel ready to speak. Still, he moved to the steps and up to the podium. Crow followed him and stood behind, slightly to his right, saying quietly, "Go get 'em, Buddy." Chris smiled with a glance back over his shoulder, then moved behind the microphone. As he scanned the crowd, it seemed even bigger than he had noticed before. There were many people sitting on hoods of cars across the street and in other yards. He even saw a few children sitting in trees. The roof of the casino looked enormous behind them, higher than the trees, up on top of the hill. The wind seemed to suddenly get stronger, and darker bands of clouds moved rapidly across the gray.

For a moment Chris stood silent, fumbling with thoughts, until he began.

"I'm not here to talk about Native Americans. I'm not going to talk about taxes, or the evils of gambling, or even the school system struggling with its budget. I'm going to ask everyone listening to think about some things that are a little bigger than what's going on here today, beyond the boundaries of your daily lives." He paused and looked across the faces in the crowd. Though some people shifted and seemed to look confused, there seemed to be fewer angry expressions compared to when he first arrived.

He continued. "There is an enormous problem in the world, a problem that is so automatic, that is so ingrained in you and me, that we don't even think about it. That problem is the tendency of people to fragment the world by perception, by thought. We love to put things in groups and categories, including ourselves. Probably because it makes the world seem more ordered, maybe because it makes things less confusing and easier to understand. And maybe it helps give each of us our own sense of identity and our own unique place in the world.

"What does that mean?" he continued. "Well, let me give you some examples. Race is a good one. I know it's hard to understand, but the whole concept of race is totally fabricated by human perception. Yeah, people with certain physical characteristics are descended from groups of people that lived in certain geographic areas, either recently or a long time ago. But you know what? Why is that important anymore? The whole world can communicate now, in a matter of seconds. The distances and boundaries just aren't there anymore. Isn't it time to start paying more attention to how similar we all are instead of how different we all are? Why argue about who did what to whom hundreds of years ago? It's over. It's gone. Instead of separating people into groups, whether it's by perception or by law, isn't it time to say, 'we're not black or white or red or yellow or whatever?' We're all brown. Brown. We're all basically the same, it's just that each individual is a slightly different shade of brown from the next."

He paused, trying to gauge reaction and reception in the crowd. He couldn't read their faces, not sure if he saw indifference, boredom, or confusion.

Across the street and slightly up the road in the direction of the Gold, parked in a driveway beyond the direct sight of Chris, was a black, pickup truck. Hector sat in the driver's seat, a can of beer in his lap, five empty cans on the floor on the passenger's side. His window was open, and, above the low music of the radio, he could only occasionally hear enough of what the speakers were saying to make sense of it. Not that he cared. He had just cleaned out his locker at work, had gotten tired of waiting in traffic, and had pulled into an empty driveway to wait until the cars thinned out and to have a few beers.

Now he straightened in his seat, turned the radio off and watched intently, not quite believing what he saw. His pulse quickened as he understood, leaning his head closer to the open window to listen over the low noise of the wind. Unbelievable, he thought. It's that faggot with the kids. How's your mailbox, dickhead? Get any mail today? He laughed to himself. And, holy shit, could it be? Is that Johnson standing next to him? Both of the assholes who ruined my life standing side by side in the same place, right in front of me. This must be my lucky day. Unbelievable.

Hector quickly looked up and down the street.

He thought, I still won't be able to move my truck much, but maybe that doesn't matter. Maybe this is a good spot. For the first time, he noticed he was parked under two large, oak trees, one on either side of the driveway, and it occurred to him he was probably mostly hidden from view under the branches. He thought, there are those two police cars between me and those shitheads. That's a problem. But, maybe, if I move my truck up a little behind that tree, or out into a break in traffic, maybe I can get a clear line of sight.

He opened the glove compartment and took out his .38 caliber pistol. The six chambers were still full.

"Religions of the world is another one," Chris continued. "They all overlap to some degree, based on a higher power that deals in love or compassion and gives guidelines on how the world should get along, and all that. But, it's the differences between those religions that everyone focuses on, not the similarities, to the point where it has led to numerous wars in the past, and still does. As incredible as it sounds, more people have been killed because of the worship of God than the worship of the devil. Why? Because, to most people, it seems that believing or not believing in your own religion is more important than what the religion is saying in the first place!

"The same is true about political parties. Even though the goal should be to make the quality of life better for the people of whatever country or state it is, differences are drawn along party lines and those differences become more important than what can be accomplished through laws and policies that are being discussed."

"What the hell are you talking about!" someone yelled from the crowd. "What does that have to do with the casino!"

Chris didn't respond but tried to continue. "It's time to look at the similarities, to look for agreement and compromise, instead of concentrating on the differences between groups of people and arguing in favor of our own position or group." He thought a second. "Imagine what would happen to your body if the differences between the different types of cells became the priority instead of all of them trying to work together to keep the body working and running as a unified whole. Each cell has its specific role, but each one only takes its share of the energy and other resources it needs. Or it creates only the amounts of waste that are absolutely necessary, no more than the body can handle. And the goal, the purpose of each cell is to maintain the homeostasis, the balance and order in the body. They're all from the same source, from the same egg and sperm, so they're unified by a common bond, a common spirit, if you will.

"And that's what we need to do, how we need to be. Except we're all the cells, and the Earth is the body. We are all slightly different in our own way, with different abilities and knowledge, to contribute to making things better. To get enough to keep us comfortable and living well, but not so much that it takes more than our share of resources away from others that need them."

Chris paused and looked around. Confusion was pretty much what he saw on all the faces in the crowd.

"Another way to look at it is love. Well, what is love? Everyone talks about it like it's such a certain, known thing. Like it's water or something like that. Well, I have a pretty good idea—"

"Shut up, you asshole," someone yelled. "What the hell are you talking about!"

Chris couldn't ignore that comment. It was too loud, too harsh. "Excuse me! I'm talking here. Do you mind? Why don't you listen and try to understand what I'm saying instead of—"

"Yeah, I mind a lot," the man yelled, and stepped more into an open spot, where Chris could see him. He was an older man with gray hair and glasses. "No one here even knows what you're talking about. We're here to talk about Passemannicans stealing our houses to build blackjack tables, and you're talking about cells and love!"

"Are you even trying to understand what I'm saying?" Chris yelled back, anger propelling his voice as his tone rose to a higher pitch.

"No! Because it sounds like a bunch of bullshit!"

"How dare you—" Chris started, until Crow put his massive hand on his shoulder.

"Say it with love," Crow said quietly. "Try and keep calm, keep in control."

Chris turned back and looked at him briefly. Crow smiled. "Thanks," said Chris, "you're right. Thanks."

"Get off the stage!" the same man yelled.

"Just a minute," said Chris calmly, regaining composure. "Give me a couple more minutes. Like I was saying, one way to define love is: any action done by choice that improves the quality of life for everyone involved. Sharing whatever resources we have, what we know, what we own, what we can do, instead of only using them for our own personal gain, will be a step towards making less conflict and greed in the world.

"Now, I'm not saying we can't have businesses that make money or that people shouldn't sell products or services. It's a matter of being reasonable, a matter of compromise. If you have something that many people need, you don't have to just give it away. But sell it for how much you need, not how much you can get."

Three gunshots shattered the air.

Before Chris knew what was happening, wood from the podium splintered in a shower all around him. There was a loud, metallic clang from the microphone stand and sparks flew in all directions. Piercing ringing and feedback blared from the speakers. Chris flinched and ducked away.

Crow yelled in pain, grabbing his side and falling to his knees. "Damn it. Damn it," he said, clutching the wound as blood immediately poured out between his fingers. "Aah! Oww!"

"Crow! God damn it! Crow!" Chris yelled, scrambling back to him.

Screams exploded from the crowd. People ran in all directions, stampeding from the lawn.

Around the side of the podium, while kneeling at Crow's side, Chris saw the top of a black, pickup truck driving away. The yellow fog lights on the roof were unmistakable. He stood quickly, watching over the mass of panicked people, as the truck drove over grass and around parked cars, quickly vanishing from view behind trees and around the curve. Chris saw Officer Crooks jump into the cruiser and attempt to turn it around. Instantly the sirens blared, and the lights blazed as she worked the car back and forth until it was facing the other direction. Cars in the road tried to pull off to the side, but parked cars and running throngs of people prevented them from moving, clogging the path Liz tried to follow. She finally worked her way to an opening and swerved sharply onto the grass, trying to follow the same route Hector had taken.

The two policemen who had been standing near the road ran through the scurrying people to the podium. "How are you? Are you hit?" one of them yelled while running up the steps.

"He's shot!" said Chris.

One of the officers knelt beside Crow, trying to examine the wound, saying, "How bad is it? Let me see."

The other pulled a phone from his belt, demanding immediate medical assistance.

"Aaah! Damn it!" said Crow, his face wincing in pain. "It feels like my belly's on fire! Damn it!"

"Hold still," the officer said. "Hold on. Let me get the kit from the car. More help will be here in a second."

"Hurry, would you?" said Chris to the officer, helping to support Crow's head and shoulders. "Hang in there. You're okay. You'll be fine."

Chris' mind raced. He hadn't fully comprehended what had just happened, how lucky he had been.

All he could think was, why? Why did this happen? Who is that guy in the truck?

The wind blew harder and a rumble of distant thunder could be heard over the screams of the crowd.

■　■　■

The cruiser bounced and jostled over rocks and gullies as Crooks jammed the accelerator to the floor, the engine screaming in protest, the rear tires spinning wildly on gravel and pine needles. The rear end swerved from side to side as she tried to maintain control, her eyes fixated on the black truck. Still not close enough to read the license plate numbers, she desperately tried to gain ground. But the truck had pulled off the dirt road it had been following and was now going through uncleared forest.

Soon, Crooks couldn't go any further as the brush thickened. She couldn't work her way back towards the paved road that was visible over the crest of the short embankment. The truck was now long gone, able to easily transverse rocks and logs her cruiser couldn't drive over.

"All units! All units!" she snapped into the radio. "Crooks, here! APB on a black, Dodge, pickup truck, Mass. plates, ID unknown, last seen heading south on Pescatello Way, one point five miles southeast of Passemannican Drive. Driver considered armed and dangerous." She repeated the alert rapidly, hung the microphone back on the dashboard, and swore quietly to herself. Then she slowly backed up the cruiser and headed back toward the protest area.

Chapter Twenty

esus walked slowly through the olive trees. The rich fragrance of the new blossoms saturated the spring air. Colorful blooms of perennial flowers lined the path on either side. He knelt for a moment to inhale deeply of their perfume, then lifted his head back and closed his eyes as if drinking deeply of the aroma, wanting to commit it to memory. The recently-set sun splashed red and lavender across the wisps of high, still clouds filling most of the darkening sky. Jesus opened his eyes briefly, but closed them again as sadness overwhelmed him.

Impatiently standing behind him, Peter, James, and John waited for him to walk. When he didn't, James said urgently, "Master, it is best we keep moving. If we are to sit in privacy in the garden, we should be among the trees and bushes there before darkness falls."

"Everything is so beautiful," Jesus said to none of them. "Why must we continue to bring such ugliness into the world?"

"For your own safety, if you please," insisted James.

"You, yourself, have said Judas will return and attempt you harm," agreed Peter. "If we are to help keep you safe, it would best be done in the sanctuary of the garden."

Jesus opened his eyes and looked at them again. He said nothing for a few moments. With a heavy sigh he said finally, "If you would, my friends, stay here for a while. I would very much like to be alone in the garden to think, to try and understand all that is happening and has happened."

"How will we keep you—"

"The only way to the garden is to follow this path. Stay here, but watch over the path, so I may be alone."

John and James looked at each other, and then to Peter. It was John who said, "Very well, Master, we will wait for you here. If you need us, you will call for us?"

"Thank you. My heart is very heavy. It is a weight I best carry alone right now."

Slowly he turned and continued up the path. His three friends, swords still sheathed, sat on small rocks just off the path and talked nervously to each other.

Darkness fell rapidly as the full moon rose to the east.

The confusion, the feeling he was out of place, that he did not belong here, still haunted Jesus. After all the years, throughout his entire life, this feeling still consumed him, forming the restless foundation of his existence. Though he ate and slept like all people, sweated and felt pain like all people, it had always been clear to him that his mind, his thinking, was very different. All the things he knew, all he tried to teach. Not only did no other people know of these things, most could not even understand them after hearing him speak and explain. And most thoughts in his mind seemed to have no clear words to explain them in the language that was spoken. After all he said, after all he had done to try and set an example, still the confusion of people was the most apparent factor governing everything that was done, in what their priorities were, in how people lived their lives day to day, year after year, generation after generation. What he possessed, that everyone else did not, was an awareness of things, a knowledge of the ways of the Earth and of living things, of the role people should have on Earth. Other people viewed him as magical, divine, possessing powers to heal or command the natural elements. Even though he tried to explain in every possible way that no such forces exist. The sun, the stars, the Earth, and its natural elements are just as they are and not under the command of any spirit or being. God is life, and all living things are the expression of God's essence, God's spirit within them. And God made living things to best utilize the elements and energy of the Earth and sun. This, his most important and basic message, he did not believe any but a handful of people were able to understand and accept.

Now, as he sat alone in the garden, only the full moon for light, this frustration, the failing on his part to teach people this most basic concept, weighed heavily upon him. And, after all he had said, speaking of all the goodness and beauty in the world, he was to be betrayed by one of his own friends! Consumed by sadness as he sat, several times he fell to his knees, holding his face in his open hands, weeping in powerful, convulsing sobs that racked his body.

He thought of these things, and many others, for hours as he sat alone, quietly, in the garden among the olive trees. Finally, now in want of the company of his friends, he walked back down the path. When he came upon them, he was disappointed to see they were asleep on the ground, resting their heads upon rocks.

"Even this one simple thing I have asked of you, you could not do!" he said loudly, waking James, John, and Peter with a start.

Peter leapt to his feet, his hand on the grip of his sword still in its sheath, looking around quickly for anything of danger. He finally looked at Jesus and understood what was happening. "We are so sorry. It is just that it has been such a tiring day at your side, and you were in the garden for so long. We would have heard anyone approaching."

"And yet, you have not heard. But it does not matter, now. The traitor is here!" and he pointed down the hill.

The others watched in dismay as the light of many torches became clearly visible through the trees, moving toward them. Peter and John stepped forward quickly, in front of Jesus, when the first men came into view. All were armed with swords and clubs, or carrying burning torches, except for one. This one man stepped forward in front of the others.

"Judas!" called James, upon recognizing him. "What is happening? Why have you—" But his voice trailed off.

Judas was not armed, but he stepped forward quickly, directly face-to-face with Jesus. Without a word, he grabbed hold of Jesus on both shoulders. Their eyes met for only a moment, but Jesus saw the look in his eyes, a look that was a strange combination of pain and anger and, yet, excitement and exhilaration at the same time.

Judas leaned forward and kissed Jesus on the cheek.

Instantly, two armed men hurried forward and held Jesus firmly by both arms. He stood still, silent, without a struggle. Other men advanced, swords drawn.

Seeing this, Peter drew his sword and swung at the closest man. Not armed, but carrying a torch, the man tried to avoid the path of the blade. It struck a glancing blow down the side of his head, separating the top of his right ear from his skin. Blood poured from the wound as he yelled in pain and fell to his knees. Others drew their swords, and clubs were raised as the men advanced. James and John drew their swords and raised them in preparation to fight. There was much yelling and confusion.

"Stop!" yelled Jesus. "Put away your swords, all of you!" Only now did he use his strength to pull free. Peter had raised his sword to strike again, but Jesus quickly grabbed his elbow, holding his arm firmly. "Stop it, I say. I will not have any man harmed for my sake!" He turned to the guards who had been holding him and said, "I will go with you. Put away your swords. But, first, let me help this man." With that, Jesus tore off a narrow strip of cloth from the bottom of his toga. He knelt next to the injured man. "Fear not. So you do not lose your ear, let me help you."

The man looked up, his teeth clenched, his face contorted in pain, both hands cupped over his injured ear. He knew of Jesus and what people said of him, so he slowly moved his blood-covered hands. Jesus wrapped the cloth around his head, covering and tightly securing the ear, then said, "When you return to your home, wash this well with warm water and aloe, and wrap it again as I have done. It will heal well if it is cleaned in this way."

When he had finished, the man nodded weakly, still grimacing, and said, "Thank you, Lord. I will do as you suggest."

Jesus stood and freely walked the three steps back to the guards. "Do with me what you must. I will go with you now. There is much I am prepared to give to make people understand the goodness of which I speak. I am even prepared to die if need be. But there is nothing for which I am prepared to kill. Or to have anyone kill while defending me." And even as he spoke these words, he had the vague feeling that he was not speaking complete truth.

Hesitating at first, the two guards took hold of his arms and slowly led him away, out of the garden. Dozens of men followed, torches blazing in the still air of the spring night.

Again Caiaphas asked Jesus, this time his voice higher and louder. "Are you the Son of God?" Caiaphas glared at him, as did other members of the Sanhedrin. Their patience was wearing thin.

"What do you say to this?" one of them yelled in anger.

And, again, Jesus was silent. He stood with his head down, his hands still bound behind him, his feet shackled in iron chains.

For the third time, now leaping to his feet as he shouted, Caiaphas cried, "I say, are you the Son of God?" He pointed in accusation, his finger trembling.

Jesus finally raised his head slowly and looked him in the eye. "I am. As are you. As are all m—"

"As such! He admits it!" one of the council called from the back of the room. "We have all heard it. He admits he is the Son of God!"

"No more!" cried Caiaphas. "We need hear no more! No man can be the Son of God! To think that any man and any woman could create the Son of God insults Him. Insults His very power! His very existence!"

His will crushed and gone from him, his body drained from hunger and thirst having spent the past day and night in prison, Jesus said weakly, "As I have said, all living things are—"

"Silence!" thundered Caiaphas. "You have admitted you believe yourself to be the Son of God, and you have insulted God by doing so. To insult God is blasphemy! And the punishment for blasphemy is death!" Venom dripped from the tone of his voice as he spoke this last word.

Jesus bowed his head in silence as there was a chorus of agreement from the council.

Caiaphas said his final words, ending the hearing. "So is the judgment of this council. Guilty of blasphemy."

With that, several members of the council moved forward and surrounded Jesus. The first one to reach him spat on his face, saliva splattering across Jesus' beard and nose. But he did not flinch, did not blink, did not speak.

"Oh, Son of God, the soles of my feet are most sore," someone else mocked. "Can you not heal them, so I may walk home without pain?" There was a chorus of laughter.

"Yes, my Lord," another council member laughed, "why do you not walk across the Mediterranean and ask the governor of Rome for forgiveness? Or do you need to wait for winter's return, like the rest of us, so it will freeze solid?" There was more laughter.

Two others then spat on him, and someone else shoved him backward while saying, "Why do you not ask your Father to come and help you?"

Through the laughter of the others Caiaphas exclaimed, "Enough of this! Guards! Take him away! Tomorrow he will be taken before Pilate!"

In the judgment hall, Pilate sat surrounded by guards from Rome who were assigned to protect the Governor of Judea as he passed sentence on all prisoners brought before him. As he finished his meal and a chalice of wine, Barabbas, the first prisoner, was in the process of being brought out to stand before him.

"Crime?" he asked one of the guards as he wiped his mouth with fine linen.

The two guards holding him pulled Barabbas gruffly forward to directly face Pilate. As he laid down his napkin, Pilate looked up into wild, black eyes—eyes with no fear, no remorse. With his black, matted hair, long but patchy beard and yellowish brown teeth, Pilate thought Barabbas appeared more like an animal than a man. His muscular arms rippled and strained against the chains that bound him, and the two strong guards held him tightly by the elbows.

"This man has caused numerous disturbances and caused much mischief throughout much of Judea. But, just two days ago, he drank very much wine and strangled one man with his hands and brutally beat two others to their deaths, because they laughed at something he said."

Pilate's eyes narrowed. "Have you anything to say in your defense?" he asked impatiently.

Barabbas leaned his head forward, straining against the chains and guards. In more of a growl than a voice he said, "If I could get free, you would be next." And one of the guards struck him on the back of his head with the handle of his sword, cutting off his threat. Barabbas ducked briefly but quickly straightened, regaining eye contact with Pilate.

"Death by crucifixion," Pilate said calmly, evenly. "Take him away." He turned toward other guards and called, "Next prisoner!"

With Barabbas snarling and fighting them, the guards dragged him to the holding cell in the next hall. Slowly walking past them toward Pilate, led by two guards, was Jesus. His head was lowered, his walk weak and listless, his feet dragging as the chains binding them rattled slowly across the marble floor. The guards positioned him to face Pilate.

Pilate looked up, and his first expression was confusion. "Crime?" he asked one of the guards, though his eyes never moved from Jesus.

"Blasphemy, sir. This man has insulted God by claiming to be His son."

Recognition lit Pilate's face. "Ah, yes. I have heard of this man." He thought a second. "Jesus Christ, is it not?"

Jesus' head remained bowed, and he was silent.

One of the guards pushed at the back of Jesus, indicating he should answer, but Jesus remained silent.

After a few moments the guard finally said, "Yes, sir. It is he."

"I have heard much about you, Jesus. To hear the stories people tell, you should be able to cause those chains to melt and have your freedom. Is this true?" A slight grin curled Pilate's mouth.

Jesus was silent for a moment, then said quietly, without lifting his head, "No man can do such a thing, unless he has a very hot fire."

Still smiling, Pilate said, "Well spoken. But you are not a man, or, apparently, so you have said."

"I am no different from other men."

"Are you not the self-proclaimed king of the Jews?"

Now Jesus looked up at him. "You may believe whatever you desire," was all he said, returning his gaze to the floor.

"So it is, as others have said," smiled Pilate, noticing the expression of complete submission in the blue of his eyes. Unlike with Barabbas, Pilate felt a wave of pity for this man that now stood before him. "But you do not admit this yourself?"

Jesus was silent.

"The crime you have committed is blasphemy for insulting God. Is it true you claim to be the Son of God?"

Jesus was silent, continuing to look down.

"You have nothing to say in your defense?" asked Pilate.

Jesus said nothing.

Pilate's eyes narrowed. "I would be prepared to show you pity if you renounce this claim, to be the Son of God. Will you not do this?"

Jesus said nothing.

Pilate paused for a moment, thinking. He then said, "I have heard tell that you can cure leprosy just by the touch of your hand. You have allowed the lame to walk simply by touching their legs. That all manner of fever can be cured simply by the wave of your hand, if it is your will. That the sound of your voice may allow the deaf to hear. Are all these things true?"

Jesus said nothing.

More confused than before, Pilate looked at him for several moments, studying him, his demeanor, his expression. Then he asked, "Why are you before me, Jesus? Has the Sanhedrin sent you before me in error? Or out of envy of the power and influence you have over the people of Jerusalem?"

Still, Jesus remained silent. He did not move, did not change expression.

"The political and social unrest you are causing is quite clear, though it is my opinion you have not done so of your own desire. People in this territory of Rome seem to be quick with rumor and story. I cannot believe all that I hear, but I have also heard of your kindness and honesty. Can you not even verify this in the least?"

With this, Jesus raised his head again and repeated, "You may believe whatever you desire."

"And what of this crime of blasphemy? Do you deny it?"

Jesus, once again, was silent.

After a long pause, Pilate said, "Very well. In this matter I have no choice but to uphold the conviction of the council of Jewish elders. Guilty of blasphemy."

When he turned to the guard and called for the next prisoner, he was informed that Jesus and Barabbas were the only two to be judged that day.

And when Pilate started to call for the guards to have Jesus join Barabbas in the holding cell, he remembered the Passover celebration in the streets outside the judgment hall. "You may have the will of God with you after all, Jesus. It is customary during Passover to release one prisoner. The choice is to be made by the masses." Then he called to the guards, "Bring Barabbas out. And Jesus. Out to the balcony."

He turned and walked slowly out to the railing that overlooked the streets below. Crowds of people milled about. Musicians played in front of doorways and on street corners. There were carts and tables lining the streets selling food and other wares. When Barabbas and Jesus came out behind him, Pilate addressed the crowds in a thundering voice that projected far out over the streets.

"Good people of Judea! In celebration of Passover, I ask you to aid me in my judgments this day! There are two prisoners before me: Barabbas, the rebel and murderer, and Jesus Christ! I ask in your good faith, whom do you wish for me to set free?" Pilate, still feeling pity for him, but feeling nothing but fear and revulsion for Barabbas, thought, with this introduction, the people would surely call for Jesus to be set free.

But a small group of priests and councilors standing in the street, aware of Jesus and afraid of his power and influence, yelled out quickly and loudly, "Set Barabbas free!" They turned to face the center of the street where most people were milling about and called again, "Jesus must not be allowed to continue to insult God and the good people of Jerusalem any longer!"

There were a few scattered calls of agreement.

"You would have me set a murderer free, instead of Jesus?" asked Pilate.

"Set Barabbas free! Set Barabbas free!" the group of priests called, and soon others called out for Barabbas to be freed.

Pilate looked out over the people, stunned. After listening to the calls for a minute, he raised his hands for silence. Then he asked, "And what should be done with Jesus Christ?"

Instantly, a single call came out, "Crucify him!"

"Why?" asked Pilate, "What crime has he committed to justify such a punishment?"

But a loud chorus began to rise from the crowd, yelling, "Crucify him!"

Pilate shrugged. Motioning to servants, he asked for a bowl of water and clean linen.

"Take note," he called out, symbolically washing his hands in the water, "that I am innocent of this man's blood!" There was a round of calls and yelling from the people in the streets.

After drying his hands, Pilate motioned to have Barabbas released but commanded this be done beyond the walls of the judgment hall.

And he motioned for Jesus to be taken away and prepared for crucifixion. With his head bowed, his postured slumped, his walk slow and shuffling, Jesus was led away by the guards.

CHAPTER TWENTY-ONE

"They think he'll be okay," said Chris, on the phone talking to Kathy. Sara had answered his call, but he quickly asked to talk to Kathy.

"Oh, my ... thank God!" she said, tears welling in her eyes.

"They took out the bullet, and they're stitching him up. He lost some blood, and it nicked his small intestine then embedded in abdominal muscles on the right side of his stomach. They're getting IV antibiotics going now."

"I'll be there as fast as I can," she said. "You're at Hargus Memorial?"

"Right. I think he'll be in the ER for a while, at least until he's stable."

"I'm leaving now. Here's Sara again."

Chris listened to silence for a second, then heard Sara's voice talking firmly to John and Mary. "You have to come in. There's nothing to discuss. Now! 'Bye Kath. Good luck!" Then the receiver rattled, and she picked up. "Chris?"

"Mom!" Mary said in the background.

"Just a minute!" she snapped at her. "Just wait right there for a second!" Then she spoke to Chris, questions pouring out. "What in the world happened? Are you all right? Kathy looked like she just got news of a death in the family. Is Crow all right?"

"Hold on, hold on," said Chris. He waited until she paused, waited an extra couple seconds, and then said coldly, "It was him."

"What the—What did he do?"

"He shot at me. I was talking at the protest. He drove by and just shot wildly at the podium where I was standing. It missed me and hit Crow."

Sara was silent, her mouth hanging open. Then she said stiffly, having trouble speaking, "I ... what ... how is Crow?"

"He'll be okay. It hurt him, but not too serious. He'll have to stay here for a while."

"Thank God," she said quietly.

"What, Mommy?" Chris could hear John in the background.

"Just a minute, would you please," she said to John. "Chris, are you all right?"

"I'm shook up, but I'm not hurt."

"Why is he doing this?"

"I don't know. I still don't even know who he is."

"Didn't they arrest him?" she asked, her fear rising. "Weren't the police there?"

"The police were there, but I don't know if they arrested him."

"What do you mean, you don't know? What happened?"

"I saw Liz jump in her car and chase him, but I don't know if she caught him. I followed the ambulance to the hospital in Crow's truck."

"Come home. Now. Jesus, Chris, I'm scared to death."

"I'm just going to check on Crow for a second, let him know Kathy's coming. Then I'm leaving."

"What about your car? Where is it?"

He had forgotten all about it. "Uh, still where I left it, I guess, on Passemannican Drive. I'll get it later. It's not important now."

"Could you hurry, please," Sara pleaded. "The wind's picking up, and it looks like it could rain any second."

"I'm leaving in a minute. And Sara?"

"What?"

"Stay with the kids, would you please?"

"Count on it."

Chris hurried back down the hallway into the emergency reception lobby and headed through the double doors into the treatment area. A Littleboro police officer stopped him.

"You're Magnuson, right?" he asked.

"Yeah. Chris."

"Can I talk to you for a second? About the shooting?"

Chris hesitated, anxious to talk to Crow and then leave. "I really need to get home to make sure my family is okay. You're more than welcome to come talk to me there in a few minutes."

The officer studied the look in his eyes, then said, "Just one quick question, then we'll catch up with you later."

"Sure."

"Do you know who did the shooting?"

Chris told him what he knew, then said, "But I still have no idea who it is."

"Uh-huh. I'll stick around for a few minutes to talk to," he looked at a page of a small notebook, "Johnson. Henry Johnson. If you remember anything, give the station a call."

"Will do. Thanks." The officer headed back out into the reception area. Chris hurried around the corner then peered through the glass into the operating room. The final stitches were being sewn into Crow, but, after a few moments, he made eye contact with an aid who was cleaning instruments in a sink along the near wall. Asking her with his expression if he could talk to Crow, she held up one figure to indicate "just a second."

"How's he doing?" Chris asked, when she finally came out.

"We just finished dressing the wound. It came back together pretty clean, so there's no reason it shouldn't heal well. We just started the IV, plus a sedative."

"Can I talk to him for a second?"

She hesitated, looking over her shoulder through the glass. "For just a second. When the ileum was lacerated, some chyme leaked out. We were able to clean it and close it effectively, but he's pretty weak. From that, and from the blood loss. And the sedative will take effect quickly, so he'll get pretty drugged up."

"Thanks."

Chris walked through the door into the operating room, the doctor nodding briefly as she passed him. Crow was lying on the table on his back with his eyes closed. "Hey, Crow," Chris said quietly. "You awake?"

Crow turned his head slowly, opened his eyes and forced a smile. "Hey. How'd you get here?"

"I've been here. Waiting. How do you feel?"

"Tired. Weak. Like I'm drunk."

"That's the sedative. I think they want you to sleep for a while."

"Yeah. Uh, Kathy here?"

"She's on her way. You'll be fine, you know. Did they tell you that?"

"Not really. Just 'lay still, this will sting a little,' stuff like that." He closed his eyes.

Chris looked at his massive form, lying still, and thought it was amazing a small, lead ball could injure him enough to keep him down. "Oh, Crow," he said quietly, almost whispering, "I'm so sorry."

He opened his eyes again. "You're sorry? Why are you sorry?"

"He was shooting at me."

"No he wasn't. If it was who I think it was, he was shooting at me."

Chris' jaw dropped. "What?"

"A guy I used to work with. It looked like his truck. If I know him, unfortunately, I do, he probably thinks I had … with him getting fired." He closed his eyes and winced momentarily. "A week or two ago. That would make him mad … to shoot at me. He's the type."

"Crow! That's the guy who knocked over our mailbox. And tried to get Mary into his car!"

"Oh, shit," Crow groaned, his eyes still closed. "Why would he try to hurt your family?"

"I don't know, I just don't know," said Chris, looking away, shaking his head.

"Name is … Hector Torrez. Don't know where he lives. Remember his truck at work. We happened to leave together on some days."

"Torrez, you said?"

He nodded weakly. "Hector. Seems like he's worked there forever."

Chris suddenly felt like a man on a mission. "Listen, I have to go. The police haven't found him yet. But, now, maybe they can catch that bastard when I tell them who he is."

"Be careful, will you?" Crow said, weakly lifting his hand.

Chris took it firmly with both his hands and held it tightly. "I'm sorry this happened. Kathy will be here in a few minutes. I'll see you at home later. I'll just leave your Ford in the driveway."

"Thanks. See you." Crow smiled then closed his eyes. "Watch your ass," was the last thing he whispered.

Chris hurried to the reception area, and before the police officer could turn around Chris said, "Torrez. Hector Torrez."

"What's that?" he said, turning to face him.

"The guy who shot at us is Hector Torrez," said Chris eagerly. "I don't know where he lives or anything, but he used to work at the Gold." He anxiously looked toward the door. "I have to go."

"Thanks," said the officer, writing. "I'll call you at home later."

"Great. Thanks."

Chris ran outside and across the parking lot, noticing the wind was even stronger. He leapt into the Expedition and pulled away just as the first rain drops hit the windshield.

■   ■   ■

"It's raining!" called Sara. "John, get those other toys from the sandbox! Mary, will you help me carry this last chair into the garage?"

"Okay." She hurried over, gusts of wind tossing her hair about. As Dudley watched, sniffing the wind vigorously, Sara lifted the heavy end of the wooden, chaise lounge, but Mary was barely able to hold up the lower end. Together, they walked slowly into the garage and set it down against the back wall. Just as they placed it down, the phone rang.

"Damn it," Sara said between clenched teeth. "That might be Dad again.

Help John with those toys, and come right in. Go ahead, now. Hurry." She motioned her out of the garage toward the sandbox then turned and ran up to the kitchen. Yanking the receiver off the wall, she barked, "Hello?" while straining to peer out the living room window to see if Mary and John were coming back into the house.

"Hi. Sara? Liz Crooks, Littleboro Police."

"Hi, Liz," Sara said quickly. "What can I do for you?"

"Is Chris home yet?"

Outside, a gust of wind blew a small, green, plastic bucket, rolling it across the sand and into the driveway. Clutching an armful of plastic sand toys, John ran awkwardly after it. Just as he reached for it, another gust of wind blew it a few feet farther, onto the grass.

Dudley began barking just as the racing engine became audible. The black truck sped across the front lawn and bounced over the edge of the driveway.

John froze in fear, dropping the toys.

Mary turned to see it and instantly screamed, "Mommy! Mommy!"

Rain began to pelt harder as the driver's door opened. Hector reached out and grabbed John, pulled him into the truck, and slammed the door. Dudley's barking reached a frenetic crescendo, and he strained vigorously against the chain holding him to the tree. The truck backed up onto the road and began speeding away.

Sara, leaping out the door, knocked Mary backward and down the steps as she was running up into the house. Mary fell back hard and landed on her back on the cement, screaming in pain and immediately beginning to cry. Sara screamed a piercing, "NO!" as she leapt over Mary and sprinted across the grass to the street. She ran frantically in the direction the truck was headed, but it accelerated away rapidly, rounding the corner and vanishing from view. "NO!" she screamed again, continuing to run down the street, her eyes wide in terror. But she stumbled and fell and slid to a stop on the wet pavement. At first, she leapt to her feet and started to run again but then stopped and stood there, feeling panicked and helpless. Understanding it was pointless to chase the truck, she turned and hurried back to the house to see if Liz was still on the line. Or to call 911.

And just as she turned, down the middle of the street ran Dudley, bolting by her, trailing a broken length of chain, giving pursuit.

■ ■ ■

Chris was having trouble seeing through the windshield as the wipers slapped away the rain. He was driving as fast as he could to get home as quickly as possible. But the rain and wind were increasing. Thankfully, traffic was thinning since most of the people who were leaving due to the storm had already left. The Expedition handled rougher than it should have, leaning to the left and not cornering very well. He pulled the car off the town road and onto Jefferson Drive, heading toward his neighborhood.

An oncoming car approached rapidly, headlights cutting through the rain, making it even harder for Chris to see. As it came closer, just before it passed, he saw the pair of yellow fog lights on the roof.

His blood ran cold.

He turned to look as it passed but couldn't see inside the cab. Rain and condensation clouded both his window and the windows of the truck. Slamming on his brakes, his mind became a confused mass of speculation, thinking of a hundred things that could have happened and a hundred more about what he should do.

Then, appearing in the rain about two hundred yards behind the truck, running at full speed, was Dudley.

Instantly, Chris' heart thundered in his chest. "No," he whispered. "Please, God. No." For a split second he was frozen, confused, too over-whelmed to react.

Then, it became all too clear. Dudley would only chase the truck for one reason.

Chris screamed, "My GOD!"

His foot pounded the accelerator to the floor, and he yanked the wheel hard to the left. The right wheels bounced over the curb as the Expedition reversed direction, the front tire spinning momentarily in mud. Chris pulled the lever for the four-wheel drive to engage, and the wheels instantly grabbed the pavement and gravel and propelled the car headlong with a forward thrust. Chris' right foot was still on the floor.

Rapidly, he gained speed, the engine whining in protest. His eyes were fixed on the blurring taillights that now rounded a corner to the left and off Jefferson Drive. Soon he had caught up with Dudley. Chris looked down at his dog as he passed, galloping at full stride, splashing through collecting puddles. He was soaking wet, his fur matted in clumps, his mouth open and tongue hanging out, swinging freely as he ran. Chris considered slowing to pick him up but, instead, continued to accelerate, reaching the corner and cutting it close to the inside curb, barely slowing at all.

At the red light on Route 14 at the bottom of the hill, the truck slowed to turn right. Chris rapidly approached, closed the distance between them, and came up directly to its bumper. In the beam of his headlights, silhouetted through the window covered with condensation, he saw a small figure moving back and forth, and the arm of the driver reach out and pull the figure down.

"Oh, my God. John," he uttered through a constricted throat. His entire body tensed. "You son of a bitch," he growled.

Jamming the transmission into park, he kicked open the door and leapt out into the rain, running to the truck. Just as it was beginning to move forward again, Chris grabbed the driver's door handle and pulled the door open, crying, "John! John!"

"What the fuck?" Hector said. "Where did you—Get out of here!"

"Daddy!" came a terrified cry from inside the truck. "Help! He's hurting me!"

Hector accelerated more rapidly and Chris' left arm, still clutching the door handle, was pulled hard, feeling as if it was being tore from its socket. "Hold on!" he screamed in pain, having to release the handle as the truck sped away, the door slamming closed again. "No!" he cried, stumbling forward a few steps.

Blinded by rage, clothes now soaking him to the skin, Chris ran back, jumped into the Expedition, and pounded the shift back into drive, flooring the accelerator again. Now the truck was speeding away much faster, and even though the tachometer of the Expedition was close to red-lining as the transmission hurtled through each gear, Chris couldn't make up the distance between the two vehicles.

The truck sped through a red light, continuing north. Chris didn't even notice there was a light as he kept his foot to the floor. "John. John," he repeated over and over, tears welling in his eyes, making it harder to see.

Rain battered the windshield, and a distant flash of lightning illuminated everything with a blue-white flash of strobe light. Dusk was falling, unnoticed, above thick, gray clouds.

■　■　■

"Sit the fuck down, you shithead!" Hector screamed, pushing John away.

"Daddy!" he called, standing up on the seat, trying to look back through the window. "Daddy!"

Hector pulled John down and pounded on his back with his right fist as he spoke each angry word, "I—said—sit—down!"

"Ow—ow—ow—" John cried, grimacing with each word. But he didn't cry out on the last hit, even though it was harder than the first three. He wasn't crying now, and, suddenly, he wasn't afraid. He lifted his head up slowly and turned his eyes to look at Hector, to look at this bad stranger. He remembered something his father had told him. "Don't hit me any more," he said evenly, with cold anger.

"What? Fuck you, you little faggot," Hector hissed, incredulous, pounding his back again.

John flinched momentarily, but quickly straightened. Slowly getting to his knees on the seat, then to his feet, he said, "Don't—hit—me—again!" and he leapt at Hector, grabbing the steering wheel and yanking it with his full weight.

■　■　■

Chris saw the truck suddenly swerve to the right, bounce hard over the stone-laden shoulder, and careen into a grove of pine trees lining the road. It skidded momentarily on pine needles and mud and slammed to a stop against one of the trees. Another flash of lightning washed everything in a bright glare as he swerved and slid to a stop with his headlights showing full beam on the truck. As he quickly opened his door, inside the truck he saw thrashing movements, diffused shadows through the condensation on the back window of the cab. Who was where or doing what was completely indiscernible. As Chris was running the few steps, in an instant, from inside the truck there were two bright flashes simultaneous with a muffled *pop-pop*. Just for a second, he was confused.

Then, he understood. He tried to scream, but his fear of the absolute worst strangled him.

When he pulled the door of the truck open, Hector was turned away from him, and Chris couldn't see John. "You bastard!" Chris screamed, grabbing Hector's left arm. But Hector quickly pulled away, the speed and strength surprising Chris.

For a second, in the raw glare of the headlights from behind, their eyes met.

Evil. The empty, cold, satisfied look in Hector's eyes was evil.

Chills knifed though Chris' spine.

"John!" he screamed, as he lunged into the truck. "John, are you okay?"

But Hector pushed him away, first with his left forearm, then with his left leg. "Fuck you, faggot!"

Chris lunged again, but Hector put both legs out to deflect his charge and sent him sprawling on his back, splashing and sliding into the mud.

Hector quickly leaned to his right and lifted John off the seat, pulled him across in front of him, and threw him out the door. John tumbled limp through the air like a rag doll.

"John!" screamed Chris, struggling to get up and reaching up to catch him. His hands grabbed John at arms' length, and he quickly pulled his son to him, saying, "John! Are you all right?"

There was no answer.

Chris felt it first, warmth running over his hands and down his arms. Holding John up into the light, he saw his eyes were half open but not looking at him. And his little chest was blown open, a tangle of cloth, skin and shattered ribs, blood soaking the entire area.

"NO! JOHN! NO!" His jaw locked, his tongue quivered, tears poured from his eyes, lost in the rain. Chris tightly clutched his dead son's body to his chest, lying in the mud in the rain, his anger and strength diffused. His mind now was a tangled mass of terror and dread.

"I just wanted to make sure you saw him before you go to join him." Now Hector was over them with the pistol pointed directly at Chris' face. A flash of lightning reflected the gleaming wet metal of its short barrel.

"Why?" Chris said weakly. "Why are you doing this?" He clutched John's body tighter.

"Why. You ruined my fucking life, that's why. I didn't understand a fucking thing you said, but you kept me from getting a better job, then made me lose the one I had. Ever since then, my life is a fucking nightmare." Hector leaned closer. "Anyway, fuck that. I sure got nothing to lose now."

Chris' face was contorted in confusion. When he tried to speak, his jaw only quivered. Hector pulled back the hammer of the pistol with his thumb. It clicked into position. He moved it closer, straightening his aim, closing one eye. Chris was paralyzed with fear. Holding John tightly, he closed his eyes, whispering, "God, no. Please. Why?"

Hector's finger tightened on the trigger.

Dudley leapt from the darkness at full speed, his teeth clamping on Hector's right forearm. He snarled deeply and shook his head, ripping the skin on Hector's arm.

"Ahhhh! What the fuck!" Hector squealed, stumbling back. Reaching up for Dudley, he grabbed a fistful of fur on his neck. "Get the ... Owwww!" Hector managed to hold onto the gun, knocking Dudley away. The snarling dog rolled over quickly and leapt again, knocking Hector down, scrambling on top of him, snarling and snapping at his neck and face.

"No ... ahhh ... shit." Hector struggled, keeping Dudley at length with his left forearm. He tried to work his right hand, holding the gun, underneath the dog, but couldn't. Dudley clamped down hard on the skin of his forearm again, and Hector yelped in pain.

Still in shock, Chris didn't realize fully what was happening. Then he became more aware and said, quietly at first, "Good boy, Dudley." And then, quickly but gently, he laid John to the side and rose to his feet. First to a crouch and then slowly to standing, calling, "That-a-boy, Dud!" He took a step toward them.

But Hector had grabbed the front of the base of Dudley's neck, holding him at arms' length. Bending his right elbow, he brought the gun in front of Dudley's face. Snarling and snapping, he tried to bite Hector's hand holding the gun. When Dudley's open mouth was momentarily in front of the barrel, Hector pulled the trigger.

The top of Dudley's head blew open in a shower of blood, teeth, and bone, killing him instantly.

The shot caused Chris to flinch and duck again as Hector knocked the limp body of the dog off of him. Before Chris could move any closer, he had the pistol raised quickly, pointed to the center of Chris' chest. As he stood he said, "Now. Finally. See you in hell, shithead."

Surprised by the quickness of Hector's movements and by the pistol aimed at him, Chris froze again. Then he realized, just for that second, that he didn't care. Tears still flowed from his eyes as he raised and spread his arms, not moving.

Hector pulled the trigger.

The hammer slammed on an empty chamber. Hector glanced at the gun, then pulled the trigger again. Same result.

Quickly, he pulled the trigger six more times, and each time there was a hollow click.

Laughing, he flipped the gun at Chris, bouncing it off his chest harmlessly. Then Hector jumped through the open door of his truck. He jammed it into reverse and pulled away from the tree, leaving a broken piece of grill embedded in the bark. With the tires spinning just for a second in the mud, he was able to maneuver between two trees and swerve back around onto Route 14, accelerating northward.

Chris was left standing in the mud, pelted by rain and wind, his dead dog to his left, his dead son to his right.

He collapsed to his knees and wept bitterly.

CHAPTER TWENTY-TWO

Chris' clothes were heavy with water as he knelt in a crumpled heap in the mud. Rain rolled in heavy sheets from his hair and shoulders, a steady stream dripped from his nose. Now the wind increased in strength and was more sustained, howling from the northeast, hissing and whooshing through the pine boughs above him.

It grew from deep inside him.

He remembered. Remembered everything he had ever heard, ever read, ever experienced. The stupidity, the hatred, the pointless destruction of what was good; the arbitrary division of the Earth by the ill-found thoughts of men; the fragmentation of everything living, of the society of mankind—to the point where the differences between groups became more important than any good common bonds or goals.

His eyes lifted slowly at first, then higher until he saw his dead son, covered in rain, in mud, in blood.

And he hated.

He hated everything that had been wrong before, and that was wrong now.

Most of all, he hated the man who had killed his beautiful son.

Chris' rate of breathing increased, slowly at first. His head raised fully, and, soon, he was on his feet, every muscle in his body tensed. His brow was lowered into an angry wedge, his teeth clenched tightly, his hands curled into fists. Yet gently, gingerly, he picked up the body of John, opened the back door of the Expedition and laid him on the seat. There was a blanket curled up in a heap in the back cargo area. Chris pulled it forward then gently covered John, tucking it in around the sides to secure him underneath. After closing the door, he deliberately, tensely slid in behind the wheel and put the Expedition into drive. He accelerated slowly at first, then more rapidly. The tires grabbed and pulled the car around and back onto Route 14, heading north. Then Chris pounded his foot to the floor, and kept it there.

There were no other cars on the road. The rain was blinding, and it was all but dark, the dusk made night by the storm. The high beams of the Expedition reflected back off the rain, making it harder to see.

But Chris was unaware it was hard to see. He was blinded by tears. Tears of anger and hate, of numbing sorrow. He didn't know where Torrez had gone, or how far, but he kept his foot to the floor and drove on.

Route 14 divided, the main road curving to the northwest, with 14A heading more straight and to the east. At the last second, Chris yanked the wheel to the right, the wheels gripping the pavement and pulling the car around the curve. Chris dipped even further downward as the car sagged on the worn springs, leaning to the left. John's body slid across the seat and thumped against the door. Gaining speed, Chris soon had the car going eighty-five miles per hour through the rain on the narrow, two-lane road. His knuckles were white on the steering wheel, his legs tensed, his back hunched slightly forward, his head leaning over the steering wheel.

A faint pair of taillights became visible through the rain. Chris gained on them as rapidly as he could. The road curved to the right, then sharply to the left, and the right wheels of the Expedition clattered over gravel on the shoulder before Chris could yank the wheel hard to the left and recover. Only the double, yellow line was visible in the glare of the headlights. His gaze locked on it as he turned the wheel, left, right, left again. But always, his foot heavy on the gas pedal.

The distance decreased between the two cars until Chris' headlights shown brightly on the tailgate of the truck. His grip tightened on the wheel, his heart raced faster, his teeth clenched, the muscles of his jaw knotted beneath his beard.

Suddenly, the truck accelerated faster, jets of blue smoke shooting from the tail pipe.

Chris tried to accelerate, but the distance between the cars widened. The road snaked along another series of curves. Chris was able to drive through the curves faster than the truck, making up the distance between the two.

Chris accelerated with a rapid burst, and the front end of the Expedition slammed into the rear bumper of the truck with a metallic thud. There was a brief burst of sparks, and pieces of plastic and glass sprayed over the hood and tinkled up over the windshield. The headlight on his side died suddenly, and now only one beam was left to help him see. Chris fought to keep the Expedition straight and maintain its speed as it wavered from the shock wave of the collision. Blue-white lightning exploded above, blinding him for a second.

The distance between the cars lengthened again. Suddenly, the truck braked hard, the rear end swerving forward and to the left. Chris braked as well, maintaining a straight course in the center of the road as the tires skidded but held their direction. As the truck slowed, it cut hard to the right and drove off the road, over the shoulder, down an embankment into darkness. But Chris was able to follow, pulling hard to the right and giving the

Expedition gas again. It bounced down a steep hill, bushes and branches scraping at glass and metal, the beam of the headlight dancing wildly as he drove over rocks and logs. The taillights of the truck were visible just ahead, bouncing through the rain. It cut to the right, around a tree, and back left, just missing a huge boulder. When the trees thinned for a distance, the two cars accelerated, driving unimpeded for several hundred yards. Chris followed closely, not able to pull alongside, but not falling behind.

The truck slid on mud as it turned right to avoid a small cluster of trees that were suddenly blocking its path. The left rear fender slammed hard into the biggest, closest tree, sending a shudder through the truck bed. The tree was jolted hard, water falling in a burst from its branches, scattering in the wind. The impact bent the wheel there, jamming it into the axle, disengaging it from the drive shaft. When Hector tried to drive, the mechanism slipped, and the drive shaft spun uselessly, falling from its housing and spinning in the mud.

Chris accelerated while maneuvering the Expedition, aiming directly for the door on the passenger's side. He slammed into the side of the truck, his arms absorbing the impact as the airbag burst open in front of him, buffering him from the windshield. As the hood accordioned and the airbag deflated, he recoiled back into the seat. The engine died instantly, the remaining headlight going black.

Now he threw open the door and leapt out, quickly running around the open door and scrambling over and through the bed of the truck. Instinctively, without seeing it, he grabbed a long, thin, heavy object on the floor of the bed as his hand reached down to maintain his balance. A crowbar.

Hector had opened his door and was starting to run around to the front of the truck. Chris jumped from the bed, darted between the open truck door and the trees and with a leap and quick plant of his feet, swung the crowbar. It clipped Hector's left elbow, and he cried out, staggering to his right. Chris shuffled forward and swung again, the metal landing full force across his left shoulder blade. The bone there shattered and Hector stumbled and slid in the mud and pine needles, his left arm flopping limply as he fell to his back. Now many yards away from the truck, the two men were just in the outer fringes of the headlight beams.

Without a word, without a sound, Chris was on top of him. He lifted the crowbar and swung down hard, but Hector was able to catch it with his extended right hand. They struggled with it, yanking and pulling, until Hector was able to pull it away. He tried to swing while lying on his back, but Chris caught his arm. They tugged and pushed until Hector released his grip and the bar was flung several feet away into darkness. Another brief flash of lightning gave the glow of midday.

Hector struggled to defend himself with his only good arm as Chris' fists began pounding. Blinded by anger, by hate, unthinking, unseeing, he pounded. He saw nothing, felt nothing as his fists worked, up—down—up—down—up, again and again. Hector parried the first few blows, uttering a muffled cry, rolling his head from side to side as he flinched. But the next fist down shattered his mouth, cutting off his cry. He was swallowing teeth and blood as the next fist hit his right eye, and he saw a bright flash as it went blind.

Chris pounded. Pounded. Pounded. Up and down. Again and again and again. His fists were covered with blood, cut and bruised from jagged edges of teeth and bone. Hector had stopped struggling and gone limp. Chris still pounded.

■　■　■

Minutes later, exhausted, now starting to feel the pain from the cuts on his hands, Chris slowly crawled off the body of Hector and knelt in the mud.

"Oh, God," he said quietly aloud, "what's happened?" He buried his face in his arms. "Oh God ... Why?"

He remembered it all again. Crow. Dudley. John. "Oh, no, no. John."

He lifted his eyes slowly skyward, to the rain, to the wind, and saw a golden glow above him through the tops of the trees that bowed and swayed in the wind.

The Gold. He was in the woods, near the bottom of the hill below the main entrance to the casino.

Slowly, he stood and walked to the Expedition, but knew it couldn't be driven anymore. John was still wrapped in the blanket but, now, on the floor in front of the back seat. Gathering him up carefully, making sure he was secure in the bundle, Chris picked up John and began walking. Occasionally, lightning helped him to see, but he stumbled several times as he walked through the darkness toward the gold light on the hill.

■　■　■

Sara had hurried back to the house and called 911. Though Mary had landed on her back on cement, she wasn't hurt except for a couple of bruises.

A burly officer with a dark complexion and black mustache, Eric Murphy, had come over and was asking her everything she knew about what had happened. She sat nervously in the living room on the sofa with Mary clinging to her. Murphy asked who this guy was, what had he done this time, that time, what did they see, did they know anything else?

The phone in his belt rang. He pulled it out. "Murphy."

He listened briefly. "Okay, thanks. Yeah. Right." He hung up and looked at Sara. His expression had changed.

"What?" she asked, her fear rising again. Panic edged her voice. "What happened?"

"They found your dog. The collar and tag with your name and address were still on him."

"What happened? What do you mean, 'still on him?'"

Murphy looked away. "He's dead. It looks like he's been shot."

"NO!" screamed Mary. "Dudley!"

"Oh, no." Sara covered her mouth with one hand and pulled Mary closer, and she buried her face against Sara's blouse. "What about John? Have they found him?" Then her tone changed to anger. "Why can't you stop this creep? Where's my son?"

"There was no sign of him. There were a lot of tire tracks and some foot prints around where your dog was found, but it was too muddy to tell what kind of cars were there, or even how many. It looks like whoever they were went north on 14. There's a unit following it up now."

"Damn it!" she snarled, leaning forward. "Why is this guy still running around loose?" Then she looked away, toward the front door, and said to herself, "Where is Chris? Damn it."

Murphy looked at her thoughtfully. "Look, I can't stay here. The wind's starting to knock out power here and there, and it'll only get worse. There's already flooding over the west bank of the Chelsea in the center of town." He shook his head slowly. "It's going to be a hell of a night."

"What?" Sara gasped. "My son's been kidnapped ... and ... and you're worried about a power outage?"

"Look! I'm sorry! I can't do anything right now!" Murphy snapped, his nerves frayed from an already demanding day and the prospect of a tougher night. "The other unit is following up. If there's anything to find out, or anything to do, they'll take care of it. I've got to get downtown."

"What are we supposed to do? We don't even have a gun! What if he comes back?" She clutched Mary.

Murphy thought a second. "Kidnapping is a federal offense. In most cases the FBI gets involved. When it's determined to be a life-threatening situation they get involved as quick as possible. What I strongly suggest to you—no, I insist that you come with me right now and I'll drop you off at the station on my way downtown."

"No! My husband doesn't even know yet, there's—"

"Look!" Murphy cried, his voice edged in anger. "I'm not asking you. This is a police and a federal matter. I'm bringing you to the station right now. You can tell everything you know to an officer there. And if we can get the local federal guy to come out in this storm, he can start on it right away from their end. And, besides all that, it'll be safer for the both of you."

Sara understood the logic of what Murphy was saying. "Yeah," she said, nodding, "We'll go with you now. But I've got to let my husband know. He still doesn't know anything about this. How am I supposed to do that?"

"You don't know when he'll be back?"

"I thought he'd be home half an hour ago."

"You can call him here when you get to the station, if he comes home between now and then. Or just leave him a note. Or do both."

"That's a good idea. I'll leave him a note, now, and I'll call here when we get to the station. Should we follow you in our car?"

Murphy stood from the chair. "With this storm, why don't you ride in the back of the cruiser. That would be simpler. Your husband can come get you later, since he'll need to come down and talk to the federal guy anyway."

Sara stood, gently setting Mary down on the sofa. "All right. Let me write the note and then we'll go."

"I'll be in the cruiser," said Murphy. "I've got some radio calls to make to the other units."

Sara stepped closer and looked him in the eye. "Find this bastard, would you please," she growled. "And find my son."

"With your help, we will," he said, and turned and walked down the stairs and out the front door.

She watched him walk out, and then thought to herself, where in the name of God is Chris?

■   ■   ■

The golden glow from the roof of the casino now seemed to be directly overhead, but was still mostly a blur through the driving rain, high above him on the hill. Branches at face level clawed across Chris' face, leaving red trails of broken skin on his right cheek. He flinched momentarily but continued, stumbling forward. Clutching John wrapped in the blanket tightly to his chest made walking more difficult, unable to swing his arms for balance. And the ground was uneven and wet. His feet often landed at a different level than he expected, jamming his ankles or hips awkwardly. Several times he stepped on loose mud or wet, lichen-covered rocks, slipping and buckling to his knees. Once his feet flew completely out from under him as wet dirt and moss gave way. He landed flat on his back, but still managed to keep John from falling to the mud. And the only time he could see well was during random one-second intervals whenever the sky was pierced by a jagged tine of lightning. Though he had only walked a few hundred yards, it seemed endless to him as he dragged through the woods, numb and unthinking. His clothes were heavy with water, as was the bundle he carried. Moving toward the light, somehow, he knew there would be help there.

He was walking up an incline when more lights became visible. Smaller, point sources of light, dancing in and out of moving tree branches. Then he realized they were from houses and he was standing on the edge of a road. Turning left, still he continued heading for the light from the Gold, now just ahead.

There was a car parked on the edge of the road to the right. As he came upon it, a wave of recognition swept through him. His Toyota! Still where he had left it in the afternoon. He thought, was that today? It seems like a lifetime ago.

Seeing the car ignited a spark of cognition in his mind. He remembered, rationally. I'm carrying my dead son, and I need to tell someone, bring him to a hospital, something. I've killed a man. I need to tell the police that, tell them where Torrez is. And Crow's been shot.

Sara. Oh God. She doesn't know anything about this. Maybe that Torrez had John, and nothing else. I've got to tell Sara.

Panic and dread crept back into his mind. Tears formed again, but he fought them. He had to take care of too many things now. He had to get home. But how?

His keys! He felt his right front pocket through his jeans. They were still there, where they always were. With difficulty, he slipped them out of his wet pants while still holding John, and unlocked the doors. As rain beat on his back, he laid John in the back seat.

He started the car and turned it around in the road, driving slowly, anxiously towards his home.

■ ■ ■

"What if Daddy doesn't see the note?" asked Mary, struggling into her nylon windbreaker.

"If I leave it on the table where we usually put notes, he might not see it. I'll tape it up somewhere more obvious," said Sara, sitting at the dining room table, finishing writing.

"The rain will wash it off the door, won't it?"

"Yeah, it will. He'll probably come in through the front door, like he always does. I'll tape it just inside the door, on the edge of the handrail going up. He'll see it there."

"What does it say? Did you tell him about John getting taken?"

"No!" Sara snapped, then realized how loud she had said it. "Oh, I'm sorry, Honey," she apologized. "I'm so upset I can't even think straight. No, I don't want to tell him that in a note. I just said we're out and we'll call him back in a few."

"Why isn't he home already?"

"I don't know what could've happened. Maybe the storm is blocking roads. That policeman said there was some flooding already."

"How will you know when he gets here?"

"We'll just keep calling until he answers," she said. "We'd better go. He's waiting for us in the police car." She folded the paper and wrote on the outside, in big, block letters, *Chris*. Then she tore a piece of cellophane tape from the dispenser on the table, hurried down the stairs and taped the note to the railing. Coming back upstairs, pulling a jacket out of the closet, she said, "Are you ready?"

"I've been ready."

"Then let's go."

Mary followed as Sara hurried down the stairs. When she opened the front door, a burst of wind and rain hit her in the face, causing her to flinch. She had to grab the door with both hands to hold it open. Over the wind, she called, "Go ahead! You hurry through and get in the police car!"

Mary stepped forward to the door, the rain and wind lashing at her, and hesitated only a second before lowering her head and running toward the car parked in the driveway. About halfway to it she let out a squeal as the rain soaked her, but she continued as Murphy jumped out of the driver's seat and yanked open the back door. She jumped in the seat, and Murphy waited a few seconds for Sara to follow, slamming the door behind her and jumping back in behind the wheel.

After Mary had run past her out the front door, Sara had pulled it closed, but a stronger gust of wind had kept her from closing it all the way. With one final pull, it had finally slammed closed and locked. She then turned and quickly followed Mary to the car.

The closing door had deflected the strong gust of wind to the right and up the stairs slightly, carrying a rush of rain with it. The note on the railing had flipped up, exposing the underside of the tape to the rain. When the adhesive got wet, its grip gave way. The note came loose, fluttering and darting downward, landing on the bottom step at the entrance to the family room downstairs. Sara's handwritten *Chris* was face down on the carpeting.

■   ■   ■

As Chris drove, his mind was a plethora of disjointed thoughts. His dead son was in the back seat. How would he tell Sara and Mary? What would he say? Mary's little brother was gone. So was her dog, his head blown off. And Hector was dead. After all Chris tried to say about love, he had killed a man. His mind had gone completely blank, and all he could feel was hate. Not that Chris could have controlled himself. And why the hell was Hector doing all those things to his family? That was the cause of it all. Whatever were Hector's intentions, only he knew the reasons. And now Chris probably would never know. He had killed Hector, and that was something he would have to deal with for the rest of his life.

Lightning flashed across the sky, cracking thunder following two seconds later. Chris realized he was in his neighborhood and that he had got there without ever paying attention to the road, even with the rain and wind. He pulled the Toyota into his driveway and parked at the end of the walk leading to the front door. Leaving John in the back seat, he ran up the steps. At first he was surprised by the locked front door but then realized Sara should be keeping it locked. She thinks Hector is still driving around, he thought, as he found the right key and unlocked the door.

"Sara!" he called in a weak and cracking voice as he stepped in. "Sara! Mary! Where are you guys?" The lights were mostly turned off, except for the light over the kitchen sink, the one they always kept on, and the hall light at the top of the stairs. His heart sank as he began to realize they weren't in the house. "Sara!" He ran quickly upstairs, to the kitchen, down the hall, looking in each bedroom. "Sara! Mary!" His pace quickened, and a wave of panic swept over him. "Oh, please be here." Now running, he hurried downstairs into the family room, calling again, never noticing that he stepped on a piece of paper at the bottom of the stairs. Then into the furnace area, and the storage closet. He ran back upstairs and outside, and looked in the garage. "Sara!" he called in panic, on the verge of tears, when he saw the van was still there. "No! Where are they?" he said aloud. Could Hector have got to them, too, he thought. Oh, no. No. Where else could they be?

More panicked, he ran through the house again, this time searching more carefully. Looking under furniture, in closets, even in the crawlspace attic. Searching for Sara and Mary, expecting to find them in a state where they couldn't have heard his calls. Searching for their bodies.

When he didn't find anything, he became even more confused with increasing dread. He slowly walked out to the Toyota, not noticing the rain that continued to soak him, picked up John, and carried him carefully into the house. Chris walked upstairs and down the hall, entering John's room. Kneeling, he gently laid him in his own bed, adjusting and smoothing the blanket as though he was tucking him in for the night. He gently kissed John's forehead.

Chris was suddenly overcome by an all-consuming feeling of loneliness. Not knowing where his wife and daughter were, and looking at John laying there, he collapsed, falling to the floor and weeping loudly. Again, all that had happened ran through his mind in a blinding confusion of fragmented thought. As he cried, the tears pouring out freely, he lay in a crumpled heap on the floor. He agonized over why this all had to happen. Why John? Why did he have to be killed? If there was only some way to get him back. If only I had known how serious it was all becoming, I could have done things differently, done something to prevent it.

"Oh God!" he yelled aloud. "My God!" An exultation consumed him, and he leapt to his feet, his heart instantly thundering in his chest. His eyes flew open wide, and his mouth hung agape. Confused at first about what to do, he quickly remembered the advisement rosters for his classes of the past semester. Running to his room, he unzipped his pack of school papers and flipped through to the correct, inside pocket. He pulled out the sheet he was looking for and scanned down through the names and phone numbers listed.

MacIntyre, Margaret Lisa ... 327-7717

He picked up the phone and dialed.

Chapter Twenty-Three

he crushing weight of the enormously heavy wood ran across his shoulder and down his back. The bottom of it dragged on the dirt road, grinding in the sand and across gravel. Any small stone or wheel rut it dragged across brought him completely to a halt, causing him to stagger and sway. Three times he fell, but guards, or the people they ordered that stood nearby, helped him back to his feet. Thorns digging into his forehead and scalp had previously opened gaping wounds from which blood had poured freely, leaving thick crusting streaks of scarlet angling down his face and neck. Though his body was wracked by the stress of his physical exertion, he was so dehydrated that sweat no longer could cool him. His mind was a blinding frenzy of confusing thoughts. People he passed along the road often spat at him, yelled insults, threw stones. Only a few offered words of pity or thanks. But for the most part, he was unaware they were there.

Except for one. A beautiful woman, weeping openly, her long, dark hair flying wildly as she followed along most of his path, working her way through the throngs of people.

"Jesus!" she cried often, though only once he actually heard her.

That one time he recognized the voice and was able to lift his head enough to make eye contact with her. She stopped and knelt so he could better see her, and she even managed to force a smile, hoping it would please him.

"Why have they done this to you?" she whispered, tears flowing freely.

Though he didn't hear her words, he recognized the face, and remembered. The beautiful face he loved so much to look upon, the only face he had ever kissed, the face of the only woman to whom he had allowed himself the luxury of physical love. He vaguely remembered he could have been her husband, and for a fleeting second he wondered how his life would have been different had he done so.

But the crack of a guard's whip stung his back, and he flinched and closed his eyes. And she was gone from him. He tried to walk again, staggering forward, managing to keep his balance and move on.

Still on her knees, she reached for him, but he passed by. She was unable to follow as the throngs of people thickened on either side.

An old man standing behind her soon helped her to her feet, saying, "You know this man?"

Through tears, not looking at him, Mary said, "I love this man."

"What crime has he committed to be put through such punishment?"

Mary sobbed heavily, trying to catch her breath. Soon she said, "He is too beautiful a person, that is his only crime. He tried to love all people, too much, too completely. More than anyone can understand."

The old man just looked at her in confusion.

Though it was difficult, Mary tried to follow Jesus through the noise and confusion all around her.

The dull, iron spikes felt as if they were tearing the hands from his arms as they ripped through skin and muscle, crushing and separating bones. Blood pored out the wounds, drenching the splintering wood. Still, he did not cry out in pain. He was barely aware when they were doing the same to his feet.

The cross was hoisted into the hole on the top of the small hill and secured upright, guards and attendants working to fill in dirt and pile stones around its base.

He drifted in and out of consciousness as the searing pain in his hands and feet gradually gave way to a dull burning. More from the dehydration and complete fatigue than from the pain, he quickly weakened. It became more difficult to keep his head up, his eyes open. Occasionally, he was vaguely aware of activity below him, but his senses were all but gone from him. He was unable to comprehend who was there or what they said.

On the ground, people stood and stared, coming and going. Some spat, but he was too high to reach. Others threw stones until a friend or guard chased those people away.

A few stayed very close to him, all morning.

"Mary!" said Jesus' mother, seeing Mary of Magdala sitting on rocks just below the crest of the hill. She stood and ran to her, and they embraced deeply, holding each other for several seconds.

"Oh, you must be broken with grief," said Mary, "to see this done to your son."

His mother could only shake her head and bite her lip, staring at the horrible image of her son on the cross. Dark clouds were forming in the sky above them. A bolt of lightning flashed in the distance behind the hill.

Finally, his mother spoke in broken sentences, cracked with emotion. "I have loved him always, Mary. Even before he was delivered to us, I loved him. But I have not been able to understand most of his life. He has been so different, what he has said, what he has done. I have not understood most of it."

"But surely you understand that he is a great and beautiful man. You must have been aware of this." Mary paused for a second, carefully examining the mother of Jesus. "And more than any one person, you must have influenced him to become the man he is."

"But I have not," she insisted. "He was as such before he came to us. I have watched him grow to manhood, but it seemed he was already the person he was to become."

Mary from Magdala considered this, and understood.

"But this," his mother continued. "I … he …" And she collapsed into tears again. Mary embraced her.

A crack of thunder tore Jesus from unconsciousness. He lifted his head, and for a few seconds he had clarity of thought. He looked to his mangled hands but could not feel them, his own weight draining the remaining blood and feeling from his arms. His breathing was spastic as each attempt to fill his lungs became a greater effort.

But, at that moment, he remembered. He remembered everything.

And with the breath left in his lungs he cried, "Oh God, when will we stop this? When will we understand the love You have given us?" And his head slumped back to unconsciousness.

"Did you hear?" said Mary of Magdala, pulling away and looking up to the cross. "He spoke!" She stepped quickly over the stones and stood directly below the cross, looking up. "Jesus? Jesus? Did you speak? Can you hear us?"

His mother soon came up behind her. "What did he say?"

She had heard it clearly. "After all they have done to him, after all the misunderstanding and pain, still, what he asked of God was, why do not people love. Not about why this has happened to him, nor for help for himself. Still, his thoughts are with the people who are to live after him—" Emotion overcame her, and she began crying again.

His mother did not fully understand what Mary had just said, but moved closer to the cross and looked up. The sky was darkening rapidly, lightning was closer, louder, more frequent. Wind was gusting now, blowing dirt and dead grass across the ground and over the hill.

"Son?" Mary said weakly. "Jesus?" But his head remained slumped against his chest, and the wind made her voice no louder than a whisper.

Mary of Magdala raised her head and spoke to her. "He was most wise, Mary. Your son was aware. Aware of too many things. He spoke of things that most people could not understand."

Mary looked down at her. In confusion she said, "But he spoke mostly of love. And of God."

"Yes," she said, "these are the things people do not understand." She lifted her head to look upon the dying man nailed to the cross, ridiculed and misunderstood. "But he did," was all she finally said.

On the cross, Jesus died quietly, the blood, the water, the spirit of life drained from him.

The sky blackened. The intensity of the storm grew and consumed the land. Wind gusted, rain drove in pelting torrents that flooded the ground. Violently, lightning flashed and thundered, incessantly, illuminating the dead man hanging in the middle of the raging storm.

CHAPTER TWENTY-FOUR

As they had arranged over the phone, Chris stood just inside the front door of Lennon Hall, waiting for Margaret. The building and the entire campus were essentially devoid of people. Students, faculty, and maintenance people would have been sparse anyway between semesters, but Jeremy bearing down on the inland counties of central New England kept everyone either inside or evacuated from the area. As Chris watched, the wind howled through the trees, the boughs and branches bending and heaving in the gusts that were now sustained over seventy miles per hour. Rain thrashed at the front of the building and on the pavement of the campus street and parking lot. Deep, collecting puddles in any depressions of the previously parched lawn splattered and danced as the rain shattered their surface. The lamps along the walks and narrow driveways shown as nothing more than dim flecks of light hidden by rain blowing sideways, occasionally washed out by a bright flash of lightning.

Part of Chris was numb, part of him anxious for Margaret to arrive safely. Often he paced and fidgeted, or he constantly crossed and uncrossed his arms, rested his hands on his hips, grabbed the door handle in front of him and released it again. His emotions drained dry, he felt like he had nothing left to lose, or to give.

Finally, headlights were visible coming up the drive onto campus toward Lennon Hall. The white Neon slowed and stopped in front. After what seemed like several minutes to Chris, the driver's door opened and Margaret dashed out and ran up the steps to the front door of the building. He quickly opened it for her, having to brace himself against the wind, and pulled it closed when she was through.

"Damn it!" she cried, shaking the rain off her nylon windbreaker and her hair. "For Christ's sake, this better be good! It's almost nine o'clock, and in case you haven't noticed, there's a hurricane out tonight." Then she stopped, seeing the expression on his face, the look in his eyes. "What's wrong? You look like you've been crying. Jesus, you look like you've gotten ten years older since I saw you a few days ago."

Chris gave a slight nod of understanding and tried to speak but could only force a twisted grimace. Finally, he managed to say, quietly, "I need your help. Very badly, I need your help."

"You said that on the phone."

"I, uh, I don't even know where to start." He bit his lower lip, trying to stop it from quivering, then lowered his face into his hands. Fighting back tears again, he coughed and inhaled through his nose with a loud gurgle.

"Chris. It's okay. You listened to me when I needed it. Come on. Tell me."

"God, Margaret," he whispered, unable to catch his breath, "it's so screwed up. Everything is such a fucking mess."

"What. Tell me." She reached out and put her hand on his shoulder. "Can I get you anything? Do you want to go sit down somewhere?"

"You brought the keys to your lab?"

"You asked me to, I have them."

"Let's go there," he said, straightening and taking a step toward the stairwell that was just down the hall. Then he said, "I need to ... borrow Dr. Leonard's machine."

"I ca ..." she started to protest, but stopped and remaining silent for a moment.

Chris looked at her, his gaze piercing. "It does work, right? The time relocation equipment?"

"Yes, it works," she said slowly. "What's happened?"

"My son, John, my four-year-old son, was murdered tonight."

Her jaw dropped. "What?"

"I think maybe I could have stopped it. I didn't know, but there were so many things I should have seen."

Margaret stared at him, wide-eyed, her mouth open.

"And John—" It welled up in him again, overpowering. He collapsed to his knees. "Oh, God! My son is dead! NO!" He convulsed violently as the tears racked his body. "My son is dead!" Unabated, tears poured out, liquid ran out of his nose and clung to the floor. He buried his head between his knees.

Margaret stood over him, gaping helplessly, her hand over her mouth. She knelt beside him then touched his back lightly, reminding him she was there.

Slowly, he looked back up at her and stood. After explaining what had happened in sentences broken by emotion, he said, "You have to help me. Please. The equipment. Send me back. I don't know how far, a few months, a year. This time I'll know. You said Dr. Leonard remembered you, at least a partial memory, even though it was hundreds of years. If I go back and do it again, this time I'll know."

"It doesn't work that way!" she interrupted. "At least that was Dr. Leonard's hypothesis. The data supports that everything happens only once. You can't go back and change anything."

"I have to try!" he yelled. "I have to! I've got nothing to lose anymore."

211

He started to walk slowly up the stairs, and she followed.

"What about your wife? Your daughter? You've got a whole life here! People who love you!"

"I don't know where they are. They're gone. The car is still there, but they're gone. For all I know, he could have got them, too." Then he repeated, emphatically, "My son is dead! And because you have this machine, I have a chance to keep it from happening. Please. I have to try."

"I told you," Margaret said firmly, "it doesn't work that way. All events happen only once. Time progresses. You can't change that."

"But you said yourself it's just a theory."

"Yes, it's just a theory! But all the data support it. It's the testable hypothesis of the man who built the machine. And everything Dr. Leonard said seems to be accurate. Like I keep saying, things happen just once. If someone is relocated, it happens that one time, to whenever they relocated to. You can't coexist with yourself. That doesn't even make sense."

He looked at her intensely, his large, blue eyes leaving no doubt of his conviction. "I have to try," he said coldly, his voice firm and even.

She looked at him, into his eyes. She felt pity, and understood his suffering at that moment. "All the data support what I'm saying, but I'm not positive that it's true."

They stopped at the top of the stairs on the seventh floor. He turned to her and said with finality, "Margaret, I have to try. If there's even the slightest chance to save John, I have to. Please help me."

She had been listening and debating in her own mind. A sense, a feeling in her had changed and she knew what she had to do. "There is a chance," she said. "I'll help you."

Finding the right key, she unlocked the door to the lab.

■　■　■

"It's the only capsule I have," Margaret said. "But I guess that doesn't matter now."

"You've got everything written down, right?" asked Chris, as they walked toward the old observatory. "Dr. Leonard kept complete records?"

"Oh, he kept complete records all right. Yes, the design of the cylinders themselves is well documented. The only thing is, Dr. Leonard had the worst handwriting in the history of the Earth."

"What did he do, write everything by hand? Why didn't he use software?"

She shrugged. "He preferred using his hands. Pencils. Paint brushes.

That's just him. Part of my job is to rewrite all that into software documents that can eventually be used by other people." She looked at him hard. "We'll send you back in the other capsule. When I'm ready to publish his work, more can be built by others, or by me with somebody's help."

"Okay," Chris said soberly, the reality of what he was about to do finally sinking in. "What do we do?"

Margaret walked to the bank of electronic equipment. The sound of the rain pounding on the domed roof of the observatory echoed between the walls. A crash of thunder, not more than a mile or two away, sounded dull and metallic from where they stood. "You don't have to do anything, except lay down in the capsule when it's ready for you." She hesitated, looking at him from head to toe.

"What?" he asked blankly. Though he didn't remember because of his state of mind, her expression was the same as the time she had made a pass at him.

"You'll—you have to be naked to get in the capsule."

"Wha … why?" he asked.

She turned her head slightly around, looking back at him with narrowed eyes. "One of the rats we sent back, we wrapped it in cotton cloth. We're not sure what happened to the fibers when they relocated in time, but that was the rat we found dead, in China. It looked like the cotton fibers had regressed, constricted, and probably suffocated the rat." She turned back to the bank of circuits and lights. "It may increase your chances of living through this, that's all. It's that simple." She turned a dial and then flipped up a series of six switches. The panels of the machine lit up like a Christmas tree. Green numbers on various displays, red lights in several rows, glowing, yellow dials with needles that jumped to life, twitching back and forth. A hum from behind the panel started low but, quickly, increased in volume. "This will take a minute to warm up. Then we have to program in the date. Once the computer calculates the correct location in time and space, that gets fed into the software on the capsule. Then I have to initiate the atomic diffusion reaction."

Chris was staring blanking at her, but not really listening. He started to undress, pulling the shirt over his head, exposing his chest covered with dark hair.

Margaret smiled. "You don't have to do that yet. You have a few minutes." She turned back to the machine. "But I don't mind if you do," she said quietly.

Chris became aware of what she said and managed a stiff smile. He stepped out of his sneakers without untying them.

Margaret was watching the dials quietly, needles moving slowly to the right as power increased. On another display, digits rapidly scrolled upward, the green numbers flickering past too quickly to read. She turned slowly and walked the few steps to Chris, who had started to unbuckle his belt. She stood very close to him.

"This is dangerous," she said, looking him in the eye. "Like I told you before, we never found five of the small prototypes with rats and mice. We have no idea where they went."

"Dr. Leonard got where he wanted to go. He is, was, Leonardo da Vinci. Right?"

"It looks that way. All data is consistent with that."

"And I'm only going back a year. He went back hundreds of years."

"That's true," she admitted. She looked up, listening to the rain and wind through the roof of the dome. "We didn't do it in the rain, and I'm not really sure what will happen."

"You think it will affect the capsule, like its direction of movement or something."

"Actually, no. I don't think it will matter. Once the reaction gets going and the cylinder departs, it shouldn't be affected much by physical forces, other than its own. Once it's to full power and traveling close to the speed of light, it definitely won't matter, but that should happen when it gets beyond the present day atmosphere."

"I'll have to take your word for it," said Chris dully, looking down as he fumbled with the button of his jeans.

Margaret moved closer, until their faces were inches apart. When Chris looked up, she reached out and took his hands in hers, just in front of his zipper. They stared for a second, until Margaret said, "You're sure? If there is any chance this will work, it's slim."

He looked back into her eyes. "I have to," he said, so close to her she could feel his breath on her lips. "I don't know why, but I know this is just something I have to do. Maybe everything that's happened in the last few days is some kind of, I don't know, wake up call. I know things no one else seems to know. This will give me more time to let people know, to teach people, and not just students." He swallowed. "But most of all, if there's any chance I can keep my son from being killed, I've got to try, even at the risk of my own life."

"I hope we're doing the right thing," Margaret said, backing away slightly. "And I hope you're successful in getting where you're going and doing what you need to do."

"Thank you." Chris looked past her to the equipment. "What do we need to do now? Is it ready?"

She turned, inspecting several of the dials. "It is. I need to put in the date, and it will take just a couple seconds to calculate the location. Then, once the correct date registers on the display of the capsule, I can start the atomic diffusion reaction."

"What should I do?"

"The only thing you need to do is, once the location is calculated, pull down that lever there," and she pointed to an aluminum bar protruding from the wall, tipped with a black rubber handle. "Hold it until the dome opens so there's enough room to let the capsule lift out."

"How will I know how far that is?" said Chris, stepping out of his wet jeans, leaving nothing on but his white, cotton briefs, still wet and partially transparent.

Margaret stared, momentarily losing her train of thought. "I ... I'll let you know. It's about forty degrees of arc."

"Okay."

"So, what's the date? Where do you actually want to go?" she asked.

"About a year ago? Maybe a little more?"

"Sure. Let's start with the minutes first." She clacked on a keyboard in front of several digital displays. "Those aren't important, but we need them for the calculation. I'll leave in the default setting, all zeroes, at the even hour." She simply hit *return*, and *0000* showed on the minutes output display. "For the hour, how about 8 A.M.? So when the capsule touches down you'll have a whole day to get your bearings and figure out where you are and what's happened. Remember, it could land anywhere on Earth."

"Okay. Whatever." Chris stepped closer, watching her, standing in his underwear.

She entered *0800*, hit *return*, and it registered on the next display down on the panel. "Now, the day is critical, and it needs to be numerically assigned."

"Which means?"

"January first is day one, February first is day thirty-two. The computer calculates the location on a four-dimensional, numerical grid system. The words *January* or *Thursday* don't mean a thing to it."

"So, what? August first?" Chris tried to add up days in his head, but couldn't think straight.

But Margaret had been adding as well. "That's day two hundred and thirteen, I think." She hit the keyboard, saying, "Zero, two, one, three," then hit *return*. "All right. And the year is two, zero, zero, six." She watched as the correct numbers glowed on the bottom display. "Great. Now, the fun part." She rechecked the power levels, which were at maximum. She hit the keyboard one more stroke, looked at two other dials, then hit *return*. "That ought to do it," she said, watching the dials.

Chris could see numbers scrolling on another display, and several lights were blinking on and off. He noticed a faint whirring sound rise to an audible level. "What's happening?"

"It's calculating the location," smiled Margaret, turning to look at him. "It should only take a few seconds." As she spoke, a green light came on, and a *beep* emitted from a small speaker. "All right. It's done with that. Now to tell the capsule where to go." She hit several more keystrokes, flipped three switches, and hit *return*. "I think you can open the roof now," she said. "That will take a minute or two."

"Sure." Chris walked to the far right wall, inspected the lever briefly, then slowly tried to pull it down. There was some resistance, but, with a *kwack*, it engaged. He heard a motor whine to life, and, with a loud *thud*, the doors of the roof began moving, separating in the middle. When the space widened, there was a sudden shower of falling water that landed on the floor to the side of the capsule. "Is this important? The water? Will it hurt the equipment?"

"Not as long as it doesn't get on the electronics. Looks like it's not a problem."

Chris looked up at the gradually enlarging opening as he held the lever down. It soon became apparent that the wind was driving the heavy rain sideways across the opening, and not much was coming into the observatory. Just a few drops dripping in along the edges, rolling off the roof. "It's okay here," he said. "How's that part going?"

Margaret was watching the display on the capsule as the same numbers, indicating the date and time, registered there. "Communication between base unit and capsule is established and maintained. And transfer of calculated data completed. Time to start the diffusion reaction."

"How do you do that?"

"That's plenty. The roof," she said, pointing to the rain-swept sky beyond the open dome. "You can release the lever now."

He did so, and the motor stopped, the halves of the ceiling grinding to a halt in that position, about forty-five degrees of the room open to the sky. Howling wind was audible, and frequent lightning was visible outside.

Margaret had gone to a small, locked drawer in a cabinet to the side of the main unit. Unlocking it, and then putting on heavy, lead-lined gloves, she took out a small glass and metal rod. "This is the starter fuel tablet."

Chris stepped closer, but not too close. "What is it? Like plutonium or something?"

"No, but it is radioactive. It's a mixture of several isotopes of the metallic alloy that the capsule is made of."

"Titanium?"

"I know titanium is one of them. I'm actually not sure of the others. It's all written down." She walked toward the near end of the capsule. "I think there's a little uranium, a little aluminum for strength and stability, some iron, some cobalt."

"And it's safe?" asked Chris, his mouth hanging open.

"No, it's dangerous, but most of the danger is not because of the radioactivity. It's because of what you're doing—relocating in time and space. Dr. Leonard thought there might be some minimal radioactivity exposure. Emissions would go off in all directions, but in the diffusion reaction, this tablet aligns them along the plain of the capsule, so exposure to you is much less. The emissions from the entire metal structure supply it with its own energy, to power the propulsion unit."

"It's so small, the propulsion unit. That's the engine that makes it go the speed of light?"

"Yeah, the engine," she smiled. She opened a small chamber in the base of the cylinder and slowly, carefully slid the rod in. Once she was sure it was in place, she closed the chamber again. She looked at him hard, then said, "This is it. Once I start the reaction, it can't be stopped until the location is reached. Part of the calculation is energy usage." She hesitated for a second. "You're absolutely sure?"

Chris didn't hesitate. "I've never been more sure of anything." Then he lowered his head and said, quietly, "Except for the love of my children."

A flood of warmth swept over Margaret. She flipped a switch and slowly turned a dial. Lights illuminated on the control panel of the capsule near the chamber containing the fuel rod. A humming started immediately, emitting from the entire cylinder structure.

"How do I get in?" asked Chris, more alert than before and fascinated by it all, leaning closer.

"Don't worry about that. The hatch will lift open when the power increases enough, when it's close to departure. Then I have to close it with a keyboard entry. It will only take—"

Over the rain and wind, a siren could be heard outside. Chris hurried to the open roof. By holding onto the edge of the roof panel tracks, he pulled himself up and leaned out into the rain, peering down. Looking to the left, he could see a police cruiser that was pulling up in front of the building, directly behind his Toyota. It was difficult to see through the rain, and lighting was poor. A gust of wind, the strongest one he had felt, tore sideways across the front of the building. Lightning flashed, causing him to blink, and thunder followed three seconds later. The roof panel track dug into his stomach just below his rib cage as he leaned out.

"What is it?" called Margaret, still in front of the main console, monitoring power levels.

Chris turned his head in. "Police. They probably found the cars, and Hector's body. Hang on a second." He turned back out into the wind and rain and watched. After a moment he saw an officer get out of the car and hurry forward to Chris' car, searching through the windows with a flashlight. Then the officer trotted up to Margaret's car and did the same. Another bright flash of lightning, followed almost immediately by a deafening crack of thunder, split the night. Chris flinched. A second officer had exited the cruiser and was moving towards the building. The first had left Margaret's car and, also, headed towards the front door of the building. They both disappeared from Chris' field of vision around the corner of the building. After several seconds, a very distant knocking was barely audible over the storm.

Chris lowered himself back down, dropping the last couple of feet to the floor with a thud. "They're probably looking for me." His voice was edged with urgency. "Can this thing get ready any faster? If they get up here, they won't let me go."

"No, it can't. But the cycle can't be stopped, either. The hatch should be opening any second. You should get naked right now. Once it opens, get right in. Then it's just a minute until departure."

Without hesitation, Chris pulled his briefs down and slipped them over his feet, tossing them aside. Margaret was compelled to look, but was only struck by how vulnerable he looked.

There was a hissing sound, and a previously invisible seam appeared on top of the cylinder. Hydraulic hinges slowly lifted the two halves of the hatch upward, and the opening in the capsule widened. "It'll just be another few seconds."

There was a blinding flash outside, simultaneous with a deafening, all-consuming explosion of thunder. Chris and Margaret could feel the electric shock wave in the air, and the floor of the room vibrated for a second.

The room instantly fell into total darkness. All humming and lights from the relocation equipment fell silent and dark.

"The power!" yelled Chris as his heart sank. "No! God damn it!"

The only light in the room was the glow of the cylinder. The diffusion reaction continued to progress causing an eerie, metallic, silver-blue glow to be emitted from the entire surface of the capsule.

"No!" Chris repeated. "It can't be." Though they had only been in darkness for a couple seconds, it seemed an eternity to him. Margaret stood in shock, not knowing what to do, or what would happen.

With a hum and a loud click, the room lights came on. A split second later, the relocation equipment burst back to power, all the lights and dials illuminating again, the humming audible, starting low and quickly building to its original level. Only the room lights seemed slightly dimmer than they had been.

"What the—?" muttered Chris, looking around. His anticipation quickly returned.

"Emergency power!" exclaimed Margaret. "This whole building is on a back-up generator system, set to come on whenever community electricity is lost. The cell culture incubators, the minus eighty freezers, some of the physics equipment—they can't ever be without power."

"Right! Oh, thank God!" Chris cried. As they watched, the hatch of the capsule slowly resumed opening. "The computer's okay? Will it still be able to generate enough power?" Somewhere in the building, the vibration of a door closing could be felt in the floor.

Margaret heard it, but quickly inspected the dials. "It's okay! They've returned to optimal power. Maybe you'd better get right in, and be ready when I close it."

"I will." He stood in front of the capsule, waiting for the hatch to completely open.

Another crack of thunder, farther away, shot through the night. The power in the room remained on.

Now, they could clearly hear voices, first a man's, then a woman's. Anxious and naked, assuming it could only be the police, Chris stepped on the rear edge of the capsule, even though the hatch wasn't completely open. He hesitated and turned to face Margaret.

Though distracted by the voices, Margaret noticed him and said, "It's all right. Get in. You can't do anything to hurt it. Just lie flat on the cushions. I think the only way you'll fit in is to fold your arms over your chest and keep your feet together."

Chris nodded just as the doors of the capsule reached a completely horizontal position and stopped there. He stepped over the edge, into the chamber inside. First kneeling, and then sitting, he extended his legs to one end and laid back. Having to squeeze his shoulders into the space, his body fit snugly against the nylon and acrylic padding. The thought that he was lying in a coffin was prominent in his mind.

"That's it," called Margaret. "Just lie still. The reaction is progressing, so I'll have to close the hatch in a few seconds." She hurried over and looked over the edge of the open cylinder. "Hey," she smiled down at him.

"Thank you so much. It's going to work out," he smiled. "I just know. I know it's what I have to do."

Continuing to smile, she glanced up and down at his naked body, then looked him straight in the eye. "You're such a beautiful person. I admire you for doing this. But I'm afraid for you, too." She leaned over to kiss his forehead, but couldn't reach. He lifted and tilted his head and kissed her once, quickly, on the mouth. "Good luck, Chris," she said. "I don't know what this will solve, but, like I said, I hope it works."

Voices were clearly audible coming from the stairwell. "Police! Anyone in the building? Mr. Magnuson! Police!"

"I'd better close the hatch now," Margaret said with urgency. "Then I have to remove the fuel tablet before you depart."

"Good bye. Thanks again. I hope I can see you again, teach you again, or before, or whatever. Whenever." He gave her one last smile.

Margaret hurried to the back end of the capsule and pressed a toggle button. The hatches slowly, irreversibly, began to close. The glow caused by the reaction in the metal was brighter now, visible even in the room light.

Inside, Chris closed his eyes. Not knowing what to expect, what he was about to experience, he thought of John. The worst that could happen was he would be killed. The best, his son would live again. He knew that was worth the risk. And maybe he would have more time to teach people what he knew, what they didn't seem to know or understand about love, about God.

Margaret slipped on her gloves, flipped open the hatch of the fuel rod chamber and using a thin pair of pliers, removed the rod carefully. As she was setting it gently back into its container, she noticed something out of the corner of her eye, almost subconsciously, that was different about the settings on the capsule. But it didn't register with her right away.

Then, she looked again, and the change in the settings became all too clear.

She shuddered. A wave of panic swept over her. "No," she said, quietly at first. Then, "No! Chris!" She hurried back to the capsule, but the hatch was just sealing, the seam becoming invisible as the glow from the metal intensified.

Inside, Chris thought he heard Margaret call his name. But the hatch closed, and he was plunged into darkness, except for the glow from the metal around him. The humming grew in volume and consumed him.

"No! Oh, my God!" Margaret whispered, through a tightened throat. "What have I done? Chris. My God."

"Police!" came a loud call through the door of the lab. There was knocking, thundering on the metal. "Open this door! Now!"

The reaction in the metal of the capsule reached a critical point. The wires connecting the capsule to the main console automatically disengaged. The glowing of the metal intensified. The humming from the power source increased in volume.

Margaret stood back, her eyes wide, her hands over her mouth. All she could do was watch. The knocking on the lab door continued.

The capsule glowed bright. Brighter. It lifted, slowly at first. Then more rapidly, and soon it was glowing so bright she could no longer look at it as it lifted toward the open roof. The humming continued to increase in pitch and volume.

She turned and looked at the main console to confirm what she had seen on the capsule.

Yes. It was true. When the electricity had gone out and then come back on, the reaction and the power of the machine had resumed at their normal levels.

The time settings had not. They had returned to the default settings, and the computer had automatically recalculated the different relocation information. On the main unit, and on the cylinder, the time settings read:

Minute: 0000

Hour: 0000

Day: 0000

Year: 0000

The capsule glowed brightly and ascended, heading west. It moved through the night, through the violence of the storm.

EPILOGUE

Outside, rain pounded against the glass as the wind ripped sideways, clattering loudly against the panes and plastic siding of their little house. Mike stood from the sofa, walked over to the window, and peered out. Another storm, he thought. How much rain can we get in one spring? His teeth were clenched into a grimace, exposing his capped incisor tooth, a slightly different shade from his others, just a little too white. He fingered his tooth gently, thinking how young he had been then. Carving a tooth! What a ridiculous thing to do.

The sky was growing dark rapidly as dusk approached. A few cars were parked on the street. One drove by as he watched, its headlights piercing the rain pounding the pavement and front lawn, countless splashes dancing over every surface, shifting in intensity as wind gusts came and went.

Kristin, his wife, was on the phone, sitting on the sofa in front of the television with the volume low. Mike walked back to the sofa and sat down next to her. He watched CNN and waited for her to finish.

"We'll talk about it and let you know. I love you, too, Mom. Bye-bye." She hung up and turned to Mike.

"How's your mom doing?" he asked.

"Not bad. Her hip is better. She says that new arthritis drug is working wonders." Kristin's face became more serious, and she looked away. "Mom wanted to know when we're going to have Lauren christened. She'll help with the arrangements and everything, but she's very anxious and says we probably shouldn't wait much longer."

Mike frowned. "I'm sure she is anxious." He stared at the television.

Kristin looked back at him, studying him briefly. Changing the subject, she said, "It's really something, isn't it? What they're talking about on the news?"

"Hmm?" he asked, having been thinking about something else. "What's that?"

"The sea wall they have to build in Manhattan. The ocean level has risen, what did they say? Eight inches in the last five years? And that's enough to cause flooding and damage in some parts of the city. They're scrambling around, trying to build a wall that will keep waves in a storm like this one from washing onto the streets. I guess the damage on the FDR is pretty bad."

Mike nodded his head. "Yeah, I heard that. And it's getting worse. I heard yesterday that they found a huge chunk of polar ice as big as Delaware, floating somewhere northwest of Greenland. It had broken away and is melting so fast that it has a bunch of rivers running over the surface of it. The ice is getting cut so deep by the canyons forming in it that they think it will start breaking apart in less than a month. And they think the ocean levels will keep rising, even faster than before."

"It's like it's out of control," said Kristin. "So many weird things are happening. They're talking about needing sea walls in Boston, Baltimore, even Washington. Parts of Miami and most of the barrier islands on the coast of the Carolinas had to be evacuated. And, before you got home, they said there was some country near India or somewhere—a bunch of little islands or something—"

"The Maldives?" suggested Mike.

"Yeah! That's it. The Maldives. That whole country is basically gone. Every island had to be abandoned. The whole place is just about under water. And here, it just keeps raining and raining."

Mike shivered. "It's pretty scary." He looked back to her. "I guess I really don't care whether Lauren gets christened right now. It just seems so unimportant."

A flash of lightning, followed an instant later by a loud crack of thunder, shattered their conversation.

Kristin was startled and lurched in her seat. Then she turned back to Mike, her face sunken in disappointment. "She's your daughter. How could you say that?"

"Oh, you know she means more to me than anything. She's the most important thing in my life."

From the baby monitor on the end table came a quiet, cooing sound. Soon it increased in volume and intensity until it became insistent crying.

"I'll get her," said Mike, standing. "The lightning woke her up." He walked out of the living room and down the short hallway to Lauren's nursery.

Peering over the edge of the crib, his eyes met those of his three-month-old daughter as she lifted her head to see him. "Hi there!" he chirped happily. Her crying stopped instantly, and a toothless smile spread across her face. He returned the smile and that feeling returned, the one he always had whenever he saw Lauren. Though he loved his wife deeply, what he felt when he looked at Lauren, a new life he had helped to create and now nurture, was a deep warmth that was something completely new to him, completely indescribable. Reaching into the crib and tucking the receiving blanket around her tightly, he picked her up and cradled her across his left shoulder. The clean, sweet fragrance of her tiny body was evident as soon as she was near his face, and she continued to smile and coo. Soon her eyes caught the movement of rain running down the window of her nursery, and they darted back and forth, trying to focus.

"Did that nasty storm wake you up? Want to go see Mommy?"

As they returned to the living room, Kristin called, "Hi!"

Mike sat down, cupping Lauren in the hollow of his bent arm so Kristin could see her face. Kristin cooed and talked in a singsong voice for a moment, taking Lauren's tiny hand in her own and jiggling it gently as she spoke.

Then she looked up, reached out, and took Mike's hand in hers. "About this christening business, I'm sorry for saying that. I know how you feel about her. Just like I do. I've seen the way you look at her, the way you hold her like you are now. And how you sing to her." Kristin smiled broadly.

"I never understood what having a kid was all about," said Mike, looking away and out the window behind the TV. "And I never really thought much about it or whether or not I was ready for it. But I realize, now, that I am. And it's such a great thing. And a real important job."

"Not to sound condescending, but, I'm so proud of you. That's such a sign of maturity."

"Thanks," he said, looking back to her. "That doesn't sound condescending at all." They kissed briefly.

"So, what should I tell Mom? We should decide, one way or the other."

Mike was silent, thinking for a moment. "You know, there's something a college biology professor taught me in undergraduate school, before I met you. When was that class, six years ago? Anyway, he explained some things that really stuck with me, that I've always remembered."

"Like what? Something that has to do with a christening?"

"No. That's just it. He explained what God is, what love is, in such a simple way. Almost too simple." Mike laughed. "He explained the nature of God, the meaning of life, and the definition of love in just a few sentences. And I've always remembered it. It made a lot of sense. Not some belief or idea or viewpoint with magic or fantasy or the supernatural. It was just the way it is, the way it's always been." He looked back at her. "But, until we had Lauren, I don't think I've ever really seen good ways to use it, other than being nice to people and working hard and all that."

"The nature of God and the meaning of life have to do with raising a kid?"

"Yeah. Completely. They actually have to do with everything we do, or should be doing. Since we've had Lauren, I can see that the simple definition of love, like he explained it, makes perfect sense. What we need to do is make her life as good as possible by sharing everything we have, everything we know, with her."

"Of course we'll do that. She's our daughter."

"I know, but what most people don't understand is where it all started, and why. And that has to do with what God is, a very real thing, and how life and love are such amazing gifts." He motioned toward the window. "And the screwed up state of the world right now is because eight billion people don't understand what that love is or because they're not doing very much about it. They're just going about their day in pursuit of short-term gain and gratification, or maybe survival."

Kristin watched him closely. "Whatever that teacher said obviously means a lot to you. But I guess I still don't get what that has to do with whether or not Lauren is christened."

"Right. Well, the ritual and symbolism of religion don't mean much of anything, really. What's important is the way we all live our lives, every minute of every day. That's all that matters. To what degree we return the love God has given us, by making the quality of life just a little bit better for as many people as possible, is how we need to live every day. It should be the motivation that guides all our actions. It doesn't have ritual, it doesn't have a denomination. It's just the way life is, and the way we should be." He smiled slightly. "Seeing as the world seems to be falling apart, dabbing Lauren's forehead with blessed water seems like a pretty silly thing."

Kristin watched him for another moment. "Why don't you tell me about it, now, so when Mom argues I'll be able to tell her why we decided what we decided."

"Sure. I've wanted to talk to you about it before, but the situation just never seemed right. We always seem so busy and preoccupied with what we need to do next in our busy days." He paused, trying to remember, then said, "Well, one thing I can say is, though the ability to love is a gift, what we do with that gift is always a conscious choice. One we all have to make, individually."

Author's Note

ith the exception of Jesus and other Biblical characters, and Dudley, all characters in this book are fictitious. And as you have seen, I have taken liberties with traditional writings that describe the historical events, teachings and personality of Jesus. Those of you who know Dudley personally see I did the same with his personality.

Though some Biblical scenes were familiar to you, the story itself is a work of fiction. I have not been able to reconcile traditional religious dogma with the world I continue to observe. What I have tried to accomplish is to present, in the palatable medium of a novel, a different perspective on some fundamental questions and issues at the core of the human existence. I believe they offer a common link between science and religion. For, as I would be willing to discuss rationally with anyone, regardless of what anyone thinks or believes, there is a singular nature of things, including God. All people, including myself, have hugely varying perceptions, opinions, beliefs, ideas and prejudices as to the nature of the universe and the world around us. I offer this as a starting point for a new perspective, drawing on evidence that has been accumulated for thousands of years, and my own observations. I believe it is consistent with any perception, whether it be scientific or religious. I understand that both science and religion exist in, and attempt to describe the nature of, the same world. Life is real, our world is real, as are all forces and matter in it. It is time we begin to understand what that means and how to approach living and loving with that perspective.

The emotional nature of the content of this book will affect each reader to varying degrees. You may come away from this with an entirely different outlook on life and living, God and spirituality. You may have enjoyed it as an unusual story, put it down now that you are done, and will never give it another thought. Either way, I hope you have felt even just a small fraction of the emotion I have felt in thinking about this, and then finally being able to write it down.

Absorb the ideas. Savor them. Think about them in your own time and context. Though it all wasn't pleasant reading, I hope what I've written can have a positive influence on your life, and inspire you to do the same to those around you.